Benjamin Had Strange Powers . . .

In the morning Lenora still tingled pleasantly. She sensed a change beginning in her, a change within the essence of herself.

Was this what it felt like to fall truly and totally in love? . . . She felt as primal as an animal. Never before had she merged with a man in such a hauntingly thrilling exchange of lust and satisfaction.

The bite at the base of her neck tingled like the other sexual parts of her. It seemed to feed delicious post-coital sensations directly into her brain . . . Instead of annoying her, it pleased her that Benjamin had left her a love wound, a souvenir of his erotic domination. Rather than wearing a halter today, she planned on wearing her white blouse so the collar would conceal the tooth marks. . . .

Books by John Russo

The Awakening
Black Cat
Bloodsisters
Limb to Limb
Midnight
Night of the Living Dead

Published by POCKET BOOKS

The Awakening

JOHN RUSSO

PUBLISHED BY POCKET BOOKS NEW YORK

This novel is a work of fiction. Names, characters, places and incidents are either the product of the author's imagination or are used fictitiously. Any resemblance to actual events or locales or persons, living or dead, is entirely coincidental.

Another *Original* publication of POCKET BOOKS

POCKET BOOKS, a Simon & Schuster division of
GULF & WESTERN CORPORATION
1230 Avenue of the Americas, New York, N.Y. 10020

ISBN: 0-671-45259-2

First Pocket Books printing April, 1983

10 9 8 7 6 5 4 3 2 1

Printed in the U.S.A.

For Alex and Karen. With special thanks to Ralph Intrieri of the Pennsylvania State Police, and thanks also to Robert Trombetta and John Connolly of the Fort Pitt Museum.

In letting of blood three main circumstances
are to be considered, who, how much, when?

—Robert Burton,
The Anatomy of Melancholy

The life of the flesh is in the blood.

—*Book of Leviticus*

The earth was heavy on his chest and limbs, but his grave was shallow and the dirt was loose. He began to claw his way out. They had hanged him, but somehow he had not died. He remembered the jerk and snap of the rope, the blinding pain, and nothing after that. They must have buried him unconscious, thinking he was dead. But the noose hadn't broken his neck. He still had air in his lungs. The shallow, loosened earth must have enabled him to breathe just enough, his need for air reduced while he was in a coma, like Indian fakirs he had read about, who could let themselves be buried for days on end. He had survived, he had cheated death. He pulled himself up, his body rising through clods of moist yellow clay.

He hadn't opened his eyes yet; unused to anything but darkness, they hurt even with the lids shut. By the rough feel of dirt and stones against his skin, he could tell that he was nude. The gravediggers must have stolen his clothing and his good leather boots. And they must have decided to save his coffin for somebody else—as if his remains didn't deserve to be treated with modesty and respect. Well, their penny pinching had saved his life. He could hardly have clawed his way out of a nailed-shut pine box.

In a half crouch, he brushed his thighs and calves, rubbing the dirt off with his hands, awakening the good tingly sensations of muscular living flesh. He opened his eyes slowly, and they hurt till they got used to the light. Tears coursed down his cheeks. He blinked. He blinked again, trying to convince himself of the reality of his surroundings.

He was standing amid a vast expanse of torn-up, devastated ground. Weeds, stones, and even trees had been plowed and uprooted to completely clear an area of at least two acres all around. Would his executioners have ordered all of this dug up in order to obfuscate his exact place of burial? He'd put nothing past them. Their minds were in the Dark Ages. They had convicted him of sorcery and vampirism, and were so terrified of him that they had talked of driving a stake through his heart, stringing cloves of garlic around his neck, and burying him at a crossroads. They wanted to make sure he stayed dead. How ironic that their noose hadn't even strangled him as he twisted and dangled in front of their superstitious fear-maddened eyes.

His feet sank in and it was hard to walk till he groped his way to firmer ground. Squinting against the bright sun, he held out his arms and felt the hot rays on his skin, convincing himself that he was flesh and blood. He touched his neck, wondering why it didn't hurt, why the rope hadn't even left any burns. Perhaps his coma had had a healing effect. Benjamin Latham was still alive, up from the nameless grave to which he had been unjustly consigned. But he had no time to revel in his rebirth. He must find some clothes to wear. He must get away from here in all haste, lest his enemies spot him and finish the job they had left undone.

Benjamin made his way toward a patch of woods that was still intact, at the edge of the devastation, and hid in a thicket of trees and weeds. He didn't know exactly where he was. Which direction was Hanna's Town? The sun was straight up in the sky—giving no clue to where it had risen or where it would set. He couldn't get his bearings, couldn't tell east from west. Surely they wouldn't have buried him far from the outskirts of town, the site of the jail and the gallows. Yet nothing looked familiar. He thought he might have been able to recognize a landmark or two if the acreage around his grave hadn't been so rudely and utterly denuded.

Maybe the townspeople had taken the time and trouble to disguise and obliterate all this place, as a substitute for burial at a crossroads—which was supposed to confuse the spirit of a risen vampire so it wouldn't know which way to go to return home. Benjamin scoffed at the superstition. He wasn't a vampire. But for the moment he was surely lost, and his joy at surviving the noose was beginning to be eroded by desperation.

Taking another look around, he suddenly realized what was so odd about the woods where he was hiding. The trees were all *young*—he could tell from the thinness of their trunks and branches. Where, in the vicinity of Hanna's Town, was there any substantial growth of new forest? Nowhere. The answer seized him with unreasoning panic. Where *was* he? He couldn't be near Hanna's Town, for it was a frontier settlement, carved out of ancient wilderness. Nothing had lived there but Indians and animals until a few years ago.

He wondered if they could have carted him far away to bury him, a hundred miles or more, back toward Philadelphia where some of the forests were younger. But then why hadn't he regained consciousness during such a lengthy journey? No. He must be close to home. Maybe he'd realize it soon. His ordeal must have disoriented him, confounding his senses. It would be wise not to make a move till he got himself under control. He might stumble into the arms of his persecutors. His freedom would depend on keeping his wits about him. Even if he could get away, he'd have to struggle and scheme to make a new life. Everything he had owned was gone. His home and all his possessions had been burned to the ground. The crazed mob had destroyed his medical supplies and equipment—"the wicked tools of the vampire sorcerer."

When he had first heard the shouts, the clattering hooves, and the pounding of fists on his cabin door, he had thought they were coming to tar and feather him because he was a Tory. He had no intention of running from them. Since the start of the Revolution, he had lived with the possibility that they might turn on him this way, and had resolved to face up to them with a showing of courage and dignity.

They ought to be ashamed of themselves. They ought to skulk away with their tails between their legs. They *needed* him here. He was their only doctor. And he was a skilled Indian fighter, from his experience in the French and Indian War. Out here in the wilds of western Pennsylvania, diseases and tomahawks were more to be feared than redcoats.

Maybe his neighbors had hated him for being against independence from Great Britain, but they still should have been grateful for the lives he had saved last summer when the Shawnees had attacked Hanna's Town, murdering settlers and burning their log houses. They hadn't called him a Tory traitor then—when he had been loading and firing his musket alongside the best of them, and giving medical care to the wounded while screaming savages were beaten off from the fort. When times got tough, they had accepted Benjamin Latham as a damned valuable member of their frontier community, regardless of his loyalty to King George.

He had figured that he could make them see the light of reason by reminding them of all the good he had done. Coming to the front of his cabin, he had taken his time lifting the heavy wooden bar out of its iron brackets. Let them wear some skin off their knuckles, let their voices go hoarse from yelling and swearing. It might sober some of them up and blunt their cowardly "patriotism."

When he opened the door, they had pounced on him, pummeling him to the floor and binding him in coils of coarse hemp. He had been knocked unconscious and his mouth had been gagged. He had had no chance of defending himself. He had come to as they hoisted him onto the bed of a horse-drawn cart, and by that time his cabin had been torched—wild flickering tongues of fire made the faces of his captors look weirder and crazier. Instead of lynching him or immersing him in tar, they had dragged him to the jailhouse and had locked him inside.

The next morning, before a panel of three judges and a roomful of noisy, gawking spectators, he had been accused of bleeding Patience Rutherford, an indentured servant, sixteen years of age, and of drinking her blood and using it in occult experiments. Patience and her younger sister, Sarah, age fourteen, had sworn out a complaint before a magistrate, in which they said that they had spied on him through his cabin window and had witnessed him drinking the blood that he took from Patience on several occasions, and on other occasions had seen him treating her blood with "salts and potions that caused it to separate into three layers, all the while mumbling a charm over this devil's work," which caused Patience to suffer "agonizing headaches at night, and horrible contortions of her limbs," so that she could not remember the words to her prayers or even kneel to say them.

Benjamin had realized that he could not hope to reason with the pandemonious mob that filled the spectators' benches, gibbering and gasping over the sensationally embellished testimony of the Rutherford girls. But the three judges were learned men, his peers, and he had thought that by being candid he could make them understand him. They would see that he was actually much like their hero Benjamin Franklin, whom they revered for his great inventions and his daring experiments with electricity.

After considerable pounding of the gavel and threats to evict some of the more unruly spectators, the judges had allowed Benjamin Latham to arise and testify in his own behalf. They had listened intently, restoring order as best they could whenever some of his statements provoked the ignorant mob.

He had admitted that indeed he had tasted blood from time to time, in order to test the effect of its nutrients upon himself. He had made the point that the judges and everyone else in the courtroom tasted blood every time they ate freshly butchered meat—it was what made the meat red. They also tasted blood whenever they licked a cut finger, and no harm was ever known to arise from this universal human reaction to bleeding. As far as the experiment the Rutherford girls had witnessed, the separation of blood into three layers, that chemical procedure had been discovered hundreds of years ago, by Hippocrates; Benjamin had been making use of it in order to arrive at a better understanding of the ingredients of human blood, for he believed that by such knowledge many diseases might someday be cured.

He had confessed that, as a doctor who liked to keep up with all the latest discoveries of his profession, he no longer truly believed in the efficacy of phlebotomy—the letting of blood for medicinal purposes. He had explained that human blood, and the blood of all creatures, did not stay in one place but circulated throughout the entire body, as had been proved by William Harvey, the eminent physician of the Royal Society of London. "If the blood does not lie still in the vessels, but is constantly flowing, then how can we heal a swollen arm by letting some of its blood out of it? It would merely be replaced by blood from other parts of the body." He had allowed some time for this concept to sink in, and for the furor to die down.

He had gone on to say that in recent years he had continued to bleed patients who insisted on it; and he had used this fluid, which would have been otherwise discarded, to try to learn more about its life-sustaining properties. And, furthermore, he had drunk some of it—at great risk to himself, as some might have thought, since it had come from patients who were ill. But he had never contracted a disease from any of his patients so treated—as he would have if their illnesses had been caused by so-called bad blood. On the contrary, he believed, though he couldn't verify it as yet, that the small amounts of blood he ingested had nurtured him and contributed to his overall well-being.

Summing up his defense, he had quoted from the

preface of William Harvey's monumental contribution to medicine, *An Anatomical Essay on the Motion of the Heart:* "I only wish, by this work, under God the Creator, to contribute something pleasing to good men, and appropriate to learned ones, and of service to literature." He had hoped that his invocation of God would please everyone in the courtroom and convince them that he could not be a sorcerer.

He might as well have saved his breath. The judges had listened to him, giving him their rapt attention, not because he held them spellbound with his cleverness and his obvious innocence, as he had thought, but because they believed in his guilt wholeheartedly and were content to let him expound it in public. In their opinion, he had hanged himself by his own testimony. The fact that he was a "damned Tory" had no doubt added to their glee in bringing him to "justice." He had been condemned to die at sunrise, on the morning after his trial.

How long ago had he stood wearing the noose around his neck?

Yesterday?

The day before?

A week ago?

He had no idea how long he had been buried. If the stories about the Indian fakirs were true, he might have remained in a trancelike state for an incredibly long time. It would have taken weeks and weeks and a large party of men with their beasts of toil to clear the field he now looked out upon. But maybe it had already been cleared by farmers far away from Hanna's Town. And now it was ready to be plowed and planted. His executioners must have expected his corpse to feed the roots of new vegetables.

But their deepest dread had come true. He *had* risen from his grave, like a vampire of legend. Except that it was daylight instead of nighttime.

He started when he heard some voices. Then laughter. He cowered down behind some foliage. Maybe some brave, ignorant souls were coming to show off by dancing on the vampire's grave.

The voices were coming from the left, about a hundred feet away, but back among some trees. Then Benjamin heard a great chugging and grinding sound that he couldn't identify. A huge smoking monster rolled out of the woods.

He couldn't believe it. His mouth gaped open.

Two men were riding the monster, and they were dressed like no men he had ever seen in his life. Strange caps and bibbed leggings. Riding a great yellow behemoth of plated steel. It wasn't a creature of flesh and blood, but a machine of some kind. But no horse was pulling or pushing it—and, judging by its bulk, it would have taken several teams of horses. It had an enormous blade in front, which lowered itself and began scraping over the ground, smoothing out hilly places. In a flash of inspired bewilderment, Benjamin realized that this incomprehensible beast, mastered by the men on top of it, must have been what cleared the land and helped free him from his grave.

At that instant, one of the machine-masters looked up and spotted him. In his befuddlement, Benjamin had neglected to keep his head down. Totally panicked, he rose up in full view, exposing his nakedness.

"Flasher! Flasher!" one of the men called, pointing at him, gesturing angrily.

The machine stopped and the men jumped down. They began running toward Benjamin. He bolted, crashing through foliage, hurting his bare feet on twigs and stones as he strove to run faster. He had never been so scared in his life. He did not understand who or what was coming after him. They looked like *men,* but not of this planet.

If he wasn't on earth, then where in the devil *was* he?

He pushed the question to the back of his mind and kept running. He tripped over a root and went tumbling down a ravine and into a creek with a hard rocky bottom. The water was shallow, and the creek bed treacherously slippery. He picked his way across gingerly. He was lucky not to have broken any bones in his fall. He had lost his lead, and he could hear the men's footsteps getting closer.

On the other side of the creek, he found a path. He kept running till it dawned on him that the sounds of heavy pursuit had died away.

His heart pounding, his breath coming in short, painful gasps, Benjamin took refuge under a tangle of thick, leafy vines that formed a canopy between a cluster of trees, shutting the world out. He couldn't be spotted easily if anyone came by. Encouraged by this degree of safety, he began to relax a little. He stopped perspiring. His breathing and his pulse rate returned to normal.

He was sweaty and dirty, and insects buzzed around him and nipped at him. He was almost grateful for their torment: the mundane peskiness of it seemed to prove that he was alive on earth, and not on some bizarre planet or in some unearthly spiritual realm. He had *not* died. He had survived hanging. Whatever else had happened to him would soon become clear. He must have imagined the strange men riding that monstrous yellow machine—they were probably ordinary farmers working a horse-drawn plow, but his addled brain had transfigured them into something fantastic. Perhaps if he concentrated on calming himself down, putting the past behind him, he would begin to see the present in its proper perspective.

Whatever his mental problems might be, he had certainly given good account of himself in a physical sense. He had done splendidly for a fifty-five-year-old man. After all, he wasn't in top condition anymore. Yet he had outdistanced two men who looked much younger than he, and his lungs hadn't burst, his heart hadn't given out. His stamina had been absolutely marvelous.

Maybe this was because he had lost weight, living off his own flesh while he was in his underground trance. He was at least twenty pounds lighter than he remembered himself. His thighs were lithe and powerful, his abdomen lean and hard and ridged with muscle, as it had been in his youth.

Looking at his stomach, he suddenly noticed something that gave him a jolt: he had no navel, no belly button.

Something told him, like a voice whispering from deep inside him, that his past was now lost and irretrievable. Maybe this feeling would go away. Maybe it was all the extraordinary result of beating the Grim Reaper, of being, in a sense, reborn.

He touched his own cheek. Then, slowly and carefully, he felt with his hands and fingertips over his whole face. His skin felt taut, youthful, responsive to touch in a sensuous way that was denied to old men.

He didn't know what to make of the changes in his body. He felt like a *young* man, not a man of fifty-five. Maybe he did not need a navel because he was not born of woman but was reborn from the earth. Where had that idea come from? It had just popped into his head. It sounded logical but insane. No more insane, though, than being alive when he ought to be dead. Was he dreaming all this? Or had somebody worked a spell on him that had caused him to go mad?

He didn't believe in spells. Or witchcraft. Or vampirism. Those superstitions were for the ones who had condemned him to hang. They had accused him of being a vampire, and he had refuted it because it was pure poppycock. He had never bitten into anyone's neck with long fangs. He had never slept in a coffin. And he had always been able to get around quite well in the daylight, without disintegrating to dust. He was *not* a vampire, not in the supernatural sense. He had occasionally drunk blood, as one might take medicine. He had never believed that drinking it might make him immortal. . . .

But maybe it had.

Preposterous.

Preposterous, he told himself.

But still, he was alive—very much alive—and he felt like a young man. His vim and vigor were extraordinary. He hadn't felt better when he was in his early twenties. He reached up and touched the top of his head—he felt hair. His bald spot was gone! Surely this couldn't be his imagination. He was truly young again! The thick curly hair running through his fingers was as real as the navel he no longer had.

He couldn't remain hiding in these woods forever, that much was for certain, whether he was crazy or sane. He had a need for clothing and shelter, and a need for food. He had to disguise himself lest the two men who had chased him come back with helpers, shouting and beating the brush in search of the "naked vampire." If they didn't shoot him on sight, they might very well lynch him again. Or they might lock him up in an asylum, where they'd try beating his madness out of him or hosing him with ice-cold water till the devils that caused his lunacy were driven out.

Which reminded him that he needed a bath.

And more than that, he needed to find his way to familiar people and places and worldly concerns.

Ordinary reality.

The reality he had known.

He got his first look at himself in a small pond. He knelt down till his face was inches from the water and saw himself reflected as a young man, no more than twenty-five years old. He touched his brows, his cheeks, his nose, his chin—his bald spot now covered with hair—and he didn't know whether to be happy or sad. He was an old man with an old man's memories in the body of a youth. If this dramatic change had been magically wrought in him, then what awesome changes had been wreaked upon his world? Was the yellow machine-behemoth only a small sample of worse horrors to be encountered?

No.

He must be mad. He'd almost prefer it.

Or dead. He might be dead and undergoing the tortures of hell. Part of the torment of it might be this devilish mockery of making him think he was still alive and on earth. Even to the furnishing of mosquitoes and gnats.

Exasperated, he smacked the water and his image

dissipated. It occurred to him that if he were a vampire he would not have been able to see himself at all. *They* were supposed to have no reflection. He waded into the water, splashing himself all over, getting his body clean of sweat and soil. He drank handfuls of water, quenching his thirst. It was *real* water. It felt and tasted the way he remembered it.

He started walking again, eschewing easy pathways and keeping to denser parts of the woods where he could not easily be seen. Hiking over the rough terrain was tough on his bare feet. He took time to urinate, and this simple bodily process consoled him because of its indication that he was not in the spirit world. Maybe it gave him courage, too. The courage of his own vitality, his own flesh and blood. Because he soon admitted to himself that he couldn't *stay* in the dense part of the woods; he'd have to take to the paths if he expected to find civilization.

Eventually, he sighted a clearing, through the trees. He crept up toward it and hid behind some bushes, peering out.

He was behind a row of houses that all looked alike—remarkably so. They were uniformly two-storied and of clapboard construction. The clapboards had such neat, straight edges that they were almost unreal; in fact, they had a metallic sheen. The houses didn't appear cheap, yet they were crammed closely together, as if property were scarce. Some of them were painted white, some green, some yellow, some tan. Each one had a little wooden back porch, facing either left or right. The funny thing was that none of the houses had chimneys. Some of the yards were fenced in, and some weren't. The most common kind of fence seemed to be made of silver wire, and Benjamin had never seen anything like it before.

There were clotheslines strung up here and there in some of the backyards. Benjamin perked up upon noticing this and let his eyes wander up and down, scanning the housing area. He got a thrill when he spotted a great assortment of clothes and bedsheets hanging on a line.

Staying back among the trees, he skirted the edge of the woods till he was directly behind the yard containing the clothing. For a long time he peered through the windows of the pastel green house, and he detected no movement behind the filmy curtains. Two houses down, a little black dog was chained by a doghouse, and he'd be likely to bark at anything unusual. For the moment, the animal was preoccupied, munching something out of a rusty tin plate.

His heart beating quickly, Benjamin worked up the nerve to venture forth; he had his eyes on a pair of blue trousers and a red-and-blue plaid shirt fluttering on the clothesline. Instead of darting forward—since it would have had the most chance of alarming the black dog—he stepped purposefully out of his hiding place and strode briskly toward his objective, painfully aware of his naked vulnerability. But the dog didn't bark. Nobody came out of any of the houses. He grabbed the trousers and shirt, clothespins flying, and darted back behind the bushes.

He glanced around nervously, afraid that someone might still come after him. Gradually his fears subsided. Skulking back farther into the woods, he tried the stolen garments on. The trousers seemed to fit well enough, although he was used to knee-length breeches and high silk stockings instead of these things that came down to his instep. The shirt was a little snug for him; he kept fingering the buttons, which were made of something white, shiny, and almost translucent, like a sort of artificial bone. At least the apparel was dry. Funny how the stuff held its creases even though it obviously hadn't been ironed yet. He tucked the shirttails inside the pants, wishing he had a belt to thread through the loops. But if he had his choice, he'd take a pair of shoes ahead of a belt. No matter. He was certainly less conspicuous now than he had been at any time since his resurrection, and might even venture into the open, if need be.

However, he wasn't about to take any unnecessary risks. He skirted the edge of the woods once again, stepping gingerly because of his bare feet, keeping an eye out for a way around or through the housing area.

In the yard of a white clapboard house he spied a little girl playing in a sandbox. He almost hadn't seen her because she was behind a white picket fence. She couldn't have been more than six years old. Concealing himself behind a tree, he studied her, enthralled by his intimate proximity to an innocent, unhostile human. She was scooping sand with her hands and piling it up in the shape of a pyramid. She seemed a strong, energetic child, plump and healthy. Her hair was ash blond. She was wearing a tiny red garment no larger than a diaper.

Following a compulsion that went against his instinct for self-preservation, Benjamin forsook the cover of the woods and walked slowly up to the white picket fence. The little girl turned around and looked at him, her blue eyes widening in a quizzical way, then continued nonchalantly patting sand. He wanted to talk to her. It had occurred to him that he might ask her questions without arousing the sort of suspicion that would come from adults.

"Hello!" he called out cheerily, startling himself by the sound of his own voice. She glanced up and flashed a tentative smile, showing her dimples.

"My name is Benjamin," he said. "What's yours?" Trying not to appear furtive, he scanned all the houses in the immediate vicinity, assuring himself that he had attracted no unwanted attention.

"Stephanie," came the little girl's answer. "Want to help me build a big sand castle?"

"I'd like that very much. Will you let me into the yard?"

"Uh-huh."

She stood up, not bothering to brush herself off, and came to the gate and undid the latch. "Mommy thinks I don't know how," she said proudly. "But I'll let you in so you can be my playmate."

"Where is your mommy?" Benjamin asked, trying to sound calm and collected.

"In the cellar ironing."

Relieved, Benjamin followed Stephanie through the gate, leaving it open in case he had to make a hasty exit. She climbed into the sandbox, and he sat on its wooden ledge while she knelt before her sand heap and resumed patting it. Having shaped it into a lumpy mound, she started poking rows of holes into it with her index finger and calling the holes windows.

"What do you want *me* to do?" Benjamin asked, trying to ingratiate himself by entering into the spirit of the thing.

"Nothing. Just watch."

"I thought I was supposed to be your helper."

"No, my *playmate.*" She pursed her lips, thinking it over and deciding not to be so selfish. "If you want, you can build your own sand castle over there." She pointed to the opposite corner of the sandbox. "Want to use my shovel and bucket?"

"Okay."

"In the shed." She used a sandy, grubby finger to indicate a tiny building a few paces from the sandbox. It was as white and metallic-looking as the house. The front door of the shed was open, and Benjamin went inside, looking for the shovel and bucket Stephanie meant for him to fetch. The first thing that caught his eye—and gave him a shudder—looked to be a miniature version of the great yellow machine-behemoth driven by the two men who had chased him. It had no blade in front, though. Its fat black wheels and other parts of it were soiled with greenish grass stains and clumps of dried grass. It was the main piece of equipment in the shed, although there was lots of other junk, too. Benjamin had no idea of what most of it could be. But he did spy a pair of beat-up, grass-stained leather boots that interested him considerably. He found Stephanie's shovel and bucket, tiny ones made of painted tin, and brought them over to the sandbox.

"I'm too tired to dig," he said. "Let's just talk for a while."

He sat on the ledge, near where Stephanie was working. She was putting some smooth sticks that looked like tongue depressors all around the roof of her castle, so that they stuck out like guns. He put her bucket and shovel on the grass by his bare feet, hoping she'd forget about them.

"Don't you want to make a sand castle to show Mommy?" she chided.

"I'm sure I could never build one as nice as yours. For a

little girl, you are really bright and clever. How old are you?"

"Six. I just finished kindergarten. When summer's over I'll go to the first grade."

"What year were you born in?"

"I can say the month, the day, and the year. Daddy taught me. Want to hear me say it?"

"Surely. I'd love to."

She stopped patting sand, drew herself a deep breath, and recited proudly by rote: "My name is Stephanie Kamin. I am five . . . I mean, *six* years old. I was born on April fourth, nineteen hundred and seventy-six, in Pittsburgh, Pennsylvania." She let her breath out in a rush and gave a big dimpled smile, pleased with herself for being able to say all the numbers.

"Don't you mean seventeen seventy-six?" Benjamin probed, trying not to sound desperate.

"No, *nineteen!* Nineteen seventy-six. Daddy helped me memorize it for my teacher." She rattled it off once more: her age, her birth date, and the fact that she had been born in Pittsburgh, Pennsylvania.

"Is this Pittsburgh, then?" Benjamin asked hopefully, stifling his rising panic, hanging on to the name of Pittsburgh—a name he recognized—the way a man capsized and being swept over a falls will clutch on to a piece of driftwood.

"This isn't Pittsburgh, silly!" Stephanie informed him. "Pittsburgh is a big city, real far away."

"Have you ever heard of Hanna's Town?"

"Nobody lives there."

"You mean it's a ghost town?"

"What's that?"

"Well . . . I mean . . . why doesn't anyone live there?"

"Because it's too *old.* Mommy and Daddy took me there. It's not for living, just for looking. It's no place you'd want to *live.* They have an old fort and a flea market, and lots of people dressed up like Indians and pioneers. They sell homemade bread and apple butter and funny, lumpy soap."

"I . . . I s-see," Benjamin stammered lamely. "What . . . dear me! What country is this, then?"

"America!" Stephanie exclaimed, looking at him as if he were a lunatic. "The United States of America!"

He didn't have the heart to ask her any more questions. It was too much like asking to be hit over the head with a sledgehammer. She was an intelligent, well-informed child. Everything she had told him had the ring of truth. It tied in with all the other farfetched things that were happening to him. He believed her without knowing exactly why.

If she had been born in 1976, then *this* year, right here and now, was 1982—two *hundred* years in the future! In other words, he had been hanged two centuries ago. And by some god-awful fluke he had come back to life in an alien epoch—an epoch of mad machines and metallic houses.

On the bright side, all his enemies were probably dead. But his milieu, his way of life, was vanished! How in the world was he going to cope?

It dawned on him that America must have won the Revolution. The thirteen colonies were now states, independent of Great Britain: Stephanie had called them the United States of America. The rabble had triumphed—the slavering cretins who had hanged him as a vampire instead of tarring and feathering him as a Tory.

Oh! It was too much to take! He felt depleted, used up. His situation was worse than hopeless. It would be better not to be alive at all, not to have survived the noose. As if his blood had drained right out of him, he succumbed to an overpowering tiredness, a weakening of the flesh and the spirit. He wanted to disintegrate, to seep back into the earth.

He looked at Stephanie, who was scooping up sand, getting ready to build a brand-new sand castle. She was as unreal to him as if she existed in another dimension, across the threshold of a thin, elusive dream. They were two creatures of separate realms, juxtaposed by an intangible quirk of fate. If he tried to touch her, would she disappear? Or would the joining of his flesh with hers substantiate his own existence? Would his reality be confirmed and enhanced? Would his vitality be restored?

He wanted to fold her into his arms . . . to hug her close to his chest . . . to . . .

. . . to sink his teeth into her . . .

. . . and to drink her blood . . .

. . . so that, by absorbing the essence of her, he could add to his own substance. He could substantiate himself. His mind and his body, his entire being, filled with the concept of taking sustenance from her. It became a vivid, instinctual lust, almost sexual in nature. The ravening power of the urge scared him as much as it tantalized. He was like a child at puberty, awakening to the possibilities of eroticism . . . a dimension of himself and of the world that had hitherto been nonexistent.

Yet he shrank from the prospect of biting her. That was taboo. He wasn't that kind of animal. She was an innocent child, and he didn't have it in him to hurt her.

But what harm if she should cut herself and he should lick the wound for her? If such a thing should happen, he could comfort her, could kiss the laceration and make it better.

As if fate were in compliance with his dreadful desires, sunlight glinted in his eye and he spotted an object in the grass—a piece of a broken bottle. He reached out surreptitiously and secreted the sharp fragment in the palm of his hand. Then he asked little Stephanie a question to distract her.

"That machine in the shed—what is it used for?"

"What machine?"

"The large yellow thing with wheels."

She giggled as if he must be teasing. "You know what *that* is, silly—it's the grass-cutter." She giggled again and reflexively glanced toward the shed. Benjamin had just enough time to bury his chunk of broken glass in sand, near where she was playing. Now, if she dug in there with her hands . . .

She was doing exactly what he hoped. Scooping up handfuls of sand and funneling them into another conical mound. She did it once . . . twice. . . .

He was practically salivating. Surely she must have scooped the glass fragment out by now. He hadn't buried it very deeply.

He watched her patting and shaping the sand she had already piled up, till it resembled the same sort of lumpy mass she had built earlier. "This one is going to be my best one," she said as she started to poke holes for the windows.

"Don't you think you should scoop up some more sand . . . make it a lot bigger?" he encouraged.

"Oh, I don't think—ouch!" She jumped and screamed, yanking her hand back as if it had touched a hot stove. "Oh, oh, oh . . . I *cut* myself!" she whined, looking terrified and ready to bawl. She stared at her index finger.

Benjamin stared, too. At first he saw only the jagged line of the incision, obscured by grimy sand . . . then it began to ooze red. He was fascinated, entranced, while at the same time a part of him wondered how he could be so captivated by the phenomenon of bleeding; he had seen it many times before without being so profoundly intrigued.

Stephanie emitted a sob, her eyes wide, looking for sympathy.

"Don't cry," he cajoled hastily. "Don't cry, Stephanie. It's not a bad cut. Here . . . let me take care of it."

She struggled to be brave, to hold back tears. Biting her lip, she held out her hand, the bleeding finger stiffly extended. He wiped it on his shirttail, then took it into his mouth, surprising himself by his greediness.

Her first impulse was to yank the finger away, but he had seized her wrist and he held on to it tightly till she calmed down. He lapped at her blood with his tongue, using just the tip at first. The fluid tasted incredibly warm and sweet. He closed his eyes and sucked on her finger as if it were a nipple. A dreamy, half-somnolent feeling came over him. He became lost in the automatic, sleepy rhythms of his cheeks and lips . . . sucking . . . sucking . . . puffing in and out like the cheeks of an infant being suckled at his mother's breast.

Stephanie wasn't crying anymore, but he was barely aware of that. His eyelids fluttered dreamily, remaining lightly closed. His head followed the little girl's body downward as she collapsed, sinking into the sandbox. He made himself stop after taking what to him seemed like a small amount of her blood. The tiny cut wasn't bleeding anymore. He gave it a final lick, then pulled his lips away. At the same time he relinquished his hold on her wrist and heard her hand smacking the sand with a limp thud. It was an unnerving sound, and he opened his eyes.

He saw Stephanie lying flat on her back in the sand, her pupils dilated, staring glassily into the harsh sun. Timidly reaching out to touch her cheek, he found it cold and pallid. Her mouth was wide open, a whitish froth on her lips. Her protruding tongue was a sickly color, almost bluish white. He felt her wrist, but he already knew there would be no pulse.

"Stephanie . . . Stephanie," he moaned.

He kept his hand on her arm as it lay there in the sand, as if his touch might bring her back to life. He couldn't believe that she was gone . . . that he had caused her to die. He never, ever had had any intention of harming her. Surely it couldn't be his fault. He hadn't taken enough blood to do this to her. Maybe she had died of fright—a hysterical overreaction to her harmless little cut finger. Or perhaps she had been harboring a dread disease that had coincidentally killed her right at this moment. Or what if the piece of broken glass was poisonous—a fragment of a bottle that was used to store a powerful poison?

Backing away from the sandbox and the tiny, pathetic corpse, he was overwhelmed by misery and guilt. Was he no longer a human being? Stephanie had been so young and innocent. Now she would never smile or play in the sand, ever again. He had destroyed her. However unwittingly, he was to blame.

He had to get out of here. He had to run. People would come after him now, eager to put him to death. This time they would be justified. He deserved to die.

But—and he cursed himself for it—he wanted very much to live. The startling thing, the cruel thing, the thing he wished he could deny, was that the taste of blood had made him feel strong, refreshed, keenly and vibrantly alive. He didn't want to let go of that feeling; it coexisted with his feeling of remorse, his dread concerning what sort of creature he had become.

Looking all around, assuring himself that no one was watching, he went to the shed and took the pair of beat-up leather boots he had coveted earlier. Then he walked out through the gate and back into the woods.

He didn't stop to put the boots on until he had put a considerable distance between himself and the scene of Stephanie's death. They were at least a size too big, and the leather felt cold and clammy on his bare feet. He couldn't figure out how to close the slits in the uppers till he tugged on a metal tag and—presto!—the tiny metal teeth on both sides of the slits sealed themselves shut. The more he walked, the more the stiff leather loosened up, and the more comfortable the boots became, but he still expected them to give him some blisters.

Stephanie had said that Pittsburgh was a big city. Benjamin decided he'd try to get there. A large settlement would offer the best chance of evading capture.

He still felt guilty and sorrowful over Stephanie. But he couldn't repudiate the sense of well-being he had obtained from drinking her blood. Yet his desire for it scared him; it had been so animalistic, so profound. In his previous life he had experimented with blood as a nutrient and had observed its effects on himself in a scientifically detached way—but this time it had been something he absolutely *craved.* Maybe, he desperately told himself, the craving was a one-time thing—a surge of nourishment needed at the outset of his rebirth. Still, a child had died because of him. When he had performed phlebotomies—bleeding people—he had not been doing them any permanent harm. He had thought it would be the same with Stephanie, but he had turned out to be terribly wrong.

The sun was lowering in the sky; by its position and the angle cast by his shadow, he could tell east from west. He figured that since he had crawled out of his grave at noon, it must be about three o'clock now. He was keeping close to the edge of the tree line, heading in a northwesterly direction, looking for a way around the housing area.

Presently the houses petered out, but so did the woods, and he found himself crossing a field. He picked up his pace, but he didn't dare break into a run, for fear of calling attention to himself. Some teenage boys at the far end of the field were playing a game that involved a lot of running and yelling and hitting a ball with a stick. To Benjamin's relief, they didn't seem to take any notice of him, and he was glad they were so involved in their sport.

The field bordered on a road. It was quite wide, and paved with a blackish gray material. Yellow lines were painted down the center and at the edges.

Benjamin's spirits were lifted by finding the road. It stretched far away toward the horizon, in the westerly direction that he wanted to go. What a good omen! He decided to cross to the other side, which was bordered by tall weeds and then more trees. He could make good time by walking on the paved surface—and dash to cover in case he saw anyone coming his way.

Satisfied with his plan, he stuck his foot out into the road—and was transfixed there in mind-boggling terror as a monstrous whooshing roar thundered in his ears and he was almost run over by a thing bigger and faster and more awesome than the machine-behemoth that had peeled the top off of his grave. Huge as it was, it was possessed of devilish speed, ripping and roaring into the distance, leaving a cloud of foul-smelling smoke. It was yellow, like the machine-behemoth, but it was shaped more like a box on fat black wheels, and he could have sworn he saw little children gaping and grinning at him from behind its large glass windows. But he couldn't believe that any society would risk its children's lives that way.

Well, it made his mind up that he wasn't going to walk right on the road. He kept off to one side, where the ground was smooth for the most part. Although he didn't come across any pedestrians for the first few miles, he did run for cover every time he was threatened by a vehicle. And the ones that bore down on him were of all sizes and descriptions, some less noisy and more speedy, others bigger, uglier, and more ponderous.

Keeping his eyes and ears peeled so he would not be caught off guard by one of the awful machines, he rounded a bend and was startled to see a bearded young man stepping out from among some tall weeds, buttoning his fly. Benjamin backed up a couple of steps and ducked to one side, behind the weeds. The young man kept on walking down the road. A bright red pack was strapped to his back. Over his shoulder was slung a shiny rectangular metal box, into which he slid a smaller rectangle, slowing his stride momentarily to attend to it, and immediately some loud, rhythmic noises issued forth, seeming to be composed of musical instruments sorely abused and over-ridden by discordant human voices.

Benjamin heard a humming of wheels behind him and turned his head to see a small sort of vehicle approaching and then speeding by. Whipping his head around to follow it with his eyes, he saw that the young man up ahead had stopped walking and was gesturing at the vehicle by holding his arm out and extending his thumb. When the vehicle passed him he pulled in his thumb and extended his middle finger. Benjamin figured *that* must mean the same thing it had meant in his own time—and it echoed his sentiments about *all* the vehicles.

He wanted to let the young man get way ahead of him and out of sight before venturing out of his hiding place, but, to his consternation, the young man shuffled along slowly, as if he lacked energy, and kept sticking out his thumb, followed by his middle finger, at every passing vehicle. Finally, one of the smaller, brightly painted traveling machines screeched to a stop in front of the young man, and he opened the door and got in, and it sped off with him, disappearing into the sinking sun.

It dawned on Benjamin that the thumb-up gesture must have been a pleading for a ride, and the use of the middle finger an expression of displeasure at each failure. Did he have the nerve to try the same thing himself? It was a frightening prospect. But it offered a chance of rapid escape from the imminent danger of his present surroundings. Also, he knew that in his own day Pittsburgh was about fifty or sixty miles from Hanna's Town, and there was no reason to suppose that it had been moved any closer. If he dared to wangle a ride in one of the twentieth-century traveling machines, it might cover the distance in question by nightfall or sooner.

He finally worked up the nerve to stand by the side of the road and stick out his thumb. The first few vehicles whooshed right on by—he jumped back each time—and he started to wonder if the thumb-up gesture really meant what he thought; perhaps something else had actually done the trick for the young man. But finally a little tan machine stopped for him. He was so taken aback that he stood rooted for several seconds; then when he reached for the door handle he didn't know how to work it. Breaking out in a sweat from fear and nervousness, he finally pressed a button that was built into the handle, and the door opened. He got in awkwardly, fitting his buttocks to the snug leather seat and tucking his legs in tight so that his kneecaps were only about an inch away from the interior front paneling.

"Shut the door!" the driver called out urgently.

Benjamin did so, and the vehicle lurched out just in time as one of the huger and more monstrous ones bore down upon it. The grinding noise and the mad honking caused Benjamin to turn around and see the danger, but he was too frightened to watch the outcome. In ten or fifteen seconds, however, the thing he was riding in had accelerated greatly and then stabilized its speed, and when he dared look back the bigger and uglier thing was much farther behind.

"That truck damn near hit us," said the driver. "Good thing this little baby has some pickup."

"I—I thought w-we wouldn't make it," Benjamin managed to comment.

The driver chuckled as if he had enjoyed the thrill of the narrow escape. "He wasn't even in sight when I stopped, but you took your good old time getting in. Could've gotten us both killed."

"I'm sorry," said Benjamin with deep sincerity.

The driver shrugged and let the matter drop. After a while he said, "Where do you want to go?"

"Uh . . . P-Pittsburgh," Benjamin stammered.

"I can take you to Route Thirty, as far as Irwin, then you can hitch another ride. My name is Joe. What's yours?"

"Benjamin."

"Mind if I just call you Ben?"

"No, not at all."

Benjamin thought that the proposed informality might open up further conversation, but Joe lapsed into silence. He behaved rather nonchalantly, considering he was handling such a fast, dangerous machine. His arm hanging out the window, he negotiated curves and other road peculiarities effortlessly. Benjamin guessed the driver's age at about thirty-five, going by his thinning and graying brown hair. His short-sleeved shirt, pale blue in color, was stretched over a round little paunch. He didn't keep his eyes on the road at all times, as one might have expected, but instead let his gaze wander upon whatever else there was to look at.

Though he wouldn't have thought it possible, Benjamin found himself gradually relaxing. To his surprise, he eventually discovered that he rather enjoyed riding in Joe's machine. He wished he might ask how it could go along by itself without any animal pulling it, but of course he couldn't reveal his ignorance. From inside the vehicle, the speed didn't seem so terrifying; one got accustomed to the rate at which the scenery whisked by. It was fascinating to observe how the steering was done by means of a wheel. In the front panel there was a dial and a needle which registered MPH—and Benjamin deduced that to mean miles per hour. For the most part the needle stayed at 40 or thereabouts—a fantastic enough velocity, though the limit was apparently much higher.

The thing that was still scary, even when Benjamin got used to riding, was when other vehicles approached head-on. The road appeared too narrow; it seemed impossible not to collide. The passing whoosh was always a relief. The worst of these incidents happened as Joe was maneuvering to overtake a slower machine, and just as he got beside it another one came over the hill from the opposite direction. Benjamin couldn't watch—he stared wide-eyed at the MPH gauge as it climbed to 50 and 60 with heart-stopping rapidity. Nothing happened. No crash. Benjamin didn't dare look up till long after he heard the passing whoosh. By a miracle, they had swerved back onto their side of the road. Their speed eased up. They were safe.

Joe didn't seem the least bit perturbed. "This car has what it takes," he commented with a yawn.

Now Benjamin knew that Joe's vehicle was called a car; the other machinery that had thundered up on them from behind had been called a truck. The differentiation must depend on size and hauling capacity, the smaller vehicles being analogous to stagecoaches in that they were primarily used to transport passengers.

Joe was driving through hilly country with scattered clumps of woods and occasional farms. Some of the farming machinery reminded Benjamin of the thing that had overturned his grave, only he was less awed by it now. Here and there were a few houses, and sometimes a store with a car or two parked in front. One kind of store was particularly intriguing to Benjamin because he noticed a man sticking a hose into the side of a little red car—he couldn't imagine why and he didn't dare ask.

Presently, Joe made a right-hand turn past a sign that said YIELD and got on a ramp that funneled them onto an even bigger road, four lanes instead of two. Now there was more traffic, zigging in and out crazily, and a great number of business enterprises lining the highway. Many vehicles were crowded into the lots of brightly painted restaurants advertising exotic-sounding foods like Burgers, Fries, Tacos, Pizza, and Big Macs. It occurred to Benjamin that it must take a lot of people to eat so much food—more than a dozen eateries whisked by within a space of five miles or less.

"What is the population of America?" he ventured to ask, hoping it was not the kind of question that might expose him to ridicule for not knowing the precise statistic; probably a good many of Joe's contemporaries did not know it either.

"Oh . . . let's see," said Joe, scratching his head, leaving only one hand on the steering wheel. "What was it the last census? Over two hundred million . . . close to two hundred and a quarter million, I believe."

Astounding! Surely Joe had to be wrong. How could so many persons be crammed into thirteen colonies . . . er . . . states? At the outbreak of the Revolution, there were only eight million in all of Great Britain, versus two million of her subjects in the New World—and even then gadflies like Daniel Boone never had enough elbowroom.

"Which state has the biggest population?" Benjamin probed.

"California."

Well, Benjamin had never heard of it. And he couldn't think of any way to try to enlighten himself without asking something that might make Joe think he was crazy. So he took a new tack: "Joe, have you ever been to Hanna's Town?"

"Just to look at the fort and nose around at the flea market. Lots of folks'll be moving into that area once they get the roads enlarged and the new mall put in."

"New mall?" Whatever that was.

"Yep. Two hundred new stores. A helluva complex. The bulldozers have already torn out the old Hanna's Town crossroads, and now they're leveling off the acreage so they can start laying foundations."

That stunned Benjamin to silence. Now he knew why his grave had been uprooted. And why he had been lying under the earth naked, without a coffin. . . .

The pine box had been waiting for him beside the gallows. The lid was off, lying in the grass next to the gaping, beckoning box. On top of the lid lay the necklace of garlic, the heavy iron hammer and iron nails, and the sharp wooden stake. The executioners wanted everything handy so the vampire would have no chance of coming back to life.

The fall through the trapdoor *had* killed him, the thickly knotted noose had snapped his neck. That's why he didn't remember anything but a flash of blinding pain, didn't remember suffering and choking to death. But now he could picture the aftermath. He could envision what must have happened, as if seeing it through a sixth sense.

They cut him down from the gibbet and laid him in his coffin, leaving the iron shackles and chains on his ankles and wrists. Then they placed the necklace of garlic cloves around his broken neck. And they drove the stake into his heart. Then the coffin was nailed shut and hoisted onto a horse-drawn cart, which carried it several miles through the woods to the crossroads outside of town—the roads in the shape of the holy cross upon which Christ had died. There a hole was dug, and the vampire was buried. To make sure he would never rise again, mumbo-jumbo prayers and charms were recited over his grave.

Then came the passage of time. Fifty . . . a hundred . . . two hundred years. Two centuries of rotting under the earth. Benjamin Latham, the unjustly convicted vampire, moldered in his grave, worms devouring his flesh. The cloves of garlic tied around his neck slowly turned to green, powdery mold . . . and disintegrated to dust. The boards of the coffin became waterlogged and termite-infested, and rotted to pieces around his corpse. The irons on his wrists and ankles rusted to reddish flakes. The wooden stake decayed and fell through its cage of bone, since there was no longer muscle or sinew to hold it in place.

Thus were the charms of the garlic and the stake

destroyed by the elements, through the natural effects of two centuries under the earth.

Then new flesh began to grow on Benjamin Latham's skeleton. As he lay senseless in his grave, which had evolved into a supernatural womb, skin and organs materialized around and within his bones . . . he became a complete organism, shaped into the image of himself as a young man.

But he was not alive, not yet . . . not quite. He had no awareness that he had been re-formed.

The crossroads was a talisman powerful enough to prevent the spark of life from being breathed into him. The shape of the cross remained a guardian against the creature's rebirth.

But this year the crossroads was suddenly obliterated. The bulldozers tore up the intersection and cleared the area all around, to make way for the new mall. By this preparation, the last obstacle to the rebirth of the vampire was removed. And Benjamin Latham rose from his grave, with the help of the machines that had partially excavated him from the earth.

But why had this happened to him? It made no rational sense. He had never believed in vampirism. He would have detested those creatures of fangs and bloodlust had he known that they really existed. Had he made himself into one accidentally, by experimenting with blood? By drinking it?

No. His conscience rejected that burden of self-incrimination, self-guilt. It was too much like giving credence to his persecutors.

He preferred to believe that the charms they had worked upon him—the stake, the necklace of garlic, the burial at the crossroads, the babbling of spells—must have acted opposite to the way they were intended: instead of preventing the vampire from rising, they had made Benjamin *into* a vampire by somehow preventing an essential part of his spirit from leaving his body. Thus, he was created by ignorant superstition.

By this logic, vampires would not exist were it not for the fear-crazed imaginings of the uneducated mob. First they had unjustly put him to death; then they had transformed him into something he did not wish to become, by means of their superstitious devices and rituals—which were far worse than the science he himself had reverently pursued.

If one vampire could create another, as foolish legend would have it, then perhaps little innocent Stephanie would come back to life, too. Benjamin didn't know whether to wish it on her or not. It would absolve his own guilt somewhat—or would he feel guiltier knowing he had put her into the same dreadful predicament he found himself in?

"I'm going to make this right turn toward Irwin," said Joe, breaking into Benjamin's macabre reverie. "I'll let you out across from the car dealership. This is a major intersection, perfect for hitchhiking. You shouldn't have much trouble catching a ride into Pittsburgh. You're only about twenty miles from downtown."

But the thing overhead that Benjamin had come to recognize as a traffic signal turned red. By what magic was the device powered and rigged to change colors at timed intervals? Joe had to stop while other cars were given the right-of-way. When the green light came on—did it work by electricity?—Joe made his turn and pulled off the road at a convenient spot, and Benjamin got out of the car. Before slamming the door, he gave Joe his thanks, and they told each other good-bye.

What Joe had called the car dealership consisted of a large glass-enclosed building, with half a dozen shiny mint-new-looking cars of various colors and designs displayed behind the glass. The building was situated in the center of a sizable paved lot which was also filled with cars. Benjamin wandered around looking at them, allowing himself to be momentarily absorbed by the opportunity of examining the wondrous vehicles close at hand and harmlessly at rest. They were multicolored, and all had shiny metallic labels like Skylark, Century, and Riviera. It was a puzzle why they were called so many different things when, in a general way, they all looked so much alike.

Sunlight glinted off one of the exterior rearview mirrors

of the cars, causing Benjamin to notice such an accessory for the first time. He stooped over and crowded in close to the vehicle to look at himself. Would he have a reflection or not? To his relief, he saw his own face. Actually, he had reason to be quite pleased by his countenance, which was the way he remembered it from his youth. His hair was brown and curly, his nose not overly large and only slightly hooked, his jawline firm and square, his chin modestly cleft. He had alert blue eyes, a wide and full mouth, and a ruddy complexion. His good looks made him smile. Whatever problems he had been saddled with, it was still marvelous to be young and energetic again, facing a future full of challenges and complexities he never thought he'd live to see.

The sad part was that he'd never see his son, his daughter-in-law, or his grandchildren again. They had been far enough removed in Williamsburg, Virginia, where Robert had gone to set up his law practice, but now they were removed not only by miles but by the space of two centuries as well. Before, there had been the hope of an occasional visit by means of a rough trek across the Shenandoah Mountains; Benjamin had even considered moving to Williamsburg himself in his old age. Now he had his youth back, but his nearest kin were all dead. The full realization struck him with such utter melancholy that he wanted to sit down and weep.

"Two-thousand-dollar rebate on the LeSabre, sir," a voice behind him said, making him jump. "Can I put you behind the wheel and show you how she handles?"

Benjamin spun around and found himself facing a thirtyish gentleman crisply dressed in a green suit, a white shirt, and white-and-green-striped neckwear. His shoes were shiny and black. His bald head was shiny, too. Powdered wigs must have gone totally out of fashion, or else this obviously stylish person would have worn one.

"Uh . . . are you the proprietor of this establishment?" was the first thing Benjamin thought to say.

"No, just a lowly salesman, I'm afraid. Harry Klein, at your service, sir." He extended his hand for a shake. "Are you thinking of buying a new LeSabre?"

"No, I was just looking," said Benjamin.

"I can make you a tremendous deal right now," offered Harry. "If you saw our TV ads, you know what I'm saying."

Benjamin merely nodded.

"These great rebates are too good to pass up," Harry persisted. "They won't last forever."

"I'm sorry. I don't have any money and no way of earning any at present," Benjamin confessed, hoping the despair in his voice would discourage the salesman.

Harry became immediately sympathetic. "I understand you. I hear where you're coming from. People like you and me *want* to buy new cars, we just can't afford to. I can't make a go of it anymore—I'm damned lucky if I score more than one commission a month on this lot. God! Where did we all go wrong? You don't see the politicians starving, do you? We all used to believe the United States was the land of opportunity. But I swear I don't know what's happening to us. Sometimes I think we're all going to hell in a handbasket."

The salesman walked away muttering how he couldn't afford to make the payments on his own house and car, and shaking his head disconsolately. His mournful diatribe had made Benjamin realize that he must have been at least partially right, years ago. As he and other Tories had predicted, all was not peaches and cream just because independence had been won from Great Britain.

Benjamin caught a ride in a green car, bigger than Joe's, labeled Oldsmobile Cutlass. The driver's name was Norman Willoughby, and he said he was going all the way into Pittsburgh to pick up his son, who was coming home for the summer vacation from college. Norman looked to be in his late fifties; he was all dressed up in a black-and-white checked suitcoat and black, sharply creased trousers, and he smelled of a strong but pleasant cologne. "Hope Jimmy remembered to put a necktie on," he enthused. "I want to take him to my club for prime ribs. He deserves it for making the dean's list."

"He sounds like a gentleman and a scholar," said Benjamin, hoping the expression was apropos in the twentieth century.

"Say, you have some accent!" said Norman. "Are you a Johnny Bull, Ben?"

"Johnny Bull?"

"All right—an Englishman. Don't let my slang bother

you. I poke fun at all the nationalities. You should hear me tell Polish jokes."

"I'm English," Benjamin admitted. Fleetingly he wondered if he ought to consider himself an Englishman now or a United Statesian. He had been born under English rule the first time around. He had always been a loyal subject of the Crown. He remembered that at the outbreak of the Revolution even the so-called Patriots weren't unanimous in their aims; some of them claimed to be fighting for the rights of Englishmen rather than the right to independence from England.

"What are you doing in the States?" Norman asked.

"Er . . . uh . . . I'm sort of an amateur historian. I've been traveling here and there, visiting historical sites that date back to the time of the thirteen colonies. For some reason that period holds the greatest fascination for me."

"My wife and I used to sort of be history buffs, when we had time for it," said Norman. "Visiting some of these old places used to be a cheap vacation for us, but now they're all jam-packed with tourists. Ever since *Roots* was on the TV, people have been out in swarms delving into their heritage."

"I guess that's true."

"Certainly. Not that I mean to put *you* down for it, if you have a sincere interest or hobby or whatever. Something must've put a bug up your ass to make you come all the way from overseas just for the sake of looking into the past. I imagine you intend to visit Fort Pitt?"

Benjamin's heart started pounding. He hadn't dared to hope that Fort Pitt, where he had served as a soldier and a physician during the French and Indian War, would be still standing after more than two centuries. "I was there once, but it was a long time ago," he said, with a wistful tremor in his voice.

Norman Willoughby chortled. "Couldn't have been *that* long ago, Ben! You're no more than twenty-five or so, are you?"

Benjamin chuckled, too, as if he and Norman were sharing a joke.

"History can be a dynamite subject," Norman said.

"My wife and I, when Jimmy was little, we took him around to Fort Pitt . . . Fort Necessity . . . Braddock's grave. Now, that Braddock must've been some asshole! Trying to fight ambushing Indians as if he and his redcoats were on a parade field in Europe! Served him right to get shot 'cause he wouldn't take advice from George Washington."

"On the contrary," Benjamin said, his hackles rising. "General Braddock was a fine soldier, more than competent. The day could have been saved if his men had regrouped the way he ordered them to. Many of the colonial troops turned coward and fled, and Braddock had five horses shot out from under him, trying to stop the desertions. He ran one traitor named Fawcett through with his sword, and Fawcett's brother Tom turned around and shot Braddock in the back. The general wasn't killed by the French or the Indians, but by one of his own men."

"Well, I'll be damned if I ever heard *that,*" said Norman with heavy skepticism and indignation. "That might be the way they teach it Johnny Bull country, but not in the history books over *here.*"

Benjamin realized too late that he should have kept his mouth shut. Of course, he knew the truth of the matter firsthand. But the true version had only served to make Norman mad. Miffed, he continued to drive in silence, his fingers clenching the steering wheel. Finally he reached out and turned a switch and loud noises started up like the syncopated noises that had issued from the metal box carried by the young man with the backpack. After a while, with great reluctance, Benjamin admitted to himself that these sounds must constitute what this day and age thought of as music. Apparently the abomination could be always at people's fingertips if they so wished it. My, how nice it would be to listen to a Bach sonata out in the peacefulness of the wilderness! But the stuff filling up Norman's car could have no appropriate setting. It was nothing but jangle and discord—and on second thought maybe it *did* express what Benjamin so far had seen of this disturbing, frantically paced twentieth century.

The tempo and excitement of his own expectations

heightened minute by minute as he and Norman approached Pittsburgh. The land on both sides of the road was so utterly transformed that he didn't recognize any landmarks, though he had surely traversed this area before on foot and on horseback. Now there were rows of stores and complexes of stores with gaudy signs advertising products he had never heard of. The men that he saw walking around, carrying packages or pushing wire carts full of purchases, were for the most part conservatively dressed. But the attire—or lack of attire—of the young women was absolutely scandalous; many wore very short trousers and bodices that exposed practically all of their charms, leaving little to the imagination. Benjamin couldn't help gawking at them.

However, the business district seemed to peter out suddenly, and Norman drove the car up a ramp and onto an even bigger and faster highway which, for some reason, was not lined with stores. They zoomed along for a mile or two, then flew over a mammoth span of steel and concrete and into a brightly lit mile-long tunnel straight through the side of a mountain.

Emerging into daylight again, they zigged and zagged in the thick of the traffic and soon were barreling alongside what appeared to Benjamin to be the Monongahela River. But it wasn't fringed with forest anymore—instead, for miles it was lined with huge black buildings and belching smokestacks.

"Those are all steel and chemical plants," said Norman with unabashed civic pride. "Pittsburgh is the iron and steel capital of the world, you know. Did you say you were here when you were a little boy? If so, you can see that great progress has been made in cleaning up the smog and pollution."

"Very . . . impressive," Benjamin murmured.

"There's a citizens' group called GASP that keeps on the politicians' backs," Norman explained.

As they approached the city proper the sky was a beautiful shade of blue. Tall, shiny buildings clustered together en masse, their tips poking through puffy white clouds. Traffic patterns became more complex, more geometrical, as intertwining roads looped over and under each other, supported by massive steel girders and concrete buttresses.

To Benjamin, it was an awesome, fantastic spectacle. He remembered Pittsburgh as a grubby, unsavory hodgepodge of log huts and mud streets, with hogs oinking and wallowing at their pleasure, and drunken woodsmen and rivermen staggering about hooting and hollering, shooting off their mouths and their muskets.

"I'll take you right to Point Park," offered Norman, being gracious. "That's where the old fort and the museum are, if you recall. I have plenty of time to drop you off before I pick my son up out at the University of Pittsburgh." As he spoke he tugged his coat sleeve up and glanced at a tiny instrument on his wrist. At first the dial looked totally black; but then it lit up, showing the time in hours, minutes, and flashing seconds.

Gawking all around at one architectural and engineering marvel on top of another, Benjamin couldn't help being both intrigued and frightened by this modern society whose vast technology encompassed everything from miniature luminous watches to buildings that touched the sky.

5

State Trooper Ronald Vargo, a plainclothes criminal investigator from the Greensburg barracks which had jurisdiction over Hanna's Town, stood on the back porch overlooking the yard where Stephanie Kamin lay dead in her sandbox. He had just finished interrogating her mother and father, and his insides were churning. The porch was a no-man's-land between the grieving parents and the pathetic little blue-eyed corpse that awaited his further attention.

Vargo was six feet two inches tall. His athletic build came from trying to work off tension every night in his basement weight room. But the tension never seemed to go away; it was in the way he stood and the way he moved his shoulders. At age forty-two, his wavy hair was still thick and dark, except for some gray in the sideburns. His complexion was swarthy, not from tanning but from his southern Italian heritage. His face was craggily handsome, marred by a nose that was too broad and flat, as if someone had intentionally flattened it. His black deep-set eyes glinted with a penetrating mixture of curiosity and skepticism that usually managed to hide his deep inner sadness.

Resting his hand for a moment on the porch banister, he scanned the scene of the investigation, noting that the coroner hadn't arrived yet. Two R&I men (Records and Identification) were finishing up with their job of taking photos and dusting for fingerprints, a meticulously slow procedure since the aluminum shed, the wooden bench going all around the sandbox, the toy shovel and bucket, and the gate to the picket fence all had to be dusted. Trooper Jim Hoskins, a uniformed detective—black trousers, dark gray shirt with epaulets, black Smokey-the-Bear hat—stood by the gate making sure nobody touched it and that no unauthorized persons tried to enter the yard. The picket fence made it easier to keep neighbors from trampling all over any possible evidence; clusters of curiosity seekers were milling around in both adjoining yards, but the fence blocked them off from the death scene more effectively than the usual makeshift barricade of ropes strung between bamboo stakes.

Vargo felt the eyes of the onlookers staring at him as he stood on the porch pretending to examine a page in his notebook. He didn't really need to look anything up, but he wanted to unwind a little and didn't want to appear to be doing nothing. People were always looking for an excuse to criticize the police. He could picture the neighborhood gossips in their coffee klatches, berating him for not coming up with some miraculous deduction and not living up to their image of TV supersleuth.

"I thought it was Georgie Stevens," Rita Kamin had said, her voice hoarse, her pretty face red and puffy from constant weeping. Looking at her, Vargo could see where Stephanie had gotten her blond hair and blue eyes. Finally Rita had broken down utterly, her petite body wracked with inconsolable sobs while her young husband held her and patted her, like two lost souls on an island of sagging corduroy sofa, trying to ward off the awful fact that their beautiful six-year-old daughter was dead. The mother had found the body. Vargo's questions had been necessary even though they added to her pain. He had gotten everything out of her that he could under the circumstances. Her grief reminded him too much of his own.

Three years ago his daughter Kathy, aged seven, had been raped and stabbed to death in the woods behind her grandparents' house. The perpetrator had been caught, found guilty, and confined to Laurel State Hospital for the criminally insane. Vargo didn't believe in insanity as a defense plea. He believed instead that if all heinous crimes carried the death penalty, then many of those who were going insane would subconsciously orient their insanity in a milder direction. And the fiends who were caught wouldn't get loose again, like the one who had murdered Kathy.

"I thought it was Georgie Stevens, because he was wearing Georgie's clothes," Rita Kamin had said. She must have repeated it ten or twelve times, trying to absolve her own guilt over not checking more closely on who was sitting beside Stephanie while she played in her sandbox. "I glanced out the back door when I came up to get a blouse I wanted to iron. I saw him, but I thought it was Georgie. He was wearing Georgie's jeans and his red-and-blue plaid shirt—the same as I've seen him wear dozens of times after school. But school wasn't out yet, and I didn't even think—it was too early for Georgie to be home."

"Are you *sure* Georgie didn't come home, Mrs. Kamin? Maybe he was sick, or maybe there was an early dismissal."

"No . . . no," she had wailed. "It *wasn't* Georgie. His mother told me he wasn't home yet, but his pants and shirt were missing from the clothesline. She was taking the clothes down and came running when she heard me screaming, and she stayed with me till my husband got here. She was the one who telephoned the State Police barracks. After . . . after the worst had happened . . . I realized that my mind had registered what I expected to see when I looked out the back door. But it really wasn't

Georgie. At the time it didn't quite sink in . . . but there was something different about him."

"What was different?" Vargo had asked gently.

"The hair . . . longer and darker than Georgie's. And the profile. Georgie has a receding chin. I was looking at him through the screen door . . . all the way across the yard. It was natural for me to assume that nothing bad was going on."

"You're not to blame," Vargo had said.

He wanted to talk to Mrs. Stevens and her son Georgie. Presumably they would be able to accurately describe the stolen clothes. From Richard Kamin, Stephanie's father, he already had a description of the boots missing from the shed.

From an earlier call that had come into the Greensburg barracks, he knew that a flasher had been reported wandering around in the woods near the construction site of the new mall, not far from here. If the report was accurate, the suspect wasn't just an ordinary flasher, but someone with *all* his clothes off. Vargo wondered if it could be an escaped inmate from nearby Laurel State Hospital. It would have to be checked.

Hell, Vargo didn't even know yet just how Stephanie had died. He reminded himself not to jump to conclusions. But he had a gut feeling that this was murder. The missing clothes, the report of the naked flasher, the mystery man sitting on the sandbox, all added up to too much coincidence surrounding the death of one little girl.

Coming down off the porch, Vargo glanced at his wristwatch: almost four-thirty. The coroner ought to be here any minute. The R&I men appeared just about ready to wrap up. Vargo crossed the yard to the gate and stopped to talk with Trooper Hoskins.

"Do you mind keeping a watch here by yourself for a while longer, Jim? A couple of neighbors should be interviewed immediately. It won't take long. I can fill you in when I get back."

Hoskins nodded, pursing his lips grimly. "Go ahead, Ron. I'll hold down the fort."

Vargo went out through the open gate, and the onlookers watched him. He heard a few nosy questions blurted at his back, but he didn't answer. At least the nearest neighbors had sense enough to keep their kids inside, if they had any. Farther along, some tots were playing in their fenced-in yard, but they were too small to look over the fence and too far away to see anything very disturbing. Still, if they were Vargo's kids he'd have kept them in the house.

He and his wife hadn't tried to have a second child after what had happened to Kathy. Somehow the subject never even came up. He just kept using a condom. But they didn't have sex so often anymore, either. He tried to push all his energy into his barbells.

Perspiring in the hot sun, he kept scanning his surroundings as he walked, in case he might spot something. Maybe more than a pair of trousers and a shirt had been swiped from the clothesline; maybe an article of clothing had been dropped. But he didn't see anything. When he arrived at the Stevenses' place he paused to wipe the sweat from his brow and looked up at the clear blue sky. It was a beautiful day in mid-June. Hard to believe that an innocent child could die on such a beautiful day. Earlier the State Police helicopter team had been out flying over this area, looking for the flasher reported by the bulldozer crew. They hadn't been lucky enough to spot him because at that time he was probably sticking to the cover of the woods.

Vargo smelled something cooking as he came through the yard. The clothesline was still up, strung between galvanized steel poles, but the clothes had been taken down. The house was similar to all the others in the development; its aluminum siding was pastel green. He went up onto the back porch and knocked at the door. Mrs. Stevens opened it right away. She was short and frumpy, in her mid-forties. "Come in," she said. "I'm baking a meatloaf. It seems almost like an irreverent thing to do. I keep trying not to think about what happened to poor little Stephanie." She kept nervously wiping her hands on her frilly flowery apron.

"I know how you feel," said Vargo. "This kind of thing

isn't easy for me either. But unfortunately it's part of my job. Just to clear up a few things, I'd like to speak with you and your son."

"Come into the living room. Diane Jacobs—Georgie's girlfriend—is here, and you'll probably want to talk to her also."

"Why?"

"She was with him in homeroom. And then she rode home with him on the bus. They didn't get here till a half hour ago."

"I see."

"My gas dryer is on the blink," said Mrs. Stevens. "I could have taken my wet clothes next door, but rather than pestering Mrs. Barnett I decided to just hang them in the fresh air."

Vargo followed her into the living room, which looked just like the one at the Kamins' house except that it was painted a different color and the furnishings were newer and might have cost more. Diane and Georgie were sitting on the sofa with the TV going. Mrs. Stevens shut it off. Then she joined the two teenagers on the sofa. Vargo introduced himself and sat down opposite them on a tan vinyl armchair.

Georgie didn't look like he had anything to hide. He had probably never been questioned by a detective before, but he didn't display an inordinate amount of nervousness. He was an average-looking sixteen-year-old.

Diane was a knockout—a black-haired, voluptuous beauty who looked as if she should have been paired with someone a lot older and far more manly and sophisticated than Georgie Stevens.

Diane unhesitatingly confirmed Georgie and his mother's story. After talking with the three, Vargo was convinced they were telling the truth.

The two teenagers had left school together at three o'clock and had ridden together on the school bus, since Diane had been invited to the Stevenses' for dinner. Georgie had been in school all day. Vargo would confirm that tomorrow, but he believed that the alibi would hold up.

Georgie Stevens was five feet eleven inches tall and weighed one hundred and forty, which should be a fair approximation of the height and weight of whoever was wearing his clothes. Using the phone in the Stevenses' kitchen, Vargo called the Greensburg barracks to ask them to put out an all points bulletin and to get the helicopter flying again, now that he had a better idea of what the suspect looked like—probably of medium build, wearing a red-and-blue long-sleeved plaid shirt, light blue Levi trousers, and scuffed-up brown Dingo boots full of grass stains. He also put in a call to the director of Laurel State Hospital. Every inmate was supposedly present and accounted for; but he had little faith in the information since the institution's security had been bad enough to allow Kathy's killer to escape little more than a year ago. Finally, he phoned the Greensburg Fire Department and requested that the two firemen who worked a team of bloodhounds get themselves and their dogs out to the scene of Stephanie Kamin's murder. He didn't call it a murder out loud, but privately he had stopped thinking of it as anything else.

When he returned to the Kamins' yard, he saw that County Coroner Ed Stanford was in the middle of the sandbox, crouching over the little girl's corpse. In his early fifties, Stanford was lean and wiry, with a shock of thick gray hair, and wire-rimmed eyeglasses perched over a sharp, inquisitive nose.

Vargo watched Stanford take his thermometer out of Stephanie's mouth and read it, comparing the drop in body temperature with the temperature of the air, which would help in estimating the time of death. Stephanie still lay flat on her back in the sand, her eyes wide open to the sun. She was wearing only a pair of red shorts, the bottom half of a sunsuit. Her face was puffy and whitish blue.

"You didn't cover her hands," Stanford accused.

"I wanted you to see the cut on her finger," Vargo replied. Normal police procedure would have been for him to put plastic bags over Stephanie's hands, in case she had died in a struggle and had scratched whoever was attacking her, getting skin particles under her nails.

"The cut isn't too deep," the coroner said. "Doesn't look like it bled much. Looks like she must have put it in her mouth, the way kids do, and licked it clean."

"How do you think she died?"

"Hard to say. If somebody choked her, he didn't bruise her throat. Asphyxiation can make the face puffy and blue the way hers is, but so can certain types of snake venom. Another possibility is anaphylactic shock—an acute reaction to a bee or hornet sting. You can see that the cut finger is swollen twice its normal size, and some of the swelling moved into her hand. If the wound looked more like a fang mark, I'd feel pretty certain about what must have killed her. But it doesn't—it looks like an ordinary cut. Maybe some poisonous insect stung her right on top of the cut. An experience like that might frighten a little girl into shock. Extreme fright can paralyze the vagus nerve, stopping all bodily functions, including breathing."

"Could there have been poison on whatever cut her?"

"Possibly. If so, lab tests might find traces at the wound site—and in her mouth, assuming she licked the cut. But it would be a very difficult test to run, since saliva would have diluted the poison."

"It would help if I could find what cut her," Vargo said.

"It certainly would," Ed Stanford agreed.

"I don't think it was a snake," said Vargo. "If a snake bit her, she'd have run screaming to her mother right away. Same thing if she was stung by a bee or a hornet."

"Depends on how quickly she sank into shock," Stanford contradicted. "In extreme cases it can be all over in a matter of seconds." He pursed his lips, thinking. "You notice there are some spiderwebs under the bench of the sandbox? A poisonous spider might have bitten her without her noticing. The tiny prickle of pain would have merged with the stinging of the cut."

"Quite a coincidence to get bitten right on top of the cut," said Vargo.

"Yes. But human fingers are particularly vulnerable, always getting hurt in various ways. We are always using them, always poking them into things."

"She had lunch at noon," said Vargo. "A peanut butter

and jelly sandwich and a glass of milk. She didn't have a cut on her finger at that time. I asked her mother."

"We'll have the stomach contents analyzed to determine how much digestion took place," said Stanford. "It'll help narrow down the approximate time of death."

He took two small plastic bags out of his black leather kit and secured them over Stephanie's hands. Then he put a larger bag over her head to stop sand or other contamination from getting in her mouth. That done, he turned the body over on its stomach. There were no unusual marks on her back, no wounds, no signs of a struggle or an attack. With a soft brush, Stanford brushed away sand from the child's back and legs. "No abrasions from squirming in the sand," he remarked. "It's very odd. Looks like she just fell down and succumbed, with hardly any fuss."

"Could have been knocked unconscious," Vargo ventured.

"If so, the autopsy will show a skull fracture or a concussion," Stanford said. "But I don't see any outward signs of it. No bruises or swelling under her hair."

Right then two white-coated ambulance attendants carrying a body bag and a collapsible stretcher rounded the side of the house. When Stanford was ready, he signed some papers, releasing the corpse so it could be taken to the Allegheny County Morgue in Pittsburgh, where the autopsy would be performed.

After Stephanie's body had been carried away and the coroner had departed, Troopers Vargo and Hoskins stood waiting for the two firemen and their bloodhounds. "What kind of scent are you hoping to pick up?" Hoskins asked. "We've got to give the dogs something to work with."

"Maybe something off the sandbox bench," Vargo told him. "Or off the toy shovel and bucket. I'm also considering the boots—Mr. Kamin's scent would be on them."

As he talked he was looking at the place where the little girl's body had lain, as if the depression in the sand could tell him something. He stared at the two sand castles, one at either end of the sandbox. Each one had holes, like imaginary windows, going around the perimeter. Ed Stanford had said that people were always poking their fingers into things— Suddenly Vargo realized how Stephanie might have cut her finger.

He found a lawn rake in the shed and began raking through one of the sand castles, very slowly and carefully. When he heard a tinkle, he uncovered a piece of greenish glass, possibly a fragment of a pop bottle. He picked it up, using a corner of his clean handkerchief, and wrapped up the item of evidence. He tucked it into his inside jacket pocket. Then, while Hoskins watched, he continued raking through the sand in the sandbox, hoping to turn up something else valuable.

6

Norman Willoughby dropped Benjamin Latham off in front of the Hilton Hotel in the heart of Pittsburgh's Golden Triangle—a complex of shiny green, gray, and golden skyscrapers at the Point, where the Monongahela and Allegheny rivers flowed together to form the Ohio. In the 1750s the French had built Fort Duquesne here in an attempt to control access to the rich and fertile Ohio Valley. And after the English drove the French out, they erected Fort Pitt, named after Prime Minister William Pitt, to safeguard what became known to pioneers as the Gateway to the West.

In 1776, at the outbreak of the American Revolution, Pittsburgh consisted of about fifty ramshackle log cabins clustered around the fort. There might have been three hundred people living in the vicinity, including soldiers. Daniel Brodhead, a Patriot officer considering how best to make use of the existing fortifications, suggested that the first step in defending Pittsburgh should be to burn the settlement to the ground.

Well, Benjamin Latham thought to himself, Brodhead would have a jolly tough time of burning it now. Who would have imagined such a colossus could have grown up out of the mud? It was a gigantic, clamorous sprawl of honking cars, foul-smelling trucks, and angry, sweaty pedestrians swarming and shoving in and around and through an oppressive milieu of steel, aluminum, and concrete.

Norman's glowing watch dial had said five o'clock. Benjamin didn't realize that this was the peak of the evening rush hour. Later he would find out that for most of the day the city wasn't so congested, so tumultuous. In his day, Philadelphia had been an awesome, booming metropolis, its population of forty thousand making it the largest city in the New World and one of the largest in the British Empire. Looking all around him at this modern city of Pittsburgh, he imagined that it must hold at least half a million people—a figure so staggering that he felt silly even thinking of it, although the evidence was before his very eyes.

"There's Point Park, right across the street," Norman had said. Benjamin wanted to visit the site of the old fort. More importantly and urgently, he wanted to get out of the clash and clamor of the city proper. He could see the grassy sprawl of the park over the tops of the cars, so close he could almost taste it. But he remained rooted in front of the Hilton, scared to cross the boulevard in the crush of ongoing traffic. Finally he got up the nerve and darted across, zigzagging frantically as horns honked and brakes squealed, and by some miracle he reached the curb without being smashed to the pavement.

Gradually his heart stopped pounding so fiercely as he entered the park by means of a wide concrete walkway. Within earshot of the traffic jam, he found a measure of peacefulness. Young men and women strolled or lay together in the grass, disporting themselves lewdly in public. He averted his eyes from such couples. He watched boys and girls running after a thing that they tossed back and forth—a green, saucer-shaped thing that floated wondrously through the air at a skillful flick of the arm and wrist.

Over the trees and grass of the beautiful park loomed enormous concrete buttresses and steel girders of bridges filled with traffic. Gray, green, and gold skyscrapers formed a backdrop for the entire scene, which seemed like a pastoral oasis in the midst of urban grotesqueness.

The first reminder of Fort Pitt that Benjamin encountered was a reconstructed portion of the Music Bastion and Curtain Wall, where the drawbridge had been located. There was no need for a drawbridge anymore, since there was no longer a moat. A bronze plaque on a wall of red bricks set into the grassy earth stated that these were the remnants of one of five bastions built between 1759 and 1761 under General John Stanwix. Obviously they weren't the original bricks. Benjamin remembered how the bricks used to build the fort were made out of clay dug from Ayres's Hill, across the Monongahela, and were a dirty white instead of red.

Feeling like a man walking in a dream of his previous lifetime, he left the remains of the Music Bastion and headed toward a concrete footbridge about twenty feet wide, with shiny steel handrails. He clutched on to one of the rails to support himself, for he felt dreamy and woozy. The footbridge passed under the huge concrete arches of a much larger bridge supporting a highway choked with traffic. Underneath was not any bubbling brook but instead a mosaic of cobblestones arranged in geometric patterns. On the other side stood the Fort Pitt Museum and one of the original blockhouses. The museum was built right into the earthworks of another of the five bastions of the old fort. It was closed. Benjamin walked up to the glass doors and read the schedule of visiting hours—which had ended at four-thirty.

The blockhouse was closed, too. A plaque in front of the five-sided windowless brick structure explained that it was a redoubt with rifle slits and firing platforms upstairs and down, built by Colonel Henry Bouquet in 1764, purchased with the site of Fort Pitt by General John O'Hara in 1805, and presented to the Daughters of the American Revolution in 1892. The dates on the plaque seemed to flit through more than a hundred years of history like a pebble skipping over a pond. Benjamin could not make the transition so easily. The litany of years dead and gone, nothing but numbers etched in bronze, put him into a melancholy state. He stared at the stone tablet over the heavy wooden blockhouse door, and the sight of Colonel Bouquet's name nearly worn away by the elements, when he remembered it freshly carved, made him feel old and out of place.

Not knowing what to do with himself, he walked deeper into the park, following a trail that led past a series of stone benches. Nothing more of the old fort greeted his eyes.

At the Point itself, the very tip of the triangle of land at the forks of the Ohio, he saw a huge fountain shooting foamy geysers of water a hundred feet into the sky. He stood apart from everyone and looked across the Allegheny River. Smoky Island, where Indians used to torture prisoners, had disappeared.

The log stockade of Fort Duquesne, the French fort, would have stood almost right on top of the Point Park fountain. Benjamin was held prisoner there from 1755 until 1758; he had been captured during Braddock's defeat. His life had been spared by the French victor, Captain Ligneris, who needed a physician to treat some of his sick and wounded soldiers. Fourteen other English prisoners hadn't been so lucky. The Delaware and Shawnee Indian allies of Ligneris had stripped their captives naked, tied their hands behind their backs and tarred their bodies, then forced them to make a barefooted eight-mile march over rough trails to Fort Duquesne, prodding and beating them all the way for their sins against the Great Spirit. Benjamin had been allowed to keep his clothes and dignity.

Captain Ligneris had Benjamin protected by a guard of musket-bearing soldiers as he tended the enemy wounded who were brought inside Fort Duquesne on litters. He tried to immerse himself in his work of healing amid the cries of war-painted heathens and the roar and stench of celebratory gunfire. Several of his patients had arms or legs so badly shattered by leaden musket balls that the limbs needed to be amputated. The screams of the men under the surgeon's saw blended with the hideous war whoops of the drunken, frenzied Indians.

As a blood-red sunset hovered over the towering southwestern bank of the Monongahela, the naked prisoners were taken by canoe over to Smoky Island. Benjamin had to go with them. "I have ransomed your life from Chief Pontiac," said Captain Ligneris. "The chief has given his sacred word that you will not be harmed. But he insists that you must be an eyewitness to the fate of the others, so that you can warn all Englishmen to stay out of the hunting grounds west of the Three Rivers."

Made to stand with his hands tied behind him, Benjamin was bound to a tree, coils of rope knotted around his chest, waist, and ankles. A band of rawhide was tightened around his forehead so he'd have to keep his head up, facing the area where the torture of the other prisoners was to take place. "Do not close your eyes," Chief Pontiac said. "Every time you do, you will bring increased suffering to your countrymen, for we will prolong the release of their spirits to the white man's heaven."

Pontiac had straight black hair, a hooked nose, and yellowish pockmarked skin. His face was painted in streaks of red, white, and purple. Outside of beads and feathers and a necklace of animal teeth, he wore only a breechclout and a bloody, bullet-riddled scarlet coat. He did not take part in the atrocities on Smoky Island, but stood by explaining them to Benjamin and watching that his eyes did not blink shut.

"They will now run the gauntlet," Pontiac said. "This is part of our welcome to them, the mildest part, just our way of saying how do you do."

The Indians, men and women of the Shawnee, Delaware, and Ottawa tribes, formed two long files facing each other, all armed with knives, tomahawks, or clubs. Flames flickered eerily on their barbarically distorted faces as they brandished their weapons and kept up an incessant pandemonium of war whoops and hysterical chanting. One by one, the prisoners were forced to run the gantlet, while the Indians tried to rain hard blows on their naked, tar-blackened bodies without hitting them on the head so they wouldn't be put out of their misery too soon. Surprisingly, all fourteen managed to survive this "mild" part of the ordeal, though some had to be dragged to their feet, half conscious or half dead.

Bleeding and groaning piteously, they were mocked and derided by Indian braves who had to hold their sagging bodies upright till they could be tied securely to stakes ringing the bonfires in the island clearing. Having survived the gantlet, they were now subjected to the most fiendish tortures their captors could devise. Fiery embers were heaped about their feet. The women thrust red-hot sticks into their nostrils and ears and seared their genitals, shrieking hilariously when the hair took fire. Even the children joined in, coming up close with their half-sized bows and shooting arrows into the prisoners' arms and legs.

By an effort of will, Benjamin kept his eyes open, but he was so dazed and sickened that what he was seeing scarcely registered. His eyes were frozen open in abject terror. He heard himself mumbling a prayer, begging God to put the sufferers to rest mercifully.

Chief Pontiac laughed sarcastically. "The Great Spirit will not hear you," he jeered. "You are wasting your breath, white man."

"Then the Great Spirit must be a spirit of evil," Benjamin said in a hoarse but defiant voice.

"The Great Spirit belongs only to the red man," said Pontiac. "We are Lenni Lenape—God's Original People. The white man is a mongrel with hair and eyes of ugly unmatching colors—like a dog of an inferior, mixed breed."

A young and beautiful Indian maiden who had been one of the most enthusiastic and inventive torturers now approached one of the men tied to a stake, who seemed to be dead or near death. In her right hand she held a sharp, gleaming knife, and in her left hand a gourd. Deftly she slit the man's throat—and he had *not* been dead, for he emitted a gurgling scream as jets of bright red blood spurted from his jugular vein. The Indian maiden collected as much as she could in her gourd, her arms streaked red as the spurts ebbed to tiny pulsating streams . . . and then to a lifeless trickle.

Kneeling in the dirt at the feet of the dead man, she raised the gourd high, offering it to Chief Pontiac, the foremost warrior on the island.

Before striding forward to accept the maiden's gift, the chief said to Benjamin, "We drink the blood of our vanquished enemies, but only if they die bravely without begging for mercy. We do not want the milk of cowards in our veins. You white men will never conquer us red men, because each of us will grow stronger and more fierce every time we feast on the blood of one of you."

For the better part of two hours Troopers Vargo and Hoskins tramped through the woods, chasing after the bloodhounds. There were four dogs and two firemen handling them, armed with shotguns and heavy-caliber pistols. The dogs had been given the scent of Mr. Kamin's overalls—basically the same scent as on his missing boots. They started off sniffing and yelping, their noses to the ground—but they lost the trail on the other side of the woods, on Route 819.

"Could have hitchhiked from here," one of the firemen said. A big burly man, he was huffing and puffing from the hard trek behind the dogs. "Probably caught a ride out to Route Thirty, and from there east or west—your guess is as good as mine."

"Got a good four-hour lead on us anyways," the skinnier fireman said. Accepting defeat, he jerked a cigarette out of a flattened pack and lit it, watching the yipping disappointed bloodhounds racing back and forth futilely hunting for the lost scent.

"We've got to get this into the newspapers," said Vargo. He wasn't breathing hard, but his insides were churning with as much nervous energy as the dogs gave off visually. "This guy could be on the other side of the continent in another three hours. I'm not letting him get away, like John Hampton."

Hampton was the one who had raped and stabbed Kathy. When the man escaped from Laurel State Hospital Vargo had pushed himself almost to the point of a nervous breakdown, trying to hunt him down. He wished he had shot him in the back the first time, so he wouldn't ever have gotten loose again. He itched to correct the oversight. But the leads petered out. In the past ten months, no new clues had turned up. Unless . . .

Hampton might be prowling his old territory again, like a beast returning to familiar hunting grounds. He could be the one who had killed Stephanie. The physical description was scanty, just an idea as to height and weight—but so far Hampton wasn't ruled out. He was about the same size as Georgie Stevens.

Vargo wanted the killer so badly it made his blood race, made his temples throb. Wanted to grab him. Wanted to smash him. Tear him apart. Never mind reading him his rights. Unless he could hear the criminal-coddling Miranda warning after he was dead.

"If he made it to Route Thirty he could have gotten onto the turnpike," Hoskins said. "In which case he could be damned near to Philadelphia already."

Watching Hoskins's Adam's apple bob and listening to his slow, half-unconcerned drawl riled Vargo to an even greater pitch of frustration. "That's my point," he snapped. "We're not going to pick up his trail again without the kind of lead that we can only get by going public."

"You're the boss," Hoskins muttered.

The two firemen had leashed their dogs and started back through the woods with Hoskins and Vargo following. Since they knew exactly where they were headed this time and didn't have to wait for the bloodhounds to sniff and circle, it took them less than an hour to get back to the housing area where Stephanie Kamin had lived. Somehow it looked even more dismal now that the sun was going down and the rays weren't glinting so brightly off the various pastels of aluminum siding.

"Wonder if he even knows he killed her," the burly fireman said.

"What do you mean?" asked Hoskins.

"Some of these lunatics go around in a trance. High on dope or their own screwed-up thoughts. It's like they're in a different world altogether. A fifth dimension or something, where they're not aware of or responsible for their actions."

"We're going to explain to this guy what responsibility means," Vargo said softly.

Hoskins could barely hear the words, but he shivered with worry as he saw Vargo's white knuckles clenched around his pistol.

"Hey, my man! Can you let me hold a dollar?"

Benjamin spun around and found himself confronted by a gang of scruffy young men in ragged denim. There were four of them. Two were black and two were white.

"I don't have any money at all," he told them.

One of the blacks snickered. "Hey, you talk funny! You from England or what, my *man?*" He laid on the word "man" with a heavy, threatening drawl while his pals closed in tighter, hemming Benjamin in.

He looked around for help. He wasn't far from the fountain and its small crowd of people. But he sensed that if these young men were to pounce on him, no one would come to his rescue; nobody else would get involved. That's why the rascals were so openly insolent, ready to perform any outrage with impunity. The black fellows baldly lacked the passive demeanor of slaves. Were they freedmen? Had the slaves *all* been set free, as Tom Paine, the author of *Common Sense,* had advocated back in 1776? It was one small point upon which Benjamin Latham the Tory had agreed with Paine the rabble-rouser. Benjamin's father, a Philadelphia Quaker, had always been against slavery and had raised his family accordingly.

"If you comin' on straight, lemme see the insides of your pockets," said one of the blacks. "Come on, turn them inside out for us."

"If his pockets is empty, then he could have a wad stuck inside them big boots," the other black reasoned.

Benjamin sized up his adversaries. One of the whites—the big one with the evilly handsome face and a jagged scar on his cheek—hadn't spoken so far, yet he seemed to be the leader. It was in the way he smirked, black eyes glinting coldly, while he hung back from the action just a couple of steps, with the air of someone who didn't need to get his knuckles skinned unless he wanted to. He was the chief and the other men were the braves. Sticking around debating with them would be like trying to talk a renegade war party out of taking a scalp.

Letting his shoulders slump and sag, Benjamin started turning his trousers pockets inside out. The young toughs grinned at each other, taking perverse pleasure in their power to intimidate.

"Hurry up, man, show us what you holdin' and we might even let you keep some," one of the blacks teased.

"Don't try to jive us, now," said the other black. "You can't hide your wad from us. We gonna make you take your boots off come hell or high water."

Suddenly Benjamin uncoiled, plowing his shoulder into the one he had diagnosed as leader. Scarface grunted and sagged, the wind knocked out of his lungs, and Benjamin practically ran right over him as he hit hard on his buttocks. The others were stunned for a few seconds, but then they leaped into action. Benjamin sprinted across the green, heading for the far side of the park, with the gang—minus one—coming after him. Glancing back over his shoulder, he saw Scarface dragging himself to his feet, swearing and groaning. The leader could do no more than limp along slowly for the time being, but his henchmen were in hot pursuit.

Benjamin whizzed past a couple embracing and kissing on a stone bench, and they didn't even look up at him! There was no place to hide; the park had few trees. He zigzagged around the blockhouse, trying to use it to temporarily shield whatever change in direction he might choose.

"Split up!" the leader called out, his voice weak in the distance. "Come at him from both sides of the building!"

Pivoting sharply to his left, Benjamin ran past the museum and across the long concrete footbridge. He was out of the park now.

He dashed across Commonwealth Place, making the cars squeal their brakes. When his foot hit the curb he glanced back—his pursuers were still coming, dodging cars too. Then he darted across Stanwix Street, perpendicular to Commonwealth Place, doing a wild dance to avoid getting run over. Again brakes screeched and horns honked. He flung open the glass door of a building called Allegheny Tower and ran inside.

People were standing in the lobby. When a pair of gray metal doors slid open magically with a soft whoosh, exposing a boxlike windowless cell, people entered the cell, so Benjamin did too. The gray doors shut just in time to prevent one of the thugs from getting a hand in. Then the cell moved, giving Benjamin a sinking feeling in the pit of his stomach. He noticed the other people were all watching some digits that lit up in sequence, signifying various floors—apparently the purpose of this cell-like device was to lift people up so they would not have to climb stairs. One man got out on level 2, but the doors opened and shut too fast for Benjamin to make a decision. At level 3 the doors slid open again, and he got out along with a middle-aged couple who moved off at a brisk pace.

He was in some sort of elevated concrete catacomb filled with parked cars, but he had barely had time to glance around when an orange door burst open and one of the thugs came at him, wielding a knife. Benjamin backed away. From behind him somewhere, a woman screamed. "Come on, it's none of our business!" a man barked. Their voices and footsteps trailed away, echoing hollowly in the bowels of the car catacomb.

The thug chortled confidently, a leer on his face as his knife blade glinted and flashed. Benjamin continued to backpedal, stalling for time. He heard car doors slam and an engine starting up. The strangers who might have helped him were instead leaving him to his fate. He decided against turning and running, which would only expose his back to the thug with the knife.

Even while he was sidestepping and backing away down an aisle between rows of dusty parked cars, he was studying his opponent's style of attack, hoping to spot an opening for a well-timed feint—followed by a skillful switch to the offensive. He focused all his attention on seeing into the rhythms and nuances of the encounter, until it was as if he and the other man were locked together in an eerily menacing waltz that transcended any ordinary concept of time and space.

Benjamin slipped into a feeling of slow motion, a state of being in which he had extraordinary control over his five senses and heightened awareness of every perception. He saw it all—every thrust, every flicker, every glint of the knife blade—as if it were all slowed down, measured and timed for his own particular rhythms and reflexes. He was completely at home in this sudden and strange milieu, and his opponent was an awkward interloper. He could resolve the conflict at his leisure. He could capture or avoid the knife. He could do whatever he wanted. Because he was able to see everything at a much slower speed than his opponent, he could seem to move faster, even though such an ability was illogical and irrational. It was the kind of power that one sometimes enjoyed in a dream. He even doubted that it was real, although at the same time he knew that it was.

He looked the thug unblinkingly in the eyes. Not only did he feel a remarkable control over the pace and sequence of events, he also felt a trancelike force exerted by his mind over the mind of this other, inferior creature. The thug flinched. Then he began to tremble. Deep inside, with the certainty of despair, it dawned on him that his weapon was now useless. He made an effort to stab, but Benjamin saw it so clearly that he simply reached out and seized the thug's wrist, as easily as if the man didn't even try to avoid being grabbed. The wrist was squeezed in a vise so tight that the veins swelled blue, and the knife was dropped. Then, a hand on the thug's throat, Benjamin forced him to the concrete floor, which smelled of tarry dirt and carlike fumes. The black eyes began to glaze as Benjamin's fingers tightened . . . and tightened. . . .

Kneeling over his victim, he stared into the dying eyes and thought to himself that he would like to know where the other three gang members were . . . and from the thug's mind to his passed an image of the others searching for him on two upper floors. The thought image faded slowly as the thug died.

Benjamin went through the dead man's pockets and pulled out some bills and coins. He examined the stuff before putting it into his own pants pocket. He was sure that it must be modern currency.

With the sharp knife that had been dropped on the floor, Benjamin slit the thug's wrist, and since the heart was no longer beating the blood didn't spurt out but instead oozed and trickled. Benjamin drank some, finding it exceptionally satisfying. He was reminded of what Chief Pontiac had told him about the benefits of drinking the blood of one's enemies.

And even though he still felt guilty about killing the little girl, this man's death brought no remorse.

Vargo and Hoskins had split up, each taking half of the houses in the development, but their interviews turned up no new information.

Using a wall phone in the kitchen of the last house on his agenda, Vargo put in a call to State Police headquarters. The desk sergeant told him that the helicopter team had not sighted anyone matching the suspect's description. The all points bulletin to municipal police departments had not netted any result either. Dave Fein, the lieutenant in charge of the Criminal Investigation Section of the Greensburg barracks, had punched out at about six, leaving word for Vargo to phone him at home to brief him on the Stephanie Kamin case. Fein was Vargo's boss. The lieutenant's approval would be necessary before information about the suspect could be released to the media in detail.

But it turned out that the lieutenant did not want to "overreact."

"Our best shot is to go on TV and radio with this," Vargo argued. "The sooner the better. We've got to take a chance that he was picked up hitchhiking, and whoever picked him up will contact us if we get his attention—if we make him realize that the guy he picked up is the same one we want. If we don't do it right away, our suspect is going to fade out of somebody's memory."

"We don't have much to raise a fuss about so far," said Fein. "A possible flasher. Not a case of murder, not till the coroner says so. How can we go on the air looking for a murder suspect for a murder that doesn't officially exist?"

"We can call it suspected murder. I don't care what we call it at this point, but we can't wait. If we don't get a better description of him from someone who saw him close to the scene of the crime, he's going to escape into the anonymity of a big city like Pittsburgh or Philadelphia."

"Well," said Fein, "if a better description is what's going to capture him, we can still get it tomorrow or the next day, when we're likely to be certain exactly what crime has been committed. And by then the lab may be able to identify our suspect by feeding a fingerprint analysis into a computer."

"Providing they've got anything better than smudges," Vargo countered. "Besides, it may take them days to eliminate the dozens of prints that must've been left by the Kamins and their neighbors."

"We'll have to hope otherwise," said Fein. "Letting the media label this murder when we're not really sure would be crying wolf."

When Vargo hung up, he was angry and frustrated. He hated Fein's kind of attitude: a careful, plodding professionalism that protected him from making a false move in public. Fein's constipated approach to crime solving kept his mistakes few and his successes unspectacular. He would rather make an error of omission than one of commission—which would be so much easier for his superiors to spot. He tried to appear patient and methodical in the performance of his duties, but he was really overly cautious and uninspired. Part of his conceit was to treat Vargo as an officer whose reckless impulsiveness must be reined in and controlled.

Vargo dialed his home number, and his wife, Norma, answered. He told her he wouldn't be home till after midnight, he was working late on a new case. He didn't tell her what the case was, and she didn't ask. He knew she wouldn't. She didn't care so very much anymore what time he came home, whether he made it for dinner or not. Sometimes he felt that she cared less than he did himself. Her voice on the phone had sounded remote and lifeless. It had sounded that way ever since they had lost Kathy.

Vargo tried to remember the time, in the first eight and a half years of their marriage, when he and Norma had been reasonably happy together. When they had made love regularly and passionately and tenderly, and had shared the birth and rearing of their baby daughter. His memory of himself and his wife and child in a snug, cheerful family unit was like a hazy recollection of strangers he had once known intimately, who had become separated from him by a curtain of unkind years.

In his pocket, wrapped in his handkerchief, he still had the piece of broken glass he had removed from the sandbox. After he and Hoskins got done comparing notes, finding out that their interviews of the neighbors had produced no worthwhile information, Vargo asked Hoskins to take the article of evidence with him to the State Police crime laboratory at the Greensburg barracks.

"Where are you going—home?" Hoskins asked.

"Yeah," Vargo lied.

The truth was, he had decided to drive into Pittsburgh. He couldn't relax, couldn't simply go home to dinner and bed. He'd prowl around the city by himself, even if it was only to still his anxious restlessness. But Vargo had to be out doing something. Not lying in his bed, suffering from insomnia, listening to his wife tossing and turning beside him.

It was after dark when he said good night to Hoskins and got behind the wheel of his unmarked black Chevrolet sedan in front of the Kamins' house. Pittsburgh was the likeliest place for the suspect to run to.

His first stop was the Greyhound station. It was a hangout for transients and shady characters looking for new arrivals from out of town who might be easy prey. Groups of these human vermin clustered together on benches, intimidating ordinary people waiting for buses; or leaned against walls of metal lockers, passing joints back and forth; or loafed at the lunch counter and in the lavatories, dealing dope and sex, or just jiving and sneering and motherfucking each other and everybody and everything.

Most of them froze into poses of nonchalance and silence as Vargo approached, because they figured him for a cop. He glowered at each and every one of them, letting them know they were right. Moving slowly and deliberately, he checked out everybody in the Greyhound station, but he didn't spot what he was really looking for. He almost hoped one of the current crop of creeps would give him some trouble so he would have an excuse to smash the hell out of him.

He left his car parked in the lot across from the bus terminal and began cruising the rest of Liberty Avenue on foot. This section of downtown Pittsburgh was like New York's Times Square area—a conglomeration of massage parlors, pornographic bookstores and movie houses, squalid saloons and greasy-spoon restaurants, surplus stores and fleabag hotels. Vargo prowled past one joint after another, elbowing his way through crowds of loiterers, poking his nose inside some of the places to peer through thick, sour booze and cigarette fumes at the hostility, drunkenness, and despair of bitter, desperate people. He didn't see anyone wearing blue Levi's and a red-and-blue plaid shirt. Most of the costumes worn by the denizens of Liberty Avenue were either a lot shabbier than that or a lot more bizarre. Like the pimps in their white suits, lavender shirts, and white Panama hats. And the hookers in slinky red satin dresses and red spike-heeled shoes.

Vargo walked up and down both sides of Liberty Avenue and on some of the side streets, till it was close to midnight. He was tired and thirsty, and although the night had cooled down some, it was still hot. He had put in a long day. And he had to reluctantly admit that he probably wasn't going to accomplish anything more.

He drove to Freddy's Place, a small saloon on Second Avenue. It was a hangout for cops. Freddy, the owner, was a redheaded Irish ex-cop with a whiskey nose and a huge beer belly under an expanse of white apron. He was tending bar when Vargo walked in.

"Whatsay, Vargo," Freddy called out gruffly over the din of the jukebox and the clanging of pucks on the bowling machine. "What brings you to town? Working on a case?"

"Yeah. Had to do some nosing around."

"You want the usual? Frozen fishbowl?"

"Yeah, Freddy. Please."

"You look like you can use it," Freddy said as he poured foamy draft beer into a large ice-coated fishbowl glass. He set it in front of Vargo and watched him drain about half of it in a few thirsty gulps. Then he said, "Working late is a pain in the ass. But it's better than coming in here to testify in court against some asshole punk who ain't never going to do any time anyways after his lawyer gets done jerking everybody off."

"Right you are, Freddy," Vargo said. He pivoted on his stool to see if he knew any of the guys playing the bowling machine. He thought he recognized two of the four from seeing them before in Freddy's Place, but he didn't really know them personally.

"Your buddy Jack Harpster is in the booth back there," Freddy said. "He's been working late, too, on a homicide thing. Maybe you ought to go back and keep him company so he won't swill his booze down too fast."

"I wouldn't mind talking to Jack," Vargo said. "Why don't you give me a refill first?"

"Don't buy him a round," said Freddy. "He doesn't need any encouragement."

"I know."

Harpster, craggy-faced and gray-haired in his mid-fifties, was wearing a rumpled tan suit and a chocolate-colored tie loosened at the knot. He had a half-full mug of beer in front of him, and an empty shotglass. "Well, well . . . sit down and join me, Vargo," he said, his speech a bit slurred. Over the past ten years he had developed a drinking problem, after his wife divorced him and took their two children to California. Most of the cops who knew him tried to help him stay sober whenever they could, in hopes he could last till his retirement. It didn't seem so wrong to do him the favor, since he never got drunk on the job. "What brings you to town?" he asked after Vargo slid into the booth, facing him.

Vargo recounted the details of the Stephanie Kamin case, including the cut on her finger, the mysterious swelling of her finger and hand, and the coroner's uncertainty as to just how she had died. Harpster listened intently. He even seemed to become sober while he was listening. His gray eyes flashed intelligently, and he didn't sip his beer or order another shot.

"I just couldn't let go of it," Vargo told him. "I can feel in my bones that the little girl was murdered. We just don't know how yet. On a crazy impulse I drove all the way to town, hoping I'd spot the flasher."

"No such luck," said Harpster.

"No. Of course not."

"Funny thing," said Harpster.

"What is?" Vargo responded.

Harpster pursed his lips, trying to get his thoughts together. "The homicide I'm working on is a bit odd," he said finally. "Young black guy found strangled on the third floor of the Allegheny Tower parking garage on Stanwix Street. It was real easy to get an ID on him since the asshole has a rap sheet a mile long. Elijah Alford, age twenty-six. Been in and out of reform schools and jails ever since he was thirteen—everything from breaking and entering to attempted rape. He was out on bail on a burglary charge when he turned up dead. The punk is nobody to cry over, not like your little girl. But the odd thing is he had a cut on his wrist that seems totally unrelated to cause of death. You say little Stephanie had a cut on her finger?"

"Yeah," said Vargo, becoming interested. "Her finger

and hand were swollen, too. Ed Stanford thinks it might have been poison. Or a bee sting or a spider bite. But that's too farfetched for me. That would make the flasher a total coincidence—and I don't believe for one minute that he was around without being involved. If Stephanie was poisoned, I'm betting that the lab is going to find traces of the poison on the piece of broken glass that I found buried in her sandbox."

"Elijah Alford was choked, and choked *hard,*" said Harpster. "Whoever did it to him has an extremely powerful right hand. I mean strong as a vise. There were deep purple contusions in his neck—some deep enough to bleed—and his windpipe was crushed like a paper straw. And it was all done with *one hand.* You can see it from the imprint of the thumb and four fingers."

"Then Alford's wrist was cut?" Vargo asked.

"That's what I said was so odd. It must've been done after he was already dead, because it hardly bled at all."

"Any swelling around the wound?"

"Not so you'd notice," said Harpster. "I don't know if tissues can become inflamed and swollen after death. We don't have the weapon he was cut with, but it looks like it was done with a sharp knife or maybe a razor."

"In his preliminary examination," Vargo asked, "did the medical examiner find anything else that seemed odd?"

"Only that the cut on Alford's wrist was sliced so deep that more blood ought to have drained out before it coagulated. I would've expected to find a puddle of blood on the floor, but there wasn't any."

Vargo and Harpster thought that over. They each took a sip of beer.

After a while, Harpster said, "It makes me think of those ritual murders that are going on down in Florida . . . you know what I mean? Apparently some cult of crazies down there is collecting human blood and using it in voodoo ceremonies. I swear, it's enough to make you sick, the kinds of things that are going on today. This is the age of wretched excess—drugs, sex, religion—even the maniacs are crazier than they used to be."

"Do these voodoo people collect the blood and wipe the wound clean?" Vargo wondered.

"Hell, I don't know," said Harpster. "I guess you could call the sheriff down in Dade County and find out."

"We should compare the autopsy reports on Elijah Alford and Stephanie Kamin," said Vargo, "on the off chance we're both looking for the same man."

"Lizzie Borden took an axe, and gave her mother forty whacks," Harpster said, a glint of perverse nostalgia in his eyes. "Talk about the good old days! In today's fucked-up world, nobody would bother to write a song about her—she wouldn't even make page three. Too mundane."

"She had one thing in common with today's lunatics," Vargo said.

"What's that?"

"Her lawyers got her off scot-free."

10

Benjamin Latham slept on top of the Monongahela Bastion, which now formed an enclosure and roof for the Fort Pitt Museum. The modern brick-and-glass building was built right into the earthworks of the bastion itself. There was a wide pavement sloping to the top of the bastion, so tourists could go up and examine reconstructed firing parapets for cannon and musketry.

When Benjamin had climbed the slope, just before dark, he was going on the premise that this was the last place that the three hoodlums who were still after him would think to come looking. They probably wouldn't figure he'd backtrack to the park. Maybe finding their cohort dead would scare them off entirely; or maybe it would make them all the more zealous for revenge. Benjamin almost didn't care. He had a knife now. And more than that, he had the knowledge of the special power he had called on when he choked the one hoodlum to death.

After the sun went down he felt that he would be reasonably safe as long as he didn't fall into a heavy sleep. The park was closed, and its perimeter was patrolled by uniformed watchmen with dogs. Lampposts were lit up all over the grounds down below, and the watchmen carried sticks of light that they could shine into dark places. They probably wouldn't think to check for stowaways on top of the Monongahela Bastion. If Benjamin heard someone coming up the paved slope, he could escape by hanging and dropping over the fifteen-foot-high rampart wall.

Dozing and waking, dozing and waking, he managed to get some rest even though he was damp and cold. When he sat up, just at dawn, everything was wet with dew, including his clothes. He stretched and rubbed his eyes, looking out over the parapet at the Three Rivers, getting used to the reality-fantasy that his life had become, and letting the new sunrise bring him dryness and warmth.

When the sun burned off the morning mists, and people started coming into the park, he decided he could start moving around just as though he were one of them. He ran his fingers through his hair and over his stubble of beard. Maybe he looked and felt a bit seedy, but not enough to attract any special attention. In fact, coming down off the slope of the bastion, he noticed several young men who were more unkempt than he was, and it appeared to be their normal condition. They reminded him of backwoodsmen who refused to bathe and dress up even when they came to civilization.

He drank from a fountain and splashed water on his face and let it dry in the sun as he strolled. He came upon a man sitting on a bench reading a newspaper and asked him what time it was. Nine-thirty. The museum would be open in half an hour. According to the sign on the door, the admission price was one dollar. Benjamin stopped on a path when no one else was around and took from his pocket the folded currency he had appropriated from the dead hoodlum. Two bills had pictures of someone named Lincoln, and each was designated to be worth five dollars. Another bill was engraved with a rather poor likeness of Alexander Hamilton, and its denomination was ten dollars. Three lesser bills bearing George Washington's portrait were only worth a dollar apiece—and Benjamin thought even that was too dear a tribute for the turncoat who had led rebel troops against King George.

When he walked back toward the museum, he saw an old man sweeping up around Colonel Bouquet's blockhouse. He asked if it was time to go in yet; the old man said it would be okay, but he grumped that it was five minutes early for opening.

"How much?" asked Benjamin.

"Blockhouse is free. Museum costs a buck and a half."

"The sign says one dollar."

"I know what it says, but it isn't so. We get hit with inflation same as everybody else."

Limping slightly, the old man swung open the heavy wooden barricade of a door on its creaking hinges, and Benjamin followed him into the blockhouse. It was pretty much the way he remembered it, except for the placement of glass display cases, one containing relics of the 1700s and the other containing trinkets for sale to tourists. In 1764, when Benjamin had served as post physician during Pontiac's War, Colonel Bouquet had ordered this redoubt built to command the moat on the Allegheny side of the fort, because when the river was low and the moat was dry, Indians could crawl up the ditch and shoot any soldier who showed his head over the parapet.

"I suppose the underground passages no longer exist," Benjamin said to the old man, who had leaned his broom against the wall and stationed himself behind one of the glass display cases.

"What underground passages?"

"Why, the ones built by Bouquet's engineers. One led to the Monongahela River, and the other exited behind the stockade of the fort, so that if the defenders of the redoubt needed to escape they could do so by either route."

"Never heard of such a thing," the old man said with considerable indignation. Clearly he thought that Benjamin was making it up. "Do you want to buy a souvenir?" he asked impatiently.

"I don't think so," Benjamin said. Actually, he was horrified by the price tags of three, five, and ten dollars on letter openers in the shape of bayonets and swords, toy cannons and muskets, and dolls dressed up like little colonial soldiers and their ladies. Ironically, these stilted mannequins conjured up in Benjamin's mind an image of the balls held at Fort Pitt every Saturday evening, which he and his wife Clarissa would attend enthusiastically, as a respite from the monotony of garrison life and the ever-present danger from Indians prowling within war-whooping distance of the stockade.

Moving away from the souvenirs, he spent a few minutes looking at the display case full of relics—so old and decrepit that they made his former life and his memories of it seem weirdly remote. There were pieces of rotten leather labeled as fragments of shoes dug up by archeologists; rusty flintlock pistols without handles; a rusty bayonet blade; a rotted and rusted tomahawk; and a rusty musket with a worm-eaten stock.

He left the blockhouse and stood outside for a while, breathing deeply and feeling a bit numb. Looking at these artifacts of the past was like walking on his own grave.

"Would you move out of my way, please?"

He jerked his head around. An attractive young woman had called out to him. She had long, straight black hair and wore leather sandals, a crisp white blouse, and a blue skirt. In her hand was a boxlike device secured to her wrist by a leather strap; a shiny black tube with glass in the front protruded from the body of the thing, like a foreshortened telescope.

"How can I be in your way," Benjamin asked, "when you are at least twenty feet away from me?"

She held up her boxlike device and frowned exasperatedly. "I want to film the blockhouse!"

She raised her device to her face and started twisting the tubular part of it, as one might focus a telescope. With alarm, Benjamin saw that it was pointed almost directly at him. He scampered out of the way as fast as he could. Instinctively he feared the device, without knowing why.

But he was attracted to the young woman. In any time and place, she would be considered beautiful.

He stood to one side watching her. Her device was making a soft whirring sound, and she was moving it very slowly from side to side, then up and down, so that the protuberance that looked like a lens swept all over the blockhouse—yet nothing happened to the building that Benjamin could see. But he was convinced that he was right in thinking the device was dangerous when a man who noticed he had inadvertently walked in front of it immediately darted away.

"Damn!" said the young woman and started sweeping the device over the blockhouse again. But this time she only did the up-and-down part, which was the part that had been interrupted by the man. Then she pushed a button and the device stopped whirring.

She pivoted. Benjamin followed her into the museum. An attendant—a handsome young black man in a green suit—was selling tickets at a desk just inside the door. He smiled with extra effort, the way most men smile at exceptionally beautiful women, and said, "Good morning, Lenora." As far as he was concerned, Benjamin wasn't even there.

"Hi, Lenny," she was saying to the black man. "How are things going? Is the boss in his office yet?"

"Yep. He just came in," said Lenny, still smiling. He gazed admiringly at Lenora as she swept by. Then he looked up at Benjamin. "One admission, sir?"

"Yes, please." Benjamin put two one-dollar bills down in front of Lenny and was given two silvery coins in change. They weren't *real* silver; they were too light. Benjamin dropped them into his pocket, noticing that they didn't make a satisfying weighty clink.

He moved past the desk and into a foyer, where there was a marble bust of Prime Minister William Pitt. He loitered around it for a while, hoping that Lenora would pop out of the nearby office into which she had gone. Peeking in through the open doorway, he couldn't see her at all; but he could see a swivel chair and a desk piled with books and papers. On the green desk blotter lay the device she had used to "film" the blockhouse. He stared at the bust for a few seconds more, long enough to read the inscription: William Pitt, 1708–1778. When he turned back, Lenora was sitting in the swivel chair. He wished he had a way to make her speak to him.

She raised her eyes from the book she was reading and looked right at him. Then she arose and walked up to him as he stood by the marble bust. She had the most striking eyes. They were lambent violet, set off by the glossy black curls that framed her oval face. She had lovely high cheekbones. Her nose was aquiline. Her pink lips were wide and full, and the cleft of the upper one formed a perfectly sharp V. Around her neck she wore a delicate gold chain against the lightly tanned skin that showed under the snow-white collar of her blouse. When she had walked in front of him into the museum, he had noticed that her calves were so exquisitely shaped that they couldn't be improved by any slight change of weight or muscularity.

"I'm sorry I snapped at you outside," she said. "I don't know what made me so impatient."

"Beautiful women are sometimes given to haughtiness," he teased, hoping it was a provocative enough line for flirtation in this day and age.

"You sound like you're from England," she responded, with no attempt at a coy or clever rejoinder.

"Yes. My name is Benjamin Latham," he said, struggling with the realization that perhaps modern women did not enjoy witty repartee.

"I'm Lenora Clayton. Pleased to meet you." She extended her hand and he took it and bent to kiss it, and when he looked her in the eyes she seemed wryly amused. She asked, "What brings you to America?" Her voice was soft, melodious, but still frankly assertive. She was charming but certainly not demure, not in the manner that eighteenth-century women would have prized. Still, he remained captivated by her extraordinary poise and beauty.

He fell back on the same lie he had told Norman Willoughby on the drive into Pittsburgh. "I'm an amateur historian, interested in the period of the thirteen colonies. I've been traveling around visiting museums and archeological sites."

"I'm a history major," she said. "Do you have a degree?"

"Yes." He was referring to his diploma from Franklin Academy in Philadelphia, where he had studied the humanities and the medical arts. Too late, he realized that he probably should not have answered in the affirmative, for any knowledge he could display would probably be classed as abysmal ignorance in twentieth-century terms. "But not in history," he added. "I'm afraid that someone with formal schooling, such as yourself, would find me to be a mere dabbler."

"Oh, you're being modest, I'm sure," she said, smiling. "I'm always glad to meet someone who's sincerely interested in the Fort Pitt Museum. I'll show you around, if you like—and try to prove that we Americans aren't always churlish and sassy whenever we get foreign visitors."

"I'd like that very much," he told her quite truthfully.

He had the strange feeling that she really wanted to be with him, as much as he wanted her. In fact, he was almost ready to believe that his thoughts had compelled her to arise from her chair and come out and speak to him. He had wished it, and then it had happened. She had responded to an inner command, a force that passed from him to her. He was reminded of how he had looked into the dying thug's eyes and had known where his cohorts were as if he had read his mind. Did he now possess an occult power over the thoughts of others? Where was the limit of the eerie and marvelous changes that had been wrought in him along with the ability to rise up out of his grave? He was both awed and gratified by the notion that he might be superhuman in some ways. But he didn't want to be too superhuman. He had no wish to lose his humanity entirely, and with it the ability to relate to a lovely human being like Lenora Clayton.

He had a strong desire to know all about her. And, as if answering the desire, she talked about herself while showing him the various exhibits of the museum and managing to talk about them, too. Her magical presence insulated him from the nostalgic sadness that would have struck him so profoundly had he been looking at the exhibits on his own. Together they viewed life-sized mannequins of French and British soldiers, dioramas of battles and pioneer life, displays of weapons and utensils, reconstructed models of a fur trader's cabin and a barracks interior. As they chatted, enjoying each other's company, he found out about Lenora and she discovered that he truly knew as much as she did, and more, about the historical period to which the museum was devoted.

She said that she was studying for her doctoral exams at the University of Pittsburgh. She had been lucky enough to land a summer job assisting the curator of the Fort Pitt Museum while she worked on writing her thesis. She was from Marietta, Ohio, a town steeped in pioneer history because of its role as the first settlement of the Northwest Territory. An ancestor of hers had been one of the earliest settlers, having accepted land at the junction of the Ohio and Muskingum rivers as payment for soldiering in George Washington's Continental Army. As a child, she had loved visiting Marietta's Riverboat Museum and sites such as the General Rufus Putnam House, preserved just as it was in 1805.

"So it's no wonder I decided to become a historian," she said with a laugh. "Have you ever been to Marietta?"

"No," said Benjamin. "I'm afraid I've never gotten that far west."

"Oh, you simply must go!" Lenora exclaimed. "It's a charming little town, quite apart from its historical value."

"It must be quite charming to have produced you," Benjamin told her.

"Thank you. Will I see you again?"

In his time, that sort of question would have been his to ask, not hers. But he was becoming accustomed to her directness.

"My plans aren't very firm," he hedged. "I have to find

a place to stay and a means of supporting myself. That is . . . if I'm to remain here for more than a day or so."

"Do you wish to stay?"

"Now that I've met you, indeed I do."

She smiled. "Maybe I can help you. The curator told me he'd like to hire two more knowledgeable young people for the summer."

That she would make such an offer pleased him enormously. He was tempted to take her up on it, but he feared getting involved too deeply. He needed more time to learn about modern things so that he wouldn't appear the fool. And he needed to be sure, somehow, that there was no way he might inadvertently harm her, if in fact he was responsible for what had happened to the little girl.

"I have a friend here who has offered me a job," Benjamin lied. "And I believe he's expecting me to stay with him. In fact, I have to see him this afternoon. What time is it? It must be getting late. You've made it so easy for me to let the hours fly."

She glanced at a tiny gold watch on her wrist. "Gosh, you're right—it's ten minutes to one. I have a special museum program that must go to the printer by two. I'll have to get on it right away. You're not the only one who lost track of time."

She blinked and shook her head as if coming out of a mild trance. Benjamin felt himself relinquishing whatever hold he had maintained over her. He realized that he had been able to influence her behavior to a considerable extent; that was why she had spent so much time with him. He didn't know how he felt about having such an odd, compelling power. If used indiscriminately, it could be a mixed blessing. Maybe it would be all right as a way of beginning a relationship. But in the future he would rather that Lenora come to him of her own volition, instead of at the behest of a subtle but irrefutable mind control.

"Good-bye," he told her. "I must be on my way."

"S-stop back again," she said shakily.

"I'll do my best," he said. Then he pivoted and walked

out, under the disapproving gaze of Lenny at the admissions desk.

Later, Lenora thought about Benjamin. What had she seen in him? He was good-looking but unkempt. His shirt didn't even fit him properly. His boots were soiled and scuffed. He hadn't even bothered to wear a belt. If clothes make the man—she smiled to herself—she ought to forget about Benjamin Latham. Why did she have a strong feeling that there was much more to him? He projected a mysterious intelligence, an eerie sensuality, a hint of wildness coexisting with gentility and charm. Telling her life story to a man after being in his company for just a few moments simply wasn't her style. But she had been intrigued by Benjamin Latham . . . she might almost say he had held her spellbound. And he knew it. She liked to be more in control.

What was it about him?

Animal magnetism?

Charisma?

Love at first sight?

Ha!

She scoffed at the idea. She was a practical, capable woman. Not that there wasn't room for romance in her life; but she had always kept it in a reasonable perspective. Some people thought she was standoffish, or even sexually frigid; but these were the ones who didn't get to know her intimately.

Benjamin Latham had commented several times on her beauty, and it hadn't bothered her, when normally it would have tended to turn her off. If she was beautiful, so what? If it was a blessing, it was also a curse. It prevented most men from noticing anything else about her—her quick mind, her broad spectrum of social and cultural interests, her sense of scholarship and professionalism. In other words, they refused to take her seriously. And that infuriated her.

But in the very short time they had been together, Benjamin had seemed to look deeply inside her and to appreciate that she had more to offer than just the physical thing.

She shivered, remembering how she had surrendered to him in some subtle, magnetic way, as if he had taken over a part of her mind and body. An odd sensation had come over her, as if she were moving and reacting in a force field emanating from him; yet she wasn't subjugated, she still had her own force and her own personality, enlivened and enhanced in his presence. Their two electricities had touched and merged—two auras glowing and vibrating more brightly, more intensely, because of each other.

Was this how it felt when the absolutely right man came along?

She found him terribly exciting and sexy and . . . and . . .

Dangerous.

She couldn't wait to see him again.

11

Benjamin walked up Stanwix Street, glancing warily at the parking garage. The corpse certainly would have been found by now, and he wondered what sort of official inquiry was going on. It seemed highly likely that the dead man's friends might not tell what they knew to the authorities but might instead seek revenge on their own.

He walked through the crowd of shoppers and looked at the smartly dressed men and women. They made him feel grubby. When he passed G. C. Murphy's Five and Dime, he realized that he should buy some more conventionally fitting clothing. He was amazed at the plethora of goods filling the shelves and showcases. Nothing was cheap. "Five and Dime" apparently didn't mean five and ten cents.

He took his time browsing, mingling with the other customers, because for him it was a learning experience. Much as he hated to spend the cash, he ended up parting with more than sixteen dollars for a blue long-sleeved shirt, a pair of white socks, a black belt that looked like leather but wasn't, and a pair of blue-and-white shoes called sneakers that were similar to the footgear he had noticed on the thugs who had chased him out of the park. He changed clothes in a cubicle inside the store and threw his old stuff away in a garbage can out on the sidewalk. Then he went into the Original Oyster House and had a delicious fish sandwich and a glass of cold buttermilk—and was skinned for almost two dollars.

With his hunger appeased and in his new apparel he felt more comfortable and less conspicuous. Crossing the cobblestone street, he sat on a park bench, realizing he was down to seven dollars and change and wondering how best to begin making his way in the world.

He was jarred out of his thoughts by the sounds of an argument taking place among a group of derelicts fifteen feet away, on the corner. One fellow seemed almost sober and was better dressed than the other four, and he had something in a brown paper bag that he was clutching lovingly and protectively to his bosom—obviously the something was a bottle of alcoholic spirits, and the man was defending it against the rest of the motley crew, who were practically salivating in their zeal to wrap their lips around it.

The four covetous derelicts were emaciated, red-eyed hulks with ashen, corpselike complexions, stubbly jowls, and greasy shaggy hair. Their trousers were baggy and soiled, gathered in ravels at the waist. Their shirts and shoes were grimy and frayed and falling apart. Their personalities, like their apparel, seemed mean, dirty, worn-out, and beaten. The one with the bottle clearly did not consider himself of exactly their ilk—he was trying to hang on to some dignity and not sink down to their level, while the others sneered as if they knew it was only a matter of time before he lost the struggle. Benjamin couldn't help rooting for him. He was short and wiry and gray-haired, but his clothes still fitted him reasonably well and he had a lot of spunk left. He had stiffened into almost a fighting stance.

"Oh, no you don't!" he cried out defiantly. "Don't

come around trying to bully Andy Bonner! I'll put you in your place, I will! All you bums ever have is cheap rotgut, and now I got me some good Seagram's Seven and you act like you expect me to share it. Well, it ain't fair—it don't come out even-steven. I went to work for Manpower, bustin' my ass and stayin' sober, and now I got cash in my pocket and I mean to live it up some. You guys won't ever work with me—oh, no!—you'd rather hang around and bum quarters and roll in the gutter with a quart of Thunderbird. Well, you had *your* kind of fun. Now you can just watch me relax and enjoy myself like a gentleman!"

"Yeah, like a stingy prick!" one of Andy Bonner's adversaries jeered.

"Goddamn you, we oughtta beat the piss outta you!" another declared. "It's okay for you to play buddy-buddy till you got somethin' we ain't—then you turn highfalutin on us so's you can have an excuse to keep it all to yourself!"

"You said a mouthful, Max!" echoed a cohort, leaning on a garbage drum to keep from falling down.

"Darn tootin'!" slurred another.

"Just don't let us catch *you* down and out," warned a third.

"Get out of here! Beat it! Clear the square! Leave a decent, hardworking citizen alone!" Andy Bonner harangued, glowering and posturing like a banty rooster.

Just when it looked as if the other four might gang up on him, a policeman in a blue uniform, with a pistol and a nightstick on his belt, came up on them from behind and butted in. Perhaps Andy Bonner had spotted the policeman approaching all along, and that had encouraged him to sound off so bravely.

"Okay, fellows, break it up!" the policeman said in a stern, no-nonsense voice. "Move along, or I'll haul you all in. You'll spend a couple days in the slammer—miss out on all the nice weather." He stood watching till the four seediest derelicts obeyed, shuffling and grumbling and moving down the sidewalk in a pack, while Andy Bonner gave a contemptuous snort to their backs. "Cool it," the policeman said, "or I'll haul *you* in."

"They was picking on me," Andy said.

"Try telling it to the magistrate," said the policeman.

At that, Andy retreated and sat on the opposite end of the bench where Benjamin Latham was sitting and assumed an innocent, harmless pose. But the policeman didn't wander away for several more minutes. During this time, he gave Benjamin a close scrutiny, and Benjamin tried to appear unconcerned and nonchalant. But he didn't really relax until the policeman crossed the street and started walking toward the far end of the square.

"Did you get a load of what I had to put up with?" Andy Bonner blurted indignantly. "I was just tryin' to mind my own business—but those freeloaders figured they'd crowd me into parting with what I worked for, just 'cause I chewed the fat with 'em on the square a couple of times. I seen 'em pick food outta garbage cans—all four of 'em—and I'll be a monkey's uncle if *I* ever sunk that low. Not by a long shot. Not by a helluva long shot!"

"I don't blame you for being so upset," Benjamin said, commiserating.

"You can see it. You ain't blind," said Andy Bonner. "Go on, tell the truth, now—do I look like one of them garbage-pickers?"

"Not at all," said Benjamin.

It was true. Andy Bonner was wearing a pair of clean brown trousers and a yellow-and-brown plaid short-sleeved shirt. His complexion was pallid, but his bony face was clean and freshly shaved. His short gray hair was neatly parted and combed. He looked like a tough old codger, his stringy right arm clutching the brown bag that contained his bottle.

"*They* ain't nothin' but a pack of raggedy bums," he ranted. "They got their nerve callin' *me* stingy! I ain't no such thing. I just don't want to drink after *them*. Don't want to catch their diseases. Scabies, rabies—you name it, they probably got it. Know what I mean?"

"Of course," said Benjamin. His eyes and Andy

Bonner's eyes met and locked. Benjamin concentrated forcefully: Make this man open his heart and mind. Heighten his desire to be my friend. Cause him to trust and confide in me, so that he will help me without being afraid.

"That cop's clean on the other side of the square," Andy Bonner said. "What say me and you have a little snort together, just to prove I ain't stingy? You look like a clean young gentleman. I ain't afraid to drink after *you.*"

He uncapped his bottle, pulling the neck an inch or so out of the bag, and handed it to Benjamin, who obligingly took a swig. It burned at first, but then it warmed his insides and gave him a pleasant glow.

Andy Bonner swigged, then wiped his lips with the back of his hand. "Now we're buddies," he said staunchly. "My name's Andy Bonner. What's yours?"

"Benjamin Latham. Pleased to meet you, Andy."

They shook hands.

"Shit, Ben, you ever do any *work?"* Andy said. "Your hand is softer'n a baby's ass!"

"Er . . . I've been sick," Benjamin lied. "Out of circulation."

"What kind of sick?" Andy shot back, squinting suspiciously. "Don't tell me you got somethin' catchy after we just got done sharin' the same bottle?"

"No, no—not catchy," Benjamin ad-libbed. "A blow to my head. I was unconscious for weeks. And then afterward I couldn't remember things."

"Amnesia?" Andy asked, titillated by the idea.

"I think that's what it's called," said Benjamin. He congratulated himself for taking this tack. It had been a spur-of-the-moment inspiration. One of his medical texts—he almost wanted to think of it as a recent one, since it had been published at Oxford in 1778—had described the symptoms of patients who underwent long bouts of forgetfulness. It was a perfect ruse. It would give him the opportunity of asking Andy Bonner all sorts of questions without appearing insane or stupid.

"Goddamn! Amnesia! Sorry to hear it," Andy said. "Here, go on and have another snort—it might not clear up your amnesia, but it'll sure fill your head with lots of funny little thoughts to replace the ones that are missing."

He winked and chortled. Benjamin laughed with him. They passed the bottle back and forth a couple of times, keeping a lookout that the cop didn't sneak up on them.

"Ahhhhh! This is a helluva sight better'n the rotgut those filthy winos guzzle," Andy said, smacking his lips.

"You said a mouthful," said Benjamin.

"Look here . . . where was you born?" Andy asked him.

"I don't know."

"How old are you?"

"I don't know that either."

"What kind of work did you use to do?"

"I'm sorry, but I'm at a loss to tell you."

"Hmmm . . . I guess it's true, then," Andy said.

"What is?"

"Your memory's gone. You sound somethin' like a limey—you might be from England or someplace like that. You look to be in your mid-twenties. You got a Social Security card?"

"I'm afraid I know nothing about it."

"So you ain't got a job either?"

"No, Andy."

"*Damn* these doctors! How'd they expect you to make a go of it with your handicap? You mean they discharged you from the hospital with nothing to your name *but* your name and the clothes on your back?"

Benjamin nodded, outwardly glum but inwardly pleased that he was eliciting sympathy.

Andy Bonner pursed his lips, thinking hard. After a moment his eyes twinkled and he got a determined set to his jaw. He said, "Don't you worry, Ben. I'm gonna take you under my wing . . . show you the ropes. You better stick with me for a while. Fellow with your particular affliction, folks'll be quick to take advantage of you. But you're gonna be okay, with me on your side. I'll show you how to get a Social Security card so's you can work with me at the Manpower joint. You got a place to stay?"

"I'm afraid not."

"Well, I'll show you how to check into the YMCA."

"I'd be most grateful," Benjamin said warmly and sincerely. "Thanks, Andy. Thank you for being my friend."

"Amnesia ain't so bad," said Andy. "Don't let it get you down. I got lots of things I'd *like* to forget but can't, except when I'm two-thirds crocked."

Benjamin murmured something agreeable.

"Look at it this way," his new friend told him. "This is a golden opportunity for you to accumulate only pleasant memories. The bad ones are gone. All you have to do is not let any more bad ones in. Filter them out, and just keep the good ones."

"I never thought of it that way."

"Sure. Stick with me. I'll teach you everything you need to know."

12

The body of six-year-old Stephanie Kamin lay on the stainless-steel autopsy table. Her blue eyes were fixed in a wide-open sightless stare. Her mouth was open, too, in the O-shaped rictus of death. Her face was puffy and bluish white. A large manila tag dangled from her right big toe. She reposed flat on her back on a metal grating over a long, shallow basin with constantly running water to flush away blood and other fluids exuded during the postmortem.

As the detective in charge of her case, Trooper Ronald Vargo had to be present for the autopsy procedure, much as he'd rather not be. He could never get used to the feel and smell of the morgue. With its cold white tiles and stark fluorescent lighting, it reminded him of a grotesquely large refrigerator filled with decaying human meat. He tried to forget that the corpse to be cut open this morning had yesterday been a lively and beautiful little girl.

Ed Stanford, the Westmoreland County coroner, was attending the autopsy, too. It was being performed by Dr. Peter Coleman, a pathologist on the staff of the Allegheny County Morgue in Pittsburgh, which had better forensic facilities than were available in Westmoreland County. Stanford was there to follow the case through since it had initiated under his jurisdiction, to take notes, and to contribute whatever advice or assistance seemed tactful and appropriate.

Dr. Coleman or one of the morgue assistants had bathed Stephanie's body in preparation for this morning's work. Her skin was no longer dotted with grains of sand. Sand had been combed out of her ash-blond hair. Her tiny curled-up hands were no longer covered with plastic bags. Lab men had already taken scrapings from underneath her fingernails and had saved samples of the soil that had been on her body, and now the body had to be clean so that tissue and fluid samples collected by Dr. Coleman would not be contaminated.

Late last night, after getting home from Freddy's Place, Vargo had phoned Ed Stanford at home to tell him about the homicide that Jack Harpster was working on and to point out the similarities to the Stephanie Kamin case. "I know this is going to sound crazy," Vargo had said. "But after talking to Lieutenant Harpster, I started wondering —suppose we really *are* dealing with a psychopath who has a fixation on blood. It certainly wouldn't be the most bizarre case that's ever happened. Remember the so-called vampire killer convicted and hanged in England a while back? He was slicing people's jugular veins and sipping their blood through a lemonade straw. So maybe Stephanie didn't lick her cut finger the way kids do. Maybe somebody else did it for her. If a pervert like that got hold of her and wouldn't let go, I believe it *could've* scared her to death."

Leaning against his kitchen wall, the phone clutched to his ear, in the wee hours of the morning, Vargo had waited for Stanford to react by being angry or patronizing. Instead, after a long silence, Stanford had simply said,

"Are you proposing that we should try to take a saliva sample from Stephanie's wound site?"

"Not only from Stephanie," Vargo had replied, "but also from Elijah Alford—the man strangled in the parking garage."

"All right, I'll make the necessary phone calls to get clearance," Stanford had promised. "And I'll make sure that the morgue staff doesn't bathe the bodies until a serologist gets there to try to take the saliva samples—if there are any."

"You're not just humoring me, are you?" Vargo had said to Ed Stanford.

"No, not at all. Your hunch might pan out."

And it might not, Vargo thought now. If there wasn't any saliva around the wounds, the serologist would be looking at plain distilled water.

Dr. Coleman, a short, fat, swarthy fellow in a white morgue coat, was lifting Stephanie's left wrist, holding the swollen tissues of her hand and finger closer to the bright overhead light. "I had a very close look at this earlier," he told Ed Stanford. "You know what it reminds me of, don't you?"

Stanford moved to Coleman's side and peered at Stephanie's wound after pushing his wire-rimmed eyeglasses firmly in place on the bridge of his sharp, pointy nose. "Hmm," he said. "It looks like snakebite."

"Exactly," said Coleman. "See how the capillaries have burst?"

"What!" Vargo blurted. "What on earth are you two talking about?" He came around to the left side of the body and stared in amazement at Stephanie's finger and hand—which were now bruised and mottled in a purplish spiderweb pattern, like an old woman's varicose veins. "Ed," he said to Stanford, "we didn't notice anything like this yesterday and—"

"Whether you did or not," Coleman interrupted in a tone of haughty professionalism, "the phenomenon is clearly apparent at this moment. The blood vessels are ruptured at the wound site, and the flesh is badly swollen.

This is exactly the way that some snake venom behaves—rattlesnake venom is a good example."

"But it usually acts much faster," said Stanford. "It goes to work as soon as the victim is bitten."

"Unless it's a weak or dilute dose," said Coleman.

"I'll bet it was on the piece of broken glass," Vargo said, his black eyes flashing angrily. "The guy we're after must've poisoned her with snake venom."

"If so, any traces of it can be analyzed," said Ed Stanford. "A swab can be taken from the glass fragment."

"The effects will show up in her heart and circulatory system, too," Coleman said. "So let's get on with the postmortem."

Vargo wished he could turn his head away, but he had to watch. There was nothing in the morgue that he could pretend to be distracted by. The place was utterly sterile. Nothing but cold white tile and stainless-steel apparatus.

Using a gleaming scalpel, the pathologist made a thin incision across the top of Stephanie's head. Then he peeled the skin back, turning it inside out, so that what had been her forehead almost touched her chin; and the skin and hair from the top of her head was peeled back halfway to the back of her neck. "Just like peeling a grapefruit," Coleman commented, grinning with self-approval over the deftness with which he performed the ghoulish maneuver and the way he didn't let it get under his skin. Vargo was tormented by the knowledge that his own murdered daughter had been treated this way on the autopsy table—like a piece of cold meat on a butchering block. He gritted his teeth, trying to maintain a bland expression on his face, while Coleman used a whining electric saw to cut through bone and remove the top of Stephanie's skull.

"No sign of fracture or concussion," the pathologist said after examining the underside of the skullcap and the convex exposure of gray matter.

Ed Stanford made note of the observation, writing on one of the autopsy forms attached to his clipboard.

Coleman scooped the cadaver's brain out of its cavity and placed it on the morgue scale. "Um-hmm," he intoned appraisingly. "On the underside of the temporal lobe I see an oblong bruise, approximately one inch by two inches. The rupturing of blood vessels—probably due to poisoning—obviously proceeded to this part of the brain."

Vargo looked at the bruise in question. "How do you know this isn't evidence of a concussion?" he asked Ed Stanford, who was sketching the injury into an outline of the human brain on one of his forms.

"Because," Coleman replied acidly, as if his expertise had been questioned, "by probing with my fingers and by looking at X rays taken prior to this autopsy, I can assure you that there is no break in the skull bone corresponding to this precise area of the temporal lobe. Besides, the bruise is not typical of the kind caused by a blow from a sharp or blunt instrument. On the contrary, the blood vessels appear to have been ruptured from within, by internal pressure from coagulating blood—which, again, is what happens with certain types of snakebite."

"I see," Vargo muttered, barely controlling his irritation at being talked down to.

Coleman made a Y-shaped incision in Stephanie's torso, the prongs of the Y crossing her chest and the stem extending down to her groin. He used his circular saw to cut through her sternum. Then he flapped her chest over her face and turned her abdomen back on both sides to expose her internal organs. Her heart, lungs, stomach, and intestines were all visible as the fluids surrounding them drained away.

Coleman severed the pulmonary vessels, the aorta, and the vena cava, and extracted Stephanie's heart. Washing it, he turned it over and over in his hands. "There's a great deal of tissue destruction," he announced with the unmitigated glee of a technician having a hypothesis confirmed. "You could almost call this an induced heart attack."

He used his scalpel to open the left and right ventricles and found both chambers caked with a solid brownish mass. He reported that the blood had mortified and coagulated, and Ed Stanford made note of it on one of his forms.

"Like a carburetor full of dirty motor oil," Coleman

said, turning to Vargo with a slight grin that made the detective want to punch the pathologist's fat face. Vargo was sure that Coleman used his metaphors not to elucidate but to entertain himself. Coleman went on: "Another way of putting it is that it's like what happens when you dump sugar into somebody's gas tank. It chokes and binds the engine. In this case, the blood coagulated into thick lumps, and the heart could not keep on pumping. In trying to continue its function, it literally exploded—tore itself apart. At the same time, this little girl was being asphyxiated because her lungs had stopped working—that's why her face is puffy and blue. I'd say we're dealing with a poison that is both hemotoxic and neurotoxic—like rattlesnake venom. It attacks the blood vessels, the muscle tissues, and the entire nervous system, including the brain."

"Doesn't sound like she had much of a chance," said Vargo.

"Not any chance at all," said Coleman. "Judging from the extent of damage at the wound site, I'd say the venom was weak, like that of a baby rattler. An adult human might have survived. But for the little girl even a weakened dose was fatal."

"I don't think she was bitten," said Ed Stanford. "You'll agree, won't you, Dr. Coleman, that the cut on her finger was not made by a fang?"

"Not unless the fang grazed her in some sideways fashion," Coleman hedged. "It might have even been a broken fang, more jagged and sharp than usual."

"With all the bulldozing for the new shopping center," said Ed Stanford, "the snakes and other wild animals are being forced out of their natural habitat. I suppose something could have crawled toward Stephanie's sandbox. Our diagnosis would be so easy if only we had a puncture wound instead of a small, jagged incision."

"That's why a broken fang might be your answer," said Coleman. "A broken fang might have splashed the poison instead of injecting it, which would account for the weakened dosage."

The theory sounded plausible, but Vargo could not bring himself to admit it. His gut feeling still told him Stephanie had been murdered. And he didn't want Coleman to be totally and triumphantly right about everything. "I'm still betting we'll find traces of poison on the broken glass," he reiterated stubbornly.

"Maybe, maybe not," Coleman countered, unwilling to give much weight to anybody's prejudgments but his own.

"If the poison is on the glass, it'll prove she was killed by a *human* snake," Vargo said more heatedly.

"Not necessarily," Coleman contradicted. "It still could have been an accident."

"Which would make it manslaughter," said Vargo. "If somebody didn't dispose of poison properly."

"And you'd stand a snowball's chance in hell of finding out who," Coleman said, smiling. "If I were you, I'd be much more comfortable with the idea of snakebite."

"We're not here to buy what makes *us* feel comfortable," Vargo snapped.

The pathologist chortled as if the detective oughtn't to have made such a self-righteous statement. Vargo chafed. His muscles tightened.

"This debate is accomplishing nothing," Ed Stanford intervened. "Whether there's poison on the glass fragment or not, the lab report will tell us. Then we can proceed on the basis of that information."

Meantime, in the serology lab, the swabs taken from Stephanie's wound site were being studied and compared with swabs taken from inside her mouth, from inside Elijah Alford's mouth, and from around the cut on Alford's wrist. The serologist, Ken Beransky, a skilled scientist with twenty-seven years' forensic experience, was trying to figure out the strange patterns that were showing up on his microscope slides.

He was using the technique called electrophoresis, which is based on the fact that the amounts and types of proteins in human beings differ significantly from individual to individual, according to genetic inheritance. When a saliva, semen, or blood sample is placed on a glass plate covered with a special gel, and a direct-current voltage is applied to the plate, the protein molecules separate out according to weight, size, and electrical charge. A chemical is then added that reacts with the proteins, producing spots visible in ordinary or ultraviolet light, forming a pattern that is as distinctive as a fingerprint in characterizing the individual the sample came from.

About eighty percent of all human beings are secretors —which means that their saliva, semen, and other body fluids carry the same factors present in their blood. Both Stephanie Kamin and Elijah Alford belonged in this category, as Ken Beransky found out when he analyzed the swabs taken from the insides of their mouths. Upon subjecting these swabs to electrophoresis, he found nothing out of the ordinary. Stephanie was type O and Alford was type A. Their protein characteristics did not match, and that, of course, was to be expected since they were two different individuals, unrelated to each other.

The surprise came when Beransky analyzed and compared the swabs taken from Stephanie's finger and Alford's wrist. He got a perfect match! The protein patterns were so distinctive! Beransky had never seen anything like them before. Since the two samples matched so precisely and did not match either of the samples taken from the cadavers' mouths, the inescapable conclusion was that a third person, another secretor, had come into contact with both Elijah Alford and Stephanie Kamin.

What had this unknown person done? Licked the dead persons' wounds?

The problem in this case, or in these two cases, was that the substance on the swabs taken from around the cadavers' wounds did not exactly resemble human saliva in its reactions to test procedures. The blood-type reading was normal enough: it was type AB, the universal recipient, able to be mixed with any other type of blood without causing the red cells to clump together and clog veins and capillaries. This was the best type of blood to have if one needed a transfusion. But there seemed to be some strange enzymes present. Skeptical of his results, Beransky cut two more pieces from his swabs and again subjected them to electrophoresis. The same unusual protein patterns were produced once more. Under ordinary light nothing exceptional was apparent; but under ultraviolet light some factors were revealed which defied classification.

If this was human saliva, it must be mixed with something else—some other proteinaceous substance. But what?

Beransky looked at his watch. Almost noon. Deep in thought, he shut off his lab lights and put on his suit jacket. On his way to lunch he remained preoccupied with the task that would face him upon his return: how to analyze the organic material on his swabs to discover its exact chemical composition.

Around five o'clock of that same day, Stanford and Vargo stopped by to pick up Beransky's report. They sat in a small office across the hall from the serology lab, Beransky behind a gray steel desk and the other two men facing him on gray steel folding chairs. The office was a sterile cubicle unadorned by family photos or other personal items.

Beransky matched the office in his sober unadorned appearance and mannerisms. His complexion even had a gray tint from not getting outdoors too often. There were permanent frown lines on both sides of his wide, thin-lipped mouth. He handed copies of his report to Vargo and Stanford and started discussing it before they had a chance to look it over.

"Well, this one is a real humdinger," he said in a thin, squeaky voice that conveyed none of the enthusiasm implied by his choice of words. "Yes, sir, a humdinger," he repeated. "I guess it would have thrown me for a total loop if I hadn't checked with Dr. Coleman before going ahead with a chemical analysis. I phoned the State Police laboratory in Greensburg, too, right after I got back from lunch—but it didn't do me much good. No traces of anything but the little girl's blood on the glass fragment. No usable fingerprints—nothing but smudges."

"You mean there's no poison on the glass?" asked Vargo, revealing his disappointment.

"Nope. Not at all. But that's not to say it isn't what cut her. It did. That's why her blood type shows up there."

"I understand that," said Vargo, a bit testily.

"That's good," squeaked Beransky, leaning forward and touching the tips of his thumbs together over the green desk blotter. "Because it's one of the few things you or I or anybody will be able to make heads or tails of.

"Let me explain a little bit," Beransky went on. "Like I said, I talked to Coleman in the morgue soon as I got back from lunch. He gave me the clue I needed when he said he suspected something in the nature of snake poison. He had found brain, blood vessel, and heart damage in the little girl that would be consistent with that type of poisoning. Elijah Alford didn't show the same thing in his internal organs, but there was some partial digestion of tissues right where his wrist had been cut. The poison apparently never got any farther than that because by the time it was applied he was already dead."

Ed Stanford grimaced. "Now, let me get this straight," he said, glowering at the report. "You say in here that something resembling human saliva came in contact with the incisions on both corpses. What do you mean by 'resembling'?"

"I mean that I never saw saliva with those particular protein characteristics," Beransky answered, enunciating his points in a squeaky rhythm. "It has most of the same enzymes that you'd expect in human saliva. But some are different. And the basic secretion is toxic."

"Are you saying that the saliva itself is poisonous?" Stanford said in amazement.

Beransky shook his head in consternation, not in refutation. "It seems that way," he said reluctantly. "I told you we had a humdinger going for us. At first I figured that the saliva had mingled with the poison after the fact. But there's an organic bond there. It's all part of the same secretion."

"I don't believe it," said Stanford, getting to his feet abruptly. "There *has* to be something wrong with your analysis, Ken."

"I wish there were," Beransky replied sadly. "I hate things I can't get to the bottom of. I checked and double-checked my results, trying to make them come out in some way that made sense."

"Ed, is it possible for human saliva to be poisonous?" Vargo asked.

Stanford pursed his lips, trying to formulate some sort of answer.

"I never heard of such a thing," Beransky interjected. "If it could happen, it would have to be due to some kind of congenital aberration—like sometimes a baby will be born with a tail, or even gill slits. We're dealing with something pretty weird. The chemical bonding proves that this isn't saliva mixed with poison, but poisonous saliva. It has some of the properties of snake poison, though I couldn't match it with any of the poisons I have on hand. It has some unusual chemical properties. All of this is hard to believe, I know, but there you have it." Beransky pushed himself away from the desk and sat up straight in his chair as if daring anybody to challenge him. Maybe his report contained bothersome facts, but they *were* scientific facts, and he wasn't about to alter them to suit anybody.

After a long moment of silence, Vargo said, "Do you mind if I ask a foolish question?"

"Shoot," said Beransky.

"What would happen if this guy's saliva touches somebody accidentally? I mean, what if somebody eats after him? Or what if he kisses somebody?"

"You mean, would they be poisoned?" asked Ed Stanford.

Vargo nodded.

"Well," said Beransky, "snake poison is fatal only if it comes in contact with an open wound. If you take the venom orally, it makes your nose tingle for a few minutes, and that's about it."

"But I gather that what you analyzed wasn't exactly like snake poison," said Vargo. "It may have other strange properties that we're not aware of."

"It may have," Beransky squeaked. "But that's the type of speculation we don't get into in the serology lab."

13

After two weeks under Andy Bonner's tutelage, Benjamin Latham was beginning to adjust to his new world. The amnesia excuse enabled him to ask a lot of questions; and since Andy loved to ramble on, showing off his worldly wisdom, Benjamin extracted a wealth of information.

During the weekdays, he and Andy worked for Manpower, Inc.—a storefront office on Market Street which hired men out for odd jobs on an hourly or daily basis. Once they worked for half a day folding newspaper ad inserts as they came off the press; another time they had three straight days of hauling enormous drums of refuse out of an old office building that was being gutted and renovated. The minimum wage was legally over three dollars an hour, and that's what they were paid. Benjamin was shocked at the extent the federal government meddled in people's lives. At first the mandatory sum astounded him because it was so high, but he was even more astounded by how little it bought. By the time he paid for his room at the YMCA and his YMCA meals, he barely had anything left. Still, he managed to save, rolling bills up and hiding them in his hollow metal bedposts.

Often when he was involved in the routine of hard physical labor, Benjamin daydreamed about Lenora Clayton. But he stayed away from the Fort Pitt Museum. He didn't want to see Lenora again until he felt more at ease in this strange society.

His free time was spent strolling and wandering around the city, observing and learning through osmosis. Or else he would read one of the books he checked out of the library. He avidly devoured every kind of literature—but especially history. Through his reading and by watching documentary movies at the library, he had acquired an understanding of how and why the world had changed at a rate no one would have predicted two centuries ago. Global population had exploded from less than a billion to more than four billion. New countries had been born and old ones obliterated from the map. Marvelous inventions and discoveries had launched an Industrial Revolution that was still continuing, altering the way men lived and the way they looked at the future. Men could not only fly, they could walk on the moon. They could transmit sights and sounds electronically. Diseases like smallpox, polio, and diptheria had been conquered. Science and technology had, along with their benefits, brought the threat of destroying everybody and everything on the face of the earth at the touch of a button.

Maybe that was why, with all the material comforts of the twentieth century, a kind of zest was missing. There was an undercurrent of gloom and depression that Benjamin didn't remember feeling back in the 1700s. People preached and talked and wrote about the decadence of the new age, but it seemed so pervasive that complaining about it would probably do as much good as complaining about the weather. Pornographic pictures and artificial sex organs were sold right out in the open. Young people took drugs that ruined their minds and listened to crazy music advocating wild, destructive behavior. No wonder people were afraid to walk the streets at night: the crime statistics were terrifying. A violent crime was occurring once every twenty-four seconds. It was a wonder that the criminals had time to go to the bathroom.

As a Tory at the time of the Revolution, Benjamin Latham had believed that democracy would not work. Now he could see that he had been absolutely correct. The United States was no longer thirteen manageable colonies, but a sick giant with the highest per capita murder rate in the civilized world.

Benjamin couldn't help wondering if the outlandish crime rate might be blamed on Britain's practice of shipping convicts to the colonies. Parliament had authorized the transport to America of "rogues, vagabonds, sturdy beggars, and convicted felons"—whose sentences were commuted to terms of servitude. Murderers, rapists, highwaymen, and burglars came to the colonies by the thousands as indentured servants. Maybe the descendants of these rapscallions had an evil seed in them. Maybe their bad blood had been passed on to millions of modern Americans.

Speaking of descendants, Benjamin wondered if *he* might have some living now. Maybe he could trace his family tree, find out what had happened to his son, his grandchildren, and so on.

In the library, he began by looking up information about Hanna's Town, to see if there might be anything written about himself. When he first came across his name in print, he got a weird, trembly feeling and he ran his fingers over the ink as if it were a connection with the things he remembered from two hundred years ago.

He was mentioned as one of the fifteen signers of the "Hanna's Town Resolves," dated May 16, 1775. How well he recalled being coerced to sign the resolutions. They had pledged unshaken loyalty to King George, while opposing taxation without representation and other so-called tyrannies. Their stand was moderate compared to what some of the town's rabble-rousers had advocated, but signing anything of such a rebellious nature had gone against Benjamin's true principles, although it was better than out-and-out sedition. He was surprised that having affixed his signature to such a document still smarted, as if it had happened yesterday. In the library book there was an asterisk beside his name and a footnote which read as follows:

> Benjamin Latham, town doctor, who had served as a physician and soldier during the French and Indian War, was the only prominent citizen of the settlement to remain loyal to Great Britain after the Declaration of Independence. In 1782 he was convicted of sorcery and vampirism by the townspeople, and hanged—the last such execution recorded west of the Alleghenies. Historians suspect that it was really Latham's Toryism that aroused the wrath of the townspeople, and that their accusation of sorcery and vampirism was a pretext. However, according to Westmoreland County trial records preserved in Greensburg, which succeeded Hanna's Town as county seat, Benjamin Latham's corpse was given full precautionary rites against the rising of a sorcerer or vampire from the grave, including a necklace of garlic, a stake through the heart, and burial at a crossroads.

Reading about what they had done to him made Benjamin almost physically ill. What nonsense it had been. Sorcery, vampirism, witchcraft! It was certainly poetic justice that the townspeople's foolish superstitions had somehow backfired on them—making him into a creature with the ability to come back to life, instead of preventing him from doing so.

This extraordinary thing that had happened to him made him wonder if the limits of his supernatural powers had been reached. What else might be in store for him? Would he develop into a true vampire? Would he grow fangs? Lose his ability to move about in the daytime? Learn how to change himself into a bat or some other animal?

All of this sounded preposterous. But so did what had already happened.

Suddenly he wondered whether there were other people

like himself, who had risen out of their graves. Could he establish a kinship with them if he knew how to meet them?

Could they tell him if he was man or beast or a combination of both?

Could they say whether his master was God or the Devil?

Could they tell him how to still his growing hunger?

14

Lieutenant Harpster and Trooper Vargo were sitting in a booth in Freddy's Place, having a few beers.

"Frankly, I didn't believe Ken Beransky's serology report," Harpster said.

"Neither did I," Vargo admitted. "That's why I asked the State Police lab to run tests on the same swabs."

"And you're telling me they got the same kind of results?"

"Yeah. You want to read their report?"

"No." Harpster dismissed it with a wave of his hand, as if reading it would only aggravate him more.

"I don't blame you," said Vargo. "It's spooky."

"I thought for sure it'd turn out some loony was milking snakes, then using his own mouth to transfer the poison," Harpster said. "The Human Snake Strikes Again—I could picture the headlines in the newspapers. A thing like that would be weird, but at least you could get a handle on it. God knows, lunatics have done crazier things before."

Vargo said, "The serologist at the State Police lab says the same thing as Beransky—that it's not saliva mixed with poison. There's an organic chemical bond between the enzymes. So the venom has to be part of the salivary secretion."

"Great," Harpster said sarcastically. "If that kind of thing leaks to the press, I don't know which'll be worse, the public panic or the public ridicule." He took several gulps of beer, as if he needed it to clear his head of disturbing thoughts. "Know something? I retire in ten months. I would have enjoyed putting in my remaining time on the usual run-of-the-mill-type homicides."

"This one might be easier to solve than most," said Vargo. "Or at least easier to get a conviction if we catch the guy."

"Why?"

"Can't be too many others running around with poisonous saliva."

"Don't bet on it," Harpster said. "It'll probably turn out that some wild, crazy new drug is doing this to *all* the kids."

Vargo signaled the waitress for another round. Then he said, "My other pet theory is a washout, too. Apparently he isn't an escapee from a prison or a mental ward. At least not a recent one. I checked and double-checked Laurel State Hospital and every other institution within a three-hundred-mile radius."

Harpster said, "If he didn't have to ditch hospital or prison clothes, what in the hell was he doing in the woods naked?"

Vargo shrugged. "Maybe he was getting rid of clothing that was bloodstained. He might have killed somebody else we don't know about."

"Possible."

"But we didn't find *any* kind of clothing in the woods, even by using bloodhounds."

Mulling it over, Harpster rumpled his fingers through his silvery gray hair. He said, "Maybe the guy had a car hidden somewhere. Maybe he took his clothes off in the car."

"One thing that would explain," said Vargo, "is why nobody has come forward to say anything about a hitch-hiker, even after the description of the stolen clothes went out to the media."

"Unless whoever picked him up was a driver just passing through," said Harpster. "Or somebody who never paid attention to the news bulletin. Or didn't connect it to the guy we want."

The waitress placed two more fresh, foamy mugs on the table. "How about the gang Elijah Alford ran with? Think they'll break down and help us if we keep hauling them in and grilling them?"

Harpster shook his head vehemently. "No way are any of them about to cooperate with us. I have a strong suspicion they could probably put the finger on somebody —but the assholes want to handle it on their own. Here's hoping they succeed."

"We really don't have much to go on," Vargo admitted. "I can't think of anything we could be doing right now that might shake him loose."

"That's right," said Harpster. "We're gonna have to just sit tight and wait."

"Till when?"

"Till somebody kills him for us. Or until he kills again."

15

Lenora Clayton, her glossy black hair tied back in a ponytail, was sitting on a park bench eating slices of cheese and apple for lunch. Today was Friday. A sunshiny day, and more sunshine predicted for the rest of the weekend. Lenora was happy. She had no special plans for after work, but on a nice day like this something good was bound to happen. Sipping a Coke, she looked in the direction of the museum and saw Benjamin Latham on the path, coming toward her.

"Hello," he said. "Remember me?"

"Um-hmm. Want a piece of cheese or a slice of apple?"

"No, thank you. May I sit with you?"

"You're quite a gentleman, Benjamin. Most men wouldn't bother to ask."

He sat down. Was she fooling herself, or did he look even more handsome than she remembered? His face was clean-shaven this time, and his clothes were clean. He was wearing brown slacks and a yellow knit short-sleeved shirt.

His wavy brown hair was a bit unruly, but somehow it contributed to his good looks. She loved his cleft chin and his wide, full mouth. And his lambent blue eyes that seemed to burn right into her. She hoped he couldn't tell that he made her nervous, made her want to please him.

"Lenora," he said, riveting her with his eyes. "I want to go to Williamsburg."

"This weekend?" she asked. She had thought to stave him off by injecting much more surprise and hesitancy into her voice, but somehow her reaction was more encouraging than she wished it to be. And she knew that he meant for her to go with him.

"Tomorrow," he said. "I want to go there with you tomorrow."

He wished he could tell her he had had a son, a daughter-in-law, and two grandchildren who had lived there. He wished he could tell her everything about his life and what had happened to him. But it was impossible. She'd never believe him. She'd think he was joking. Or crazy. "I don't have a car," he said. "And it's a historical site I'd really love to visit. I thought you might be interested in it, too."

"Well, I've never been there before," she admitted. She wanted to say that it didn't have much to do with her thesis. But something kept the words from coming. His eyes were still boring into her. In the back of her mind she wondered: What strange hold does he have over me? But the notion was vague and somehow unthreatening. As if she *wanted* to be dominated by him.

"Will you drive me there?" he asked her.

"Yes . . . I have a car," she heard herself saying. "Yes . . . it will be fun . . . it's such a lovely weekend. . . ."

In his room at the YMCA, Benjamin was packing his shaving kit and a few articles of clothing into a tan vinyl suitcase that he had bought at the Five and Dime after speaking with Lenora.

He was startled when someone knocked on his door, and he closed the suitcase quickly and scooted it under his bed, pulling the army blanket down low enough to hide it. Rap-rap-rap-rap! He unbolted the door and, as he expected, Andy Bonner was the one doing the knocking.

Andy barged in, all dressed up in clean gray work trousers and a red knit short-sleeved shirt, his gray hair slicked down, smelling of hair tonic and aftershave. "Was you cuttin' logs or somethin'?" he crabbed. "Cripes, I thought you was gonna keep me standin' in the hall till the cows came home."

"Cutting logs?" Benjamin echoed, playing dumb.

"You know—snoozin'. That's what cuttin' logs means, but I guess you don't remember. You got any cash I can borrow?"

Benjamin could see that Andy was raring to go—nothing but financial embarrassment stopping him from going on a weekend binge. Payday for both of them had been a week ago, and Benjamin had hung on to most of his pay, spending hours in the library, while Andy was spending time and money in various saloons. By Thursday Andy was broke and had used yesterday evening and this morning to sober up, since Manpower hadn't hired him and Benjamin out for any odd jobs.

"I can let you have ten dollars," Benjamin said, knowing he wasn't going to get off scot-free. "I just bought a new shirt and trousers," he added, indicating what he had on. "I wish I could lend you more, but I don't have it."

"Ten bucks'd just about wet my whistle," Andy said, disappointed. "You sure you ain't got a little more stashed away?"

The phrasing of the question took Benjamin by surprise, and his eyes almost flickered toward the hollow bed rungs where he had his money hidden. But he chose to believe that Andy couldn't know about that and couldn't be hinting about it. "I barely have enough to get through till next payday," he pleaded. "If I hadn't bought these new clothes . . ."

"Well, then," Andy said, grinning and winking impishly, "looks like me and you *both* got to go to the bank."

"I don't have any bank account," Benjamin said. "I can't cash a check."

"Not that kind of bank," Andy replied with a sly chuckle.

Benjamin looked puzzled.

"All right, I guess I shouldn't pull your leg so much," Andy relented. "I didn't mean to take advantage of you, just cause you got the amnesia."

It turned out to be a blood bank.

While they were thumbing a ride across the Sixth Street Bridge, on their way to Allegheny General Hospital, Andy explained to Benjamin how they'd be paid twenty-five dollars apiece if they each donated a pint of blood. "Easy as pie," Andy said. "I do it every time I get in a tight-money spot." He held out his arm to show where the transfusion needles had gone in.

Benjamin shuddered inwardly. He wanted to *take* blood, not give any of it up. "I can't do it," he said. "The blow on my head that left me unconscious for all that time and caused the amnesia . . . the doctors said I could go into another coma worse than the first one if I suffered any kind of accidental blood loss."

"Oh shit, *this* ain't accidental," Andy said. "It's all done under controlled, sterile conditions. It won't hurt you none, and you'll have the satisfaction of helping some poor sucker who needs it more'n *you* do."

"Can't do it," Benjamin said, clenching his teeth. "I don't even know if I can watch *you* do it."

Andy chuckled good-naturedly. "You ain't gonna be a sissy, are you, Ben? I've given blood a thousand times, and I'm still hale and hearty. I ain't kicked the bucket yet, not by a long shot. They tell you you shouldn't drink afterward, but I don't pay no attention. It's great with less blood in your system, 'specially when you're low on cash. The alcohol hits you harder and you get a helluva cheap drunk out of it every time!"

Benjamin sat frozen in the back seat during their ride while Andy rambled on and on about all the weird things he had done in his life to get some quick cash. But Benjamin barely heard it. He was wondering how he was going to endure watching somebody's blood going into a jar. Just the thought of it made him queasy . . . and at the same time stimulated his desire to see and touch and taste blood . . . a desire that he had been fighting to suppress. He had hoped he could get the craving permanently under control. He had tried pushing it out of his mind by keeping himself busy, preoccupied with other things. But now he felt almost dizzy with desire. He dug his fingernails into the seat to stop himself from fainting from hunger.

At the hospital he felt better and he firmly told Andy that he couldn't go through with it. From the lurid description that Andy had insisted on giving in the waiting room, Benjamin could picture the blood-pressure apparatus, the insertion of the needle, and the flow of blood from the punctured vein through the clear plastic tube and into the jar. In his previous life he would have been intensely interested in the procedure as a medical phenomenon, a medical breakthrough. But now it gave him the creeps. On a primal level, he knew his craving for blood could never be satisfied by this modern transfusion process that required intervening tubes and needles. He needed to drink blood from a living person, so that he could feel the life-giving fluid pumping from that person's body into his own, his mouth pressed tightly against warm, suckling flesh, his tongue lapping at spurting veins and arteries, in an exchange that was overwhelmingly pleasant and sensual. The thought of receiving blood through tubes and needles repulsed him the way the artificial sex organs in the sad little shops on Liberty Avenue would repulse anyone interested in plain, basic, human contact.

Grinning from ear to ear, Andy Bonner came out of the blood-donor room into the waiting room. "Like fallin' off a log," he bragged. "I didn't even flinch. Told the nurse you'd be in to see her next. You ain't gonna make a liar out of me, are ya?"

"Drop it, will you, Andy," Benjamin snapped, glowering angrily. "I told you I *can't* give blood—I have a medical problem."

As he spoke, Benjamin stood so that his clear blue eyes stared into Andy's gray, watery ones, and he could feel the old man's urge to pursue the subject dissipate like stale air escaping from a punctured balloon.

When Benjamin broke the eye contact, Andy stammered, "I g-guess I b-better go get paid. Gotta t-take this voucher to the comptroller's office."

"I'll wait right here for you," Benjamin said sternly, as if talking to a child.

In a shambling, uncertain gait, Andy crossed the waiting area and started walking down a long fluorescent corridor.

Benjamin watched him go, then sat back down on an orange plastic chair. A low glass table in front of him was laden with reading matter. The magazines were all tattered and torn, so he reached for a pamphlet that looked new. The title gave him a start: *Blood—the Gift of Life.*

Suddenly he felt another surge of desire come over him. His heart was pounding, and the rhythmic beating seemed to be a primordial chant. For a moment he was afraid that he'd leap on someone in the waiting room. He dropped the pamphlet and slowly his body settled back into its normal state of controllable anxiety.

Suddenly Benjamin was aware of Andy Bonner's voice, barking at him.

"I said all set, ready to go," Andy chuckled. "Man, when you daydream you really go into a trance. I thought I'd go to sleep before you answered me. You was lost in your own little world."

Andy Bonner led the way out of the hospital. On the sidewalk, Benjamin kept his feet moving, but his thoughts were elsewhere. Andy didn't notice. He set a brisk pace, he was so bright and chipper about having his blood-donor money in his pocket. He said, "Still gonna let me have that ten, ain't you, Ben? If I can put it with the twenty-five bucks they gave me, I'll have a helluva good try at drownin' my sorrows."

Reluctantly, still in somewhat of a daze, Benjamin took a ten-dollar bill out of his wallet and gave it to Andy Bonner.

"Thanks," Andy quipped. "You just invested in a hangover."

* * *

The desire for blood that he felt right now was as powerful as the hunger for Thanksgiving turkey when one hasn't had anything to eat all day and the smell of the bird basting in the oven has set the salivary juices flowing. Such an appetite could be pushed out of one's mind . . . its fulfillment prolonged . . . or even denied . . .

But for how long?

Would it be like celibacy—always extremely difficult to maintain, but not impossible, in the face of sexual lust that raged at a high and constant pitch, a maddening, throbbing intensity, but then did not get much worse?

In which case it could probably be controlled.

Or would it be like the heroin addictions which afflicted so many teenagers today—an insane craving with no outer limits, just a wild, itching, twitching, pounding, earsplitting ripping and whining and clawing and prying apart of flesh and spirit?

In which case it would eventually have to be appeased.

At six o'clock Saturday morning, after a night of hot, sweaty tossing-and-turning dreams, Benjamin stood in front of the YMCA waiting for Lenora Clayton to pick him up. His tan vinyl suitcase was by his feet, in the middle of the sidewalk, and he was watching anxiously for Lenora's car. He almost hoped she wouldn't show up; he was terrified that his craving for blood would drive him to attack her.

He looked up and down the street. In one instant the street was empty, stores locked and caged, nobody up and about in the wee hours in a city that came to a bird-chirping standstill on early weekend mornings. In the next instant Andy Bonner came staggering into view, rounding the corner at the far end of the block. Obviously he had drunk up his blood-donor money and Benjamin's ten to boot, and was now finding his way home, bouncing off the walls of buildings, telephone poles, and Keep Pittsburgh Clean cans.

Benjamin wished fervently that Andy wouldn't spot him. He wished Lenora would pull up in her car so he could jump in and make his escape without having to explain anything to the drunken old man or allow himself to be hit up for another ten dollars. As if in answer to his wish, Lenora's red Fiesta popped out of a side street and wheeled to a stop at the curb. But Andy saw Benjamin just as he hefted his suitcase.

"Ben! Hey, Ben!" the old man called out. "Where you goin', Ben? Hey, *don't* leave me!"

Benjamin tossed his suitcase into the back of the car and got in next to Lenora. "Who's that?" she asked him. "Should I wait?"

"No, he'll pester us. Come on, let's get going."

She put the car into gear and pulled out.

Andy tried to catch them, staggering as fast as he could along the sidewalk, holding on to the gray stone window ledges of the YMCA building. "Ben! Please!" he cried, like a child being abandoned. "Please, don't leave your old buddy!"

He was such a tiny figure in the rearview mirror that Benjamin couldn't see the tears on his cheeks.

"He thinks you're leaving him for good," Lenora said. "How sad. You should've told him differently."

"I guess so," said Benjamin. "I just didn't want him to know where I was going."

"Why not?"

"I was scared he'd want to come with us, and I can't afford to pay his way. He doesn't have any money."

"Who is he?"

"Just an old man I befriended at the YMCA."

Actually, Benjamin suspected he might be leaving Andy Bonner for good, and the possibility gave him a twinge of sorrow. At Williamsburg he would begin to trace his family tree, if he discovered any descendants, and he was determined to go wherever the search might lead. In colonial times Williamsburg had been the capital of Virginia, and Benjamin's son, Robert, had practiced law there. Robert and his wife, Ruth, had had two children, Stephen and Patience. Benjamin had seen his grandchildren only once, when they were five and three years old, respectively. He still carried a fond remembrance of them as cute little tykes. Maybe Robert and Ruth had had more children after Benjamin died. He hoped to find out in the archives of the College of William and Mary; Robert had taken his law degree there. Surprisingly, the college was still in existence as an institution of higher learning. In this day and age where the past was often bulldozed to the ground to make way for a "better" future, that was quite unusual.

16

"I have a confession to make," Benjamin told Lenora as they bypassed Richmond on Interstate 64 which would take them southeast to Williamsburg. They were almost at the end of a four-hundred-mile trip. It was time to try to get Lenora on his side.

"Don't tell me you're married and have a dozen children back home in England," she said, smiling, but with a twinge of worry.

"No. Nothing like that. I was only going to confess that I have an ulterior motive for wanting to visit Williamsburg."

"Something other than the lure of history?" she said, still making light of it.

"Yes," he said soberly.

He watched Lenora driving, her ponytail blowing out the open-windowed Fiesta, her long, tan, exquisitely shaped legs stretched out under the dash. She was wearing a blue halter and blue shorts, a carefree modern lass out for a weekend of fun and relaxation. He wondered if, on an ordinary date, sex might normally be part of the fun. He hated to imagine her being as casual about it as most of her contemporaries seemed to be.

"Don't keep me in suspense," she told him.

Either his craving for blood was subdued when he was with her, or else it merged with his romantic, carnal cravings, so that it wasn't as noticeable as a separate, distinct passion. But it was still there, and it frightened him.

"What I have to confess is not all that serious," he said. "In fact, you might find it intriguing. You see, I might have relatives in this country. I had an ancestor who was a soldier during the French and Indian War, with the Royal American Regiment. Later he served as a surgeon under General Stanwix at Fort Pitt, and he had a son who practiced law in Williamsburg." He looked at her and, lying easily, said, "His diary has been in the family for years."

"Why, that's wonderful!" Lenora exclaimed gleefully. "You mean we might be able to track down information on him?"

"Well, on his son Robert, since he lived in Williamsburg. His father, the keeper of the diary, was named Benjamin, same as me. I guess he was my great-great-great something or other, and I'd like to find out what happened to his branch of the family tree."

"It's enchanting," said Lenora. "Why didn't you tell me about it before? It makes coming to Williamsburg doubly exciting."

"I was hoping you'd want to get involved, but I thought you might like more of a break from poring over books and working on your thesis."

"Oh, but this isn't like *work*. Especially since I know you. It'll be like tracking down clues in a detective story. What else do you know about your ancestors?"

"Well . . . Benjamin's diary makes him out to be an interesting character. Captured by the Indians, almost burned at the stake, and so on. His parents were Philadelphia Quakers. Benjamin and his father quarreled when the boy rejected the Quaker religion in favor of deism, and because he wanted to marry an indentured servant named Clarissa."

"Fascinating," Lenora said.

Benjamin went on, feeling distinctly odd, having to talk about himself in third person. "That was when young Benjamin Latham used a small inheritance from his grandfather to buy up Clarissa's term of indenture, and they married and moved to a small settlement in western Pennsylvania, where he set up practice. When the war broke out, he joined up with General Braddock."

"What happened to Clarissa?"

"She lived with Benjamin at Fort Pitt when he was stationed there. By that time their son, Robert, was in his teens. But Clarissa never lived to see any grandchildren. She died at the fort of cholera, in the epidemic of 1765. Benjamin lived by himself after his son went away to William and Mary College, and when his army enlistment expired he became one of the first settlers in Hanna's Town."

"It sounds as if his life must have been exciting in many ways, but with an overriding melancholy. I mean, in essence he lost his wife and his son and grandchildren, and eventually became almost a recluse."

Yes, Benjamin thought to himself. Even the practice of medicine had ceased to interest him very much, and he had become obsessed with his lonely experiments. He developed a fixation on blood. And his neighbors turned against him because of his odd ways and his nonconformist politics.

They arrived in Williamsburg late in the afternoon, after a nine-hour drive. The information center was swarming with tourists.

"We're in luck," Lenora said, pivoting from the information desk. "The college library and the Williamsburg Public Library are both open on Saturdays and Sundays. We'll be able to do our research."

Benjamin nodded, a far-off look in his eyes. He remembered coming into town to visit his grandchildren for the first and only time. The clopping of hooves and the creaking of carriage wheels on a dusty, uncrowded street were a far cry from this sterile hullaballoo of passing through an information center full of gawkers and gapers.

"Here it is—the Williamsburg Inn," Lenora said, looking at a wall map. "We'd better check in there, if we can get a room. I suggest we freshen up and have something to eat, and spend whatever time we have left touring the Historic Area. Then, tomorrow, we can do our library work."

"That sounds wise," he said, trying to perk up a little.

She put her hand in his as they headed out to the car. Her touch gave him a warm, tingly feeling. He wanted to be close to her and he clung to her as he walked backward through time, picking up pieces of the past.

The Williamsburg Inn turned out to be a modern motor hotel with tennis courts, a golf course, and a swimming pool. He and Lenora registered and settled themselves in their separate rooms. Then, after wolfing down cheeseburgers and french fries in the snack bar, they took the shuttle bus to the Historic Area.

Benjamin's first look at the slice of Old Williamsburg that had been preserved for posterity was a shock. Fewer than a hundred buildings remained of the once-bustling, energetic seat of colonial government. The streets were no longer packed dirt, but were neatly cobblestoned. Signs with arrows pointed out key tourist attractions. The guidebook explained that the cobblestones were a concession to modern convenience, as were the buried electrical wires, the twentieth-century plumbing, and the "inconspicuous" fire hydrants.

"Oh, it's beautiful!" Lenora exclaimed. She had an enthralled look in her eyes. "Imagine, Benjamin!" she said as they stepped down to the curb. "You had an ancestor living here at the time of the Revolution, rubbing elbows with George Washington and Thomas Jefferson. He probably stood on the Capitol steps and cheered when the Declaration of Independence was signed."

"Probably," Benjamin allowed, trying not to sound

glum. She had hit the nail on the head. It galled him that his own son *had* been an addlebrained patriot instead of a levelheaded Tory. It had been a mistake sending Robert to Williamsburg to study law. But who could have foreseen that he'd fall in with Peyton Randolph and George Wythe and the other southern Sons of so-called Liberty?

"Let's try to see as much as possible before the sun goes down," Lenora enthused, taking Benjamin by the hand.

He murmured something agreeable and let himself be led from one historical attraction to the next. Lining up behind mobs of sightseers, they traipsed through the Publick Gaol, the Magazine and Guardhouse, the Courthouse of 1770. They visited the House of Burgesses where, in 1765, Patrick Henry had made a name for himself by bitterly opposing the Stamp Act. They browsed through various homes, shops, inns, and taverns run by people in "quaint eighteenth-century costumes." In the apothecary shop someone demonstrated a pill-rolling machine. In the bakery a clerk in an ill-fitting wig sold little round loaves of "colonial corn bread." Everywhere cameras went pop, flash, and click.

The emptiness was so palpable that Benjamin wondered why Lenora didn't feel it, too. But for her it was all an enchantment, while for him it was part of the vacuum of his former life. In some of these streets and buildings, fields and gardens, his son and daughter-in-law and grandchildren had worked and laughed, cried and played.

His heart beat faster as he and Lenora walked down Duke of Gloucester Street toward the College of William and Mary.

"What's the matter?" Lenora asked. "You look like you've seen a ghost."

"Robert Latham . . . Benjamin's son," he told her. "According to Benjamin's diary, he and his family lived right on this corner."

"Oh!" Lenora said. "It's a shame his house isn't one of the restored ones!"

"It would have been nice," Benjamin said, downplaying his disappointment.

"It's getting dark," Lenora said. "Everything's closing up. What say we call it a day?"

He wanted blood.

But he didn't want *her* blood. He wanted *her*.

Lenora . . .

Lenora . . .

The tight, soft warmth of her thighs, the nubbly cushion of her breasts, the pliant receptiveness of her mouth.

His mind and soul called out for her.

Did he have a soul?

He wondered, tossing and turning, hot and naked on the hotel bed.

Maybe his missing navel was the place where the soul would have been breathed in. Perhaps only creatures with souls could ever die, because they were the only ones who could give up the ghost.

On the other hand, wouldn't his own spirit have had to form the nucleus of what he had become in his grave? If he didn't possess a spirit, wouldn't there have been nothing left when the flesh died?

His thoughts were wispy distractions, like spirits, and his aching need drove them away.

Naked need.

Naked blood.

Needed her.

Lenora . . .

Lenora!

His mind and soul cried out for her.

In the throes of a waking dream, she stood outside his hotel room. The wee hours. The blue-carpeted hallway quietly and brightly lit. She tapped the door lightly with her fingernails.

She felt naked. No excuse for being there. Could have offered a glass of sherry, but the bottle was still in her room. Her forgotten pretext.

Suddenly he stood before her, his skin as taut as her own desire.

Warm and wet and receptive, she folded herself into his arms.

In the morning she still tingled pleasantly. She sensed a change beginning in her, a change within the essence of herself.

Was this what it felt like to fall truly and totally in love? She had never come close to feeling this way before. She was a strong woman, but she knew that she had been penetrated and conquered in a way that was new, and total. She was surprised by the warmth and comfort of her surrendering, the ease and depth of her dependency. She felt as primal as an animal. Never before had she merged with a man in such a hauntingly thrilling exchange of lust and satisfaction.

The bite at the base of her neck tingled like the other sexual parts of her. It seemed to feed delicious postcoital sensations directly into her brain. Her pleasure centers were satiated. Instead of annoying her, it pleased her that Benjamin had left her a love wound, a souvenir of his erotic domination. Rather than wearing a halter today, she planned on wearing her white blouse so the collar would conceal the tooth marks.

Lenora had consumed and replenished him.

Apparently he hadn't harmed her. She was still alive and healthy. He felt a proud glow of happiness and relief. He had brought her love and pleasure . . . love and pleasure . . . in a fury of wild sensual abandonment. And she hadn't died at the crest, as he had feared might happen even as they were both screaming out their orgasms, his teeth sinking into her neck, his entire being pounding into her. Never had he reached such an intense, long-lasting climax, as if his soul were splitting out of his body . . . and then returning . . . hand in hand with her soul . . . stronger and more alive . . . and more relaxed.

The craving for blood was not completely assuaged. If that was one of the detriments of coming back from the grave, then this new sexual dimension was one of the rewards.

Benjamin and Lenora were in the cemetery of Bruton Parish Church on Duke of Gloucester Street, searching among old, weathered tombstones and monuments. The Sunday-morning church bells had inspired him to go to the cemetery before going to the library with his notebook and pen. What better place than the graveyard to find out which members of the family had lived and died in Williamsburg?

"Over here!" Lenora called out suddenly, almost gaily. "I found it! Robert Latham's grave!"

A lump in his throat, Benjamin came to Lenora's side and looked down at a stone tablet eroded by wind and rain, obscured by weeds, and sunk at an odd angle into the earth. It said: Robert Latham, b. 1749, d. 1810. Ruth's headstone was close by: she had died in 1817. Shakily writing the names and dates in his notebook, Benjamin recalled that when the noose had been placed around his neck in Hanna's Town he had imagined his son and daughter-in-law coming someday to stand over *his* grave, and not the other way around.

"Gee, here's a grave of a Patience Latham, buried in 1787."

Feeling as sad as if she had died yesterday, Benjamin approached the grave of his granddaughter.

"A little girl," said Lenora. "Eight years old. Maybe she died in an accident or a fire or something."

"More likely a disease like smallpox," said Benjamin, a tremor in his voice.

Lenora put her arm around him. "I know what it's like," she said. "An odd feeling always hits me when I see my ancestors' graves in Marietta."

"Wait a minute," he cried. He had found Stephen's grave a few yards away from his sister's. He'd died at the age of thirty-four, and he had left behind a wife, Elvira, and three children. They found no other Latham graves.

* * *

They spent the rest of the morning in the Williamsburg Public Library and the library of the College of William and Mary. It turned out that Robert Latham *had* made something of a name for himself in Williamsburg. Being on the winning side during the Revolution had furthered his career. He had done some soldiering, got himself wounded, and received a commendation from the Father of His Country. Making the most of Washington's patronage, he thrived as a lawyer and a politician. Eventually he was elected to Congress. Patience had died of smallpox, but Stephen had married Elvira Blaine, daughter of a wealthy Virginia plantation owner.

Stephen and Elvira Latham had had three children. A son, Abraham, had been killed fighting for the Confederacy at the Battle of Shiloh in 1862. A daughter, Priscilla, had died in a steamboat explosion in 1864. Their third child, John Latham, had been born in 1818. He had married a Mary Peterson in 1848 and moved with her to Philadelphia to become partners with her cousin in a railroad venture. Information about him in either of the two libraries in Williamsburg was scanty.

John Latham and his offspring, if any, might have carried Latham blood into the twentieth century. In order to continue tracing his family tree, Benjamin would have to go to Philadelphia. Back to the city where he had been born.

"It's fascinating, isn't it?" said Lenora as they stood in the shade of a sycamore in front of the Raleigh Tavern, waiting for the shuttle bus to take them back to the Williamsburg Inn. "It's just like a detective story. What makes it fun is knowing that all these people were related to you."

Benjamin impulsively kissed her, and her tongue darted quickly, mischievously, into his mouth. She giggled at the embarrassed way that he glanced around to see if people had been watching.

She had noticed that whenever they kissed, her nose and mouth tingled afterward for a time, in a deliciously pleasant way that was almost like sexual arousal.

17

There were crowds of people and clusters of pigeons in the square. Benjamin and the towheaded boy in the blue Cub Scout uniform were both sitting on a wooden bench. It was as if they were isolated in streaks of golden sunlight slanting through the branches of overhead leaves. At first nobody seemed to notice them. The boy had a penknife, and he was whittling on a hollow stick, making it into a wooden whistle of the sort Benjamin remembered from his youth.

He wished the knife would slip.

He wanted the boy to cut himself.

He wanted to see the boy's fresh young blood.

Because he willed it, it happened. Trying to punch an airhole in the wooden whistle, the boy lost control of the penknife and the fat, sharp blade closed on his fingers, cutting two of them to the bone. In speechless, wide-eyed terror, the boy unclasped the sticky red-streaked knife and dropped it to the grass. A glimpse of white bone, then blood flowing in thick rivulets and fat drops.

Benjamin seized the boy's warm, throbbing little wrist, covered the dripping fingers with his mouth, and sucked hard. The blood tasted so incredibly good! He made himself take tiny swallows so the pleasure and the instant gratification wouldn't overwhelm him.

He hoped that the boy would not die, and at the same time he didn't care. It was guilt mixed with satisfaction, like committing adultery with an extremely desirable woman. The boy's blood tasted *so* delicious. Drinking it produced a state of euphoria that made all moral considerations seem remote and farfetched. Benjamin was oblivious to everything but the pulsing elixir that could refresh his body and spirit.

But the people in the square were noticing what was going on. They started to flock around the bench where the little blond Cub Scout was stretched out flat on his back, dead or unconscious, while a man knelt beside him in the grass, sucking at the fingers of his right hand.

The people became mean. They began to mutter obscenities. Like a wall of hateful flesh, they closed in on Benjamin, wanting to smother him to death.

He woke up in a cold sweat. He was back in his room at the YMCA and he had a painful erection.

The thirst was still with him, stronger than ever. Andy Bonner would have said that he had a monkey on his back.

How much longer could he go on without satisfying his urge?

He couldn't think straight anymore. He didn't want to kill. He was almost starting to convince himself that he *could* take blood from somebody without the person actually dying. But how to pull it off without having the person going into hysterics and yelling for help? The only way might be to kidnap somebody and tie him or her up long enough to take some blood. But it would be very risky, would require careful planning and adroit execution, and if any slight thing went wrong it could get the police hot on Benjamin's tail. Killing at least had the advantage of leaving no witnesses.

But he had no wish to kill another human being. If he wasn't totally human himself, he still felt a kinship with humankind. No matter what he was now, he had undeniably once been a man. He still thought of himself as a man, or something that had sprung from man. He still empathized strongly with the struggle that all good men went through.

How, then, could he requite his blood craving if it required someone to die? How could he bring himself to end someone's hard-earned happiness, or someone's longing for love, or someone's lonely battle against despair?

If he had a *need* to kill, why couldn't he do it without moral anguish, like panthers and other beasts of prey?

Why was he half man and half beast, warring against his own nature, trying not to evolve into what he sensed he must eventually become?

At dawn he was still wide awake and suffering from a deprivation that was worse than a long-term deprivation of sex. He got up, let himself out of his room, and went down the hall to shave and shower. Afterward he tried to believe that he was feeling somewhat better. Fully dressed, he lay on top of his made bed, waiting for Andy Bonner to knock. It was Monday morning, so he expected that, as usual, he and his friend would try to get to the Manpower office by eight o'clock.

He daydreamed about Lenora. His longing for her merged with his other craving until the two hungers were intertwined and blurred, but not dulled. Trying to compartmentalize his thoughts, he went over in his mind how the exact conversation had sounded when she offered to put in a good word for him at the Fort Pitt Museum so that he might be hired for the summer as a tour guide. "You know so much about the history of the period, it's bound to impress the curator. And you'll be a big hit with the sightseers as well—at least the ones who want to *learn* something."

Andy Bonner didn't knock.

When it was ten minutes to eight, Benjamin went out to the hall and rapped on Andy's door. No answer. Nobody stirred. After rapping several more times in vain, he gave up and went to the Manpower office by himself.

Andy was already there, sitting on the curb smoking a cigarette. His clothes looked as though they'd been slept in. His hair was greasy and mussed up, and he hadn't shaved. His eyes were bloodshot and baggy. He watched Benjamin's approach out of the corner of his eye but didn't otherwise acknowledge the younger man's presence. Groups of other men were loitering on the sidewalk, and some were starting to line up at the entrance to the Manpower storefront office.

"Aren't you getting into line?" Benjamin asked.

"What business is it of yours?" Andy snarled, tossing his brown, soggy cigarette butt angrily into the street.

"I thought we were pals."

"Well, so did I."

"We still are."

"Nope," said Andy, speaking adamantly. "Any pal of mine wouldn't run off on me. A true pal wouldn't make me think I was being ditched."

"Ditched?"

"Run out on. Did the amnesia make you forget the English language? Because it sure made you forget to tell me about that pretty girl. You married to her?"

"No."

"I don't suppose you want to tell me who she is?"

"No, I really don't." Benjamin couldn't have explained why he wanted to keep Lenora's identity a secret; it was something instinctual. He didn't want to hurt Andy Bonner either; but he had been unable to stop the words that had come out of his mouth sounding so untactfully cruel.

"Afraid I'd ask you to cut me in?" Andy jeered.

Benjamin shrugged, hoping the subject would drop.

"My *true* pal!" Andy mocked. "Got yourself a piece of pussy, so you're gonna forget about me."

"Have you been drinking all night?" Benjamin asked. "Because you look like it and sound like it."

"None of your goddamn business."

"You're jealous of somebody you've never met."

"Get outta here!" Andy snapped. "Lemme alone! You and me ain't buddies anymore!"

Benjamin was too weak and distracted by his blood craving to concentrate on getting back on Andy Bonner's good side. He simply couldn't think of the proper things to say to the old man. Maybe subconsciously he wanted to drive his friend away. If he had to turn on somebody to satisfy the maddening urge that was clawing at his insides, he would rather attack a total stranger. Or an enemy.

Andy Bonner hobbled away from the curb. When Benjamin turned around, Andy gave him the finger and walked haughtily up the street in the direction of the YMCA.

Benjamin hoped that he wouldn't be given a tough assignment from Manpower today, because the craving for blood had him so depleted that he felt nauseated and feverish. But his luck was bad. He landed a job unloading boxcars full of crated furniture and stacking them in a department-store warehouse. At the end of the day he was so exhausted that his blood craving was subdued—the way that a starving man can be so far gone that he no longer feels hunger pangs.

It was late in the evening when he got back to the YMCA and found that the door to his room had been jimmied. The knob turned too easily. There were screw-driver marks all around the jamb. Closing the door, Benjamin went immediately to his bunk bed, lifted one corner off the floor, and pulled the brass cap from one of the tubular steel legs. His money was gone. He wondered fleetingly why the thief had even bothered to put the brass cap back on. None of his clothes were missing. Just his cash. Over a hundred dollars. There would have been more if he hadn't gone to Williamsburg this weekend. He was thankful that the robbery hadn't happened before he had had a chance to make the trip with Lenora.

Then he admitted to himself that it was obvious why the money hadn't been stolen until now. Andy Bonner had to be the culprit. The old man was getting even for being ditched. He had dropped a few hints about Benjamin having money stashed, had probably figured it out by observing how little Benjamin spent. It wouldn't have been difficult for Andy to find the rolled-up bills, after breaking into the room in full confidence that he would have all day to search.

Could Benjamin now think of Andy Bonner as an enemy?

Because of this transgression, could he feel justified in going after Andy's blood?

He took the elevator down to the lobby. Then he headed for Liberty Avenue. It was a hot, muggy July night, the kind that saps energy and usually makes a tired person feel even more tired. But Benjamin kept walking at a brisk pace. He was driven by anger, and he had a hunger for more than revenge. Because of what his veins lacked, his heart was pumping adrenaline insufficiently diluted, and he was beginning to feel keenly alert and alive in the high-strung urgency of the hunt.

He seemed to *know* where to find his quarry. His notion of where Andy Bonner would be was more than a hunch; it was an extrasensory perception. He knew that it would pan out, even though it didn't seem logical for him to know. When he saw Andy where he expected him to be, he would feel the inner starburst of psychic gratification that a gambler feels when he knows he's going to get blackjack before he turns over a queen and an ace.

Andy would be in the Liberty Tavern, one of his favorite hangouts. Even though it would have made a certain kind of sense for him to stay clear of his usual haunts, Andy would do just the opposite. Realizing that he couldn't avoid Benjamin forever, he'd try to pretend he was innocent—he'd have an excuse ready to explain where he had gotten so much money; he'd say he had borrowed it or hit on a number or something. He'd claim that the fact that Benjamin's room had been broken into was just a coincidence. Benjamin would be hard pressed to prove otherwise.

But of course he didn't intend to try to prove anything. Whatever was left of his money, he wanted it back. And he wanted to appease his craving. This was his opportunity to satisfy himself all the way. He ought to be able to do it now, pushing guilt and remorse aside. He had all the justification that he needed.

Still, deep inside he knew that when it came time to harm the old man, he'd have to force himself to go through with it, even though the monkey on his back was *screaming* for blood.

"We have to get the old fart out in the alley," Garth Weir whispered hoarsely, leaning over the clutter of bottles, glasses, and butt-filled ashtrays on the barroom table so he wouldn't have to talk loudly. "Then we can work him over till he tells us what we want to know."

"Right on," said Paul Hill.

"I *knew* he'd bop on in here sooner or later," said Jorell Jordan.

They were talking about Andy Bonner, who was slouched on a bar stool twenty feet away. The country-and-western jukebox in the Liberty Tavern was so loud that he couldn't have heard what was being said behind his back even if he had been sober enough to pay attention. His alcoholic mumblings were lost in the cacophony of voices, music, clinking bottles, and slurred laughter in the smoky, dimly lit saloon.

"Weird Garth" Weir, Paul "Mountain" Hill, and Jorell Jordan were the three surviving members of the quartet that had cornered Benjamin Latham in Point Park four weeks ago. They were determined to get revenge for what Benjamin had done to their crony, Elijah Alford. Instead of giving Benjamin's description to the cops, they had reserved to themselves the right to carry out justice as they saw fit.

Last Thursday, Jorell Jordan—a tall, lanky black with his hair done up in cornrows and pigtails—had spotted Benjamin Latham and Andy Bonner together on Market Square, when they were on their way to the blood bank. But Jorell had been by himself, unprepared to make any kind of decisive move.

"You should've followed them, you asshole," Weird

Garth had said, the scar on his cheek going livid with anger. "Now we'll have to twiddle our thumbs till we bump into them again."

"I *tried* to tail them," Jorell had defended. "I stayed on them like stink on shit, all the way to the Sixth Street Bridge. Then they stuck their thumbs out and got a ride, so I lost the motherfuckers."

"You think they live on the other side of town?" Mountain had asked. His nickname had nothing to do with his size; he was short and skinny, but mean. It made him feel twice as mean to be called Paul Mountain instead of Paul Hill. He liked the nickname so much that he had been the one to bestow it on himself.

"What do I look like, a fortune-teller?" Jorell had sneered, because he had to show he wasn't afraid of the little blond white guy.

"No, a fuck-up," Weird Garth had squelched.

Jorell had swallowed hard. In his opinion, Garth was the one who should have been nicknamed Mountain. Six foot four, with muscles where muscles didn't even belong. Black hair, black beard, a broken-bottle scar running down his left cheek, and wild black eyes that burned like the coals of hell whenever he turned them on somebody.

"I seen the old man around before," Jorell had offered, trying to buy his way back into Weird Garth's good graces. "I swear one place I remember I seen his sorry old ass was in the Liberty Tavern."

"I'm gonna put it on you to remind us to scout the place now and then," Weird Garth had said in his lazily threatening way.

Today the spot checks had paid off. Andy Bonner was sitting on his bar stool when Jorell and Mountain and Weird Garth had come bopping in. Now they had the old man cold. They almost liked the fact that he was alone, instead of with their primary target. It would give them some warm-up exercise, because they intended to beat the hell out of the old man until he told them the name and whereabouts of the punk friend of his who had killed Elijah Alford in the parking garage.

Slowly and methodically, as if the task demanded

infinite concentration, Andy brought a shotglass of whiskey to his lips and tossed it down, then followed it with a sip from his beer chaser. Change from a twenty lay in front of him—a ten, a five, and a one—sopping wet from a beer he had previously spilled.

"On top of what we want him for, the old coot is just asking to be rolled," Weird Garth said, grinning in anticipation. "All we gotta do is get him outside."

"Better do it before he spends all his cash," said Jorell Jordan.

"How we gonna lure him into the alley?" Mountain asked Garth.

"We're gonna buy him a friendly drink. Play it like we're his buddies. Then we're gonna suggest headin' over to the Morgan Hotel to watch the strippers—that way it'll make sense to him to take the shortcut through the alley, and he'll feel safe with his three buddies to protect him."

"Strippers?" Mountain said doubtfully. "You sure he'll be interested? You think the old dude can still get a hard-on?"

"No way," said Weird Garth. "Last time he got it up was probably when the Wright brothers flew. But all these dirty old men like to look at naked pussy and reminisce about what they're missin'."

"Dream on . . . dream on," said Jorell, with a sly chuckle.

A sticky-hot blast of stale beer-and-cigarette fumes attacked Benjamin Latham as he opened the door of the Liberty Tavern. He walked the length of the dusky barroom, looking for Andy Bonner, shouldering his way past the usual clientele of bums, winos, crooks, and hustlers. He didn't see his ex-friend at the bar or at any of the tables. Benjamin went down the dirty, rickety wooden steps to the basement and peered into the foul-smelling cubicle. Andy Bonner wasn't in the men's room, so Benjamin came back up to the bar, which now smelled fresh by comparison.

There were two bartenders working—big, baldheaded twin brothers named Big Mike and Big Tom, both with beefy forearms and greasy white aprons and looks in their green eyes that said they weren't about to take any shit from the customers. Benjamin knew he wouldn't get to talk to either of them unless he ordered a drink. He took a ten-dollar bill out of his wallet and made a show out of laying it down; it got Big Mike's attention, and he came over.

"Large draft," Benjamin said. He had purposely stood directly opposite the tap so Big Mike wouldn't go away when he poured. "Have you seen Andy Bonner today?" Benjamin asked casually.

Big Mike squinted suspiciously at Benjamin and then slammed the mug down. "Wait a minute. I recognize you. You're Andy's pal. I think he's living dangerously, but maybe you can bail him out before it's too late. He left here with three wise guys lookin' to rip him off. Andy was more flush than usual—said he had got a pension check—and these three fuckers got on him like dogs on a bone."

"Where'd they go?" Benjamin asked.

"You know where the Morgan Hotel is, down the alley on Penn Avenue?"

"Yeah."

"I don't think I was supposed to overhear—you know me and Tom, it ain't our way to eavesdrop—but hell, I like Andy Bonner, and I guess I feel sorry for him. I caught a snatch of something about going to the hotel to watch the striptease show."

"Thanks," Benjamin said, leaving a two-dollar tip and tucking the rest of his change into his wallet.

"You'd think even those three assholes would take pity on an old man," Big Mike said. "Maybe they're just figuring on taking him to the hotel and playing him for the price of the floor show and drinks."

"I hope they don't hurt him," Benjamin said.

He meant it. How much he meant it hit him as he headed for the alley. How could he have thought that he could hurt Andy Bonner? He only wanted his money back. Andy was one of the few people who had been good to him. He'd have to find some other way to satisfy his craving. If only the old man was all right!

The brick-paved alley was almost pitch dark. The only illumination came from a few lighted windows in the backs of tall buildings, in the upper stories. With a strong sense of foreboding, Benjamin pulled out of his pocket the switchblade knife he had taken from Elijah Alford and flicked it open; there was barely enough light to make a glint off the sharp blade.

From somewhere deep in the darkness, amid the smell of rotting garbage, he heard a thud and a groan. Then a faint sadistic giggle. A scuffle and a few muttered curses. And a wretched, gurgling scream. Followed by belabored grunts and soft, sucking punches. The flurry of sounds lasted only a few seconds.

Benjamin ran, banging over a couple of garbage cans and letting out a bloodcurdling war whoop—trying to make himself sound like more than one person springing into the attack. Grabbing a garbage-can lid, he used it like a shield as three fast-moving shadowy shapes came at him from behind a high corrugated-steel fence. The biggest, heaviest shape—Weird Garth—bounced off the shield with a glancing blow that almost knocked Benjamin down. His left hand stinging, he dropped the garbage-can lid, and it clanged in the alley as Weird Garth and Jorell Jordan went running by.

Mountain tried to run past Benjamin, too, but Benjamin had staggered into the little man's path after being struck by Garth. Benjamin swung his knife in a hard upward arc, like an uppercut to the solar plexus, and he felt the soft cushion of belly being punctured and heard the whoosh of air as the blade went in deep. Almost in one motion he pulled the knife away and let the stabbed man sink to his knees, kneecaps smacking the bricks.

Benjamin ignored the fallen man and went to find Andy Bonner, whose gurgling groans were coming from behind the corrugated fence.

Mountain started to crawl, pulling himself along like a snake, using one hand to get fingerholds in the brick pavement while his other hand tried to stop his life from draining away. But blood ran through his fingers and he had to crawl through it, making the going slippery. Much as he hurt, he didn't dare cry out, for fear that whoever had stabbed him would notice that he was still alive. He thought that it was unfair that he should have been stabbed when Jorell, not he, had stabbed the old man. All he had done was deliver a few kicks and punches, nothing that would kill.

Mountain thought that he didn't deserve to die. And because he could still move, he took heart. If he could get to a hospital, he figured, he might be saved. Miraculously, after he had crawled about twenty feet, he was able to summon an almost supernatural reserve of energy, and he pulled himself to his feet. On wobbly, rubbery legs hinged by fractured kneecaps, air wheezing loudly through the hole in his lung, he staggered toward the light of hope at the end of the alley.

Benjamin was aware that the man he had stabbed was escaping. But he didn't do anything about it because his primary concern was Andy Bonner. He found the old man lying flat on his back behind the corner of the corrugated fence that partitioned off the delivery docks of a high-rise office building. Andy was clearly not going to make it. He had been stabbed too many times. Benjamin knelt as close as he could to the body without getting blood on his clothes. The hopelessness of the wounds was apparent even in the dim light cast by the high back windows of the office building. Even the throat had been partially slit—an act Jorell had aborted before running away.

When he realized it was Benjamin kneeling over him, Andy tried as hard as he could to communicate and managed a few weakly whispered words. "I didn't . . . tell them . . . about . . . you . . . sorry . . . I took money . . . we're still pals . . ."

Andy stopped breathing.

There was nothing more that Benjamin could do for him, except shed the tears that he was already starting to shed.

But there was something that Andy could still do for Benjamin.

Using his switchblade knife, Benjamin slit the old man's right wrist. He cupped his mouth over the wound and drank, satisfying himself, feeling renewed strength and vitality replenishing his body and spirit. He thought of it as an act of reverence, and of love. The last rite of exchange between friends.

Walking out of the alley, he knew where his next supply of blood should appropriately come from. He would not kill any innocent people. Instead, he would go after his friend's killers. In exacting his vengeance, he would be fulfilled. He would be the angel of justice.

Inspired by his new vision of himself, he followed the trail of blood that Mountain had made in his crawling and staggering toward the end of the alley. Less than thirty yards from his goal, Mountain had sunk once more to his hands and knees and was still crawling, feebly and desperately trying to get away. Hoping somehow to live.

In a few quick strides, Benjamin caught up with the crawling man and bent over him, giving him a few moments to realize what was about to happen. Then he pushed the stiletto point of his blade in at the base of the skull and up through the cerebellum, bringing an end to all of Mountain's futile movements and futile dreams.

18

Drawing his .357 magnum, Trooper Vargo edged his body around the corner of the hallway. Seeing that all was clear, he motioned for Lieutenant Harpster to follow him. Flattening himself against the wall, he knocked on the second door to the left, the one with screwdriver marks around the jamb and light spilling out around the transom. His service revolver in his hand, Harpster covered Vargo from the end of the dimly lit hall, then moved in closer as Vargo reared back, ready to kick the door in.

With his powerful barbell-built muscles, Vargo kicked like a mule, splintering what was left of the jamb and banging plaster out of the wall as he barged into the room, aiming with both hands, itching to start shooting. Harpster followed him in, raking the area with the barrel of his pistol.

But nobody was in the room. It was cleaned out—empty dresser drawers half open, no clothes on the hooks, no covers on the bed.

Adrenaline still pumping, the two detectives holstered their weapons. They tried to swallow the disappointment of not coming up with an arrest. It was six in the morning. They had been hard at work all night on the case of the two men found stabbed to death in the alley behind the Liberty Tavern. They had examined the bodies, listened to the coroner's preliminary report, supervised the search for clues, the interrogation of the tavern owners and customers, the identification of the dead men by people who recognized them.

Harpster had phoned Vargo at home to get him in on the case as soon as he noticed the slit wrist on the old man and the absence of blood around the wound. While Vargo was driving into Pittsburgh swabs were taken from the wound site and a serology test was run by the night crew at the crime lab. The results they obtained through electrophoresis matched the slides taken by Ken Beransky from the wound sites of Elijah Alford and Stephanie Kamin.

The two detectives had discovered that Andy Bonner and a man named Benjamin Latham had roomed next door to each other at the YMCA. The description of Latham provided by Big Mike and Big Tom Danko, owners of the Liberty Tavern, made him out to be the right height and weight to have been the flasher associated with the sandbox murder.

"Latham is our man, all right," Vargo said. "Otherwise, why would he have run?"

"Looks like he didn't leave so much as a toothbrush," Harpster said, his gray eyes scanning the room once more. "Nothing to give us a saliva sample."

"What about this?" Vargo said. He had crouched down to look inside the tin wastebasket by the dresser. He saw a half-eaten apple and pulled it out by its stem. "This goes to the lab," he told Harpster, with a note of triumph. "I'll bet you a bottle of Jack Daniel's it's going to nail down our killer for us."

"It just may," said Harpster. "But I'm still looking forward to what we'll learn when we haul in Garth Weir and Jorell Jordan. Don't forget, Ron, according to the bartenders at the Liberty Tavern, Jordan and Weir and their buddy Hill had eyes to roll Andy Bonner, and they all left together—then Latham came along, acting like he was gonna try to catch up to the old man and protect him. So what happened to Jordan and Weir?"

"One thing we know for sure," said Vargo.

"What?"

"Weir and Jordan don't have poisonous saliva. They are a couple of snakes, but the ordinary human kind, not the kind that you can pin down by electrophoresis."

"Yeah. That's right. Since they both passed Ken Baransky's serology test, they appear to be in the clear so far as the murders of Elijah Alford and Stephanie Kamin are concerned. And even if they had a hand in killing Andy Bonner, they didn't suck the blood from his wrist."

"Therefore," Vargo said, "I'm betting that Latham is our man. And that this apple core will help prove it."

When she arrived at work that morning, Lenora was startled to see Benjamin waiting for her in front of the museum. A jolt of panic hit her when she noticed the suitcase next to him and the tense, distraught look on his face.

Her fear of losing him was so sudden and sharp that it made her tremble when she looked into his eyes, overwhelming her with a realization of how much he really meant to her. It was no use reminding herself that she had always been a proud and strong woman, in control of her emotions instead of being dominated by them. Now she was helpless, as if under a spell. She wasn't her own person anymore. Without him she could not thrive. He held an ineffable power over her. She was willing to sacrifice herself for him, in the name of love. She would do anything to keep him by her side. She was prepared to shamelessly beg him to stay with her or take her wherever he might go.

As she sat with him on the bench in front of the museum, his eyes locked onto hers like twin umbilical cords connecting two minds. He told her about the murder of his friend Andy Bonner and explained that the police were after him because they mistakenly thought he was the killer. She believed his story, although the details barely registered. It almost didn't matter to her whether he was guilty or innocent, she was so relieved that he wasn't going to leave her. He was asking for her help. He needed her. She had to shelter and protect him so that he could track down the persons who had actually murdered his friend.

Instead of going to bed when his wife did, after a TV sitcom that ended at ten o'clock, Vargo went down to the basement to do his exercises. He hated lying next to Norma wondering if he should make sexual advances, worrying about whether she wanted him to or whether she wished he would never touch her again.

Watching television, they had had little to say to each other. They had sat like zombies in front of the tube, letting the program's contrived dialogue and canned laughter take the place of husband-to-wife communication. He still loved Norma and believed that she loved him, but he did not know how to lead her out of the bitter, aching void they had both been living in ever since Kathy's death.

Getting into his warm-up suit and beginning the calisthenics that would loosen him up and make him perspire, Vargo thought that maybe he and Norma could have found a way to make a fresh start if only John Hampton had been properly punished. Instead, the child-rapist and child-killer had been allowed to escape. He was still on the loose. Free to stalk young, innocent victims. Free to rape and murder other people's children.

Even when Hampton was locked up in Laurel State Hospital, his spirit had hovered over Ron and Norma Vargo like the huge, dark shadow of an ogre. They were mocked and tormented by the knowledge that Hampton was enjoying three square meals a day while Kathy was moldering under the earth after suffering and dying to give the maniac his perverted pleasure. Knowing that Hampton was still alive, liable to escape or to be freed someday by a panel of well-meaning psychiatrists, created a creepy, angry tension that consistently undermined Ron's and Norma's efforts to reshape their lives into a semblance of normality. If Hampton had been put out of the way once and for all, they might have been able to decide to have another child, not to take Kathy's place but to claim a renewed portion of their love and attention. To help them reaffirm their faith in the future. They were not normally vindictive people. But they would not have felt that they had gotten justice so long as Hampton got anything less than death in the electric chair.

When he was finished with his workout he took a steaming hot shower, letting the water massage his body for a long time, making sure Norma had time to fall asleep. His muscles were pumped up and tired from his exercises; his sexual urges were temporarily muted. He thought about the case he was working on. Under electrophoresis, slivers of the apple core he had found in Benjamin Latham's YMCA room had shown traces of poisonous saliva. Latham was guilty. Although he was still at large, his chances of eluding capture were growing slimmer. By interviewing the bartenders from the Liberty Tavern, the manager of the downtown Manpower office, and clerks and tenants from the YMCA, Vargo and Harpster had come up with what should be a fairly accurate description of their suspect. A police artist had put together a composite drawing. An APB was already out through the law-enforcement network. Tomorrow morning all the newspapers would carry the composite on their front pages, with a modified account of the suspect's crimes, omitting the more shocking, bizarre aspects—which the police were withholding from the public.

"Weird Garth" Weir and Jorell Jordan had not been rounded up yet. But Vargo figured they couldn't run far. They were dumb small-time punks; the Pittsburgh cops had a handle on them, knew who they loafed with and where they hung out. Once they were arrested, they could be pressured for testimony to help nail Latham.

The case was drawing to a head. But Vargo didn't like the way the outcome was shaping up. As it stood now, with a big manhunt being launched, virtually any cop, besides himself, would stand a good chance of spotting Latham and making a lucky arrest. If that happened, the machinery of "justice" would come into play. The suspect would have a chance to plea-bargain. First-degree murder would be hard to prove. Latham could elude the death sentence, draw life imprisonment, and get out on parole after a few years. Or else, like John Hampton, he might plead not guilty by reason of insanity. He might even be able to show that some kind of drug had changed his body chemistry, making his saliva poisonous and deranging his mental faculties. He might be confined to a psychiatric hospital, only to escape, or to be pronounced cured.

Vargo hated to think that another maniac might be turned loose in the world after he had done his best to see the man caught and punished. Eliminated. He wished he could go after Latham one on one, with no witnesses and no quarter given.

When he reported to work the next morning at the State Police headquarters, Vargo was summoned into the office of his boss, Dave Fein, the lieutenant in charge of the Criminal Investigations Section. Although Fein had a desk job, he kept himself rigorously fit, fanatically fulfilling the image of the lean, hard cop. His gray-flecked crew cut was shaved bald around the ears, eliminating sideburns. His face was bony and tan. His lips, normally thin and mirthless, were clenched thinner and tighter than usual as he shoved a copy of the morning newspaper across the top of his gray steel desk at Vargo and demanded angrily, "Who leaked this? Who's the big blabbermouth?"

Vargo got just as mad as Fein when he read the stark, black headline—'VAMPIRE KILLER' SOUGHT BY POLICE—above a four-column reproduction of the composite drawing of Benjamin Latham.

"The story is loaded with all the gory details," Fein ranted. "The poisonous saliva and the blood sucking. We're going to have a public panic on our hands."

"Damn it!" Vargo cursed, clenching his fists in frustration. "I'd like to get my hands on the irresponsible bastard who did this to us. Are any names mentioned in the story?"

"Hell, no," said Fein. "Just an 'unimpeachable source.'

I sincerely hope it wasn't anybody from this headquarters." He shot Vargo a piercing, accusatory look.

"Surely you don't think it was me," Vargo said.

"Until I know for sure, everybody is suspect," Fein replied coldly. "And God help him if it turns out to be anyone under my command."

"I gave out only the information we agreed upon," Vargo defended. "If there was a leak, it could have come from the serology lab in Pittsburgh, or from the county morgue."

"Well, because of this I have to take part in a press conference headed up by the State Police commander and the Pittsburgh police commissioner. We're going to have to give the public most of the facts. If they think we're hiding anything important, they'll only be scared worse. This is a hell of a situation, Vargo. We've got to capture this guy immediately."

"Maybe the leak won't hurt us as badly as we think," said Vargo. "Maybe people won't take this so seriously. Perhaps they'll shrug it off."

"What makes you say that?" Fein asked, squinting hard at Vargo, suspecting him once more of being the one who had leaked the information.

"We've all gotten so used to lunatics on the loose," Vargo explained. "Maniacs raping and butchering people. Maybe this one with poisonous saliva isn't much more frightening than any of the others."

His cheeks grazed the insides of her thighs as he squeezed her firm, naked buttocks in the palms of his hands, arching her toward his tongue. His mouth covered the warm, wet folds of her, his breath hot and moist, and he kissed her deeply, kindling a thousand delightful barbs of arousal. He licked and sucked rapidly, and she reached lightning orgasm, screaming and thrashing powerfully against his hands and his lips. He kept swirling his tongue inside her as her bucking and moaning subsided into soft, shuddering sighs of ecstasy.

Lenora's mouth and vagina tingled from Benjamin's deep kisses. He made her feel like a wild and helpless beast, being led and taught by him, romping and frolicking in new dimensions of passion and insatiability. She wanted him to penetrate every orifice, bringing to all the virgin parts of her the same depth of lustful abandonment that she felt in the places where she had already been penetrated. She wanted to explore every erotic possibility. She yearned to do *everything;* everything that a man and woman had ever done for each other. She wanted to taste every part of him. She wanted every part of her to be caressed, probed, and anointed by every organ and every secretion he could use on her or in her. Nothing that she thought of doing with him seemed too wanton or too bizarre; and she thought about everything, every sort of variation. She was sure that in time they would perform and enjoy every act that she was capable of imagining.

After sex with him, her excitement did not die away to a low level of postcoital pleasantness; instead, her nerve endings kept glowing and tingling for the longest time, maintaining her orgasmic sensations at only a slightly reduced intensity. With other men, she had made love on marijuana and on LSD, and the hallucinogens had had the power of making the sex act and its climax seem to last forever. But Benjamin did it to her without drugs, and the effect was far stronger and more satisfying. The denouement was nearly as wonderful as the peak of her pleasure, so that making love with him didn't seem to have any definable ending.

She wanted to be with him forever. She wanted to protect and comfort and please him in every way. She was glad he had come to her in his time of trouble. Now she would have a chance to prove herself. She would show him how much he could depend on her loyalty. Even if the whole world should denounce and accuse him, she would always be his one true ally and lover.

Benjamin learned about himself by reading the newspapers. For the first time, he understood that his saliva was poisonous—it was what had killed the little girl in the sandbox. Then why wasn't it harming Lenora? Why wasn't she afraid of him? Why hadn't she turned him in to the police?

Instead, when she came home from work with the newspaper that had the headline 'VAMPIRE KILLER' SOUGHT BY POLICE, she had laid the picture of himself down in front of him and had said calmly, "It really doesn't look awfully much like you. And I can fix you up so there's almost no resemblance whatsoever." She had then cut and dyed his hair, plucked his eyebrows, and done other things to help him alter his appearance. "I don't think you should grow a mustache or a beard," she had said. "A subtle disguise is best. Overdoing it would only call attention to yourself. Besides, I don't want to entirely obscure your good looks."

He knew that she was in love with him. And, more than that, he held an eerie power over her that he did not entirely understand. But he knew it was a power stronger and stranger than love. He was awed and mystified by his ability to control the mind and spirit of another person. It was almost as unfathomable as the miracle of his rebirth.

According to the newspapers, modern scientific procedures called serology and electrophoresis had proved that he was not like other human beings. Maybe he wasn't human at all. Perhaps he was some new type of creature. One of the articles he read contained a curious hodgepodge of myth and "scientific" speculation. On the one hand, it rehashed superstitious folklore about vampires and ghouls; on the other hand, it postulated that nuclear radiation or chemical pollution might have spawned a mutant with nonhuman attributes.

Benjamin was stunned and upset over seeing himself discussed this way in print—as if he were some sort of monster. He felt normal. He felt as "human" as anybody else. He hated to think that he might be a threat to his own species.

He worried about what he might do to Lenora. And he tried to interpret the effect he was having on her.

She seemed to be becoming more like him. He felt a kinship with her, a merging of his spirit with hers, as if they were two persons evolving into one entity. In the beginning, it had had something to do with the force he exerted over her when he stared into her eyes, controlling her mind. But now something more was coming into play. He could feel the changes taking place in her, a transmutation as palpable and yet as invisible as an extrasensory perception. Did he have the power, like vampires of legend, to change her into an occult being—if that was what he was himself? Should he try not to do it to her? Or was it too late to reverse the process, if it had already begun?

It dawned on him that if his saliva wasn't harming her physically, then it must be affecting her in some other way. Perhaps the act of love itself was transforming her. His saliva and his sexual secretions were entering her, not through her veins but by other conduits. Without intending to, he was changing her from within, working himself into her, effecting a profound metamorphosis. She was becoming the same kind of creature as he. They were already sharing a deep unity and harmony of thought and being and desire. They were becoming soul mates, their destinies intertwined.

He felt a glow of warmth and pleasure, knowing that he could have another person to be so close to, sharing his struggles and his dreams. But at the same time he felt guilty and afraid. He knew what it was to be alienated from the rest of humankind, and now he was subjecting Lenora to the same condition, making her into an outcast.

But he had brought her gifts, hadn't he? The gifts of extraordinary sensuality . . . perhaps even the gift of eternal life. . . .

But if she eventually developed a craving for blood, it would be his fault.

19

Benjamin Latham was starting to believe that he could will people not to notice him. He wasn't sure that he had the ability, but he was almost sure. Tailing Jorell Jordan, he had become a bit careless and Jorell had turned and looked right at him in broad daylight. He had been crossing a busy city street, jaywalking, trying to catch up with his quarry, who had unexpectedly darted across after eyeing an attractive black woman going into a saloon. Benjamin's only thought had been *Please don't let him see me* as Jorell's head turned, looking back over his shoulder suspiciously. For the space of several heartbeats Benjamin froze, one foot up on the curb and the other still in the street. But, to his amazement, Jorell's piercing black eyes looked right through him as if he weren't even there. No jolt of recognition flashed over Jorell's face—just an odd tremor. Then he continued into the saloon.

Maybe somehow, against all odds, he had lucked out. Perhaps Jorell had not actually looked directly at him, or had simply failed to recognize him because of Lenora's disguise.

But Benjamin believed that the alterations made in his appearance were really too subtle to fool anyone who had seen him before. And the look that had passed over Jorell's face was *so* strange. It was the look of a man expecting to see something that wasn't there, or something he felt was there even if he couldn't see it.

During the several seconds that Jorell's eyes had been on him, Benjamin could feel himself being looked at. But it was as if he existed in a vacuum, where the rays of recognition could not penetrate. His presence had been merely suspected, when it ought to have been conclusively registered in the synapses of Jorell's brain. He seemed to have given his quarry not the physical impression of his form and substance but the *sense* that he was there, like a ghost crossing the street.

Half hidden behind a telephone pole down the street from the saloon, he watched the entrance, waiting for Jorell to come out. He didn't think he appeared too conspicuous; in this inner-city neighborhood there was a fairly even mix of blacks and whites loitering in front of stores or on street corners. Benjamin looked like one of the fancier dudes, in his black silk shirt and tight black trousers. His hair was dyed black and cropped short, parted on the left side, the way Lenora had fixed it for him. Even his shoes and belt were black. Once darkness came, which would be soon, he could make himself nearly invisible.

Jorell had been in the saloon for a long time. Benjamin considered going in himself and standing at the bar. Would Jorell recognize him up close? Would the bartender come and ask him what he wanted, if he willed himself not to be seen?

In his effort to appear nonchalant, he turned his gaze away from the saloon, intending to act interested in other things for a few moments, when he saw a black teenager heading toward him, bopping along with an unlit cigarette dangling from his lips. Anxious to test the newfound power he suspected he possessed, Benjamin thought to himself, very forcefully, *Don't let him be able to see me.* But the black teenager came right up to him and said, "Hey, my man, you got a match?"

Deflated, Benjamin fumbled in his pocket and said, "You can keep the pack."

"Right on, my man."

Watching the young fellow lighting up and bopping on down the sidewalk, Benjamin was disappointed and confused. Why hadn't it worked? Why hadn't his exertion of mental power been effective? He still felt that the incident when Jorell had looked right at him meant something. It had been a genuine phenomenon. He had done something special. But maybe he couldn't always control it, couldn't turn it off and on at will. Or whim. Maybe the power only manifested itself when something important was at stake—not just a light for a cigarette.

Jorell finally came out of the saloon and looked up and down the block, then started walking a bit drunkenly. Benjamin let him go for thirty or forty paces, then stepped out from behind the telephone pole and followed, very carefully, not sure of whether he could rely on any psychic or supernatural help in tracking his quarry.

The sun was going down, sinking below the skyline cluster of tall buildings. Tailing Jorell and laying a trap for him ought to be easier under the cover of darkness. Benjamin was becoming impatient. Since early afternoon he had been keeping close on the heels of his prey, but no opportunity for attack had presented itself. Jorell hadn't ventured into any secluded places.

Benjamin had thought that both Jorell and Garth would be lulled into a false feeling of security by the four weeks that had elapsed since their murder of Andy Bonner. During that time, he had kept track of their movements, getting accustomed to their routines, but had done nothing to rattle them. He was amazed that the police had let them go free. It was one more symptom of a sick modern society that didn't have the wisdom and courage to protect itself against vicious criminals.

He intended to kill Jorell and Garth one at a time and drink their blood. The craving seemed to come on him in full force at intervals of roughly four weeks, like the phases of the moon. In taking his revenge on those who had murdered his friend, he would receive two months of sustenance, without guilt. Without having to take the lives of innocent human beings.

One of the ways that Deronne Fletcher tried to keep Jorell with her was by exhausting him sexually. If she could do him enough times, maybe he wouldn't go out to find someone else. Maybe she could distract him till it got so late and he got so tired that he would fall asleep in her bed, temporarily forgetting the lure of the gambling joints and juke joints downtown.

Her nude and shapely buttocks pressed against his hip as he lay next to her in bed, flat on his back, hands behind his head, grooving on some scratchy soul sounds coming from her cheap five-and-dime record player. It dawned on her that she could have bought a new stereo with the money he had taken from her earlier. But she pushed the thought from her mind before it had a chance to make much of an impression. She wasn't greedy. Just give her some booze and dope and sex, and she was contented. For the moment, she wanted to hang on to Jorell because he gave her something else that she seldom got and liked the taste of: excitement. His contact with the Vampire Killer made her life less boring.

She turned over and snuggled close to him, letting her breasts nuzzle against his chest. He didn't say anything, just kept staring up at the ceiling. She got up on her hands and knees and bent over him, flicking her tongue at each of his nipples. Then she made a trail with her wet tongue down to his groin area. She licked the inside of his navel.

Jorell had already shot his load twice, earlier today, with one of his other girlfriends. If he came again, in Deronne's mouth, she'd be able to tell he wasn't giving her much jism. She'd wonder who had gotten it before her. But he decided not to worry about that. A jealous woman is more anxious to please. She'd probably come across with even more bread and wilder, crazier sex if she knew she was going up against some tough competition.

He thought of some exotic things he might be able to get her to do later in their relationship, and his dick started getting hard as she cupped his balls in her hand and teased him with her hot breath. He didn't murmur any sighs of encouragement. Let her learn to do it for him the way she ought to, without expecting anything in return.

He had to admit she was good at it. Her lips were fastened at the base of his fattening cock, and they were pulsing in little sucking motions, almost imperceptible except for the slight drawing and releasing of his tightening skin. So far, she had not touched his cock with her tongue. She knew how to make him long for the closing around of her mouth, the warm wetness of her saliva.

The thought of *poisonous* saliva made Jorell almost lose his rigid hard-on. He started picturing venom dripping into his peehole, killing him through his cock. He couldn't get the nightmarish image out of his mind.

He trembled.

Deronne thought she was pleasing him, even though he had gone a bit soft. She touched the tip of her tongue against the underside of his glans, and he lost his hard-on completely. She figured she had to go to work on him again in more subtle ways, so she started to kiss his scrotum.

He jumped and yelled, "No! Let me be!"

Deronne raised herself up on her elbows and stared at him. "What's the matter, honey?" There was no ridicule in her voice, only softness and sympathy.

But he didn't answer her. He just lay there, staring up at the ceiling, perspiring heavily.

Benjamin Latham stood hidden in the shadows in front of the apartment building where Deronne Fletcher lived. Hearing footsteps on the pavement behind him, he turned around and saw a policeman patrolling the sidewalk with a German shepherd dog on a leash. They were heading his way. He moved aside, giving them plenty of room to pass, crowding his body close to a black wrought-iron fence. *Don't let them see me,* he thought to himself, concentrating all his mental energy on his desire not to be seen, as if by hard concentration he could make himself dematerialize.

The dog growled, charging forward till its head was snapped back by the leash.

"Easy, Champ!" the cop yelled. "What's got you spooked?" He started shining his flashlight all around, but didn't seem to notice when the beam crossed Benjamin's rigidly frozen body.

Luckily for Benjamin, the dog was about twenty feet away and couldn't get at him, though it kept straining at the leash and growling ferociously.

"Champ! What's out there?" the cop said, grunting and struggling with his dog.

Benjamin couldn't believe that so far the cop hadn't seen him. But the dog was another matter. Was the animal using the sense of sight or smell? For the time being, it was a moot point. Not having any desire to feel Champ's fangs sinking into his throat, Benjamin sidestepped and sneaked around the corner, then started slinking across the shadowy lawn on the other side of the iron fence.

The cop let the dog pull him closer to the fence rungs. The dog poked its muzzle between the rungs and kept up a fierce barking and growling while the cop searched and probed with his flashlight. The bright yellow beam crisscrossed Benjamin's fleeing back a couple of times, casting long, man-shaped shadows blurred by wavering shadows of tree trunks, branches, and patterned wrought-iron fencework.

"Come on, Champ!" the cop commanded at last. "Let's go, boy! I don't see nothing out there for you to get so riled up about."

Benjamin kept moving as quickly and quietly as he could till he reached the other side of the lawn and hid behind some concrete pillars that framed a side entrance of the apartment building. His breath was coming in hard, panting gasps, and he hoped that the cop would not hear it. The dog was still growling and the flashlight beam was still sweeping the lawn, but its searching rays were blocked by the pillars.

Gradually the dog regained its composure, and the cop clicked his light off. "Easy, Champ, let's go now," the cop coaxed. And to himself he muttered, "Probably just a damned rabbit. Or two kids screwing behind the bushes."

After the cop and the dog were safely gone, way down the street and into the next block, Benjamin stayed in his hiding place for a while, evaluating the incident. The cop surely should have seen him but hadn't been able to, even when aided by the flashlight beam. But the dog hadn't been fooled at all. Did that mean that Champ's animal perceptions were keener than a human's?

Not necessarily. Benjamin thought of another logical explanation that felt right to him.

Reconstructing the sequence of events in his mind, he recalled that when he first spotted the cop and the dog, the dog was looking right at him—ears pricked and fur already starting to bristle—while the cop was looking in another direction. Immediately Benjamin had thought, *Don't let them see me.* It had worked with the cop, but not with the dog, because the dog already knew he was there. That must be the answer! The black teenager who had asked for a light had already seen Benjamin before Benjamin made an attempt to block his vision by the power of mental suggestion; so the power had not worked. But it had succeeded with Jorell, on the other hand, because Benjamin had transmitted his thought impulses before Jorell's head had turned completely around—Jorell's eyes and brain had gotten no chance to register Benjamin's presence before they were compelled not to do so.

If Benjamin's new insight into the phenomenon was correct—and he instinctively believed that it was—then he could be invisible, if he wished, to anyone who did not chance to see him first. Not only had Jorell and the cop not seen *him,* they hadn't even seen his shadow. Or had they? Perhaps the odd, disconcerted look that flashed across Jorell's face was caused by his refusal to believe that he could be seeing a shadow of something that wasn't there.

Vampires weren't supposed to cast any shadows. But Benjamin had discovered that in his case the reverse was apparently true. He could cast a shadow, even when his body was invisible to others. He had seen it. And he had seen his own reflection in mirrors. Did it prove he wasn't supernatural?

Not necessarily. No. It only proved that he could see his own shadow and reflection, not that others could, particularly if he willed them not to. This was a supernatural power. So was the mind control that he had exerted over Lenora Clayton, Andy Bonner, and others. His rebirth, taken by itself, was an outstanding supernatural phenomenon.

But he didn't *feel* supernatural, whatever that would feel like. He certainly didn't feel like a vampire. He didn't *want* to be one. As far as he was concerned, the only connection between himself and the creatures of occult legend was his craving for blood. He wasn't bothered by sunshine. He didn't have to sleep in a casket. He couldn't change himself into a bat. (Of course, he had never tried to do such a distasteful thing, but he just knew that he couldn't.)

He kept hoping that somehow the blood craving would simply go away. He had waited through the past four weeks, wishing they would lengthen into five . . . and six . . . and so on . . . without feeling the first stirrings of the craving, like the first tickle of an infection in his soul. But it had come, as inevitably as the rising of the moon. It was raging inside him again, as strongly and insistently as before.

He wondered if he would still be going after Garth and Jorell if his only motive was vengeance.

Jorell sprang out of bed and started pulling on his trousers. He was worried that he had shown Deronne a moment of weakness, and now he wanted to ditch her.

"Where you goin'?" she asked, in a small, hurt voice.

"None of your business."

"You oughtn't to be goin' out this late, Jorell. It's past midnight. He might be layin' for you."

"Who? Latham? If he was gonna come after me, he'd

have done it before now. If the dude has half a brain in his head, he prob'ly already lit out for some other part of the country."

Though he spoke bravely, Jorell remembered uneasily the sensation he had had all day of someone following him, looking over his shoulder. He almost was tempted to cozy up to Deronne and stay the night. But he didn't want to give in to his fears. Besides, her welfare money—which he had conned out of her earlier—was burning a hole in his pocket. He was itchy to play the big spender in one of his favorite saloons, or to get in a game of cards or dice.

"So long, Deronne. See you around."

"You comin' over tomorrow?"

"Don't know, babe. We'll see how it works out. I got to talk to Garth first. Him and me maybe got a little scheme goin' down."

"You be careful," Deronne said. "You hear?"

He chuckled manfully, making light of her worrying. He condescended to kiss each of her nipples and kiss her once on the mouth to keep her happy till next time, then checked himself in her dresser mirror and went out the door.

The Boogeyman Discotheque was six blocks from Deronne's apartment. As Jorell got nearer he could hear the loud beat and the rhythmic vocal harmonies.

He knew it wasn't wise to cut through the alley. He ought to stick to the light of the streetlamps.

But the shortcut was easier. And something, like a voice in his head, kept telling him to take it. His feet didn't want to listen. But his brain made him obey the voice. To the extent that he could still think for himself, he tried to believe he was following a good hunch.

He entered the alley, drawn not by the music at the end of it but by something else. Something he couldn't name. An icy chill came over him. He shivered. Goose bumps covered his flesh like hard little nubs, caressed by the smooth, cold fabric of his silk shirt. The hair on his head, braided into corn rows, seemed to tug at the skin of his scalp, tightening it, as if his fear were generating static electricity.

The alley was much darker than he had thought. No dogs barked. None of the decrepit ghetto houses had porch lights on. Here and there kitchen or bedroom windows glowed faintly, too grimy to let much light out. The backyards smelled like garbage and backed-up sewage.

Jorell's dread increased as he walked deeper into a web of black shadows. Something in his brain kept making him go where he had no wish to be.

He felt icy cold but his clothes were soaked with sweat, clinging to him as if he had just stepped out of a swamp.His mouth gaped open. His dry protruding tongue tried to wet his lips. The skin of his face was stretched so taut it seemed to be pulling his eye sockets out of shape.

He wanted to run.

But he couldn't.

The lump in his throat was so big and hard that he couldn't even scream.

When his weak, rubbery legs would take him no farther, he stopped. He was shaking all over. He couldn't move. He was rooted in his tracks, as if some kind of mental energy held him pinned like an insect in a case. He thought he heard footsteps, but he couldn't see anyone. At the same time he felt something encircling him like a malevolent, invisible force.

Strong hands that he couldn't see seized his throat. He struggled and thrashed feebly, feeling his fists bounce off invisible arms. His windpipe was being crushed like a paper straw. His head felt like a swelling balloon engorged with blood. He was losing consciousness. His legs had no strength left. His body was going slack. Whatever was choking him was holding him up like a rag doll.

Then the face of Benjamin Latham appeared behind the choking hands. Jorell's eyes bulged wider in recognition mixed with the pain and terror of death. His heart stopped beating from fright seconds before he would have expired from lack of oxygen.

The strong, choking hands dragged him by the neck into a darkened alcove between two garages. Then they laid his lifeless body down on the cold bricks that vibrated slightly from the loud rhythms of the nearby disco.

20

VAMPIRE KILLER STRIKES AGAIN!

The story was headlined by major newspapers all over the United States and was carried by all the national radio and television networks. *Life, Time,* and *Newsweek* ran feature stories and follow-ups. Magazines of popular science such as *Omni* and *Discover* printed articles about snakes, venom, phlebotomy, transfusion, serology, electrophoresis, the human circulatory system, and the physical and chemical properties of human blood. The tabloids hashed and rehashed every slant they could think of on witchcraft, voodooism, sorcery, and vampirism. Theories about the Vampire Killer ranged from the ridiculous to the obscene. Zoologists, herpetologists, theologians, occultists, psychologists, and criminologists all had a great deal to say. Radio talk-show hosts expanded their formats to give callers and "specialists" ample chance to run at the mouth over this hot topic about which everyone knew so little.

The public obviously enjoyed having something so exotic and esoteric to be scared about. A bloodsucking creature with poisonous saliva was, apparently, a refreshing departure from the run-of-the-mill garden variety of rapists and mass murderers who usually monopolized the eleven o'clock news.

A historian from Pennsylvania State University, Dr. Margaret Smathers, created a sensation when she announced that in 1782 a Tory named Benjamin Latham had been hanged as a vampire in Hanna's Town. Dr. Smathers immediately became a celebrity and earned thousands of dollars giving magazine interviews and paid lectures, padding what little she knew about Latham with a slide show about witchcraft in the colonies. And, of course, the little reconstructed historical site of Hanna's Town, Pennsylvania, was overrun by tourists—some of whom did a lot of damage with picks and shovels, trying to locate Latham's grave. Dozens of spurious old maps were sold to aid the grave-hunters, and quite a few metal detectors with buzzers that would sound off if they detected the iron shackles Latham was supposed to have been buried in. By digging at the spots where the buzzers went off, the grave-hunters found a large number of mundane items such as rusty ax blades, rusty pipes, rusty horseshoes, and rusty railroad spikes.

In California a cult sprung up with Benjamin Latham as its deity.

For a few demented persons, it was but a short step from believing in Latham as a true vampire to believing that they were vampires, too. Several states experienced a rash of murders in which the killers sucked their victims' blood, but these were easily isolated from the Latham case by the absence of poisonous saliva. In normal times crackpot occurrences of this kind would barely have made page three, but under the present circumstances they fired a great deal of initial hysteria, till electrophoresis proved that everybody and his brother weren't turning into vampires and Latham wasn't flying from Nevada to Michigan to Florida all in the same night. As Lieutenant Harpster told a reporter from the *Pittsburgh Press:* "We can't blame

Latham for every weirdo murder in the country. Hell, if he was drinking *that* much blood he'd be a candidate for Bloodaholics Anonymous."

Trooper Vargo had but two words for most reporters: No comment. But the newshounds kept after him, to the point where he had to get a new, unlisted home phone number and his calls at work had to be carefully screened. He felt under pressure to prove to his boss, Lieutenant Fein, that he didn't crave celebrity status. All he wanted to do was solve the case. He didn't want Fein to go on suspecting him of being the leak who had brought all the media heat in the first place. For his own part, he suspected Dr. Peter Coleman, the pathologist from the Allegheny County Morgue. Coleman apparently thought he was another Quincy. Ever since the story of the Vampire Killer made its first big splash, Coleman had hogged the limelight, touting the genius of his detection of a venomlike poison in the cadavers of Elijah Alford and Stephanie Kamin. He never bothered to give Ken Beransky any credit at all.

Vargo couldn't claim to be completely broken up over the murder of Jorell Jordan. Not only did it eliminate one very worthless and dangerous punk, but it also gave Vargo and Harpster a new angle to work with. They now gave more credence to the possibility that Andy Bonner had been murdered by Jordan, Hill, and Weir, and that Latham was going after those three one at a time, for revenge. The alternative possibility still was that Latham had something against all four. Three down and one to go. No matter how you looked at it, Garth Weir was Latham's next likely target. Weir thought so, too. He came crying to Harpster for police protection. Harpster told him, "Okay, we'll have a man watching you at all times. But he won't make himself obvious. He'll be there not only to guard your ass but to try and trap Latham if he takes a crack at you. You're going to be bait, Garth. One good thing about it, you'll have to stop mugging old ladies for a while, because you can be absolutely certain that we'll have our eyes on you."

As far as Vargo was concerned, it would be beautiful if

Latham could polish off Weir, then a hail of police bullets could polish off Latham. But it probably wouldn't work out that way. Latham would be brought in to be scrutinized by physicians, psychiatrists, anthropologists, and zoologists. The experts would pontificate about the social factors that had screwed up Latham's mind, the drugs that had altered his body chemistry. Already, on a radio program, Vargo had heard a theory blaming everything on Latham's parents, whoever they might be. A microbiologist claimed that exposure to certain kinds of chemicals or radiation could have mutated the parents' genes, producing an offspring with unusual chromosomes.

Once the experts thought they understood why something went wrong, their next step was always to try and fix it. They believed that everybody could be rehabilitated with enough love and understanding. *Everybody.* Even John Hampton.

If they thought that Latham's little problem was caused by drugs, they'd probably put him on a withdrawal program. Give him psychotherapy. Maybe a group of famous people would start advocating a parole for him, the way they did for Jack Abbott. Already the media circus was turning Latham into a bigger star than Charlie Manson or Son of Sam. Even from behind bars, he could make himself a pile of dough selling his life story as a book and a movie.

Naked, covered only by a pale blue sheet that draped itself to the curves of her body, Lenora Clayton waited for Benjamin to come to bed. The *CBS Movie of the Week* was just ending; the flickering light of the small-screen color television on the dressing table was the only illumination in Lenora's bedroom. The TV set had been a gift from her parents; they had brought it with them when they had come to visit her on her birthday, in June. She hadn't written to them since then, which was over two months ago. She barely thought of her mother and father anymore, or of her younger brother and sister. Benjamin filled her life so much these days that she didn't have time for anything else, except for her job at the museum and working on her thesis.

She didn't feel like a brash and liberated young woman anymore. She belonged to someone now. And he belonged to her. She had never thought that she could give herself over so completely to the needs of another person. In a way, it was like being brainwashed by a religious cult: much of her former sense of individuality was gone. But she didn't mind. She still took pride in her skills as a scholar and a historian; those qualities were in no way diminished. But emotionally and sexually she was changed. There was but one person who meant anything to her in those areas. And that person meant everything.

At first she had halfheartedly expected that she might put her life back in order somewhat after the initial surge of her new romance settled down to routine. But right now she didn't want the thrills of infatuation and exploration to diminish at all. In fact, in her present euphoric state she doubted that the wild, fantastic glow would ever wear off.

Merely looking at Benjamin's body as he stepped out of his trousers and briefs gave her a shiver of anticipation. She loved every curve and ridge of his flesh and all the delicious sensations he could bring to her. She smiled, thinking of his uniqueness: the way that his chemistry so thoroughly merged with hers. The more time they spent together, the more they seemed to meld into one another, physically and emotionally. His lack of a navel fascinated her, confirming her belief in him as a special being, not like other men, but stronger and wiser and better in bed. His lambent blue eyes penetrated her soul, anticipating her thoughts and desires. The orgasms that he gave her could almost be called miracles.

She loved to kiss him at the spot where his navel ought to have been. When she did so, and kept her lips and tongue pressed there for a few seconds, first she felt a warmth, then a warm vibrating glow . . . a buildup of energy passing from him to her . . . as if part of his aura were being transmitted to her, with a thermoelectrical force.

She felt that he was remaking her, enhancing her, molding her into someone brand-new. She had a clinging faith in his subconscious vision of what she ought to become.

Lenora knew that Benjamin must have murdered Jorell Jordan, but it was something that almost didn't concern her except for the increased danger it might put Benjamin in. She did not feel approbation or fear of him. Comfortable in the certainty of his love for her, she had an overriding sense that whatever he was doing must be right. Must be necessary. For both of them.

She could but vaguely remember how she must have once imagined she'd react if someone close to her—a parent, a brother, a sister, or a lover—turned out to be a murderer. Even a murderer in a just cause.

Now she only wanted her lover to remain free.

But what about others? The authorities? The police?

They were calling Benjamin a vampire. An evil, poisonous being.

If they could, they'd take Benjamin away from her. Lock him in a cage. Electrocute him.

She was his accomplice. They were two against the world. Nobody else could comprehend the depth of their attachment, their commitment, to one another.

She would do anything for him.

If she had to, she'd kill to protect him.

Logic told her that if he had killed Jorell Jordan, he must have drunk Jorell's blood. Curiously, the idea of it did not repulse her. Whatever Benjamin did, she could forgive. Such was the nature of her love.

In the flickering glow of the television, Benjamin peeled the bedsheet slowly away from Lenora's voluptuously nude body, and she folded herself into his arms. Already hard, he entered her with a swift, sure thrust that made her gasp and shudder . . . pleased and surprised to be receiving him so quickly. Just as he knew when to make her wait, this time he understood that she was more than ready and that she would find the not-waiting more erotic. She arched upward to meet him, kissing him deeply, entwining him with her long legs, touching her fingertips in the small hollow at the base of his spine, feeling the subtle rippling of the tiny muscles there as he made his thrusts.

She was vaguely aware that on the television a Dr. Harrison Lubbock was being interviewed—a bald, nervous little man with a pointy gray goatee, talking about his personal experiences in hunting vampires. "I have evidence," the doctor was saying, "that these bloodsucking creatures take the lives of at least ten thousand men, women, and children every year. Because of a genetic mutation they require one pint of blood each month for nourishment; if they don't get it, they waste away and die, just as you or I would if we had a disease of malnutrition, such as scurvy or rickets. They are freaks of nature. Some of them hold important jobs in government, here and abroad. Since they often live three hundred, five hundred years or more, they are able to amass great wealth and influence over the centuries . . ."

When Lenora was about to orgasm, Benjamin pulled out of her. She moaned in disappointment, bucking her hips as if he were still inside. Her nipples were juttingly erect, her lips parted, her arms thrown back over her mane of glossy black hair as she clutched the wooden rungs of the bed. She would have grabbed for his penis to put it back where she wanted it, but instead he crouched over her, replacing his penis with his tongue, using it like a hot, flicking spear.

On the television, Dr. Harrison Lubbock's voice was excited, intense, pitched an octave higher than it had been at the start of the interview. "Vampires obtain blood by finding people who have a fixation on the vampire legend and willingly give, at periodic intervals, pints of their own blood. But of course this requires not just one but many donors. So it is easy to see why some vampires must resort to murder when they run out of willing victims."

Lenora moaned and murmured, Benjamin's tongue and lips irresistibly drawing her toward her first climax. Exactly at her peak moment, he reinserted his penis in a long, smooth, powerful stroke. She exploded in such wildness and joy that it was close to pain, and he allowed himself to come, too, like a roaring, prancing beast, driving his energy into her, but taking from her as much as he gave.

In their postcoital haze, they could hear Dr. Lubbock's tinny voice droning on. "Vampires don't have fangs, and they don't invariably bite the necks of their victims. Instead, they often bludgeon their victims' skulls and take their wallets or purses, to make it look as if they were merely beaten and robbed, whereas the taking of blood was the primary motive. All vampires require fresh blood, not that which has been stored in blood banks in the form of plasma . . ."

Lenora kissed Benjamin's nipples, swirling her tongue in light, teasing circles, then made a trail of kisses to his belly. She nuzzled her smooth cheek against his taut skin, where the hard ridges of his abdominal muscles were relaxed but still firm. Then she opened her mouth and cupped her soft lips over the aura of his navel, the spot that seemed to emit a palpable glow. Involuntarily she moved her cheeks in and out, feeding upon Benjamin's energy, the psychic energy that came from blood. The idea of tasting blood crossed her mind. Instead of turning her off, it intrigued her. It teased and aroused her as much as the thought of oral sex. She wondered how it would feel, her lips pressed against a red, oozing slit, licking and swallowing, taking sustenance in the same manner as her lover. She sank into a dreamy, half-somnolent state tinged with the awareness that she was becoming more and more like him, and that she didn't want to stop the process but to hasten it. Her lips sucked greedily at the center of his being, as if she were connected to him by an invisible umbilical cord.

21

Weird Garth Weir was living with a woman named Angela Stone in an apartment built over a two-car garage. Benjamin Latham had been watching the place long enough to know that Angela Stone had a daughter about eight years old, named Carla. Weird Garth did not treat Carla as if she were his own child, but that might have been just his way of refusing to admit paternity. Benjamin was familiar with, and contemptuous of, the modern so-called sex revolution that permitted men to scatter their sperm anywhere and everywhere without any sense of responsibility; in his own time he had scoffed at the stuffy bluenosed Puritans of the New England colonies, but what was going on nowadays made him grudgingly admit that maybe Cotton Mather's disciples had had a point. Be that as it may, his own qualms were such that he preferred to believe that Garth wasn't Carla's father. He didn't like to think he was going to do in a parent, even though it was easy to rationalize that the little girl would be better off without having such a hoodlum for a role model.

Tailing Garth from time to time over the past eight weeks, Benjamin had observed him making narcotics connections right out in the open, on street corners or in darkened doorways. Benjamin had quickly discovered that he wasn't the only one keeping an eye on the big, black-bearded man with the scarred cheek. There was always a man lurking outside the apartment ready to follow on foot, and another man who sat a discreet distance away in a parked car, so that he could follow if Garth went anywhere in Angela's beat-up green Pinto. These watchful men must be policemen in plainclothes, assigned to protect the hoodlum, and to capture or kill Benjamin himself if they could.

Benjamin was not amused. Not only had Garth been freed after taking part in the murder of Andy Bonner, but now the taxpayers were footing the bill to keep him safe in the streets! The dregs of this "democracy" were treated better than its honest citizens. Even when Garth made his drug scores the cops let him be; they didn't even move in and bust the pushers. Benjamin had observed this phenomenon firsthand, on two separate occasions. Obviously Garth had a deal with the police not to interfere with him or any of his underworld cronies, in return for his cooperation on the so-called Vampire Killer case.

Knowing that the police were baiting him made the stalking of Weird Garth more stimulating for Benjamin. Mind control prevented him from being seen. Luckily, he had spotted the danger posed by the police stakeout the first time they had secreted themselves in the alley; intuitively he had made a wary approach, which had kept him from falling into their trap. Even now, whenever he moved in on Garth he had to be patient and careful. It was a cunning sort of game to spot new faces and new tricks of surveillance, eluding detection while setting Garth up for his final moment.

Tonight he had spotted a handsome, dark-haired man with a broad, flat nose, in a black Chevrolet sedan parked halfway up the alley from Angela Stone's apartment, and two men sitting on a bench in her neighbor's yard, who also looked fishy. He had zapped all three of them with a strong telepathic suggestion. Then he had walked softly past them without being seen and had taken up a position just around the corner of the two-car garage, on the side that housed Angela's Pinto. He was out of sight of the three cops, even if they had been able to see him.

Benjamin thought about the cop sitting in the black sedan. That particular man had often been part of the stakeout lately. He seemed to resist mind control more than the others; he might be more intelligent than they, or more determined. Each time, he seemed to resist more. Passing by him, Benjamin had seen his deep-set black eyes blinking in puzzlement, as if trying to pull in a hazy image. For a scary moment, he had felt himself almost being seen. But then his power had worked, and with great relief he knew he had gotten by safely and invisibly. Each time the power came through for him he got an odd chill from it—almost like seeing a horseshoe barely hook the stake and drop into a ringer instead of sailing on by into clanging, jarring failure. It bothered him that the power might have severe limitations. There might be people, like this cop, who could eventually become immune to it.

Vargo had put himself on the stakeout in place of another cop because he had a hunch that tonight something was going to happen. He had had the feeling before, and nothing had come of it. Three other times he had sat up half the night in his car, parked in the alley, and he might as well have been on his own back porch watching the moon. Except that all three times he had been exceptionally jumpy. As if the man he wanted were an arm's length away, like a chameleon turned green and hiding on a leaf ready to be plucked if it could only be seen.

It wasn't dark yet. Not quite seven-thirty. A warm September evening. Vargo had a clear view of the alley, the garage, and the stairs leading up to the apartment porch. If anyone suspicious entered the alley from his direction, he'd slouch in his car and try not to be noticed.

If he felt he'd been made, he'd nonchalantly start up the engine and pull out, then come right back after he circled the block. A few minutes ago he had had the distinct feeling that someone was scoping him out—either that, or something was going on that he ought to have been wise to. But he'd be damned if it was anything he could put his finger on.

Vargo snapped out of his reverie when he heard a noise and saw the door of Angela Stone's apartment swing open. The little girl, Carla, came out onto the porch. Eight years old. Only a year older than Kathy was when she died. Vargo pushed the thought out of his mind. Carla was wearing a green-and-white print dress, white shoes and socks. She held the screen door open and tugged on a red leash, pulling a little white Pekingese out onto the porch. Then Garth and Angela came out. Angela was too chunky or else she'd have been nicely built, because her proportions were good. She was as dressed up as Carla, in a dark purple skirt and a light purple blouse with some kind of shiny necklace; her hair, artificially lighter than Carla's, was done up in a shoulder-length permanent. An attractive woman, no older than thirty, with a cute little daughter. Where the hell were her brains, shacking up with a scumbag? Vargo didn't understand it and almost hated her for it. Were some women so masochistic that they couldn't be thrilled by guys who didn't fuck their lives up?

Weird Garth Weir was in jeans and T-shirt, hanging back by the door, not looking as if he were going wherever Angela and Carla were headed. Vargo watched as Angela and Garth had a few apparently friendly words that he couldn't hear, while Carla stayed at one end of the porch, petting the Pekingese. Then the mother and daughter came down off the porch, Carla picking the dog up and holding it till they got to the foot of the wooden stairs. She put the dog down outside the wire gate, and her mother swung the gate shut, and they walked out of the alley instead of getting the Pinto out of the garage, as Vargo had figured they might do.

Perfect. Garth was alone. Maybe Latham would make his move before the night was over. Andy Bonner had died thirty-three days after Elijah Alford and Stephanie Kamin. Twenty-eight days after that, Jorell Jordan was killed. Now the interval was twenty-six days. It could very well be time for the Vampire Killer to strike again. The phases of the moon might have something to do with it.

For a half hour more, nothing happened. Nothing happened except that the sun went down and it got dark, just a tiny sliver of moon in the sky. Then the porch light came on. The apartment door opened and Garth stepped out. Whereas before he had looked rather seedy, as if he were intending to spend an evening at home alone, now he looked ready for a night on the town. His shoulder-length black hair wasn't as greasy, and his beard and mustache were neatly trimmed. He was wearing designer jeans and a bright red form-fitting T-shirt.

Garth locked the apartment door and bounced down the steps jingling his keys, smirking once in Vargo's direction and once in the direction of the cops on the bench in the next-door yard, showing off that he knew exactly where his cover was. Also making it easier for Latham to spot the stakeout, if Latham happened to be around.

Angrily, Vargo told himself that Weird Garth *deserved* to be bumped off. The asshole was asking for it. He was too stupid or smug to use his own protection wisely. By not cooperating, not playing it smart, he was making it harder to trap Latham. But what could you expect from a junkie?

Garth opened the garage and backed the green Pinto out into the alley, leaving the door on the driver's side wide open while he got out to close and lock the garage door. Vargo started his engine and got ready to follow the Pinto at a careful distance. It should be a cinch. After all, Garth knew he was there and wasn't going to try and lose him. All he had to do was go wherever Garth went and be on the lookout for Latham to zero in—if Garth went to one of his regular hangouts, where Latham might be expecting to find him. Garth had been instructed to stick as much as possible to his normal routine so Latham wouldn't be put on guard and would think it was safe to attack.

The green Pinto and the black Chevrolet moved toward the end of the alley. Garth made a right turn. So did Vargo. But then the Pinto was nowhere in sight. Garth must've gunned it to the next intersection. *Damn!* Vargo took a chance and turned left, toward downtown Pittsburgh. After five minutes of fast nighttime driving he knew it was the wrong choice. He didn't catch up to Garth. The green Pinto was long gone, destination unknown.

Vargo fumed. He cursed himself for being such a sucker. He should have known not to trust Garth as far as he could throw him. But why should he have expected to be dumped by the man he was supposed to be protecting? He had no idea what Weird Garth was up to. Probably something illegal. Something he didn't want any cops watching. The only thing Vargo could figure to do was return to the stakeout in the alley and wait to see if the bait came back to the trap.

He still had a hunch that something big was going to happen. Only now he was worried that it would be happening far out of his reach, where he would have no control over the outcome. He could have radioed for help, hoping some other cop might spot the Pinto in some other part of the city—but he didn't want any flashing lights calling attention to the fact that Garth was under surveillance. Garth knew it, too. He knew that Vargo and Harpster would live up to their end of the bargain. They wouldn't put the narco squad onto Garth or any of his drug connections, even after the Vampire Killer was in the bag, or else they wouldn't be able to count on Garth as a state's witness. That kind of deal turned Vargo's stomach, but it was a necessary part of police work, though not something he'd ever get used to. It encouraged the feeling that justice *would* be best served if Latham could knock off Garth before the cops knocked off Latham. Wishful thinking.

Wherever Garth was, Vargo had to hope that nothing bad would happen to him, not just yet.

* * *

Weird Garth got a chuckle out of ditching that smart-ass hunk of fuzz, Trooper Vargo. But it was an uneasy chuckle. Garth was scared to be out without any protection, even though he couldn't logically see how Latham could stick on him if the cops couldn't. No way anybody could know where he was headed.

Jorell and Garth had scouted a job they sized up as a pushover five, six weeks ago and were ready to make it go down when Jorell got snuffed. Now Garth was going to do it on his own. As he drove to the scene of the hit he psyched himself into believing that one person could handle it as well as two. And the haul wouldn't need to be split.

He kept having the feeling that someone was watching him. But nothing suspicious ever showed up in the rear-view mirror. Still, to be on the safe side he made a couple of crazy moves that ought to shake any tail. Then he made an abrupt right turn onto a parkway ramp and raced the Pinto till there was nobody behind him as far as he could see. He left the parkway a couple of exits later and headed for the shopping center that he and Jorell had cased. One of the stores there was a tobacco shop that did a surprisingly brisk Pennsylvania Lottery business, handling as much as five to six thousand dollars in bets every single day. The shop was run by an old lady and her grandson, barely out of his teens. They didn't seem like people who could put up much of a fight. And the suburb where they had their store wasn't a high-crime district where everybody was always nervous about getting knocked over.

So far, Garth was right on schedule. He ought to get to the shopping center just before ten. Closing time. The day's receipts would be counted and bagged, just for him.

Keeping one hand on the wheel, he reached under the front seat and pulled out a garbage bag with a revolver and silencer in a smaller paper bag wrapped up inside. Angela had put it there a few days ago when she used the car to make a dentist appointment. Garth had told her to just do what he said, without looking inside the green plastic garbage bag, because what she didn't know couldn't hurt her. He hadn't wanted the cops on the stakeout seeing him stashing anything in the car; he knew they'd be less suspicious of his girlfriend.

Also under the front seat was a sturdy toy shovel that Garth had told little Carla to leave in the car. He reached down and touched the wooden handle to make sure it was there. He was going to use it to bury most of the loot in a prearranged spot. That way, he wouldn't have to go back to the apartment with a ton of stolen cash on him.

Garth congratulated himself on how well he had everything doped out. It bolstered his confidence. But for some reason he felt shaky.

When he pulled into the shopping center, he didn't park right in front of the tobacco shop but in a slot across the way, like an ordinary customer. He shut the engine off but left the key in the ignition. Not too many people were around, not too many cars in the lot. That's why it was smart to wait almost till closing time to make the hit. The wry thought crossed his mind that wouldn't it be a laugh if some wise guy stole his car before he got back to it with the loot. But he wanted the key in the ignition so he wouldn't have to fumble with it, in case he had to peel out fast.

Good. The old lady, Mrs. Hanchulak, was alone behind the counter of the tobacco shop, still open for business, anxious to rake in the last dime before closing. When Garth walked in, she was putting some new cartons of Kools into a display case on the back wall. No doubt the cash register was already stripped of the big cash, leaving just the small change with which she intended to start a new day. Where was the grandson? Gone home early? Or doing something in the back, behind the curtain? It didn't much matter. Garth didn't consider the young man—what was his name, Dennis?—much of a threat.

He nonchalantly opened the paper bag he was carrying and stuck his hand in, as if reaching into a bag of peaches. His hand closed around the butt of the revolver, the silencer already screwed on. At the same time, he strode up close to the glass counter full of all kinds of pipes and stuff. "I have a gun in this bag," he told the old lady in a low but forceful tone. "Don't make me prove it to you. I want all your money—the big cash you take to the night-deposit vault at the bank every night. Where is it—in back with your grandson?"

Mrs. Hanchulak's puffy, gray-haired face started to tremble while Garth was talking to her. But she didn't budge. She acted too scared to get her feet moving.

"Let's go," Garth barked. "Back through the curtain. I won't hurt you or anyone else back there, provided you do exactly as I say." It was a lie. Garth intended to shoot the old lady and the grandson too, if Dennis was there. They could identify him too easily. They had seen his face quite a few times before today—when he and Jorell were casing the joint.

"Dennis," the old lady mumbled, her voice a fearful croak. "Dennis . . . do as he says. He has a gun on me."

Garth moved closer to the curtained doorway that led to the back room. "You better listen to her, Dennis," he warned. "We're coming back there. If you don't hand me the money in a peaceable fashion, I'll shoot your grandmother." He pointed his weapon at the old woman, keeping it inside the paper bag. "Move!" he commanded. "You first. I'll be right behind you."

Shakily, she came out from behind the counter and parted the curtain, holding it open for Garth, showing her willingness to cooperate, hoping it would pacify him. He hit the light switch, dimming the fluorescent lights, leaving softer illumination over the counter, the way the store looked when it was closed. He'd have to take his chances on someone trying the unlocked front door. The old lady was still holding the curtain for him, and he followed her through, his eyes scanning the back room for the exact whereabouts of her grandson. All he saw were stacks of cardboard boxes and a makeshift wooden counter with two bulging canvas moneybags on top.

At that moment, when Garth was distracted by greed, Dennis jumped at him from a darkened alcove to the right of the curtain and stuck a knife in his back—up high, at the top of the trapezius muscle. It hurt like hell. Garth fired, shooting Dennis twice in the chest from a few feet away. Then he shot the old lady. Both of them hit the floor almost at the same time, bleeding like crazy, obviously dead or dying. They barely made a whimper.

A goddamn *penknife,* for God's sake! Garth winced, pulling it out of his upper back, briefly amazed that such a tiny blade could cause such intense pain. There didn't seem to be much bleeding, though. Maybe his tight red T-shirt was acting as a compress. It felt like a warm poultice over an aching wound.

Ignoring his pain, he stepped over and around the bodies on the tile floor, very gingerly, so as not to step in any puddles of blood. He grabbed the two canvas money-bags off the wooden counter. Then he came back to the curtain and peeked out. The coast was clear. The silencer had been wonderfully efficient—the gun hadn't made much more noise than a loud cough. But the paper bag was blown to smithereens; he dropped the remaining tatters to the floor, shaking them away from the barrel. Then he crept cautiously to the front door of the shop, in semidarkness. Nobody was on the sidewalk in the immediate vicinity. He juggled the moneybags in the crook of his left arm, stuffing the gun inside one of them, exciting himself by the feel of the currency that brushed his fingers. Forcing himself to take it slow, he walked as casually as he could out to the green Pinto, carrying the moneybags so they would look as innocuous as bags of groceries if they were seen in silhouette. He tossed them into the back seat of the car. Then he got in and drove off.

He still had the feeling that someone was watching him. The creepy sensation persisted even after he was safely driving down the lonely back road, close to where he intended to stash the loot. He figured he was just jumpy, too full of adrenaline. The Pinto was just about the only car on the road.

He made sure there were no headlights behind him when it came time to leave the two-lane blacktop. The turnoff was a narrow inlet, a dirt road so obscured by weeds that it was easy to miss, especially at night, even if you knew it was there. It was little more than a rutted, weed-grown path barely wide enough for a car, winding and twisting through a patch of woods, headlights playing weirdly off the dense foliage.

Garth had to drive slowly so he wouldn't pass up the spot he had in mind. He ignored the pain in his shoulder.

When his headlights searched out a big white boulder to one side of the car path, he stopped the car. He shut off the engine and killed the lights. With his fingertips he lightly probed the penknife wound. It hurt, but it didn't seem to be bleeding much. Luckily, he was wearing a red shirt. The cops probably wouldn't notice anything when he got back to Angela's apartment. Unless they decided to harass him with a frisk.

He pulled a flashlight out of the glove compartment and clicked it on. He picked up the toy shovel, and the green plastic garbage bag, which he stuffed into his pocket. Then he got out of the car, taking the moneybags from the back seat. Using the big white boulder as a guide, he started walking back through the undergrowth, letting the flashlight beam play in front of him. He took his time, watching his step. He didn't want to make a wrong move in the darkness and fall into the crumbling foundation of the burnt-down old house that he knew was back from the boulder about thirty yards. Neither did he wish to trip over any of the rusty junk that was strewn all around, slowly being obliterated by weeds.

He stopped a few feet short of the foundation of the old house and shone his light on the pit full of burnt-up junk and blackened timbers. The chimney was a mess of tumbled-down bricks. That was where he intended to bury the money. Nobody would expect anything valuable to be there after all this time. Everything worthwhile, if there ever had been anything, had long ago been scavenged.

Garth thought he heard something behind him. He whirled around and searched with his flashlight. Nothing. Just the usual night sounds. Crickets and possums and whatever. He told himself not to be jumpy.

Setting down all the stuff he was carrying, he yielded to the temptation of looking inside the moneybags. He didn't have time to count the haul, but the bundles of bank notes were so thick and numerous under the glare of the flashlight that his blood raced as he thought of the thousands of dollars at his fingertips.

He put the whole works, gun and silencer and all, into the green plastic garbage bag, which would protect against dampness. Then he moved aside some of the crumbled chimney bricks to make a space where he could dig in the ground with the toy shovel.

When he reached for the shovel, he couldn't pick it up. He tugged at it, thinking maybe it had been snagged by a root or a vine. It didn't budge. He shone his flashlight on it but saw nothing holding it down. "What the fuck?" he said and snatched at it, grabbing it by the blade, and when it didn't move it tore open two of his fingers. "Ow!" he cried out in shock and disbelief. He dropped his flashlight and scrambled for it in the weeds, seized by a powerful, irrational fear of being suddenly alone in the darkness.

When his fingers found the flashlight, he couldn't pick it up.

Then he heard someone laughing. A mocking laugh.

Weird Garth looked up and saw Benjamin Latham standing over him, laughing, and it was the last thing he ever saw with his bulging, fear-maddened eyes before a brick came down and bashed in his skull.

22

Benjamin and Lenora arrived in Philadelphia in the first week of October, at the climax of the Century IV Celebration. The city was celebrating its three-hundredth anniversary. For Benjamin, two hundred of those years were a gap in his life. He intended to try to fill in some of the gap by continuing to trace his family tree.

Lenora had finished her thesis and passed her oral exams to earn her doctorate. But she was finding it difficult to secure a faculty position anywhere. She could have stayed on at the Fort Pitt Museum. But that little job didn't pay much; it was only supposed to be a stopgap.

Benjamin told her not to worry. He had enough money that they could simply enjoy life for a while. Between what he had taken from Jorell's pockets and what had been in Garth's canvas moneybags, he had almost nine thousand dollars. Some he kept in cash and some in the form of traveler's checks; the rest was deposited in a bank account in Lenora's name.

They were registered at the Welcome Hotel, on Chestnut Street in Center City, as Mr. and Mrs. Benjamin Clayton. Their two-room suite—a bedroom and a dining and lounging area—was small but comfortable, with inexpensive but substantial furniture, high ceilings, air conditioning, and color TV. He had no idea how long they'd be in Philadelphia. It all depended on the kind of leads he might turn up in his search for his "ancestors."

Lenora liked the city. It was the first time she'd been there. She found it more cosmopolitan than Pittsburgh, and more genteel than New York. It was the fourth-largest city in the nation, yet it managed to be brisk and modern without forgetting its heritage. There was a unique kind of excitement in being surrounded by every type of contemporary diversion while still being able to enjoy a stroll in a grassy urban park or a visit to venerable shrines such as Independence Hall, Christ Church, and the Betsy Ross House. It was an ideal place for a history major to be.

Benjamin was less sanguine about it. He couldn't repress a grimace when Lenora showed him the brochure that said *Welcome to Century IV, Philadelphia's 300th Birthday Party!* On the cover was a photo of an actor made up to look like a foppish Benjamin Franklin, throwing a three-corner hat in the air and doing a silly jig in front of some skyscrapers and parked cars. The copy inside was loaded with hyped-up phrases like "Cradle of Liberty" and "Birthplace of Democracy." Center City was called "the most historic square mile in America." Well, maybe *that* was the truth, pompous as it sounded. Within the area, coexisting with modern structures, were about a thousand buildings dating back to the eighteenth century, many of them still being lived in. It always gave Benjamin a sharp pang of nostalgia to be walking along in a twentieth-century milieu and all of a sudden find himself passing in front of a home or a tavern that he remembered quite well from his previous lifetime.

The house he had been born in, on Front Street a block from Penn's Landing, wasn't there anymore. The site had been obliterated to make room for the Ben Franklin Bridge, spanning the Delaware River into New Jersey. It was just as well, Benjamin thought. He didn't need any tangible reminders of his parents to make it that much more difficult for him not to succumb to fits of melancholy. He hadn't seen his father and mother since 1748. They had disowned him when he had married Clarissa.

He kept hoping futilely that his blood craving would simply go away. He understood that he was an evolving entity: he could feel changes in himself, changes that had taken place since his escape from the grave. He was stronger now. And he now had psychic powers. Perhaps one day he would cease needing blood, the way an infant is eventually weaned away from its mother's milk.

When he was in the Free Library of Philadelphia, hunting for evidence of his descendants, he often took time to study what medical science knew these days about blood. As if the formal knowledge could help him understand his craving. As if, understanding it, he might be able to control it. But it was like trying to have an orgasm by reading a sex manual. The most he ever got from the printed word was a tiny inkling of hope. For instance, according to one medical text, modern scientists had developed and were now testing a form of artificial blood. If successful, it could be a godsend to blood banks, people with unusual blood types, and members of religious groups that prohibited transfusions. It was called Fluosol, and was the first artificial blood to have the ability to transport oxygen to body tissues. But it wasn't widely available yet. Not on the market. Not approved by the FDA. And anyway, Benjamin intuitively felt that such a synthetic product could never answer his special need. There was something too organic, too *spiritual,* about the craving he had.

Sometimes he became so angry about his affliction that he cursed the injustice of it. What had he ever done to deserve this? Searching his conscience, he thought his sins were pretty minor. He had entertained a certain uncharitability toward others; had secretly thought himself superior. In his old age he had become rather bitter and cantankerous. But that was after his son had left him and his wife had been taken from him by the cholera. Under the circumstances, his deistic beliefs had been of little comfort. He believed in God, but it was not a God who would answer prayers: a creator, not a meddler. Not the sort of deity one could cling to in the absence of human companionship. Still, even if Benjamin's beliefs made him lonely, he could not abandon them, for he thought they were intellectually sound. He had a contempt for the primitive religiosity of the masses. What a cruel irony if their superstitious hanky-panky had made him into a vampire!

He had a habit of counting the days, like a maiden waiting for her period each month, hoping it would come around and she would not be pregnant. Maybe the blood craving would stay away this time. This time and forever. Fifteen . . . sixteen . . . seventeen days since Garth. In eleven more days or thereabouts, unless a magical reprieve happened, he'd need blood again. He'd have to find some way to get it.

In the meantime, he immersed himself in the task of looking for his descendants. Since he had left Philadelphia in 1748, there was an almost poetical symmetry to the circumstance that John Latham had gone back there exactly a century later. By that time, according to what Benjamin had found out in Williamsburg, all the other Lathams, except John and his wife, were either dead or on their way, unknowingly, to a genealogical dead end.

The first break in the research was the discovery that John Latham had done well for himself after leaving Williamsburg—so well, in fact, that the library contained not only some scattered biographical smatterings pertaining to Benjamin's grandnephew but also a rather pompous autobiography, one hundred and ten crisp vellum pages privately printed and lavishly bound in blue leather, circulated in a limited edition to officers and principal shareholders of Latham Enterprises, Inc., of which John Latham was chairman of the board. His name and the title *Railroad Pioneer* were embossed in gold on the cover of his ego book. According to frontispiece information, it was published in 1888, to coincide with his seventieth birthday, and was handed out to his worshipful underlings at a testimonial dinner. Much as Benjamin deplored this blatant evidence of his ancestor/descendant's self-indulgence, he was exuberantly grateful for its numerous leads concerning all of John Latham's offspring, human and corporate—leads which could be followed up by going into such sources as census records, church logs, voter registrations, deeds, corporation histories, school enrollments, marriage and birth certificates, newspaper and magazine articles, obituary notices, and so forth.

Even with Lenora helping him, Benjamin found the follow-up work to be boring and frustrating more often than it was rewarding. But they were both driven to piece the story together, like hard-nosed detectives unearthing picayune clues. There was an undercurrent of excitement about what they were doing that carried them along, even during the most difficult times, and made them keep on devoting long, tenacious hours to the project.

Through all the grueling legwork and the poring over musty ledgers, Benjamin had the feeling that he was on the right track. He couldn't explain why, but he just had the *sense* that something vital was going to come of all this.

John Latham, who had married Mary Peterson in Williamsburg in 1848 and moved to Philadelphia to become partners with her cousin in a railroad venture, succeeded financially and in sowing the seeds that would carry the Latham genes into the twentieth century. He and Mary had had three sons, and all the children had reproduced. Benjamin traced many of them as they married and gave birth, and then married again. But when he came across another Benjamin Latham he felt vindicated.

"Another Benjamin Latham!" Lenora exclaimed. "He must be your cousin or something, Benjamin. And he must have been named after your ancestor, same as you."

This Benjamin had been born in 1927, married Julia Sipe in 1958, and had one son, Mathew Latham, born in 1959.

Benjamin didn't trust himself to speak. A queer feeling had come over him soon as he saw his name in print. Or rather his namesake's name. This other Benjamin Latham had been born exactly two hundred years after himself. It was a weird coincidence. Too *damned* weird. What did it mean? Maybe nothing at all. But, just the same, it was spooky.

If still alive, his namesake's son, Mathew, would be twenty-three years old, about the same age as himself after his rebirth. (He reckoned his own age at about twenty-five, but he didn't really know for sure.) Somehow, now that the possibility was seeming less remote, it was startling and eerily disconcerting to imagine someone of his own flesh and blood, and roughly his own age, walking around in the twentieth century and feeling perfectly at home in it.

Clarence and Jane Latham, Mathew's paternal grandparents, were both dead, according to the newspapers, one a victim of cancer and the other of pneumonia, at age sixty-seven and seventy-three, respectively, the old lady having outlived the old man, as old ladies were wont to do. But Benjamin and Lenora could find no obituary notices pertaining to Mathew or his mother or his father. Therefore, unless they had left Philadephia to die elsewhere, they were probably all three still alive and kicking.

Benjamin could shake hands with them, across the centuries. But now that he almost had what he thought he wanted, the idea of such a strange and unique meeting of flesh scared him, as if it were forbidden.

23

Lenora Clayton sat by herself in a high-backed wooden booth in the historic City Tavern, three blocks from Independence Hall. She had loved the place from the moment that Benjamin first took her there to try Red Flannel Hash, a delicious concoction of chopped corned beef, potatoes, onions, and bacon that he joked had been his favorite since colonial times. But today she needed more than the City Tavern's aura of eighteenth-century gentility to help her relax, for she had come here to meet Julia Latham, the wife of the other Benjamin.

Sipping her iced tea, she told herself there was no reason to be nervous. She wished Benjamin could be here, but he had worried that he would be recognized as the Vampire Killer if he openly probed into the Vampire Killer's genealogy.

Lenora was sitting up straight, facing the entrance to the taproom, when a slender, middle-aged woman entered, eyes darting about till they rested on Lenora. This had to be Julia Latham—she was wearing the green-and-white-striped skirt and white frilly blouse that she had described over the phone. They nodded at each other when their eyes met. Then Julia came directly to the booth and said, "Are you Lenora?"

"Yes. Julia? Please . . . sit down."

They looked at each other a bit warily. Julia had a good bone structure—nice high cheekbones—but her ash-blond hair looked brittle and lifeless and her thinness seemed not the result of dieting but of ill health. Her slender hands fidgeted with the corners of the place mat and her fingernails were all bitten down.

"Can I order you something to drink?" Lenora asked kindly. She was conscious that Benjamin was depending on her. It had taken a clever ploy to get Julia to agree to this meeting, and she might easily panic and run away.

"Yes, please, a large iced tea," Julia said. She tapped her fingers on the place mat in a nervous rhythm, then cleared her throat and said, "You do have the money with you, don't you?"

"Yes, of course. Would you like to see it?"

"I want it in my hands before we start talking. Three thousand dollars. It's what we agreed to over the telephone." Her voice didn't sound as pushy as her words. She was screwing herself up to be assertive, but obviously she wasn't used to it.

"I don't think I should give you all of it right away," Lenora said calmly. "How about half now, and half when we finish our discussion?"

"Okay," Julia said, then added determinedly, "I'll have to see your credentials too."

"Suppose we take care of everything after I order some more iced tea?"

A waitress came, and Lenora took care of the ordering. Conversation with Julia was suspended until the order came. Then Lenora fished in her purse for her wallet and took out her identification card. She was glad that she and Benjamin had thought to go for authenticity, down to the last detail. The laminated card that she showed Julia identified her as Lenora Langley, staff reporter for the *National Keyhole,* an infamous scandal sheet with a weekly circulation in the millions. If Julia had phoned the *Keyhole* to ask if there was a Lenora Langley on the staff, the whole scheme would have been blown. But apparently she had not. She was either too naïve or too greedy, or merely too needy, which was what Lenora and Benjamin had been counting on. They knew Julia was a widow, for she had admitted as much on the phone. Widows generally were in dire need of money. "My husband is deceased," Julia had said when Lenora asked to speak to him. Then why hadn't the back issues of Philadelphia newspapers contained any obituary notices? It was one of the things that Lenora hoped to find out.

She put her phony ID back in her wallet and gave Julia fifteen one-hundred-dollar bills as a down payment. When the money was safely tucked in her white purse, Julia said, "I'm not trying to take advantage of you. But you're getting something that you think is worth paying for. And I need the cash desperately. I have to get away from this city. I can't take it anymore. Living in fear of my life. By the time your article comes out and Mathew realizes I'm to blame, I'll be in some other part of the country. I'll change my name. He'll be ranting and raving, but he won't be able to hurt me if he doesn't know where I am."

Lenora didn't understand three quarters of Julia's ramblings, but she knew that she was stepping into a severe mother-son conflict complicated by the fearful reluctance of Julia and Mathew Latham to publicly admit being related to the Vampire Killer. Lenora decided not to prod her but to simply let her ramble, if she was of a mind to. A lot might be learned from a pent-up woman subconsciously in need of a stranger's shoulder to cry on.

"You've found us now," Julia said bitterly, "so obviously you and people like you are going to keep digging. I'm surprised some reporter hasn't made it to my doorstep before now. I've been a nervous wreck ever since this business about the Vampire Killer started making headlines. I was worried it might make Mathew worse—which is a sick joke if I ever heard one. How could Mathew *get* any worse? Underneath it all, I guess I was just scared to death that people might find out."

"Find out what?" No sooner was the question out of her mouth than Lenora regretted it, hoping she hadn't blurted it too alarmingly.

Julia pulled her eyes away from her nail-bitten fingers. The expression on her face was almost coy—she had a secret she wasn't sure she should tell. Lenora tried not to look too anxious to know. She wanted to seem to deserve being chosen as Julia's confidante.

"My son the murderer," Julia said, trembling and coming close to tears.

Shocked, Lenora tried not to show it.

Like a penitent making a clean breast after a long season of guilt, Julia let her story pour out. The details were even worse than Lenora feared. Benjamin, her own Benjamin, wasn't the only Latham to have his hopes and dreams contaminated by the most wicked and depraved of human crimes.

"It all happened when we were living in Vermont, eight years ago," Julia began, her voice a soft whispery wail. "We were so *happy* at first. We had nice neighbors . . . Ben had a good job teaching school. We thought Mathew would receive his diploma from the high school where his father taught biology. But then our lives started falling apart . . . turning into a . . . a *nightmare.*"

"Sometimes life isn't so easy to understand," Lenora said consolingly.

"You can say that again. I don't know where we went wrong with Mathew . . . or if it was a disease . . . or what. Maybe he has a brain tumor, like that other boy who went up in the tower at the University of Texas and shot all those people. . . ."

Lenora waited for more of the story to unfold.

"Mathew was fifteen," Julia went on. She took a deep quavering breath and let it out in a nearly inaudible sigh. "A handsome boy, not a gawky adolescent. Tall, with blond hair and blue eyes. He had the longest, prettiest eyelashes! He played the trumpet in the school band.

Always made the honor roll. Never got into any serious trouble. Earned his own spending money by delivering newspapers, trimming people's hedges, mowing their lawns. That's how *she* got at him. She seduced him, and made him fall in love with her, when he was only fifteen."

"An older woman?" Lenora asked sympathetically.

"His *English* teacher! Twenty-five years old! Married, with *two* children!" Julia's voice crackled with rekindled outrage, fresh flames licking at charred embers, hot with eternal animosity toward the memory of the woman who had corrupted her son.

"Ten years his senior," Lenora said, as if she shared Julia's indignation, although in truth the thought of such a sexual liaison didn't shock her.

"In a way, the witch got what she deserved," said Julia. "She brought it on herself. Mathew was *her* victim as much as she was his." She bit her lip, trying to get her emotions under control, struggling to understand painful events in retrospect, events that she would never really be able to cope with. "At first I suspected my husband of having the affair with . . . with Georgina. I never dreamed it was my son. She was so perfect in her sneaking and conniving. Since she couldn't have Benjamin, she would corrupt Mathew, then crush him emotionally by spurning him. At that age, boys are so vulnerable, wanting so much to act like men, yet doubting their own manhood. First Georgina gave herself to Mathew; then after a while, when she was sure he loved her, she laughed at him, mocked him in bed, and accused him of being a fairy. All because my husband had spurned *her*. She was a cold, calculating bitch, deliberately setting about to destroy a young boy. So she got what she deserved when it backfired on her."

"She sounds pretty vicious," Lenora interjected.

Julia didn't acknowledge the comment. She went on talking, as if she were no longer hearing anything but her own agonizing memories. Her eyes had a faraway look, focused on the past, and her voice had the soft, almost inflectionless drone of the human voice under the influence of hypnosis.

"Georgina was found naked, bludgeoned to death in her

own bed. The claw hammer found on the scene was full of Mathew's bloody fingerprints. It had come from my husband's toolbox. I don't know if Benjamin thought he could take the blame, in order to save Mathew . . . nobody will ever know . . . he didn't leave any suicide note. My own belief is that he was emotionally shattered precisely because he understood that the evidence against Mathew was too clear-cut for anybody else to be thought guilty. My son had acted out of rage . . . out of . . . of . . . insanity . . . and hadn't bothered to plan the crime . . . to try to get away with it. But the law in Vermont at that time didn't permit anyone under sixteen to be tried as an adult. Instead, Mathew had to be held in detention until his eighteenth birthday, then released with his record clean. He got psychiatric care while he was institutionalized, but I couldn't make him continue it after he was discharged. I brought him back here to Philadelphia. I tried to start over . . . I hoped no one would come around, digging up our horrible past. But then this thing about my husband's ancestor started making the news. At first I was afraid that somehow it was Mathew, using the Vampire Killer's name, or even his father's name, to get even with the world. But there's no way my son could have been in Pittsburgh when those first murders took place."

"Do you think Mathew still needs psychiatric care?" Lenora asked.

"Yes, I'm certain of it. He's a loner, very moody . . . and antisocial. He can't hold anything but the most unskilled, undemanding sort of job. For a while he was working as a security guard—something he couldn't have done if his juvenile record hadn't been suppressed. I was afraid that when he was fingerprinted to qualify, the fingerprint check would bring his crime to light and the spotlight would be on us, the reporters hounding us again. But nothing like that happened, and I realized that it was true—he has a clean slate, as far as anyone in the world can tell. But of course I know differently. I'm his mother, and to me it's obvious that he's still mentally unbalanced."

"But perhaps he's not really dangerous," Lenora postulated. "Maybe he's wallowing in guilt and remorse and doesn't feel that he deserves a place in society."

Julia shook her head ruefully. "No, you don't understand what I'm telling you. I *know* my own son, and he's not my son anymore, he's a stranger with a sickness festering inside. My husband was always interested in the Latham family tree—the Lathams used to be rather wealthy and famous till they lost their money during the Great Depression—but Mathew couldn't have cared less about 'ancient history'—not until the Vampire Killer started making headlines. Now he has a morbid interest in the subject, keeps a scrapbook filled with all the lurid details of the Vampire Killer's crimes. I'm afraid he's going to go off the deep end someday soon. To be absolutely truthful, I've started to . . . to wonder if he might even attack *me*."

"Why?"

"I told you, Georgina worked her evil on my son to perfection. She made him hate not only her but *all* women. All women seem to remind him of her."

"Does he still live with you?"

"No. He wants to be on his own. He lost the job with Magnum Security because he stopped reporting for duty once the fascination with the gun and the badge wore off. But he must've saved up a little money. He moved out of my place a little over two months ago. He has his own apartment, if you could call it that—it's little more than a hovel." Julia pursed her lips in a fearful, contemplative grimace. "I don't know which is worse. Having to go to sleep with him in the same house with me, yet trying to show that I trust him by not locking my bedroom door. Or having to wonder at every moment exactly where he is and what he might be up to. Is he getting ready to come after me, like that boy in Texas who went after his own mother first? Are his footsteps taking him to my back porch? Or will the police come in the middle of the night to tell me that he's killed someone else?"

"Maybe your fears are exaggerated," Lenora said, trying to offer a modicum of hope. She imagined how awful it must be for a mother to simultaneously love and fear, perhaps hate, what had sprung from her own womb.

Bitter tears rolled down Julia's face, and she dabbed at them with a Kleenex that she took from her purse. "My son will never be the same again," she said, sniffling. "Georgina made him into a monster. The only question is, how far will he go when his mind completely snaps?"

24

Fireworks were exploding in loud, continuous volleys, splaying brief ribbons and dying snowflakes of color across the black sky, as Mathew Latham wormed his way through the dense throng on Penn's Landing. It was October twenty-fourth—the climax of the Century IV Celebration. More than half a million people were packed together on the wharf, listening to the booms and bangs and watching the sky erupt in fiery luminescence.

Mathew was constantly on the move, though the going was difficult, shouldering his way through the mob, moving his eyes appraisingly over each attractive woman that he encountered.

Benjamin was keeping an eye on Mathew. Following him. Invisibly. Moving in and out of the grays and blacks and brightnesses cast by incandescent lamps, exploding fireworks, spectators' shadows.

There was no question in Benjamin's mind that Mathew was looking for a victim. Someone to murder. A woman.

His aura of coldbloodedness was repulsive . . . and fascinating. He reminded Benjamin of a leopard scouting a herd of peaceful gazelles, a glint of cunning hunger in his eye, taking his time, attempting to single out the weakest animal who could most easily be brought down. So far, Benjamin had not done that kind of hunting. His first kill, Stephanie Kamin, had been accidental. His others—Elijah Alford, Paul Hill, Jorell Jordan, Garth Weir—had been specific and not innocent targets. Not exactly helpless either.

He wondered if the mumbo jumbo that had been done to him after he was hanged had wrought a curse not only upon him but upon all of his descendants. None of them seemed to have fared too well, down through the years. Although John Latham and his kin had prospered remarkably well for a while, their business empire was sundered by the stock market crash of 1929. John's great-grandson, Benjamin, had hanged himself in his basement after learning that his own son was a murderer. Now Mathew was fixated upon the legend of the Vampire Killer and was prowling the streets like an urban predator, as if he too needed blood.

What if he did? What if *his* saliva was poisonous? What if he had inherited the curse of the crossroads? What if he and Benjamin were *both* creatures of alienation, alike in flesh and blood, but mystically different from the rest of humankind?

Somehow Benjamin doubted it. He didn't believe in curses. At least he didn't use to. But now part of him wanted to believe, because if he was suffering from a curse and if it had been passed down to Mathew . . .

It was a comfort to think that there might be another miserable being like himself in the world. But it was only wishful thinking, probably. If Mathew was a beast he must be an ordinary, human one, a product of this cold, dehumanizing twentieth-century culture where mass murders were as common as traffic violations—and punished almost as severely.

Mathew Latham was one more churlish brat gone

haywire. His English teacher wouldn't sleep with him anymore, so he killed her, bashed her brains in with a hammer. And he was going to go on killing her subliminally. Because she made the poor thing feel *rejected.* He was going to get even again and again.

Mathew zeroed in on an attractive young woman who appeared to be watching the fireworks by herself even though she was in the midst of the huge crowd. Her long blond hair was tied back in a ponytail. She was wearing white slacks and a yellow nylon windbreaker. A tan canvas tote bag was slung over her shoulder. Mathew stopped a few feet behind her and ran his eyes over her body. Her buttocks were trim and shapely, undulating seductively as she shifted her weight nervously from one foot to the other, perhaps sensing Mathew's lascivious gaze.

Realizing that he was watching a kill being selected, Benjamin started to become aroused, despite himself. It was like covertly observing two people making love, having stumbled upon them accidentally; even if one tried to entertain only decorous, uplifting thoughts, the libido was bound to be stimulated anyway. Benjamin could almost taste the prospective victim's blood. Almost a month had gone by since his last indulgence. Much as he might wish otherwise, his time of need was upon him.

When Mathew sidled up to the young woman and said something to her, Benjamin moved in closer, willing himself not to be seen. He could overhear everything being said between Mathew and his prey, as if he were eavesdropping on a seduction. It surprised him how unthreatening, how downright charming, Mathew seemed; the young woman would have no reason to suspect that he was mentally disturbed. The hungry, predatory look was submerged, and the face he presented to her was beguilingly innocent and worthy of trust. Nevertheless, she refused to respond to him. Wouldn't even tell him her name.

"I bet I can guess it," he said, flashing a boyish grin. "Is it Esmeralda?"

That was the name of one of the tall ships that had come

in in June. But the young woman either didn't get the joke or wasn't amused by it. She kept her eyes focused straight ahead, away from Mathew, at the rockets exploding above the harbor, lighting up the masts and rigging of the barque *Gazela Primeiro,* built in 1883 by Portugal and maintained as a tourist exhibit and sail training vessel.

"I know!" said Mathew, continuing his teasing. "I bet your name's Gazela!"

The young woman smiled despite herself.

"Come on, Gazela," Mathew persisted. "Give me a break and talk to me."

She reverted to her policy of totally ignoring him.

"Maybe your name's *not* Gazela," he said cheerfully. "Maybe it's Olympia. Or Becuna."

She laughed, turning to him impulsively. "It's nothing so exotic," she admitted. "It's just plain Janice." She immediately looked away at another burst of fireworks.

"Janice what?" Mathew probed.

"Janice Ridenour," she said without looking at him.

Benjamin was astounded that his descendant's trivial line of patter actually seemed to be working. It was a far cry from the sort of wit that was *de rigueur* in fashionable eighteenth-century coffeehouses and drawing rooms.

"Excuse me."

Benjamin turned toward the burly, baldheaded man in gray mechanic's coveralls who was apologizing for jostling him. He nodded his head in acknowledgment. He daren't speak, for Janice and Mathew couldn't see him and would think they were hearing a disembodied voice.

But a mere nod wasn't good enough for the burly mechanic. "I said *excuse me,*" he repeated loudly and belligerently, clenching his fat fists as if they were large ball-peen hammers.

Janice and Mathew were staring at him, through Benjamin. Mathew looked perturbed and Janice looked puzzled. "Yes, sir?" she responded meekly.

"I ain't talking to you, I'm talking to *him,*" the man said, seemingly pointing right at her.

"Sir, there's no need to be rude," Mathew interjected, knowing full well that the restraint he was displaying in this situation would help convince Janice he was to be trusted.

"Mind your own business, bub," the baldheaded man warned. "This is between me and your buddy." He jerked his thumb toward the space that Benjamin was now occupying, and since Benjamin had moved back a few steps it appeared to Mathew and Janice that the baldheaded man was jerking his thumb at empty air.

"Come on, Janice, let's get out of here," Mathew suggested, taking her by the arm.

She hesitated, glancing back and forth from Mathew to the other man. Then she made up her mind that the latter represented more of a threat. Mathew, after all, seemed like such a nice young man, and this other guy was so feisty and crude by comparison.

Mathew began leading Janice Ridenour to safety. Benjamin turned to follow. But the burly mechanic pinched him by the right bicep so hard that splinters of pain shot up to his shoulder and down through his wrist and hand.

"Hold on, bub! Where do you think you're goin'?"

Janice and Mathew had gotten thirty or forty feet away by this time. Hearing the man's shout, they pivoted and saw him tugging at thin air. They shrugged and shook their heads, then turned and kept walking, threading their way through the crowd. They were out of hearing range now, so Benjamin could talk. "I really am sorry," he said, wincing from the pain in his arm. "I didn't mean to bump you."

"I bumped *you,*" the man said. "And I said *I* was sorry. Fuck you bastards that ain't got manners enough to accept an honest man's apology."

"Bad manners are one of my peeves also," Benjamin said sincerely. "I had something on my mind. I hardly noticed that you bumped me, and I . . . I just didn't hear you at first. Please . . . I want to catch up to my friends." He was so upset that he didn't think of using mind control right away. But then his eyes and the mechanic's eyes locked, and he willed the man to release his viselike grip.

The mechanic stared at his thick, callused fingers after they let go, wondering why they suddenly seemed to have a mind of their own. "Get goin', bub," he muttered with a lack of strength and conviction. "I . . . I hope I taught you . . . some etiquette."

But Benjamin didn't hear him, because he was already hustling to catch up with Mathew and Janice. It occurred to him that he could probably use mind control to prevent Mathew from doing Janice any harm. But did he want to? He couldn't be the world's watchdog, after all. Especially in this screwed-up modern world where somebody was being raped, maimed, or slaughtered with every tick of the clock. But perhaps this line of reasoning was only a way of rationalizing his basic dilemma: if there was a humane side of him that feared for Janice and what Mathew might do to her, another, darker, side was cheering Mathew on, wanting to see him make Janice's blood run. A starving man likes to watch others eat, because there is always the chance of catching a few crumbs.

Janice Ridenour was a copywriter for a small advertising agency. She was twenty-four years old, with a degree in journalism from Pennsylvania State University, and she was divorced. The papers had come through a few weeks ago. She couldn't explain exactly why her marriage had gone bad; she was still trying to come to grips with her sense of personal guilt and failure. Yet she hadn't been unfaithful; Tom had. She had come home from work early, unexpectedly, and had caught him in bed with her best friend. So she had lost a husband and a cherished friend in one devastating blow—made all the more terrible because she wasn't at all prepared for it, wasn't in the least suspicious beforehand. Later she found out that the affair between her husband and her best friend had been going on for five months. Of course she felt betrayed and emotionally crushed. But on top of it she felt awfully foolish. Her estimate of herself hit rock bottom. How could she have considered herself such a wise and capable young woman if she couldn't even get a glimmer of a life-shattering betrayal right under her nose? In her own bed. She had tried to tell herself that the easiest thing in the world was to be tricked by someone you loved, someone who didn't love *you* enough not to trick you.

"I took my own name back after the divorce," she told Mathew. "I didn't want anything that belonged to Tom Blakely. So now I'm Janice Ridenour once again—at least in name—but I'm afraid I'll never be the same person anymore."

"We all go through changes," Mathew said. "Sometimes we learn crucial lessons from bad experiences, as long as we don't let them destroy us."

In his own case, he was thinking, he had almost been destroyed by Georgina Hartwick. But he had turned the tables on her. Now he was wise to all women. He knew what they wanted, and how brazenly they could destroy a man once they got it. That's why it was so important to strike first. Take all you could and smash them before they had a chance to do it to you.

"God, I've never talked to anyone like this," Janice told him. "But you're such a good listener, Mathew . . . and I suppose I desperately needed to open up to somebody. I've been going around like a zombie for the past six months. I haven't dated . . . haven't even made any new friends. I just find it so hard to trust anybody."

"That's not surprising, after what they put you through," Mathew consoled.

He and Janice were in Ye Olde Ice Cream Parlor on Chestnut Street. The decor included an elaborate old-fashioned soda fountain, Tiffany lamps dangling on brass chains, high-backed wooden booths, and bentwood tables and chairs.

For privacy, Mathew and Janice had taken a booth. Benjamin Latham was in the next booth, eavesdropping. Even though the parlor was noisy and crowded—jukebox blaring and patrons gabbing and laughing—he found that he could tune in on Janice and Mathew's conversation. Not that he could exactly hear it; the actual words were too muffled. But the thoughts behind the words seemed to be piped directly into his brain, so that he could understand without hearing. It was another special power, a new discovery for him, akin to his ability to influence people's behavior through mind control.

"This is good, but not as good as homemade ice cream," Janice said, "even though they claim it's made from all natural ingredients. The word 'natural' really helps sell products nowadays, so advertisers use it to the hilt. But everything on earth is natural in the broadest sense, because everything and everybody is made up of chemicals in one form or another."

"That's interesting," Mathew said. But Benjamin heard him thinking: Just like the bitch to try and show off everything she knows.

"I work on the Yukon Ice Cream account," Janice said. "We call their junk 'natural' too." She smiled wryly. "And we're not telling a lie, because all the ingredients *are* made from stuff that occurs in nature. Even the artificial colors and sweeteners that come from coal tar."

"Yuck!" Mathew said. "You have to be kidding, Janice."

"Nope. Unfortunately, I'm deadly serious. I had to do a lot of research to write copy for the Yukon Ice Cream account. The kind of stuff I found out makes me want to quit my job. It's like selling cancer. In case you don't know it, coal tar is what's used to produce cancer on the shaved backs of laboratory mice so scientists can try to find out how to cure it."

Learning all this was turning Benjamin's stomach. He quit eating his hot-fudge sundae and laid his sticky spoon down on his napkin. The gooey fudge now made him think of coal tar. He rinsed his mouth with water. No wonder so many Americans were turning into murderous lunatics. Their government was allowing them to feast on cancer!

Mathew was bored. He could see why Janice's husband had had to get away from her if she was such a food fetishist that she couldn't let him eat in peace. "It would be handy having you around all the time," he lied, "so you could keep me healthy and eating the right things."

A warm glow came over her, and she felt appreciated. It was the kind of feeling she hadn't enjoyed for a long time. Like one thirsting in the desert, she wanted to believe in her mirage. Mathew was so nice; he hadn't even taken her to a saloon, but to an ice-cream parlor. He had a boyish, innocent charm. He was as clean-cut as a college fraternity boy—the kind that didn't smoke dope or go on crazy alcoholic binges to blow off steam. His blue eyes were alert and intelligent, devoid of guile. His sandy hair was clean and neatly groomed. He was conservatively dressed in tan slacks, a yellow button-down shirt, and a dark brown corduroy sports jacket.

Trailing the romantic-looking young couple as they left the ice-cream parlor arm in arm, Benjamin could no longer tune in to their thoughts or hear their conversation. Although he had willed himself invisible so far as they were concerned, he still didn't want them to hear his footsteps behind them, so he was staying thirty or forty feet back. Thus he discovered, disappointedly, that his ESP eavesdropping power had a limited range.

He pursued Mathew and Janice through a quaint section of the "olde city" called Society Hill, in the heart of "the most historical square mile in America." Arts and crafts shops, antique parlors, fashionable boutiques, and cozy bistros lined the cobblestoned streets. It was a warm night for late October, and crowds of people were out having a good time, prolonging the festive mood inspired by the fireworks display.

Janice led Mathew down a narrow, shadowy street lined with wrought-iron streetlamps and young maple trees. The lamps, alternating with the trees at measured intervals, made the leaves, in their autumn colors, look like reddish golden plumes leaping out of blackness. The entrance to Janice's apartment was in the rear of a colonial-style brick town house. She unlatched a wooden gate and led Mathew into the dark corridor between her building and the adjacent one.

"Aren't you afraid to come in here by yourself?" Mathew asked.

"Yes," she admitted, squeezing his hand. "But don't worry about me, I know how to take care of myself," she added, with what sounded to him like false bravado.

There was a light on her back porch, a bright naked bulb. But it wasn't much protection. It revealed a small brick courtyard with a high wooden fence all around. Nobody could see into it unless he or she accidentally happened to look down from one of the rear upper-story windows of the town house that fronted on the next block.

"Nice," Mathew said.

"Oh, I'm glad you like it," said Janice, mistaking his meaning, as he knew she would. "I fell in love with the courtyard. It's lovely to picnic or sunbathe out here when the weather's warm."

Benjamin had crept around softly to the rear of the building and was watching them standing on the porch. His heartbeat quickened with mounting excitement. He knew that Mathew had no intention of leaving Janice alive. But how was he going to get into her apartment? She had let him walk her back here, for protection, but he was still a stranger to her. Surely she wouldn't be fool enough to ask him inside.

"Well, it's been nice," she said. "Thank you, Mathew. Please call me sometime. You know where I work . . . the number is in the phone book." She tilted her head for a kiss on the lips, just a friendly good-night kiss from a young man she liked and hoped to see again.

Benjamin's need for blood, now that some was about to be spilled, was so powerful that he was shivering, almost salivating.

Her eyes were closed, her bare white throat arched as she waited for her kiss. Mathew pressed his lips to hers as his fingers tightened around her neck. Quickly and painfully. So tightly and quickly that she had no chance to cry out before her larynx was crushed shut. Her eyes bulged. Under the glare of the porch light he watched her protruding eyeballs, waiting for the moment when the capillaries would burst under choking pressure and the whites would turn bright red. No. He ought to stop before then. If he could control himself. At the start his intention had been to just choke her unconscious so he could fish for her apartment key in her tote bag and drag her into the house.

Then, once she was tied and gagged, he could have all the fun he wanted to have with her . . . until he got bored.

Janice saw nothing but red pain that was rapidly turning black. Her tote bag slid off her shoulder and she clawed at the strap. At the same time she tried to kick Mathew in the groin, but he pinned her against the wall in the corner of the tiny porch, his body pressed into her so hard that she could barely move. She was desperate not to pass out, not to drop her tote bag—for inside it were the things that had caused her to joke earlier that she could take care of herself. A .25 automatic—a so-called woman's weapon that she had bought for self-protection soon after her divorce—and a can of Mace. But her bag was dangling out of reach.

Benjamin, who had moved in closer to the action, was rooted in his tracks. Neither of the two combatants could see him, but he could see them, of course, and could hear their thoughts. He knew what Janice was trying to do, what her last hope was. All he needed to do to give her a fighting chance was to lift up that purse for her, high enough for her fingers to reach inside. But that would be like playing God. So far he had scrupulously refrained from being anything but an impartial observer in this affair. Whatever Mathew was going to do, it wasn't Benjamin's fault. If Benjamin rescued Janice, wouldn't Mathew then simply go after someone else: another girl who might deserve even less to suffer and die?

As Benjamin debated these philosophical issues the tote bag dropped with a loud clatter to the concrete porch, and Janice's knees buckled and sagged. Mathew sank down with her into a configuration that was almost sexual, on top of her, still rabidly choking her. His face was so close to hers that he could feel her weakening breath against his cheek and took it as a barometer of her impending death. He doubted that he could stop choking her once she was unconscious and limp. No. He needed to go all the way. He had a powerful erection now, and he squirmed to force it between Janice's legs without unbuttoning his trousers or removing her slacks.

But now that they were lying down, the tote bag was within Janice's reach. Her arm fluttered weakly, groping, fingers trying to touch familiar fabric, and then her small hand crawled inside the bag like a frail, broken bird dragging itself into a nest. Even if she found the Mace or the gun, did she have any strength left to use them?

Benjamin didn't know who he was rooting for now. Whatever remained of his humanity wanted Janice to win. She was the underdog and Mathew was the villain. But if Mathew won there would be a source of *blood.* He couldn't drink Mathew's blood, even if Mathew lost and died. Instinctively he realized that the blood of his own flesh would be poison to him. The craving was not, and could never be, an incestuous one.

"Georgina . . . Georgina," Mathew cried out, his buttocks pumping madly as he thrust his clothed penis against Janice in a frenzy of lust for the English teacher he had killed. Potent again, and impaling Georgina in his mind, he went off in an insane orgasm, moaning and whimpering her name.

For a brief moment he wasn't choking Janice quite so hard. It was the break she needed. Summoning the last desperate shreds of her will to survive, she closed her fingers around the can of Mace and brought it up to Mathew's face, the cold can touching her own cheek as well as his. Her eyes were so popped out of their sockets that she couldn't close them, and so she was going to get a blast of Mace, too. She pressed the button. She was too weak to scream or toss, but Mathew howled and screeched, rolling off of her, writhing and kicking across the concrete porch. His hands clawed and rubbed frantically at his eyes.

She had the gun out now, and even though she couldn't see she pointed the weapon feebly in the direction of Mathew's squealing and squeezed off four rounds. Two of the bullets whined and ricocheted, but the other two hit home. Mathew screamed, then lay still.

But, with a rush of new horror, Janice discovered that she still couldn't breathe, even with his fingers no longer clamped around her throat. The damage was already done: her windpipe was crushed almost totally shut, and now the narrow usable channel that remained was plugged with bloody mucus, and she was so depleted from her exertions that she couldn't possibly get enough oxygen to her heart or to her brain.

Trying to suck air only tightened the vacuum in her throat, like a hard lump wedged into the top of her lungs. She bucked and thrashed futilely and dug her fingers into her windpipe as if it were a badly flattened straw that had to be straightened out or else the world would end. But there wasn't enough time. The world was out of breath. All the air had been sucked back to its source, in some far corner of the universe, out of reach.

Benjamin watched Janice's struggle, listening to the ugly, rasping, gurgling sound of too-little air being forced in and out of a tight place. At the end, her breaths sounded like weak whistles . . . and then whispers . . . short and faint. At last she died, and the sounds stopped.

But Mathew was still breathing. Benjamin stood over him, noting his blood-soaked shirt, his corduroy jacket raveled up and flapped open like a pair of wrinkled wings flattened on the concrete. So far the gunshots seemed to have gone unnoticed, perhaps mistaken for fireworks—or maybe, as happened so often in this inhospitable modern world, people just didn't want to get involved.

Benjamin had time to satisfy his craving. But he didn't want Mathew's blood . . . not the blood of his descendant, which would curdle in his veins.

He opened up his switchblade knife, the one he had taken from Elijah Alford in the parking garage. He knelt over Janice Ridenour's dead body, slit her right wrist, and drank. As always when he drank blood, he sank into a dreamy, half-somnolent, half-erotic state and did not hear the moans of Mathew, who had regained consciousness and was struggling half blindly to get up, pressing his fingers over the bloody wounds in his chest and abdomen.

When Benjamin had satisfied himself, he turned and, getting up into a half crouch, saw that Mathew was staring at him through reddened, tear-streaked eyes that were recovering from the temporary blindness caused by Mace.

"You . . . it's . . . you," Mathew murmured incredulously, his voice weak from the shock of his wounds. He had managed to stand and was supporting himself by holding on to a brick pillar.

"Yes," Benjamin admitted. "It is I. Benjamin Latham. Your ancestor."

"I'm . . . glad," Mathew said, gasping hoarsely. "Help me . . . please . . . help me . . ."

25

Mathew was able to walk, even though he was in terrible pain. His eyes were streaming tears, not yet fully recovered from their exposure to Mace. His chest and side felt hot and sore, as if he had been stabbed by more than one ice pick and was still carrying around the embedded steel. Luckily, his sports jacket had been flapped open when he was shot, so that now, by keeping it buttoned, he could use it to cover his bleeding wounds. He and Benjamin sneaked through shadowy side streets and dark, narrow alleys on their way to the Welcome Hotel.

Every time they passed anyone, Benjamin tried to shield his descendant with his own body. And he willed each passerby not to recognize or remember Mathew's face. He had no idea whether his attempt at this sort of mind control (for the benefit of someone other than himself) would be effective; but he tried it anyway, and maybe it worked, for they reached their destination without getting arrested, even though one of the people they passed was a uniformed cop.

Further proof that the mind control might have worked: a passenger on the elevator at the hotel chatted briefly with Benjamin but directed no remarks toward Mathew, didn't even seem to notice him. He kept his head turned away, in any event, and tried to stand up straight, as if there were nothing the matter with him.

Knowing that Lenora would be using the deadbolt for added protection while she was alone, Benjamin did not try using his key but instead rapped lightly on the door to their suite. He heard a few muffled footsteps and realized she was checking him out through the peephole. Then she unlocked the door. Her violet eyes darted worriedly from Benjamin to Mathew, who, even through his pain, gave her a look that felt strange—as if she had just been evaluated and chosen for something scary.

"Quickly! Let us in!" Benjamin whispered hoarsely. Then: "Lock the door!" When she had done so, he said, "This is my . . . er . . . my relative, Mathew Latham. He's badly hurt. We must help him. I can explain everything later." Even as he spoke he wondered exactly what he meant by "everything." Would he tell her the story of his life and death and rebirth? Sooner or later he'd have to, for on the profoundest level he wanted her to love and respect him for what he was. Maybe now, in this emergency, he could find the courage to risk her hatred or her sheer disbelief.

"Do what you have to do," Lenora told him with forthright sincerity. "No explanation will be necessary. Now or ever. I will always love you. No matter what."

Thus she avowed the fact that she belonged to him body and soul. She would stand by him and support him in anything he had to do. She knew with an atavistic certainty that he was no ordinary man. In his presence she felt supernaturally elevated and strengthened. Her life was joined to his by a bond stronger than matrimony, by a sacrament of the flesh and spirit more powerful than any earthly ritual performed by priests.

Appreciating the depth of her commitment to him,

Benjamin looked upon her with gratitude and with a deepening, expanding love. Wondrously, she had become his helpmate for eternity, as much as he had become hers.

Communing totally for these brief but meaningful moments, neither Benjamin nor Lenora noticed Mathew's tremor of jealousy. And when they looked at him he averted his tear-streaked eyes and clutched at his wounds, faking a tremor of pain so they would not see how much he coveted this thing that they shared. "I'm . . . probably . . . going to die . . . if I don't get to a hospital," he moaned.

"I have . . . er . . . a certain amount of medical training," Benjamin said. "It would be unwise for you to go to a hospital, because they would be required to report bullet wounds to the police. I can treat your wounds. Tonight the most I can do is clean and bandage them. But tomorrow I can go out and buy the things I need to remove the bullets and perform surgery."

"Surgery without anesthetic?" Mathew whined.

Thinking of the many, many amputations he had performed during the French and Indian War when there were no drugs to kill pain, and of the bravery of the soldiers he operated on, Benjamin said, "Your suffering will be mild by comparison, so make up your mind that you'll have to endure it."

"By comparison to what?" Mathew whimpered.

"By comparison to the suffering you brought to Janice Ridenour," Benjamin snapped.

"Well, you got what *you* wanted out of it," Mathew said with an insolent smirk.

Benjamin seethed inwardly, but he had no adequate rejoinder. The truth hurt. Why did he have such a dreadful compulsion to help this sniveling murderer? Was it an innate drive to keep his own genes alive? Or did he have a darker motive? Perhaps in his subconscious, where the most primal needs take precedence over moral and ethical refinements, he had already decided that he could continue to use Mathew by channeling and controlling Mathew's murderous impulses, living off of the blood of Mathew's victims, limiting the toll to one per month, thus sparing the world a potentially worse carnage and saving his own conscience from the full brunt and responsibility for the killings.

Tired and scared, Lenora came into the bedroom with her second cup of strong black coffee and sat on the edge of the bed. She hadn't slept much during the night even though Benjamin had lain beside her. She hadn't been able to stop worrying about Mathew lying wounded on the couch in the other room. Maybe he would die, and she and Benjamin would have a corpse to dispose of, come morning. Or maybe he would sneak in and murder them in their sleep. He was certainly capable of it. The nine A.M. news, on the TV while Lenora boiled a pan of water on the hotplate, had stunned her with a description of what Mathew had done to Janice Ridenour. Having Janice's pistol in the pocket of her bathrobe—Benjamin had given it to her and told her to use it for protection against Mathew while she was alone with him—instead of giving her comfort gave her the goose bumps. It hadn't made her feel safe last night when she had it under her pillow, and it wasn't helping much now—but she tried to convince herself that she would be brave enough to pull the trigger if her life depended on it.

She had the bedroom door shut, but there was no way to lock it. Now she knew how Mathew's mother must have felt, living in the same house with him. She hoped that Julia Latham had escaped safely. Lenora took a sip of hot coffee, but it couldn't dissipate the chills she got from being alone with Mathew.

She wondered what he was doing out there by himself. What he was thinking. How he might react to her barricading herself behind a closed door. Would it make his demented mind want to get at her all the more, like a spoiled child who is told he can't have something?

Much as she hated being in the same room with him, she decided she had better go out. Seeing him lying on the couch would be better than wondering what he was up to. She'd have to try to stomach the way his eyes kept following her every move, boring into her, not merely stripping her mentally the way some men seemed to do but actually *dissecting* her, peeling layers of flesh and internal organs away from her bones.

She opened the door and avoided eye contact with him as she rinsed her coffee cup in the small sink in the bathroom. Earlier he hadn't spoken a word, just kept staring at her, until he asked for coffee. She had told him that he mustn't have anything in his stomach until after Benjamin operated. He had responded with a contemptuous snort.

Now he said to her back as she rinsed her cup, "You know he's a real vampire, don't you?"

She didn't answer. The implausible remark hung on the air between them. Only she didn't think it was so implausible.

Mathew said, "Maybe you're one, too. Maybe that's why he isn't afraid to leave you alone with me."

It dawned on her, with a burst of insight, that Mathew might be scared of *her.* Or, rather, that he didn't know just how wary he needed to be. He was trying to find out exactly what kind of threat she posed. He didn't know that she had the gun, for Benjamin had given it to her in private. The only thing inhibiting Mathew from attacking her, other than his wounds, might be his fear of her supposed supernatural powers—the same sort of powers he imagined that Benjamin possessed. However, in Benjamin's case it wasn't just imagination. Lenora was now convinced of that as much as Mathew was. Yet she knew that Mathew was crazy and she wasn't.

"Surely you don't believe in vampires in this day and age," she scoffed. She faced him haughtily, trying to convince him that she probably *was* the sort of creature he wanted to believe in.

He averted his eyes sheepishly. She had succeeded in staring him down. He seemed suddenly weak and impotent. Lying on the couch nude from the waist up except for his bandages, he reminded her of a broken toy.

She wished fervently that Benjamin would return from

his errands. Thinking that surely he would be here soon, she filled a large pot with water and started boiling it in order to sterilize his new surgical instruments.

On a clean white towel Benjamin laid out the assortment of freshly sterilized "instruments."

"Pliers!" Mathew squealed, his eyes widening fearfully. "You can't *touch* me with those—I won't let you!"

Benjamin had dealt with similar fears many times before. He spoke calmly and soothingly. "I assure you that this pair of needle-nosed pliers is designed exactly like a forceps in all its essentials. Once I probe your wounds I'll use the forceps to extract foreign objects. That way you'll heal as good as new. I know what I'm talking about, Mathew. You're in good hands, believe me."

He wished he felt as confident as he sounded. When he had served under General Braddock he could hardly have been blamed if a patient died. Death had been the rule rather than the exception. The state of the medical arts had been so primitive that anyone who got wounded was likely to die of infection, even if the wound was minor. Today was the first time he had ever sterilized his instruments; he understood about germs now, from his library studies. By modern standards, there was a lot he still didn't know. But, in his favor, Mathew's wounds weren't nearly as bad as many he had dealt with under battlefield conditions, and he might even have an advantage over modern doctors who weren't used to operating without anesthetic. One's nerves had to be exceptionally steady to perform delicate surgical procedures on a patient who was writhing and screaming.

"I'm just going to remove the bandages now," he said, "so I can have a look at the situation."

"What do you want me to do?" Lenora asked, coming out of the bathroom. "My hands are scrubbed. I used the carbolic acid solution, like you told me."

"Stand by," Benjamin instructed. "Be ready to hand me whatever I ask for. You may have to swab away blood so I can see what I'm doing." To Mathew he said, "Put your hands behind you and hang on to the arm of the couch.

Squeeze it hard and it'll help you stand the pain. You can't scream, or someone might call the police. And you've got to keep yourself as still as possible while I'm working on you."

"Maybe we shouldn't go through with this," Mathew said pleadingly. "Maybe I'll be okay if we just leave well enough alone."

"No," Benjamin replied firmly. "Don't kid yourself. If I don't clean out your wounds they'll fester and go to gangrene. It's a slow death and an ugly, stinking one."

Mathew fell silent. The thought of his insides rotting and dying and turning green made him try to summon his courage. His eyes stared up at the ceiling, glazed with fear and anxiety. Suddenly Benjamin had an idea. He bent over Mathew and stared at him hypnotically. "You will *not* feel pain," he told him. "You will not feel pain from this moment forward until I am finished working on you."

"Hmph!" Mathew snorted. "What are you trying to do, hypnotize me? Good try, but it won't work. Some crazy shrink tried it on me at the funny farm in Vermont, but she couldn't get me to go under. She said it was because I was too afraid of what might happen to me if I gave up the use of my five senses. *I* say it's because I'm way too smart to let anybody have that much control over me."

"I was only trying to help you," Benjamin said.

"Sure. Maybe I believe you. But you bombed out on that one. I just hope you're a better surgeon than you are a hypnotist."

Benjamin let the insolence pass, realizing that Mathew had to act like a tough guy at a time like this. But he wondered why his attempt at mind control had failed, considering that Mathew *had* been susceptible last night on Penn's Landing. Obviously the power had strange uses and equally strange limitations. It would be nice if it were more predictable. Perhaps Mathew's psychotic brain waves tended to dull its effectiveness. Or maybe Mathew inhibited Benjamin by making him feel ashamed: they were both predators, both killers, on the same wavelength in a primal sense, much as Benjamin hated to admit it. He didn't like being in tune with a madman on any level. But he was finding it harder and harder to maintain an attitude of moral superiority by making fine philosophical distinctions between his own killings and those of his descendant.

Focusing his full attention on the matter at hand, he snipped away tape and bandages. Yesterday he had bathed Mathew's wounds with water that had been purified by boiling and had applied clean surgical dressings from the first-aid kit that Lenora kept in her car. He discarded the dressings, which were now bloody, and cleaned away coagulated blood and fluids from the wound sites. "Not too bad," he remarked, to encourage Mathew. "There's not an inordinate degree of inflammation or swelling." To himself he thought how lucky it was that Janice Ridenour's pistol had been a .25-caliber automatic. He was used to the damage done by lead balls three quarters of an inch in diameter, expanding on impact, splintering bone like lightning striking a sapling and turning bone fragments into deadly shrapnel.

There were three holes. The largest one was obviously an exit wound, the bullet having glanced off a rib and burst out through his abdomen, just below the solar plexus. The other bullet had lodged in his left pectoral, thanks to the low muzzle velocity and the thickness of the well-developed muscle; if it had gone much deeper it would have entered his heart and killed him.

Of the two bullets, the one that had cleanly penetrated was easiest to deal with. "Get ready now, this is going to hurt," Benjamin said. Mathew held on to the couch arm and gritted his teeth, groaning and perspiring heavily, trying his best not to scream out loud, while Benjamin did what he had to do. First he probed the bullet hole with a long, thin steel crochet needle that he had bought at a five-and-dime store, till he was sure he had pinpointed the exact location of the bullet. Then, using his switchblade knife for a scalpel, he made an incision to the necessary depth, widening the wound to accommodate the forceps. Thus, he was able to extract the slug. He examined it, noting that it was slightly flattened, as it had gone deep enough to strike the bone under the pectoral and might have fractured it. If so, it must be a hairline fracture since there weren't any bone fragments in the wound, just bits of clothing, shirt shreds, which Benjamin was able to remove with a tweezers. It amazed him that such scraps could be a main cause of toxemia, whereas in his own day they had been deemed harmless. Scrupulously trying to tweeze out every bit of potential contamination, he wondered how many lives he could have saved if he had known about this in the past.

Lenora assisted by swabbing away blood and generally trying to calm Mathew with soothing words. All during his agony he kept his eyes glued to Lenora as if she were something special to him: an angel of mercy, an anesthetic, or an aphrodisiac. His eyes remained glazed with pain but not so much with fear anymore, and they burned into her, trying to impress her with a fierce sexual bravado that might make her feel that he deserved a place within her loins. Fully understanding what he was silently communicating, she was both riveted and repulsed by it.

Still kneeling in front of the couch which was his operating table, Benjamin incised the second bullet wound, a much longer but shallower incision, tracing the trajectory of the slug that had struck the rib and exited. Using the tweezers, Benjamin extracted metallic particles, slivers of bone, and shreds of Mathew's shirt. Then he bathed both incisions once again and closed them up, suturing with a large curved needle dipped in oil and ligatures of tough waxed twine. He used strips of surgical adhesive between the stitches, to make sure that the wounds were held firmly closed. Then he applied dressings of clean gauze and taped them in place.

"All done!" he exclaimed, allowing himself a self-congratulatory smile. "There! How do you feel?"

"It hurts like hell," Mathew said. And for Lenora's benefit he added, "But I can take it."

In the bathroom, washing Benjamin's makeshift surgical instruments and the white towel they had lain upon, Lenora watched Mathew's blood swirling in the porcelain bowl of the sink and gurgling down the drain. The look on her face was remarkably odd, as if she were in a trance . . . spellbound by the sight of blood . . . wetting her lips now and then with her tongue . . . remaining transfixed and fascinated until the towel had been wrung out so many times that the water was crystal clear, without the slightest tinge of red.

26

When the intercom buzzed he picked up the phone and barked his name into the mouthpiece: "Vargo."

"Hello, Ron. Got your bags packed?"

Recognizing the high, squeaky voice, Vargo tried not to feel a tingle of expectancy. A phone call from the serologist did not necessarily herald a break in the case. Still, it was about time for something to happen. The Vampire Killer seemed to stick to a pattern of one killing roughly every four weeks, and more time than that had now gone by since the disappearance of Garth Weir.

"Ron? Are you there? This is Ken Beransky from the serology lab in Pittsburgh."

"I know. What's up, Ken?"

"Your man is in Philadelphia. Or at least he *was* there. A young woman named Janice Ridenour was found strangled, her right wrist slashed. Electrophoresis showed poisonous saliva."

"Are you sure?" Vargo asked, holding his breath.

"As certain as death and taxes," Beransky replied. "I just finished comparing photos of the microscope slides taken in Philly with the photos I have on file here from the Stephanie Kamin case. The slides match. Looks like the guy you're after is frolicking in a new hunting ground."

"Any chance we could be talking about *two* freaks? I mean, maybe this disease—or whatever it is—is spreading."

"I doubt it, Ron," Beransky said. "*All* the protein characteristics match. The odds would be at least ten million to one against two individuals having such a precise comparison." Beransky chuckled. "Funny that the blood type is AB—the universal recipient. Type AB makes a certain weird logic, you know, for folks who want to believe Latham is an honest-to-goodness vampire. He could take a direct transfusion from any victim, of any blood type at all, without any danger of his red cells clumping together and clogging his heart valves—but I don't know how that applies to *drinking* blood. I guess some quacky scientist with a wild imagination could concoct a farfetched theory and peddle it to the newspapers."

"I heard one the other day that almost made sense," Vargo said, "from a Dr. Harrison Lubbock on a radio talk show. His idea is that Latham could be an evolutionary throwback. Since our ancestors the Neanderthals and Cro-Magnons used to be cannibals and blood-drinkers, a species of caveman could have evolved that *needed* blood and got special powers and longevity from it."

"Heh-heh," Beransky chortled. "That *is* a humdinger! I swear, I almost pity this guy if you capture him alive, Ron, and let the crackpots have a go at him. Never mind capital punishment. I can't think of a worse torture for any creature on God's earth than to have a couple hundred rabid psychiatrists and anthropologists swarming all over him with polygraphs, X-rays, sonograms, spinal taps, Rorschach tests, and Minnesota Multi-Phasic Personality Inventories."

"How he's captured may be out of my hands if the

Philadelphia police beat me to it. Why haven't I received a call from them?"

"They don't know the results of the slide comparison yet. I phoned you first, Ron. I figured you'd want to talk to your boss about getting permission to go to Philly. You can tell him he'll have my written report in his hands by tomorrow morning."

"When was this Janice Ridenour murdered?"

"Four days ago. Time of death has been placed between late Sunday night and the wee hours of Monday morning, according to the Philadelphia County coroner's report. She was choked so hard that her larynx was crushed, and then her wrist was slashed after she was already dead. I find that interesting, don't you?"

"Yeah. Elijah Alford got the same kind of treatment."

"Exactly."

Vargo asked, "Who's the logical person for me to contact? I mean, in Philadelphia."

"Sergeant Michael Mordini and Sergeant Mary Demchak are the two detectives assigned to the Ridenour case. Hold on, Ron. I'll get you their phone numbers."

"Thanks, Ken."

Vargo wanted to find out as much as he could about the Ridenour tie-in before he went to talk with Lieutenant Fein. Today was Thursday. Philadelphia was only a four-hour drive from the State Police headquarters at Greensburg. Vargo could check into a Philadelphia hotel tonight and be ready to liaison with the detectives bright and early Friday morning.

He had been spinning wheels for the past month, and now he was itching to pick up the scent again. During all this time there had been an all points bulletin out for Garth Weir, but the logical assumption was that Garth wasn't going to turn up alive. Angela Stone's green Pinto had been found abandoned in downtown Pittsburgh with Latham's fingerprints all over it, on the passenger side as well as the driver side. Somehow Latham must've lured Garth out of the apartment, maybe by some kind of crazy phone call—although it was impossible to figure what could have made Garth pick Latham up and ride off alone with him—on what was bound to be Garth's last ride.

When Vargo got off the phone with Ken Beransky, he dialed Sergeant Michael Mordini's number in Philadelphia.

"Homicide."

"Sergeant Mordini?"

"Out on a case."

"How about Sergeant Demchak?"

"Out on the same case."

Vargo was annoyed at being given such curt, gruff answers, but he kept his temper. "To whom am I speaking, please?"

"Sergeant Baker."

"This is Trooper Ronald Vargo, Pennsylvania State Police. I believe that Detectives Mordini and Demchak are working on a homicide investigation that's connected with my own case here in Pittsburgh."

"The Janice Ridenour thing?"

"That's right. I'd like to compare notes and make arrangements to liaison in Philadelphia."

"Maybe you can save yourself the trip. The way Mordini and Demchak stormed out of here, I had the impression they were about to make a collar."

"Sergeant Baker . . . are you serious?" Vargo got a sick, sinking feeling in his gut at the prospect of having somebody else snatch Latham from under his paw.

"Bloody fingerprints on a brick pillar on Ridenour's back porch," Baker announced in gruff matter-of-factness. "An hour ago Mordini took a call from the FBI lab in D.C. They must have made an ID."

Even though such a break could solve the case, Vargo found himself hoping against it and fighting his guilt for feeling that way. He said, "Sergeant Baker, when Detectives Mordini and Demchak report in, please tell them that I called and that I'm on my way to see them in person. I've been busting hump on this thing for quite some time now, and I'd like to be in on the wrap-up if possible."

"Gotcha," Baker said. "Have a nice trip, Trooper Vargo."

Baker's sentiment sounded more sarcastic than sincere, but Vargo thanked him anyway and got off the line. Before going down the hall to Lieutenant Fein's office, he made up his mind not to tell Fein that there might just have been a big break in the Vampire Killer case. If the lieutenant learned of it, he'd surely go into a holding pattern. He wouldn't grant Vargo permission to go to Philadelphia right away. Instead, he'd want to give it till Monday morning. Sit back and wait for it to be all over, and the glory reaped by a couple of big-city hotshots who had just happened to get lucky.

It was four o'clock Thursday afternoon when Sergeant Michael Mordini and Sergeant Mary Demchak parked down the block from a three-story brick apartment building on Race Street in Philadelphia's Chinatown. Mordini killed the engine of the tan Plymouth sedan, patted the shoulder holster under his gray suit jacket, and said "Ready, babe?" with a look of tense excitement in his dark, handsome face. Mary nodded, just as keyed-up as he was, her hazel eyes sparking, a rosy flush on her fair cheeks. She glanced in her leather handbag to make sure the butt of her revolver was unobstructed, easy to grab; the tailoring of her green suit would have been spoiled if the jacket had to be big enough to hide a weapon underneath. She was proud of her redheaded good looks and her attractive figure, and she was determined not to lose her femininity in a futile attempt to convert all the men who thought she shouldn't be trying to do a "man's job."

Mike Mordini was thirty-one and Mary Demchak was twenty-seven. He was married and she was divorced. His marriage was not a happy one; his young, pretty wife couldn't adjust to living with a man who worked crazy hours and was often in danger. Mary, of course, understood and sympathized with the pressures and pitfalls of Mike's job in the way that only those who have shared a foxhole can truly appreciate the anxieties and elations of combat. Two years ago they had become partners, and lovers six months after that. They had a superstition that their intimacy made them a better law-enforcement team rather than a worse one, and indeed they seemed to have a sixth sense about each other that made them perform with uncanny coordination when working an interrogation or closing in for an arrest. On the other hand, they sometimes took daring risks in trying to protect each other, even though they tried to believe that this was not so and that they were fully able to separate their professional relationship from their romantic one.

They were both primed for what could be the biggest coup of their careers—two young detectives imagining their names in headlines, their faces on TV. Once they were so famous, they wouldn't have to worry about what other members of the precinct thought about them or whispered behind their backs. Success would silence the gossips. It might even result in money—from books, articles, personal appearances—that would help pave the way for Mike's divorce.

The FBI lab had confirmed that the bloody fingerprints found on Janice Ridenour's porch belonged to one Mathew Latham, age twenty-three. His father, named Benjamin, was deceased—a suicide. Putting two and two together, they assumed Mathew must have been using his father's name to commit a series of murders. Why his saliva would be poisonous was impossible to guess. But Janice Ridenour must have fought back and wounded him with his own knife. If he was carrying such a wound, and if electrophoresis revealed the poisonous saliva, then Mike Mordini and Mary Demchak were hot on the trail of the Vampire Killer.

Outside of apartment 304, Mordini rang the buzzer, his right hand inside his suit jacket ready to make a fast draw. Mary Demchak gripped the revolver in her purse and stayed to one side of the door, almost flattened against the wall. They heard footsteps which came to a stop, and could picture someone checking them out through the peephole. Knowing that the apartment didn't have a rear exit, just a small balcony and a three-story drop to a courtyard, Mordini barked, "Police! Open up!"

After just the slightest hesitation the door swung slowly

open and an elderly gentleman stood there holding a folded-up newspaper. He was very frail and neat, in gray trousers and vest with a crisp white shirt and a red necktie. He peered curiously at Mordini and Demchak through the top halves of his wire-rimmed bifocals. The two detectives suddenly felt foolish with their hands close to their weapons, so they converted the posture to a reach for their ID's so the old man could see that they were official personages.

He said, "Is there something I can do for you, Officer? I mean . . . er . . . Officers?"

Mary Demchak spoke up, asserting the authority that might have been taken for granted were she a man. "I'm Sergeant Demchak, and this is my partner, Sergeant Mordini. We're conducting a special investigation. What is your name, sir?"

"Er . . . Albert Hathaway is my name. Always has been." He smiled at his lame joke. "Are you looking for *me* for some reason?"

"No, Mr. Hathaway," Mary said. "As a matter of fact, we're surprised to find you here. We were under the impression that this apartment would be occupied by a Mrs. Julia Latham and her son, Mathew. Can you tell us where they *do* live?"

"No . . . no, I can't. Sorry I can't help you. I understand that a Mrs. Latham used to live here, but she moved out about a month ago. Place was vacant when me and the wife leased it. I don't believe anybody around here knows exactly where the other tenant went."

"Or her son?"

"Nope. Heard people talk about him. Most say he was a little peculiar . . . not exactly friendly. But I never heard anybody say what became of him. I expect that he and his mother are still living together . . . somewhere else."

"Thank you, Mr. Hathaway," Mordini said, fighting his disappointment. "We may come back and talk to you some other time, after we turn up more information."

"Want to talk to Margaret . . . er . . . my wife?"

"Not unless you think she can tell us more than you can."

"Nope. We never lived in this neighborhood before. We don't know too much. Not even in the way of gossip. If you don't need me anymore, why, I'll just get back to my newspaper."

"That will be fine," Mordini told him.

"Gotta keep up with the Philadelphia Eagles," the old man said, smiling. And he turned around and closed the door.

Mary Demchak shrugged and let out a tiny sigh. She told Mike, "Well, it proves nothing can ever be *easy*. But we still have a darn good lead. We'll just have to start interviewing all the tenants in this apartment building. Somebody is bound to know something critical. People don't just disappear."

"Normal people don't," Mike acknowledged. "But this guy we're after may be a different story."

"Want to start going door to door?"

"Yeah. We have no choice. But let's go at it first thing tomorrow morning. It's quitting time for normal people. Not that my wife needs to know. I told her I'd be working late."

"Dinner at my apartment," Mary suggested. "I have a nice little chicken in the crock pot. And we can stop for a bottle of white wine."

"*Two* bottles," Mike corrected. "One for dinner and one for after we make love."

"Shh!" Mary said as they headed for the elevator. "What if somebody hears you?"

The voluptuous blond airline stewardess who had stood in front of Vargo at the registration desk slowly removed her clothes while he lay naked on his hotel bed. Then, smiling sweetly, she bounced into his arms, her young, supple body hot and strong against his. He entered her with a tautness and tightness so exquisite that the fulfillment was more satisfying and more erotic than anything he had ever imagined before. Entwined around him, she eagerly received his eager thrusts . . .

. . . then she became his wife . . .

. . . he and Norma making exquisite, passionate love better than his memories of past enjoyments . . .

He woke up before he reached orgasm. Frustrated and still throbbing, he kept his hand from touching his erection. He wondered if it would ever go down.

Analyzing the dream was fairly easy, even in his agitated state. He had seen so many fine-looking young women since his arrival in Philadelphia, and he had toyed with the notion of making a move now that he was away from home. With three hundred miles between him and his wife, maybe his guilt would be less. But he knew it wouldn't. He would feel terrible afterward, even if he managed to score with the most beautiful, understanding female in the world. Cheating on Norma was like taking advantage of a cripple—the emotional cripple she had become after Kathy was killed. So Vargo would remain faithful. But he would continue to see in strange young women the image of free and pure sex that he wanted to blend with the love of his wife.

Vargo was turned off by these two so-called detectives, Mordini and Demchak. It was apparent that they were having an affair. Little looks and nuances that passed between them gave them away. They tried to carry off a self-conscious professional decorum that could only be a veneer for a deeper intimacy that could not be publicly expressed. As far as Vargo was concerned, this kind of situation was a perfect example of why it wasn't good to have women on a police force in any capacity higher than meter maid.

He denied to himself that jealousy could be prejudicing his opinion. But here he was being scrupulously faithful, which wasn't easy, while guys like Mordini took what they wanted even if they were married. Not that Mary Demchak was a prize. But most guys wouldn't kick her out of bed either. Her nose was too big; it was what kept her from being truly pretty instead of just attractive. At least she wasn't defensive about her sex the way some policewomen were; she didn't try to look and act like a man. She had a soft voice and wore a tasteful navy-blue suit with a frilly white blouse, and a touch of lipstick and perfume. Her hair was dark red and wavy. She wasn't any more than ten pounds overweight. By comparison, Mordini was skinny. If he was trying to make her work it off in the sack, the tactic was backfiring on him. He was probably wearing himself to the bone doing double duty, still trying to satisfy his wife.

Mordini and Demchak were sitting across from Vargo in a booth in a coffee shop. He had surprised them by showing up at their precinct headquarters before they even got there this morning. They had briefed him (he had been secretly delighted that they hadn't made an arrest) and then they had driven him to the scene of the Ridenour murder so he could look it over. Vargo's mind was busy the whole time trying to figure out how he could get the jump on them somehow—by pretending to work with them while hoping to stumble upon something important that he wouldn't have to let them know. In line with this strategy, he offered to canvass the apartment building where Mathew Latham used to live. "It's boring, painstaking work," he pointed out. "Maybe I ought to take it off your hands since I don't know the rest of the city as well as you two do, and it might free you to put maximum effort into areas that stand a much better chance of panning out."

"Well, at least we know now that we're looking for *two* killers," Mary Demchak said. "The prints you have from Benjamin Latham's YMCA room in Pittsburgh don't match the ones on file for Mathew. We thought for sure that Mathew and Benjamin were the same person."

"Considering the facts you had at your disposal, you had a good reason to jump the gun," Vargo said. "Let me mention, though," he added tactfully, "that our friend Mathew might not necessarily be an accomplice."

"How do you figure?" Mordini said in a contradictory tone. "Those two have the same last name, so it's logical that they must be related somehow. Therefore they're probably in cahoots. Blood is thicker than water."

"Suppose Mathew had a girlfriend and Benjamin found

out about it," Vargo postulated. "He could've attacked Janice and Mathew might've been stabbed trying to defend her."

"*Then* what happened?" Mordini challenged. "If Mathew croaked, where's his body?"

"He's not necessarily dead, Mike," Mary Demchak chipped in. "He could have dragged himself home—wherever he lives now—and maybe he died there, come to think of it. Or maybe he got himself to a hospital."

"And kicked the bucket," Mordini squelched. "Because if he's still alive and *not* Benjamin's accomplice, why didn't he report the attack on Janice?"

"You got a point there," Vargo admitted. "But suppose he *is* in a hospital . . . in intensive care . . . maybe in a coma?"

"We could go to every emergency room and show them the photo from Mathew's personnel file at Magnum Security," Mary suggested. "There aren't a great many hospitals to cover."

"Why don't you two get busy on that while I start canvassing the apartment building?" Vargo offered.

"Uh-uh," Mordini said flatly. "I think the surest way to track down Mathew is to find his mother. She's our hottest connection. And if anybody can tell us anything about *her*, it's apt to be somebody from that place she moved out of."

"Of course we might find Mathew a lot easier if we published his photograph on TV and in the newspapers," Mary Demchak said. "But then he'd realize how badly we want him, and if he's guilty of murder or simply scared to rat on Benjamin, he'd hide in the deepest hole he could find."

"And we're not releasing anything about the electrophoresis results," Mordini added. "No use panicking the public. As it stands right now, we have a sort of an advantage in that Mathew doesn't know we've got him ID'd, and the Vampire Killer doesn't even know that *we* know he's in Philadelphia."

"If he sticks around," Mary said, "and if we can find out where Mathew lives, we might be able to set a trap for both of them."

It was exactly what Vargo had in mind. But when the web was woven, he wanted very much to be the only spider in the center of it.

"We have a chance of stopping him before someone else dies," Mordini mused. "If his usual pattern holds true, we have about three weeks before he strikes again."

27

Mathew Latham didn't know much about family history. Benjamin had questioned him but was disappointed in the yield: a few paltry anecdotes, probably exaggerated, about Lathams swimming in cash during the Roaring Twenties. His ignorance of things past didn't seem to bother Mathew. But then what could one expect of a citizen of this pop throwaway culture where anything that wasn't made of plastic couldn't be expected to last more than five years?

Mathew knew that there used to be Lathams living in New York and Chicago, but he had no idea what had happened to them, or even if they were still alive. "My mother might know something," he said. "Want me to phone her?" Benjamin turned down the offer because presumably Julia Latham had skipped town on the money Lenora had paid her for the bogus newspaper article, and he didn't want Mathew to find out about that just yet. But he wished that Lenora had thought to ask some more questions during her interview with Julia.

One day Benjamin sat down with his research notes and figured out that he was Mathew's great-great-great-great-great-uncle, and after a moment of deliberation he told Mathew so—for the shock value. His idea was that he might go on to tell more of his life story in a serious way or he might play it as a joke, depending upon how Mathew reacted.

"I already doped *that* out a long time ago," Mathew retorted, his characteristic flippancy undiminished by the fact that he was still recuperating from his wounds, lying flat on his back on the couch. "I *told* you I know who you are," he added, unblinkingly meeting Benjamin's stare.

"I thought you were just babbling that night because you were in shock after the girl shot you," Benjamin said.

Mathew didn't answer verbally but let his smirk contradict Benjamin's supposition. After a while he said, "I've been keeping a scrapbook on you. I'm glad we found each other. I want you to tell me your secrets . . . so I can become like you."

Having heard the conversation from the bedroom, Lenora came through the doorway and stood by the table where Benjamin sat with his papers spread out in front of him. She placed her hand comfortingly on his shoulder.

"It would be a grave mistake to wish to become like me," Benjamin said for the benefit of both Mathew and Lenora.

"Hmph!" Mathew snorted. "Lenora is already assuming your nature, whether you realize it or not. She thinks she has to be afraid of *me,* but it's the other way around. I'm scared to wake up some night and find her sucking my blood."

"Nonsense!" Benjamin exploded. "Your rantings are those of a madman!"

"Takes one to know one," Mathew jeered.

Benjamin fought to get his temper under control and let the confrontation simmer down. When his eyes met Lenora's he saw no fear or hatred in them—only love and support. For that he was thankful. He considered himself supremely fortunate to have found such a woman.

Was she becoming like him? In his heart he knew it was so. He was partly joyful and partly fearful over the changes he had wrought in her.

He told himself that now that Mathew was recovering, Lenora was in too much danger. She had the pistol—but a lot of good it had done Janice Ridenour. Besides, if shots went off in the hotel suite the place would soon be swarming with police.

Mathew was trying to make *himself* look like the one who had something to fear—maybe this psychotic delusion would form the core of his excuse for eventually attacking Lenora. The man hated (and perhaps really did fear) *all* women. His warp was pathological. The way his eyes followed Lenora around the suite was positively unnerving. Who could predict what he might do to her if he got the chance, now that he was getting his strength back? The safest thing would be to separate the two for a while, till Mathew could be sent out into the world on his own.

Benjamin reluctantly decided to send Lenora away on a trip to New York and Chicago. Her mission would be to follow up on the family-tree leads that must eventually be pursued in those two cities.

To allay their suspicions that he might be a grandstander, Vargo let Mordini and Demchak interview the tenants of the apartment building while he questioned present and past employees of Magnum Security. He was hoping to find somebody who had an idea where Mathew Latham might have applied for a new job. But Mathew's supervisor said he had just up and quit without giving notice one day in July after he picked up his final paycheck. It seemed as if the young man had wanted to disappear—drop from sight—as far as past acquaintances were concerned. Nobody he had worked with at Magnum knew much about him. They all described him as a loner, hard to get close to.

Vargo interviewed twenty-three persons who had had

contact with Mathew when he was a security guard. Some of these people had been co-workers, while others were employees of firms where Mathew had guarded. Just getting around to all these people and places was tiring and time-consuming. Vargo kept doggedly at it through the weekend and into the following week. He didn't uncover one single fact that looked promising.

But neither did Mordini and Demchak. Vargo kept in constant touch with them. Nobody at the apartment building could tell them anything pertaining to the present whereabouts of Julia Latham. The landlord of the building happened to live there, in one of his own apartments. He said that Julia had given him no forwarding address; she had merely cleared out, letting her deposit take care of her final month's rent. On her lease application her place of employment was listed as Luigi's Palace. Mordini and Demchak spoke with the owner and employees of the beauty salon, only to find that Julia Latham had collected her pay on a Saturday about a month ago and had not shown up for work the following Monday.

"It seems obvious that the mother and son both want to vanish," Mordini said. "Maybe they're *both* involved in the Ridenour murder. Sweet old mom could be the one who turned Mathew into a homicidal lunatic."

"Sounds like a plot for a movie," Mary Demchak chided.

"But it's really not a bad theory either," said Vargo, trying to keep on Mordini's good side.

They were in the same coffee shop where they had discussed strategy on Vargo's first full day in Philadelphia. A week had now gone by. They all felt as if they had been chasing moonbeams.

"What's left to do?" Mordini asked. "Cover the hospital emergency rooms?"

"I already did," Vargo admitted. "I got a big fat zero."

Mordini and Demchak raised their eyebrows. They didn't know whether to feel relieved that the work was done or miffed that Vargo had taken care of it on his own. Of course it had been his idea. But they still had a sneaking suspicion he had been hoping to upstage them.

"What's the matter?" Vargo asked innocently. "I thought if Mathew was in a hospital we should get to him before they released him. I didn't do the wrong thing, did I?"

"No . . . no," Mordini said grumpily. "I just can't believe we're hitting so many dead ends."

"We're into another weekend already," Mary Demchak said, "and I can't think of another avenue to pursue."

"At the moment, neither can I," said Vargo. And it was the truth. Much more had been done than just the canvassing of the apartment building, the hospitals, and the people from Magnum Security. For instance, a computer check had been run through the Pennsylvania Department of Transportation, but it didn't show any vehicles registered under the names of Julia, Mathew, or Benjamin Latham. Another check through the Social Security system had failed to turn up any more recent places of employment for Mathew *or* Julia Latham.

"Maybe we should publish Mathew's photograph and description," Mary Demchak suggested. "And get all the law-enforcement agencies on an all-out manhunt."

"It would blow our chance of setting a trap," Vargo said.

"That's right," Mordini agreed promptly. "Why don't we let it rest till Monday? Give ourselves a couple of days to clear our heads—make room for an inspiration." He added, as if joking, "They say good detective work is nine-tenths perspiration and one-tenth inspiration, so maybe we ought to make room for the missing one tenth."

Vargo chuckled good-naturedly. "You got a point there, Mike," he acknowledged blithely. And to himself he thought: You're not fooling anybody, pal. You don't want some other cop to have a crack at the Vampire Killer any more than I do. The prudent thing for all of us to do would be to put out an APB on Mathew. But secretly we three have the same reason for not wanting to do so.

Going on the assumption that they all had an unspoken understanding, Vargo said to Mordini and Demchak, "What kind of heat do you take by waiting? Will your bosses in the Homicide Division give you that much free rein?"

"We don't have to file our report till Monday," Mary Demchak said.

"Besides, there are still some folks who used to be tenants at Julia Latham's apartment building that I haven't been able to reach yet," Mordini added, possibly truthfully.

"I don't think it would be wise to use our last trump until all our other cards have been played," Mary Demchak concluded with a straight face.

"Okay," said Vargo. "Let's hope that one of us lights the little light bulb sometime between now and Monday morning."

On Friday night Lenora phoned Benjamin from Chicago. He took her call in the bedroom of the suite at the Welcome Hotel. The door was closed so Mathew wouldn't hear; he was watching TV and playing solitaire at the round table in the anteroom. He had recovered from his surgery so well by now that convalescent confinement was making him fidgety.

After exchanging sentiments of longing and endearment, Lenora told Benjamin, "As near as I can figure out after running myself ragged for the past four days, there aren't any more offspring still in Chicago. How's Mathew?" she asked ominously.

"Better . . . much better. He's up and about now and starting to feel quite frisky. I expect that by the time you come home in a week or so, he'll be gone."

"I don't trust him enough to even remain in the same city with him. When I come back, why don't we both ditch him? We can drive to New York and stay for a while . . . together. There are eight million people there. We can get ourselves comfortably lost."

"It sounds like a wise move, love. Which hotel have you made a reservation for, so I know how to reach you?"

"I haven't made it yet, but it's going to be the Montclair Plaza. I'm going to relax here in Chicago tomorrow, maybe take in a movie and have a nice dinner. Then I'll catch a flight to New York on Sunday."

"Well . . . enjoy yourself without me. I miss you, and I love you very much."

"I love *you,* Benjamin."

When Benjamin came out of the bedroom and into the anteroom, Mathew said, "I'm going stir crazy. I've got to get out of here."

"Nothing is stopping you if you think you're well enough."

Mathew thought it over. Was he really as strong as he felt? Or would all the vigor go out of him once he tried to do for himself? "I don't mean to leave permanently," he said. "Not just yet. I only meant that I've got to get some air . . . and some exercise. We should stay in touch, you and I, even after I'm on my own. I want to be *like* you. We're already alike in so many ways. . . ."

"I'm not like you," Benjamin contradicted swiftly. "My needs are different from yours."

"Not *so* different," Mathew said. "You and I are both predators. We take from others, and we leave them dead."

Benjamin was at a loss for a suitable reply. The facts of Mathew's argument were unassailable, but he still felt that there was a basic difference between himself and Mathew that he could not articulate. Maybe it was wishful thinking to suppose he was any better than his descendant. Perhaps he had no right to imagine he was morally superior, as if he existed on a different plane.

"You have special powers," Mathew said. "There is an aura about you that ordinary mortals don't have. Just the fact that you didn't die back in 1782, that you escaped the noose, means that you may not be *able* to be killed—"

"You long for immortality?" Benjamin interrupted coldly. "I can tell you that I do not know whether or not I possess it. In this I am no different from any other man who wonders if he will have a life of the spirit beyond physical death."

"But at least you have had longevity," Mathew countered. "That much is beyond question."

"I did not choose to become what I am," Benjamin said. "If it has its advantages, it also has its horrors."

"I wouldn't complain if I could share your lot!" Mathew declared. "Tell me—*how* can it be done? What is the secret of the transformation?"

"I honestly don't know."

"Poppycock! You are doing it to Lenora!"

"I am being candid with you. Whatever is happening to her, I am not cognizant of the hows and whys of it. And if I knew how, I would probably put a stop to it."

"Probably?" Mathew repeated ironically.

Benjamin did not answer.

"You don't want to be alone in the world," Mathew told him. "If you truly believe that your motive for killing is more noble than mine, then make *my* need the same as yours so that *I* can be ennobled."

Again Benjamin could not think of a reply. It startled him that a man as crazy as Mathew could still be so lucid in some areas.

"How is it done?" Mathew persisted. "If you withdrew a little of my blood, a bit at a time, would that effect the transformation?"

"My tongue would poison you, and your blood would do the same to me," Benjamin said, voicing what he knew instinctively. "We both would die. The craving must never be incestuous. Blood relatives are in these matters anathema to one another."

"Then Lenora could do it for me," Mathew said. *"She* and I aren't related. Once her transformation is complete, she could help me with mine!"

"I cannot tell you with confidence that the method you suggest could work," Benjamin said. "In my own case mythology does not seem to be borne out by experience. Do I have fangs? Do I sleep in a coffin?" He paused to let these points sink in. "I counsel caution. In trying for eternal life and all the other so-called gifts that you covet, you *may* unintentionally bring yourself to a premature and permanent grave."

28

Mordini had spoken of inspiration, but all Vargo could think of doing was more hard work—boring, possibly futile hard work. The idea he had was too mundane to be called inspired. To pull it off he should have a platoon of investigators working under him. Probably Mordini and Demchak would've joined in if Vargo had asked them, but he figured that if they were too stupid or lazy to think of it on their own they might as well spend the weekend getting laid. He intended to start canvassing the neighborhood surrounding Mathew and Julia Latham's apartment building. If he got lucky and struck a lead, he didn't want to share it with anybody.

He had an eight-by-ten blowup of Mathew's ID photo from the Magnum Security personnel file. Somebody in the neighborhood ought to remember the young man; he would have been fairly conspicuous in his security guard uniform going to and from work. Maybe he had tried to impress a waitress in a restaurant, a salesgirl in a store, or even some young kids. If he was the type who liked to brag about what a hotshot "policeman" he was, maybe he bragged louder when he quit the job at Magnum to "move on to something bigger and better."

To Vargo, anybody with a gun and a badge who wasn't a real cop was a punk playing a role. Contrary to what he had told Mordini and Demchak, he was convinced that Mathew was an accomplice in the Ridenour murder. Everything about Mathew smelled: his being with Benjamin Latham, his reputation as a loner and a social misfit, his lack of any previous relationship with Janice Ridenour (according to witnesses who said she hadn't dated anyone in months, ever since her divorce). Punks like Mathew usually tried to get ego gratification in predictable ways. They were all Walter Mittys whose fantasies could turn more and more perverted with each personal frustration, each bitter failure, each confrontation with the realization that they were really ineffectual and dull.

On Saturday morning, after a hearty breakfast at his hotel, Vargo took a taxi to Race Street in Chinatown. He would start close to the apartment building and fan out, hitting the high spots.

At least the weather was good. Sunny but cool. A perfect climate for his dark blue suit, white shirt, and blue-and-white striped tie—an outfit in which he managed to look rather handsome, debonair, and "official" all at the same time. At least he wouldn't sweat too much wearing off shoe leather, walking from one commercial enterprise to the next.

There was a drugstore right across the street from the apartment building, and he went in, hoping Mathew Latham was a pill freak. Of course in this day and age that wouldn't distinguish many young people from the rest of the horde. So maybe Mathew liked to read "true detective" magazines; there were slews of them on the rack at the head of the first aisle, all with cover photos of voluptuous young ladies trussed up and being menaced by rapists, gunmen, and/or knife-wielders.

Vargo noticed a plain-looking girl of about fifteen

working the checkout register, and he knew he'd want to talk with her, but first he would search out her boss. He moved down the aisle, past a couple of browsing middle-aged ladies, to the pharmacy counter. An elderly gent in a white coat was at work filling prescriptions, but he stopped what he was doing and asked Vargo if he could help him.

"Are you Mr. Rader?" Vargo asked, because the place was called Rader's Drugstore.

"Yes. Are you a salesman?" Rader inquired, looking Vargo over, obviously taking note of the fact that he wasn't carrying a briefcase or a portfolio.

"No, I'm a policeman," Vargo answered. "May I speak with you for a few minutes?"

"Everything is perfectly aboveboard here, Officer." It wasn't said indignantly, merely factually. Vargo tentatively sized Rader up as an honorable, fastidious professional of the old school. He had a sober, grandfatherly look about him, like the trusty pharmacist of many TV commercials, but in his case the casting seemed authentic.

After introducing himself and showing his ID, Vargo explained, "A young man who used to live in the apartment building across the way could turn out to be an important witness in a case I'm working on, but he apparently moved away and I've been unable to locate him. His name is Mathew Latham. Here's his picture. I wonder if you recall seeing him in your store at any time."

Rader took the eight-by-ten and scrutinized it very carefully. "I think he was in here a few times," he said finally. "I think I remember filling a prescription or two for him. But I'm pretty sure I haven't seen him recently. What did you say his last name was?"

"Latham. You may have seen him from time to time in a security guard uniform. He used to work for Magnum Security. When he was in uniform the last name would've been on a white-on-black plastic plate over his breast pocket."

"Ah . . . yes," Rader said. "Libritabs."

"What?"

"Tranquilizers. For his mother. Wait a minute . . . I can look up the last name."

Vargo stood by stifling his urge to feel hopeful while Rader flipped through an index file of customers and prescriptions. It would be a miracle if Mathew came back here for anything after he changed his address.

"Here it is," said Rader. "Julia Latham . . . an attractive woman. Didn't outwardly seem the type to be suffering from anxiety. Now I remember her *and* her son. But the young man hasn't been in here for quite some time. As a matter of fact, you can see right here that the last time I gave Julia her Libritabs was over a month ago."

"Figures," Vargo muttered, examining the notations on the prescription record. Suddenly he brightened, realizing that the data naturally included the name of Julia's doctor. "This Dr. Abraham," he said. "Can you tell me his address and phone number?"

"Certainly," Rader answered, perking up. "I see what you're driving at. Maybe you can find out where the Lathams are living now if they're still going to the same physician. Here it is: Dr. Louis J. Abraham, 210 Broughton Court, Philadelphia. That's his home address. I can give you his professional address, too, as well as his home and office telephone numbers."

"Excellent," Vargo said. "All of this may turn out to be extremely important."

"I hope so," the pharmacist said. "Why don't you let me try those numbers for you on my phone back here. The cord reaches. If I get an answer, I'll let you take the receiver."

"Fine. Thank you."

But nobody answered at Dr. Abraham's home, and dialing the office only produced a recorded message that visiting hours wouldn't commence again until Monday morning at nine. Disappointed, Vargo resolved to continue trying the doctor's home number throughout the day and into tomorrow if necessary. As he had done so many times when he or someone close to him was ill, he puzzled over why medical professionals were so expensive and so inaccessible. He asked Mr. Rader, "Any chance we might reach this Dr. Abraham at some hospital in the city?"

"No way of telling which one he may be connected with.

Looks like he's taken the weekend off, if you ask me. But you could try calling every hospital."

"I might just resort to that," Vargo said. "By the way, are you certain any of those pills weren't for Mathew?"

"Well . . . I don't have any prescription record for him, so I know I never filled anything for him. The Libritabs were in Julia's name, so I assumed she was the one taking them. Once they leave the store, of course, I can't be responsible."

"I just wanted to be sure," Vargo said. "Because there's some indication that Mathew may be unstable. Has the girl at the checkout counter worked here for very long?"

"Marlene? Been here for six months. But only on weekends this time of year. She's a senior in high school."

"Looks younger."

"Uh-huh."

"I was wondering if she might know something about Mathew. Maybe he tried to flirt with her or something."

"Not that I ever noticed," said Rader doubtfully. "But you can certainly ask her."

"I will," said Vargo. "Thanks for all your help."

"Good luck to you."

Vargo had to wait for the line of customers to dissipate before he got a chance to talk with Marlene. She didn't strike him as being particularly bright and seemed to move in slow motion. Her face turned crimson as soon as Vargo told her he was a cop, but she failed to recognize Mathew Latham from his photo even though she must have caught at least glimpses of him from time to time when he came into the store.

For the next several hours he traipsed from one business establishment to another—restaurants, dry cleaners, laundromats, haberdasheries, five-and-dimes—giving his pitch and showing the eight-by-ten and getting zilch in the way of useful info. A few people recognized Mathew's face and had trivial recollections of him or Julia, but nobody could furnish anything that remotely resembled a lead to their present whereabouts. The only thing all this was doing for Vargo was eliminating stab-in-the-dark prospects that would have nagged him if he hadn't done the legwork.

By two o'clock he was tired and hungry. Seduced by the smell of Chinese cooking, he went into a restaurant and used the pay phone in the foyer to try once more to reach Dr. Abraham. He had dialed the doctor's home number about a dozen times while making his rounds and had never gotten an answer. This time was no exception.

He was sliding the photo of Mathew Latham into its manila envelope when the pretty Chinese waitress made a shaky move and poured tea all over the tablecloth. He scooted his chair backward so his trousers wouldn't get drenched and snatched the envelope off the table to protect the photo. "Oh! I—I sorry," the waitress babbled. "I clean up." In a dither, she whisked duck sauce, soy sauce, and utensils aside and rolled the sopping tablecloth into a ball.

"It's okay," Vargo said. "No harm done."

"So sorry," she repeated, more upset than the incident called for.

At first he attributed her excessive reaction to Oriental shyness and politeness, but then he noticed how her large black eyes darted when they fell on the manila envelope he was holding, and suspected that it was the photo that had shaken her up. He let her go away to get a fresh tablecloth and napkin, and while she was gone he tucked the envelope under his chair so the sight of it wouldn't continue to rattle her. All through the serving and eating of his lunch, he acted as reserved and gentle and mannerly as he could. The girl behaved very efficiently but did not smile. She was quite petite, with long, straight black hair and a delicate, symmetrically sculpted facial structure.

Vargo left a fat tip on the table for her. Then he paid his check at the cash register by the door and got a receipt from a handsome, slender Chinese man.

"Are you the owner?" Vargo asked.

"I wish so," he said without any accent. "The owner is Mr. Charles Yee. I am his cousin. My name is Gordon Yung. I hope that you enjoyed our Bamboo Garden and we will see you again soon."

"You certainly shall if I get the opportunity," Vargo said, returning Gordon Yung's gracious smile. "In the meantime, I wonder if you might help me." He opened his wallet and showed his ID. "You see, I'm a policeman and I'm trying to locate a fellow who used to live about a block from here. Maybe you don't know him by name, but I can show you his picture just in case he ever was a customer of yours."

Gordon Yung started to look alarmed by the time Vargo got into his last sentence. His eyes flashed angrily and his lips tightened into a grimace. Vargo had to yank the photo away when it was only halfway out of the envelope for fear that Mr. Yung would grab it and crumple it up.

"Him!" Yung spat. "The animal who tried to seduce my sister!" His eyes flashed momentarily in the direction of the waitress who had tended to Vargo and was now resetting the table.

"Do you know his name?" Vargo asked to confirm the identification.

"That animal! His name is Mathew Latham."

Since it was midafternoon there weren't any customers in the Bamboo Garden right now, but Vargo decided to opt for as much privacy as possible. He asked, "Do you have an office or a room in the back where I can interview you and your sister?"

"Yes," Gordon Yung said. "A room next to the kitchen. I must first get somebody to watch the register. Then you and Li Yung and I can have our talk. I *tried* to get the animal arrested three months ago—but the police said he had not broken the law yet, so nothing could be done!"

Vargo's hopes sank. If the incident was already three months old, then Mathew Latham must have left the neighborhood sometime after it happened. Gordon and Li Yung weren't likely to have had any contact with him after that.

Vargo waited until Gordon Yung returned from somewhere in the back of the restaurant. When he did so he was accompanied by a frail and delicate-looking old Chinese man in a gray waiter's jacket, who silently took up a post next to the cash register. Vargo then followed Gordon and his sister into the small room next to the kitchen which apparently served as an office, for it contained a card table and some folding chairs, and on the table was a black phone, a pad and pencil, and stacks of bills and purchase orders.

"I didn't mean to scare you before," Vargo said to Li, who averted her eyes shyly. "It was purely an accident. I just happened to be putting the photo away after using it all morning in my search for the man. If he's done something wrong I want to bring him to justice. Your brother told you I'm a policeman, didn't he?"

She nodded.

"Actually I'm a state trooper. I've come here all the way from Pittsburgh because we have reason to suspect that Mathew Latham may be connected with some crimes there."

"What sort of crimes?" Gordon Yung interrupted.

"I'm sorry," said Vargo, "but I'm not at liberty to say. Not until we have our man in custody."

"Probably something horrible!" Gordon Yung blurted angrily.

Trying to put Li Yung at ease, Vargo asked her some introductory questions in a soft, polite manner. He got her to repeat her name and tell him her age, which turned out to be only sixteen. To give her a chance to relax some more, he asked where she went to school, what her hours of work in the restaurant were, and so forth. At last he encouraged her to tell him what had happened between her and Mathew Latham.

"He . . . he comes almost every day here . . . at lunchtime," she began hesitantly.

She had an accent and a habit of talking in present tense that at first made Vargo think that Mathew was still coming to the restaurant. Li started to say something else, but Gordon interrupted heatedly:

"I *saw* the way he looked at her. I didn't like it, but he was a customer. If he had touched her I would have had him thrown out!"

"Please, Mr. Yung," Vargo said. "I understand how you feel. But it's important for me to get this information in Li's own words. That way your testimony can corroborate, and a court of law will have to pay attention to it."

"Sorry . . . sorry," Gordon said. "I am only trying to help, but I can't help it if I get angry."

"Li," Vargo asked, "during what time period did the incident with Mr. Latham occur?"

"In June and July," she answered after a moment. Then she went on, apologetically, as if she rather than Mathew had something to be ashamed of. "He always tells me I look nice. He pays me flattery. And I have never been out with a man . . . so his words . . . sometimes they make me feel good . . . and I smile. He starts to believe I like him. Maybe I do . . . a little . . . but what I feel, it is not how he says. It is not love. But he wants to think otherwise. He likes to sit where I must be the one to wait on him, and he always comes in wearing his uniform. Then he leaves big tips . . . two and three, sometimes five dollars . . . almost the cost of the subgum chow mein special that he usually orders. And he starts asking me to go out with him, but I tell him my father is old-fashioned Chinese man and will never allow such a thing."

"Did you tell your father or brother about Mathew's advances?" Vargo asked.

"No! She did not tell us at first!" Gordon fumed. "For this we were very angry with her when she finally came crying to us." He frowned sternly at his young and pretty sister to once again impress upon her the error of her ways. Then he said to Vargo, "Sorry. I promised not to interrupt. I won't speak again unless I am spoken to."

"All right," Vargo said mildly. "Li, so far what you've told me isn't so terrible. What did Mathew do that actually frightened you?"

"He wants me . . . to run away with him . . . to be his girlfriend. He says we will flee to New York and get married. At first I giggle when he talks like this, because we have never even kissed like Americans do . . . and we have not courted in the Chinese way either. But then he starts to scare me, because he whispers wild plans every chance he gets, every time he comes in. Finally he says he has enough money saved, and he has a gun . . . and he will come for me after the restaurant closes late on Saturday . . . and he will shoot whoever tries to stop us from being together." Li bit her lip. Tears rolled down her high cheeks and she trembled, reliving bad memories of a tricky situation that a savvy, independent American girl would have handled with far less difficulty.

"What did you tell him?" Vargo asked.

Li said, "I say I cannot go with him. I have my school and my family to worry about me, and I am needed here in the restaurant. But he gets mad and says no one will keep us apart. If I do not love him enough to defy the world, I will learn to revere and honor him more deeply after he rescues me from my prison of a life."

"That is when she told us what was going on," Gordon Yung said, unable to censor himself. "And I called the police to tell them about the kidnapping this animal was planning—and that is when they said they could do nothing until an actual deed was committed! I informed *them* that I was not going to wait until my sister disappeared. So I hired some Chinese men to talk sense to the American animal."

"You mean you had him beat up?" Vargo asked. "I won't tell on you if you did. I'm just trying to get to the bottom of this."

"I did not care to know what their exact methods would be," Gordon replied enigmatically, obviously proud that he had taken the protection of his sister into his own hands. "I merely wanted to be satisfied that Li would be safe. I believe I got what I paid for, because the animal stopped coming into this restaurant. But from that time to this we have always been worried that he might seek revenge by carrying out his design of stealing her."

"You mean that was the end of it?" Vargo asked. "Nothing worse ever happened?"

Gordon Yung shot him a piercing look. "I hope you are not disappointed that we did not endure worse misery."

"No, no, of course I didn't mean it that way," Vargo defended. "I was just hoping that you knew what became of Mathew. But you're telling me you never saw him again?"

"And good riddance," said Gordon.

"You didn't keep tabs on him?" Vargo persisted. "Even

though you were afraid of him? You didn't make sure he was occupied in some way that would keep him away from your doorstep?"

"I am sure that the fear the Chinese men put into him was far worse than our fear," Gordon said.

"I see him only one time," Li Yung piped up. "About four or five weeks ago. He goes past the Chinese grocery store and I see him through the window. I jump when I realize it is he, for he does not wear his police uniform. Instead he has on gray trousers and gray shirt, and on the back of the shirt is a red design like a circle with a Z."

Vargo perked up. Unless he was reading too much into it, what she had just described sounded like it might be the emblem of Mathew's next place of employment. "Think carefully, Li," he said with controlled excitement. "This could be very important. Was there any printing on the shirt? Like maybe the name of a company?"

"No," she answered, mulling it over. "Nothing else did I see. Just the red circle with the Z inside of it."

"You didn't see the front of the shirt?" Vargo probed.

"No. Sorry."

He decided that his questioning of the Yungs wasn't going to get him any further, so he thanked them for their cooperation. Before leaving the Bamboo Garden, he told them, "If Mathew Latham is guilty of the crimes we suspect him of, he is an extremely dangerous young man. I don't think he'll come back here, but he may. Be wary. Try to stay away from him if he shows up. And telephone me right away. The numbers where I can be reached are on this slip of paper. Keep it handy. As long as Mathew is still on the loose, you can't be too careful."

"The animal has ruined the peacefulness of our family and is yet like a dark shadow over us," Gordon Yung complained. "Do you think you will be able to apprehend him?"

"I believe so," Vargo said. "But of course only time will tell. If I'm successful it may be because of the information you gave me. I'll do the best I can."

"You have our blessing," said Gordon Yung, and Li nodded in bashful concurrence.

Outside on the sidewalk, Vargo wondered how to proceed . . . how to find out what the red Z in a circle stood for. Most business enterprises were closed for the weekend, even if he could determine which one used that logo. It didn't even have to *be* a business enterprise. A wacko like Mathew might have some kind of iron-on emblem on his shirt pertaining to a pop fad, a rock band, even a crazy religion. Maybe a cult of which *he* was the only leader and follower. A cult of insanity and murder with the Vampire Killer as its idol.

29

When Benjamin stepped out of the shower and opened the bathroom door to let out steam, he noticed a strange quietness about the hotel suite even though the TV was on fairly loud. Instinctively, and with a jolt of panic, he realized that Mathew must be gone. Still toweling himself off, he dripped water on the carpet in the anteroom as he peered through the doorway into the empty bedroom.

He dressed as fast as he could. In his black shirt, black trousers, and black denim jacket he closed the door of the suite and hurried to the elevator. He had to find Mathew and bring him back here. If the unstable young man did something to get himself arrested, the police might force him or trick him into telling all he knew.

Down on the street, Benjamin wondered which direction to take. It was ten o'clock of a warm November night, a Saturday night, and the sidewalks were teeming. In an intellectual sense it was totally absurd to hope to catch up with one individual in a city of two million people. But

Mathew must not have had time to get very far. And besides, Benjamin had come to believe in forces other than those of the intellect. Something told him he could draw an azimuth on Mathew. After a while, without knowing why, he wanted to walk toward Chinatown. An extrasensory pull which might be akin to the homing instinct of birds seemed to be drawing him toward his quarry in the same way he had been guided when he needed to find Andy Bonner on the night Andy was killed.

By the time he crossed Cherry Street, four blocks from the Welcome Hotel, he had the feeling he was getting close. On Thirteenth Street, halfway between Cherry and Race, the frequency sensation in his brain was like what a radio might feel when its antenna was being rotated in the approximate direction of the signal it wanted to receive.

Rounding the corner of Race and Thirteenth, he was in a state of high-strung alertness and caution. He didn't want Mathew to spot *him* first. He stuck to the shadows as much as possible, out of range of the tree-branch patterns of light cast by the streetlamps and the multicolored neons of restaurants, shops, and taverns. Every time a cluster of people burst out of some doorway he was scared that Mathew might be among them to make split-second eye contact, then take to his heels. He was keyed for a chase to begin at any instant.

When he found Mathew finally, he didn't see him in the conventional sense, but felt his presence in the darkness of an alcove formed by a narrow walkway between a boutique and a bicycle shop. Across the street, Benjamin ducked into the entranceway of a shoe store that was closed for the evening, the display window dimly lit, so that he could pretend to look at shoes while waiting to see what kind of move Mathew would make. At first he feared that Mathew had noticed him, but the piercing gaze he felt coming as near to him as the whine of a bullet was directed toward the pagodalike facade of the restaurant next door called the Bamboo Garden.

He tried to get a reading on Mathew's thoughts, but he couldn't penetrate. Maybe it was the distance. But he doubted it. He remembered when he had attempted hypnosis to dull Mathew's pain before operating on his bullet wounds, and it hadn't worked. He had speculated that the brain waves of a psychotic might at certain times be immune to mind control. Perhaps Mathew had gone out into the night alone because right at this moment the demons of his subconscious had an especially strong hold on him.

The Bamboo Garden had red double doors ornamented with carved silver dragons. The door on the right opened and a group of Chinese people came out and stood around gabbing and giggling. There was a frail old man, a short, plump woman with a shopping bag, two younger men, and an exceptionally pretty young lady. One of the younger men turned his key in a double set of locks and tugged on both doors to make sure they were secure. Then the group walked in a cluster down the sidewalk.

After they had gone about thirty feet, and while they had their backs to him, Mathew crept out from his dark hole. He was wearing clothes that belonged to Benjamin: a pair of denim trousers, a gray work shirt, a dark blue jacket. He crossed the street, threading his way between slow-moving automobiles. His eyes were riveted intensely upon the group up ahead, and his primary focus was the pretty Chinese girl. He was so wrapped up in her that Benjamin didn't think anything else could faze him.

As Mathew tailed the people from the restaurant, Benjamin followed Mathew. The procession got no farther than a parking lot at the end of the block. There the young Chinese man who had locked up the restaurant paid the lot attendant while the rest of his people piled into a little yellow Datsun. Then he slipped behind the wheel and drove off. Mathew Latham stood watching in a slumped, dejected way, a completely forlorn expression on his face, and Benjamin had the amazing intuition that the strong emotion that rayed out from his descendant to the girl in the rear seat of the Datsun was as near as Mathew could ever feel to genuine love.

Then, the object of that feeling gone, it warped and slithered and gleamed with slimy hatred for the other members of the sex that the love object represented.

Benjamin could feel the change as if he were watching a time-lapse film of an unhealthy organ turning cancerous. With a new and malignant purposefulness, Mathew started walking, and Benjamin followed.

Nineteen-year-old Cynthia Jensen played her violin in parks and on street corners for the small bills and change that people tossed into her open violin case. The money that she made by posing in the nude for classes at the Art Academy of Philadelphia paid for her meager living expenses, and the violin money paid for her ballet lessons. She was as talented a violinist as she was a dancer, and she loved both equally well, so deciding which area to concentrate on had been a hard choice. Every now and then she still vacillated.

She didn't want people to recognize her out on the streets playing the violin for money, since it was almost like begging. So she always wore a brunette wig and a tossel cap and a special set of old worn-out clothes that disguised her appearance and even (she hoped) wrung a bit of sympathy from her audience of passersby so they were more likely to dig deeply into their pockets.

Some people liked her playing so well that they bothered to ask which corner she might be on on certain nights so they might come around and hear her. To her delight and chagrin, she had a bit of a following. It was pleasant to think she was appreciated, but she didn't want to be remembered as a former street waif after she made her mark as a ballerina.

Tonight she was working the corner of Fifth and Walnut, opposite Independence Hall. It was a location she used frequently because of the tourist traffic. She was playing Mozart—the classical stuff fit the starving-artist image she needed to project in order to pluck the purse strings of her patrons. Every five or six numbers, she would swing into a rousing country hoedown in case there were any foot-stompers in the crowd who wouldn't cough up any cash till they heard her "settin' the fiddle on fire."

Accepting applause and donations after an excerpt from Mozart's Fifth Violin Concerto, she noticed one of her regulars coming across the street—a young man named Mathew. He hadn't been around for about a month and a half, and she was glad to see him again; sometimes he tossed as much as five bucks into the hopper. On some of the hot summer evenings, he had even brought her a Coke or a Pepsi to sip between numbers. She doubted that he could be interested in her romantically, because she always dressed so scruffily that she wouldn't have been attractive to *anybody* even if she were pretty. Anyway, he never really flirted with her, and she thought that she probably didn't want him to; that way their relationship could stay platonic and safe. He was too good-looking for her. Just a nice guy who loved classical music, even if it came from an ugly duckling.

There were only five or six people gathered around her now, as most of the ones who had stayed till the end of her last selection had then moved on. "Hi, Mathew," she said, flashing him a smile as he came and stood behind the small group on the corner.

He gave a curt nod, wishing she hadn't spoken to him, because now a couple of heads were turning, looking at him. But he told himself that they probably wouldn't remember him anyway. They were probably tourists who wouldn't linger in the city for long and would spend time sucking up historical sites instead of paying attention to news bulletins. None of them would connect him to Cynthia after she was dead.

The violinist was excellent, Benjamin realized. Her Mozart reached out and touched him, penetrating his other concerns. If she played a loud, twangy guitar she'd probably be in some huge auditorium in front of thousands of screaming young dope fiends. But here she was in rags before fewer than a dozen people. And one of them intended to kill her.

Benjamin considered just marching over there and collaring Mathew and dragging him back to the hotel. He cursed the side of himself that held back, the part of him that was fascinated by the hunt and wanted to watch the methods and maneuvers of another predator. He had felt that finding his descendant was the key to learning something vital about *himself*. Tonight, for some reason, that feeling was more vivid than ever, and it seemed that he ought not to meddle with it but to simply let matters take their course.

It was almost midnight. Cynthia decided to call it an evening. She figured she had done pretty well, around thirty dollars for the five hours she had worked. She wouldn't stick around to count her take on the street where someone might snatch it from her; instead she'd close it up inside the violin case along with her instrument, then count it back at her apartment. Before she could shut the lid, Mathew dropped in a five-dollar bill. Then he said, "Let me buy you a cup of coffee?"

What harm could it do? The night had turned a bit chilly, and she was seven blocks from where she lived. It wouldn't hurt to have a man along for protection while she covered at least part of the distance. "I know a good place," she said, "where we can get some espresso. Raffaele's, on Chestnut Street."

He was such a gentleman, he carried her case for her. She trusted him with it. Somebody who had given her a lot of money all those times wasn't going to rob her and run. She was self-conscious walking with him, though. "I look like such a ragamuffin," she said. "I really wouldn't mind if you just strolled ahead and pretended not to know me till we get to the café and can hide in one of the high-backed booths where no one but the waitress will see us."

The more he heard about Raffaele's, the more he liked it. High-backed booths, probably dimly lit for atmosphere. Probably even the waitress wouldn't remember him if he stayed low-key and mumbled into the menu while ordering. "Why should I be ashamed to be seen with a virtuoso violinist?" he said, laying it on thick. "No doubt everyone who sees us is envying me for being chosen to carry your instrument."

"Oh, I'm sure," she said self-deprecatingly. "The way they envy the queen's head eunuch."

She thought it was one of her wittier remarks, but he didn't laugh. It occurred to her that perhaps he wasn't as flippant and brazen about sex as the average young man, and that pleased her; she figured it must mean he was more sensitive and refined.

He was picturing his hands around her throat. Her use of the word "eunuch" had embarrassed and enraged him even though, on a conscious level, he didn't think of himself as being impotent. He *knew* he could get an erection when a woman was squirming helplessly beneath him and he knew he was going to punish her afterward. This was the way he always had sex, because it was the only way that all women deserved it. Hard and quick. And dead. So their last memory would be of how good he was at it. And they couldn't go around lying about it afterward . . . telling everybody he was a fairy.

Since he could no longer read Mathew's thoughts, Benjamin wondered whether he could still make himself invisible to Mathew. He even wondered if the doubts themselves might weaken the power. It might be best not to rely on it. So he exercised utmost caution in tailing Mathew and the violinist. And when they arrived at Raffaele's Café he did not dare follow them in. Instead he stayed down the block, under an awning, watching the café's front door. He hoped that they wouldn't stay in there long and that when they left they wouldn't use a back exit.

He wished that he and Lenora had the luxury of just relaxing in a quaint café. How wonderful it would be if he could really join her in New York in a week or so. Let Mathew fend for himself. Obviously he was well enough to do it. He was like a wounded tiger on the mend and on the prowl, not yet ready to attack the big game, but fully able to stalk and kill some of the smaller, weaker animals.

Benjamin was shocked by the metaphor that had just passed through his mind. Could he actually think of this little violinist as nothing but a smaller, weaker animal? Was his morality now that of a beast? Was his nature slowly becoming so nonhuman that he could feel no empathy for human creatures? Was he really not much better than Mathew—a madman who killed because he couldn't help himself?

The café was as dark as Mathew had hoped, especially after he casually placed a sugar dispenser in front of the lighted candle in its red jar. The bored middle-aged waitress in the uniform of black slacks and white blouse didn't even look up from her pad as she scribbled on it, then took back the menus. He and Cynthia had ordered Cappuccino Philadelphia before she excused herself to go to the ladies' room. With satisfaction Mathew noted how much she trusted him; her violin case was under her seat in the booth and he could have run away with it.

The waitress was taking large glass mugs of Cappuccino Philadelphia from her tray and setting them on the table, and he was winding his watch so he could turn his head away, when a pretty blonde startled him by just sitting right down in the booth opposite him. Then he saw that it was Cynthia. She had removed her wig and let down her hair, then combed and brushed it. Her bulky, raggedy sweater was gone, revealing the blue-and-white plaid blouse with a red ribbon at the collar that had been underneath. She still wore the same faded jeans, but in the context of her new look they appeared considerably less shabby.

"Well! My fair lady!" he managed to joke after the waitress departed.

"The transformation can't be *that* striking," Cynthia said. But she smiled. She was flattered.

She really was quite attractive. Maybe her nose was a little big and her chin a bit pointy, but the rest of her face was good and her complexion had a healthy glow. Mathew congratulated himself on his choice. He could tell that her breasts weren't too small now that she wasn't wearing that shapeless old sweater. Complemented by her blond hair, her eyes appeared strikingly blue, whereas the cheap wig with its unnatural brunette coloring had given her eyes an ugly, dull incongruity.

"Are you originally from Philadelphia?" he aske keeping the flow going.

"No, from Johnstown. I came all the way across state to room with my cousin because she had some connections with the Philadelphia Symphony and the Philadelphia Ballet Company. But she got married last year. So I had to move into a smaller, cheaper apartment because I didn't have anybody to share the rent with."

Mathew was glad to hear she was living alone. It confirmed what he had deduced some weeks ago after following her home a few times and maintaining some surveillance. It sounded to him that she was already comfortable with the idea that he'd be walking her the rest of the way to her apartment—she wanted him to know in advance that it wasn't so hot so she wouldn't be so embarrassed when he actually saw it.

"Do you study violin *and* ballet?" he asked, as if amazed by her versatility.

"I'm not concentrating on the violin anymore," she admitted, "because I like ballet a lot better, and they're both such demanding disciplines that it would be almost impossible for one person to excel at both." She blushed. Maybe it seemed terribly egotistical of her to imply that she had the ability to excel at either, even if she truly believed it. She didn't usually blurt out her aspirations that way, leaving herself open to ridicule or condescension. But Mathew made her feel safe, able to expose her innermost dreams. He seemed so understanding, so sympathetic, so utterly incapable of hurting her feelings.

At first, ducking back in the shadows of the awning, Benjamin wondered why Mathew was coming out of Raffaele's with a different person than he went in with. But it *was* the violinist after all. Mathew was still carrying her instrument case. And she was wearing the same faded jeans and bulky brown cardigan, even though her hair was now blond and capless. She looked much better without the wig.

Mathew must have scored points, just as he had with

Janice Ridenour. He and this new morsel were walking arm in arm, chatting chummily, she never suspecting that she was going to be devoured. Following them, Benjamin considered stepping in and saving her. But on what grounds? That he disagreed with Mathew's choice of victim? Because if he really wanted to stop Mathew the logical thing would be to kill *him*. But should tigers be rendered extinct because they sometimes pounce on college professors as well as hoboes? What value judgments ought to prevail in deciding who is to die, when in the long run no human being is exempted?

After walking three or four blocks Mathew and Cynthia entered the lobby of an apartment building, and Benjamin had a tough decision to make. He wanted to stick with them, yet there was no way he could do it without being seen—unless his mind control would work on both Mathew and the girl. He concentrated with all his mental energy, trying to generate a force field that would leap from his brain to theirs. Then he hurried into the lobby because he had to catch them before they got on the elevator.

He dashed in after them just before the elevator doors closed, trying his damnedest to be swift and silent. The girl violinist blinked, puzzled by the rush of air, but she obviously did not really see him, and he wedged his body in a corner as far away from her as possible, taking care not to trip over her violin case. "What floor?" Mathew asked, and turned around and gave Benjamin a wink and a smirk.

"Five," Cynthia said.

Mathew hit the button, and up they went. The elevator did not stop at any intervening floors, so when they reached their destination Mathew picked up the violin case and they all got off. Smart-aleck Mathew couldn't resist winking once more at Benjamin as they trooped down the hall to apartment 516. Then, after Cynthia used her key in the lock, he even held the door open like a butler while she had her back turned, to make sure Benjamin got safely inside.

"At least it's furnished," Cynthia said, already apologizing. But although the place was tiny and the furniture was old, it was serviceable and clean.

"Nothing wrong with it, Cindy," Mathew piped up exuberantly, his mood buoyed by the added spice of having his ancestor on hand to watch how he operated. "Boy, I could sure use that hot toddy you promised. Thanks for inviting me in."

"Just relax," she said, "and make yourself at home. Take your jacket off. I'm just going to get out of this sweater, then I'll boil some water for tea."

She went into her bedroom and shut the door while Benjamin and Mathew stayed in the small living room with paneled walls just about covered with ballet posters. The room contained a blue sofa that looked like it might convert to a bed, a matching armchair, a black-and-white TV with bent rabbit ears, and an expensive-looking stereo with big floor speakers. Mathew took his denim jacket off and laid it on the chair. Then he sat on the sofa while Benjamin tiptoed to the far wall and stood in the cramped space between the stereo and its left speaker, where it looked like no one would walk. Mathew crossed his legs and kept right on smirking. Softly, for Benjamin's benefit, he sang the words of a dusty disc by Paul Anka: "Cindyyy, oh Cindyyy . . . Cindy don't let me down . . ."

Miffed that such an attractive and talented girl should make herself such a pushover, Benjamin whispered, "How'd you bamboozle her so easily? Doesn't she have any common sense?"

"You sound jealous of my technique," Mathew teased. "I told her I'm a cop and showed her a photo of me in my old uniform with the badge and gun. She wants to believe in me anyway because I'm so sweet and charming. She probably thinks she's falling in love."

"Preposterous!" Benjamin scoffed.

"Shhh!" Mathew warned.

The bedroom door opened and Cynthia appeared barefooted in her same faded jeans, but she had taken her sweater and blouse off and was now wearing a green-and-white Philadelphia Eagles jersey with a number 82 on it, and no bra underneath judging by the jiggle of her breasts.

She had considered wearing just panties under her jersey —but Mathew might think it was too brazen.

She went to the record player, picked up some albums that were already on the turntable, and started them playing again. The first one to drop was Tchaikovsky's *Swan Lake,* and its lilting strains filled the room. Meanwhile, Cynthia lit some tall white candles on the speakers and extinguished the goosenecked floor lamp that had been on ever since they entered the apartment. Such a romantic setting, Benjamin thought. Such a romantic setting for a murder. What a crass, almost tacky irony if the "Dying Swan" segment should be playing at the appropriate moment.

"I'm going to start the teakettle now," Cynthia told Mathew. "I'll be right back. Unless you'd like me to fix you a snack to go with your tea."

"No, I'd just like you to come here and sit with me," he told her.

Smiling, she turned away from him, pleased that he seemed to like her so well. Benjamin despaired for her naïveté. In his former life he had been unable to lead a woman on just for sex if he wasn't sincerely interested in her. He thought it cruel to toy with another person's emotions that way. And now he thought it was even crueler to toy with a person before killing her.

She came back into the living room and sat beside Mathew on the sofa, and he didn't waste any time. He took her into his arms and kissed her. She arched herself against him, showing her willingness to receive his attentions, and he worked his hands under her jersey, rubbing her back. Then he eased her down as he kissed her ears, her mouth, and her throat. She whimpered softly as he began to work on her breasts, massaging them with his palms and tweaking the hardening nipples between his fingers. She squirmed to help him get the jersey raveled up so her breasts would be bare. He kissed them all over and sucked on the nipples. When he bent to kiss her belly, she sat up enough to get the jersey completely off. Then he picked her up and carried her into the bedroom—winking mischievously at Benjamin as he passed by.

Benjamin didn't want to go in there. He stayed rooted between the stereo and the speaker in the flickering candlelight, listening to Tchaikovsky overridden by sounds coming from the bedroom—murmurs, sighs, and rhythmic meetings of flesh that he feared would at any moment segue to the equally intimate sounds of murder. When Cynthia screamed, he jumped—banging the wall with a loud thump as he flattened himself rigidly against it. But she wasn't dying, not yet; her wild thrashing spasms and delirious outcries were not those of a death struggle but those of an orgasm. Mathew gasped and groaned and roared the triumph of his own climax. Benjamin's mouth went dry, thinking that this peak moment was when Mathew's fingers would tighten around Cynthia's throat.

The Tchaikovsky had stopped playing. Due to a malfunction, the next album had not dropped and the tone arm was suspended in midair. "Darling . . . darling . . ." Cynthia murmured. But Mathew did not reciprocate with any words of endearment.

Perspiring, Benjamin kept listening for the worst, expecting Mathew's sexual gratification to turn homicidal. He started every time he heard a voice, every time the mattress shifted. "Oh . . . darling . . . your wounds," he heard Cynthia murmur. He imagined her lightly touching her fingertips to Mathew's scars. "I know. It's why I'll never go back to being a policeman," was Mathew's reply.

Suddenly there was a shrill noise—which turned out to be the teakettle. "Lie still, I'll get it. I have to go to the toilet anyway," Mathew said. The kettle kept whining while he came out of the bedroom naked and went into the bathroom across the hall. He shut the door partway while he urinated, then flushed the commode and washed his hands. Cynthia couldn't see him from her angle, but Benjamin could. Mathew winked at Benjamin as he used a pink hand towel to wipe his fingerprints from both faucet handles. He pranced into the tiny kitchenette, shut the gas off, quieting the kettle, then turned on the tap water, running it hard, as if waiting for it to get cold enough to have a drink. But he didn't take a glassful. Instead he stealthily slid open a cabinet drawer and selected a long, sharp butcher knife. He held it up so Benjamin could see. Then, with the knife behind his back, he reentered the bedroom.

Cynthia's eyes were dreamily closed. A couple of times she had almost dozed off in postcoital pleasantness. She was dimly aware of water running in the kitchen, and she thought Mathew was still out there. She wished he would come back to her so she could snuggle against him. Her nipples, still aroused from her orgasm, tingled and became tauter from the thought of pressing against his hard chest.

She sensed Mathew's nearness and she opened her eyes, smiling. He grinned at her, a strange gleam in his eyes—and suddenly something glinted above his head. Terror exploded like a grenade inside Cynthia and she got tangled in the bedsheets and couldn't roll away from the knife. It came at her, propelled by Mathew's naked, lunging body—but it jerked aside at the last instant, his body flailing clumsily on top of her, the blade plunging into the other pillow, inches from her head. Was this a scary practical joke? Was she supposed to *laugh?* Did this mild-mannered person get his rocks off by frightening people?

He scrambled around furiously, digging elbows and knees into her, ignoring her yells and protests, and made as if to stab her again. This time the knife stopped in midair. "Damn you, Benjamin!" he cried out. "Damn you, let me be!" Groaning and struggling, his face turning insanely florid, he tried to use both hands to propel the blade.

Her scream sticking in her throat, Cynthia watched Mathew trying, but failing to stab her, as if the knife were restrained by an invisible force. She was helpless, in shock, her arms and legs rolled up in the sheets as tightly as if she had been bundled in a straitjacket, her head twisted to one side. If he wanted to kill her, he could. But might this *really* be his idea of a macabre sense of humor? Was he one of those cops whose bad experiences had driven them loony? He seemed to be wrestling with a demon, pretending or actually *believing* he was possessed. It flashed through her mind that he could be schizophrenic—a split personality—warring with the "good" and "bad" sides of himself over her right to live. All the veins in his arms were throbbing and swelling like a web of pulsing blue conduits, and there were depressions around both his wrists, so that they looked like hoses being squeezed, his fingers fat and red, engorged with blood. He gritted his teeth, and the muscles of his shoulders, chest, and throat bulged as if they would burst with the effort of making the knife plunge down. "Damn . . . you . . . Benjamin," he gasped hoarsely, seeming to lose energy with each ugly hiss. His fat, blood-engorged fingers came apart slowly and the huge knife dropped onto the bed. Immediately his nude body was jerked backward as if he were a puppet controlled from behind, and he staggered back in jerky, unwilling steps. Then he thudded and sprawled on the floor on top of his balled-up clothes, as if an invisible blow had sent him crashing.

Fearfully staring at something he seemed to imagine right in front of him, Mathew began to get dressed. He moved shakily, trembling as he got into his underwear and trousers. He was like a small boy in the presence of a stern and angry parent who had caught him doing something horribly wrong.

Cynthia rolled over and buried her face in her pillow, crying in hard, jagged sobs, somehow realizing that the danger was over for her and that she had barely escaped dying . . . without understanding how or why she had been saved. For a long time she didn't stop crying and didn't dare move. She just lay there listening to the gush of water in the kitchen, afraid to look and see if she was really alone, even after her apartment door had opened and closed and footsteps had receded down the hall.

Once on the elevator Mathew stammered meekly, "My . . . m-my fingerprints . . . on the knife . . . the . . . the violin case . . . even the stove and the sink. You . . . you didn't give me any chance to wipe everything off . . ."

"She saw your *face* and the *photo* of you in your uniform," Benjamin pointed out. "That's enough to identify you even without fingerprints."

"The photo was too small," Mathew whined. "She thought I was a cop. She didn't see the Magnum Security insignia."

"I don't care," Benjamin said. "I *want* you to be caught. You kill for no reason. Madmen like you need to be put away."

"No difference between me and you," Mathew mumbled. "No difference at all."

"I am not a wanton killer, but you *are,*" Benjamin replied harshly. He had realized that when he had not been able to stand by and let Cynthia Jensen die. It was the revelation that he had sensed might come through Mathew. Now he knew what the difference was between himself and his descendant. *He* wasn't immoral—Mathew *was.* Mathew was an enemy of his own species. He *wasted* human lives purely to gratify his own warped passions, while Benjamin had to kill for sustenance and *would* kill for no other reason. In Mathew's twisted mind, murder was erotic. All of his sex partners had to die. It was a perversion that, with proper psychological therapy, might even be cured.

But Benjamin's craving was as innate and essential as the demand for oxygen. He had no control over it, and no freedom of choice over what he had become. He needed blood from living human flesh as much as other creatures needed ordinary food and drink. Like a lion or tiger, he *had* to kill. He required fresh game. He was by nature a beast of prey. But he was a *human* beast, capable of esthetic discretion in art, in politics, in religion . . . and in his choosing of companions and lovers and . . .

. . . and victims.

He didn't have to kill randomly and indiscriminately, just for the *sake* of killing. He needed to kill in order to live. But he could select his victims wisely, applying an ethical standard, as he had done in the cases of Jorell Jordan and Garth Weir. Other beasts of prey lacked the intelligence to be so selective, but he had a moral *obligation* to exercise taste and judgment in satisfying his God-given need. Yes, *God*-given. If God had made lions and tigers and humans into carnivores, then that same God had given Benjamin the craving for human blood. He did not have to war against his own nature anymore. He did not have to despise himself or his Creator. He had a right, even a duty, to survive. Why shouldn't his *super*human species coexist with humans the way humans had always coexisted with the other animals that *they* devour? Let evolution and the struggle for survival determine whether the two human species might share the earth, both having a part in the food chain—or whether one species, the bloodsuckers or the nonbloodsuckers, must eventually supersede the other, just as eons ago the Cro-Magnons with their superior intellectual and physical attributes had caused the Neanderthals to become extinct.

30

"Homicide. Sergeant Baker."

Why did the man have to bark into the phone? Especially on a Monday morning. "This is Trooper Vargo. May I please speak with Mordini or Demchak?"

"Gone."

"Are you sure they just didn't punch in yet? It's only a quarter to nine, and I'm supposed to meet them there in fifteen minutes."

"If it wasn't them I saw, it was a couple of damn clever impersonators. They were in here, but they left."

"Do you know where they've gone to?"

"Yep. Investigating an assault on a young lady named Cynthia Jensen. Claims a fellow named Mathew tried to kill her but chickened out. Her description of him matches Mathew Latham. Mordini and Demchak are on their way to her apartment to question her."

Vargo realized that he had been purposely left out in the cold. He asked, "When did the attack happen?"

"Saturday night."

"And she's just reporting it now? Why did she wait till Monday morning?"

"Claims she was thinking it over. He seemed like such a nice guy. She wanted to give him the benefit of the doubt—after all, he didn't really hurt her. But finally she decided she'd have to tell on him, maybe help get him off the streets and into therapy before he tried to kill somebody else."

"Smart of her," Vargo said sarcastically. "Was she able to say where this guy might be living? Or where he might have run to?"

"No. That was one of the first points Mordini covered. But he came up snake eyes. He's hoping to do some more digging and maybe jog her memory."

Just as Mordini and Demchak were trying to finesse *him* out of the main action in this case, Vargo had his own tactic for doing unto them. He told Sergeant Baker the lie he had worked out over the weekend: "Well, anyway, the reason I'm calling, I was going to bow out of the nine o'clock meeting. I want to check out a pawnshop and a sporting-goods store that weren't open yesterday. Both places are in the neighborhood where Mathew and Julia Latham used to live, and I'm hoping that maybe Mathew dealt with one of them to either buy or hock the revolver he carried when he worked for Magnum Security. Please tell Mordini and Demchak I'll give them a call later if I turn up anything."

"*Got*cha."

Baker managed to make the "Gotcha" sound as mocking as a "Right on, Sherlock." Then he hung up. Bang. Without saying good-bye. Clearly he thought the idea of checking a pawnshop and a gun store at random was a stupid shot in the dark, which was what Vargo wanted him to think. He wanted all of his competition to believe he was safely out of their hair.

He sat on his hotel bed mulling over the latest twist. He figured that Mordini and Demchak were the ones who were probably spinning their wheels. If Cynthia Jensen had any idea of where Mathew Latham was living, she'd have come right out with it. At least the investigation of her assault charge had delayed the decision of whether or not to publish Mathew's photo—a move that Vargo didn't want to be made as long as there was still a chance of using Mathew to set up a stakeout for the Vampire Killer.

He hadn't been able to reach Dr. Abraham all weekend. But by looking in the Yellow Pages he had found out that a company called Zenko Janitorial Services used a Z in a circle in its ad. Window washing and floor scrubbing seemed like the type of unskilled work Mathew Latham might be doing. But Vargo hadn't been able to talk to anybody at Zenko on Saturday or Sunday. Maybe Monday morning would be a better time to get doctors and janitors to answer their phones.

He dialed Dr. Abraham's office number and was slightly shocked when he got a live receptionist instead of a recorded message. He asked her if the doctor was available.

"Are you a regular patient of his, sir?"

"No. This is Trooper Ronald Vargo of the Pennsylvania State Police. I'd like to speak with Dr. Abraham about an investigation I'm handling."

"Does it concern an insurance claim?"

"What it concerns is between me and the doctor."

"He won't divulge information about any of his patients over the phone."

"That's an excellent policy. Is he in?"

"Who should I say is calling?"

Vargo repeated his name and whom he worked for.

"Please hold for a moment, sir."

After a moment that stretched to five or six minutes of Muzak, Dr. Abraham got on the line and, although he sounded harried, proved to be much more cooperative than his receptionist. He said that Julia Latham had been a patient of his, but he had never treated her son. He hadn't seen Julia for at least six weeks. Vargo asked him if he had a file on her that would list her current address and place of employment. "Yes, I would," the doctor admitted. "But that is the kind of information I cannot give you over the phone. I hope you realize that I'm not trying to obstruct your investigation. But I'd have to see you in person and examine your credentials to make sure you really are who you say you are."

"I understand," said Vargo. "But before I make a wasted trip to your office, maybe you can just look in your records and tell me if you have a more current address for Julia than the last one that is known to the police."

"That much I can do," agreed Dr. Abraham. "Just a second till I get her file."

Sitting on the edge of the hotel bed listening to more Muzak, Vargo drummed his fingers on the telephone stand. After a while he heard the receiver on the other end of the line being picked up, then some papers being rustled. "Here it is, right in front of my nose," said Dr. Abraham finally. "What address do you have?"

"Fenway Apartments on Race Street. Apartment number three-oh-four."

"That's exactly what *I* have," said the doctor. "And I see here that her son Mathew is listed as next of kin, address 'same as above'—meaning same as Julia's. Sorry I can't help you."

"How about another doctor?" Vargo asked. "Did you ever refer her to somebody else? A specialist maybe? Somebody I might talk to to find out if he has a more current address for Julia than you do?"

"No, I'm afraid not. There's nothing like that in her records. And I certainly don't recall ever referring her to anybody."

"Too bad," said Vargo, letting his disappointment show. "I appreciate your time, though, Dr. Abraham."

"That's perfectly all right." The doctor chuckled. "After all, time is money, and I just saved myself some by being able to handle this over the phone."

The Z in a circle was Vargo's last chance. He dialed the number of Zenko Janitorial Services, hoping their logo was red instead of blue or green or purple—or black, as it appeared in the Yellow Page ad where everything was printed black on yellow.

"Good morning. Zenko." The strong male voice had answered the phone after one and a half rings.

"Mr. Zenko?" Vargo asked.

"That's me. What can I do for you?"

"Mr. Zenko, my name is Ron Vargo. I'm a —"

"If you're a salesman we don't need anything," Zenko interrupted heartily. "What we need is a couple of window washers who ain't afraid of scaffolds. You looking for a job?"

"Uh . . . not exactly. I'm a detective with the Pennsylvania State Police, and I'm trying to locate a young man named Mathew Latham who might have worked for you."

"I didn't think he'd be like the rest of them," Zenko said.

"What do you mean?" said Vargo, his spirits lifting. "You recognize his name?"

"Sure! A good worker. I thought he would stick with it for a while. But he stops coming to work one day, just like that. None of the young ones stick anymore. They all think they should be making a hundred grand a year right away and driving a Corvette. I give them an opportunity here to make something of themselves, but they don't take it."

"Mathew Latham," Vargo said. "When did he last work for you?"

"Not since the third week of October. I remember he didn't show up on the twenty-fifth, a Monday, because that was the day after the big fireworks on Penn's Landing. I still owed him about a hundred bucks in wages, so I mailed it to his place. I tried calling him, but he don't answer the phone. Is he in some kind of trouble? Hey! You don't think something bad happened to him, do you?"

"No, there's nothing to worry about," Vargo said. "I just have to ask him some questions about a confidential matter. Can you give me his address and phone number?"

"Sure, I got it right here in my Rolodex."

Copying down the information that Zenko gave him, Vargo felt the keyed-up, tingly feeling he always got when a hot lead seemed to be paying off. Now he knew where Mathew Latham had been living as recently as three weeks ago. Maybe he was still there, scared to answer the telephone. It was obvious why he hadn't shown up for work on October twenty-fifth—the day that Janice Ridenour had been found strangled.

If Mathew Latham and Benjamin Latham were still traveling together, Vargo wondered, why hadn't Benjamin taken part in the assault on Cynthia Jensen? Probably because only three weeks had gone by since Ridenour. The Vampire Killer didn't think he needed to drink any blood.

Not yet.

Not for another week.

Today was November twenty-second; the next full moon wasn't due until December first. In looking for a pattern to the killings, it had seemed to Vargo that the Vampire Killer usually struck not when the moon was full but a week or so *before* it was full. That might be a compromise between "esthetics" and practicality: maybe he felt a need to conform to a lunar cycle but also wanted to avoid the brightness of full moonlight which might blow his cover while he was stalking his victims.

Vargo wasn't superstitious. He refused to believe that there were actually humanlike creatures who needed to drink blood in order to live. They might *think* they needed to drink blood, and they might *think* that the phases of the moon had something to do with it—but that was because their deranged minds were subconsciously influenced by the vampire and werewolf myths. It was even conceivable that the moon's gravity or energy might have an as yet unexplained *physical* effect on their brain fluctuations, making them more insane or less insane, according to some kind of a lunar schedule.

In which case they could quite literally be called lunatics.

But not vampires or werewolves.

Not literally.

Not in any supernatural sense.

31

Benjamin wanted to be free of Mathew but hated the thought of killing him. Mathew's blood would be poisonous to him if he tried to drink it, but because the same blood coursed through their veins they shared a mystical bond that Benjamin was loath to break. He balked at the idea of being "his brother's executioner." But at the same time he was afraid that a Mathew on the loose would be a perpetual threat to him and Lenora. Mathew might try following them, might even persist in his desire to be "transformed."

Even if such a transformation could be accomplished, Benjamin could not bring himself to take part in it. He was haunted by visions of Mathew, still insane, still sexually perverted, but with an additional craving—for blood—and with the heightened powers that would make his sadistic mentality all the more formidable.

Benjamin considered setting Mathew up so that the police could capture him. They might gun him down. But if they took him alive, how long would he stay in jail? Or in an asylum? Probably not for long in this permissively decadent "land of the free and home of the brave" where rapists and other types of scoundrels roamed the land so freely that the honest citizens *had* to be brave just to venture out of their homes.

Mathew was the only person on earth, so far as Benjamin knew, who could connect him directly to Lenora Clayton. Julia Latham had met Lenora under the alias of Lenora Langley and believed her to be a writer for *National Keyhole;* Julia was likely to be relieved rather than disappointed when no news article came out, because she really would prefer not to have any media attention. But Mathew could tell the world that Benjamin and Lenora were traveling together as lovers. He could describe Lenora quite accurately to the police if he were captured, or if he turned himself in on an insane whim, or if he simply wrote an anonymous letter to a newspaper editor.

Fear of how Mathew might use his knowledge of Lenora was what finally made Benjamin decide that Mathew was too deranged, too unpredictable, to remain free. He would be better off dead. Not only was he the scourge of the innocent, killing for the sake of killing, but he himself was a tortured creature, like a wounded tiger or a dog with rabies. He needed to be put to sleep as humanely and mercifully as any other afflicted and dangerous animal.

Suicide would be the perfect answer. Benjamin wished his mind control were strong enough to implant the idea in Mathew's tormented brain, but he couldn't hypnotize Mathew. The young man's psychosis seemed to act as a force field, protecting him from the penetrating energy of mental telepathy.

Ever since Saturday's fiasco, Benjamin had let Mathew have the bedroom so he himself could sleep on the couch, close enough to the door to hear the bolt being slid back in the middle of the night. But Mathew hadn't tried it. For the past two days he had languished in the hotel suite, moping around, not bothering to shave or bathe or do much of anything except sleep and eat. The cockiness seemed to have gone out of him as a result of his frustrated attempt to kill Cynthia Jensen. By all appearances his spirits had sunk so low that he might even *be* self-destructive. But Benjamin wasn't buying the act. He suspected that Mathew was merely playing possum, biding his time for a chance to run out and successfully murder some young woman.

Having reluctantly resigned himself to the notion that his descendant must die, Benjamin began to seriously plan how to bring the event to fruition. He even started to look forward to it, since it would have a liberating effect. He was tired of being constantly on the alert, worrying about what sort of crazy thing Mathew might try next. The immoral aspects of the murder he was planning gradually ceased to trouble him. He was like a married woman who, having agonized with her conscience over whether or not to have an affair, has now made the terrible decision to be unfaithful and is eager to get to the good part.

The advantage of making it look like suicide would be that the police probably wouldn't look any further. Benjamin figured they would have no reason to; they couldn't connect him with Mathew, he believed, since he and Mathew had never been seen together at the scene of a crime—Benjamin had always made himself invisible when the occasion called for it. Even at the Welcome Hotel, Mathew had been confined to the suite so much that hardly anyone must have seen his face. As long as his body was found someplace else, nobody ought to come around trying to connect Benjamin with his untimely demise.

The best place to stage the demise would be Mathew's apartment. It would be logical for him to kill himself there . . . all alone and sunk to the depths of despair, self-pity, and guilt. Benjamin knew the address, on Front Street, near the harbor, but he had never been there. He needed to have a look inside so he could conceptualize his staging. Should Mathew hang himself, shoot himself, use poison? Was there a convenient place to attach a rope? A chandelier wouldn't do; the weight of Mathew's body might pull it out of the ceiling, and if he wasn't quite dead beforehand he might survive. The thought of surviving a noose gave Benjamin a chill because it was what he had inadvertently done two hundred years ago. He didn't think he could bring himself to hang Mathew. Mathew had best shoot himself. He had bragged about having a gun at his apartment and had mentioned wanting to go back and get it. He might as well do himself in with his own revolver—the one he hadn't had the pleasure of using on his victims.

The next question was: Were the police watching Mathew's apartment? He had left fingerprints—on Cynthia Jensen's violin case, butcher knife, stove, and sink—which should enable them to identify him. But probably not right away. Benjamin had read up on forensic sciences in order to know better how to protect himself, so he realized that a fingerprint check by means of the FBI computer system usually took at least several days. Only two days had passed since the assault on Cynthia. How perfect it would be if, come Wednesday or Thursday, a passel of armed policemen burst into Mathew's apartment and found him slumped over with a pistol in his hand and his brains splattered against a wall.

Benjamin decided that he would first scout out the apartment on Front Street to make sure there was no stakeout. Then he could get Mathew there by some clever ruse. Ha! He pictured himself plying Mathew with alcohol till he was helplessly drunk, then letting him stagger the whole way to the suicide setup, "helped" by invisible hands. Amusing as it sounded, it might work. The risk would be minimized in the wee hours when hardly anyone was on the streets. Once inside the apartment, Mathew could be tied and gagged. Then Benjamin would have the privacy to stage the main event properly with all the authentic details.

There was also the matter of the scrapbook Mathew had admitted keeping on the Vampire Killer. It would be to Benjamin's advantage if he could make that little bit of evidence disappear. So far as he knew, the police didn't realize that the Vampire Killer or anyone connected with the Vampire Killer was in Philadelphia. If they had thought to run a serology test on Janice Ridenour's wrist wound, they might have found poisonous saliva. But apparently they hadn't. There had been no Vampire Killer scare in the newspaper, just a routine article with a routine heading, YOUNG WOMAN FOUND SLASHED AND STRANGLED. Obviously there were so many slashings and stranglings going on day in, day out that it was hard for the police to imagine that any one of them could be something special.

The Welcome Hotel had provided the suitcase rack that Mathew Latham had taken apart to make the weapon with which he intended to kill Benjamin. Covertly searching the bedroom, he had found the rack in the closet, where Lenora had put it when she had departed for Chicago and New York. It was the folding type made of wooden slats and leather straps. Mathew had cut the straps away with a razor blade. Perfect. The legs of the rack, which had been X-shaped, bolted together in the middle, opened up into the shape of a cross when the straps were removed. To secure that shape, Mathew had used the leather as binding. Then, working surreptitiously behind the closed bedroom door, he had used his razor blade to whittle the base of the cross to a sharp point.

He believed that if he could destroy the Vampire Killer he'd be hailed as a hero. He could tell the world that *he* was not responsible for his crimes—Benjamin Latham was. The Vampire Killer had put him in a trance. All this time he had been kept prisoner, under an evil, hypnotic spell, until he was able to snap the spell and make a daringly clever escape.

Once the Vampire Killer was dead, the glory would belong to Mathew Latham. Radio. TV. Newspapers. He'd make headlines. He'd be a media star. He'd be rich. His life story and the story of his adventure with the Vampire Killer would come out as a book and a movie. He'd be the biggest celebrity of the decade.

He'd be known as the Vampire-Killer because he killed the Vampire. He'd be just as famous as the Exorcist. Getting rid of a vampire was just as awesome and scary as getting rid of a malevolent spirit. Probably a hero-worshiping cult would spring up around Mathew Latham. He'd have fans. An agent. A PR organization behind him.

Maybe he'd even go to Hollywood to play himself in one of his pictures. Starlets would tumble into bed with him because he'd *be* somebody. They wouldn't think of him as a fairy. They wouldn't dare. He'd have the confidence to screw them all because they'd be sucking up to him, trying to get him to boost their careers.

But he'd toss them aside when he was done toying with them. None of them would mean a thing. He'd take what he wanted, then leave them groveling in the gutter.

He would marry Li Yung, a pure and beautiful Chinese maiden. Their love for each other would be perfect, shining, and true. Her family would no longer be able to dim its radiant glow. They'd be proud of him for being so rich and powerful and successful—an international hero. Li Yung would worship and adore him forever.

He dreamed his dreams and waited for his chance, his sharpened cross hidden under his mattress.

Lying on the couch, where he was posed as if reading a book, Benjamin looked over at the closed bedroom door. In pondering how he might have a reasonable guarantee that Mathew would remain in the hotel suite while he went out to scout the apartment on Front Street, he decided that he would simply tell Mathew that he intended to clear the place of any incriminating evidence, such as the scrapbook, and bring back Mathew's belongings—such as the gun. He could use his power of invisibility to make sure he wasn't seen. Then, mission accomplished, he would give Mathew all his stuff—plus a thousand dollars to help him start a new life—and he and his descendant could go their separate ways.

Or so Mathew would think. His lust for the gun and the money would help con him. But, once Benjamin ascertained that the coast was clear for setting up the "suicide," he wouldn't bother trying to get Mathew drunk in a parting "celebration"—that idea was too frivolous. Instead he would just drug him unconscious, tie and gag him, and carry him the few short blocks to Front Street rolled up in a carpet. He was strong enough to manage that, but he was so unused to his new, supernatural strength that it almost hadn't entered into his planning.

He wondered why Mathew had stopped pestering him to be made into a vampire. It was a relief not to have to deal with *that* issue. But it would seem that the young man's addled ego would have an even stronger lust for occult powers now that his worldly ones had failed him in a key situation. In a way, it was a pity to see him so crushed and broken that he must have given up on his ambition of bettering himself.

Benjamin arose from the couch, laying his book aside, and tapped on the bedroom door. "Mathew . . . are you awake?"

"Uh . . . just a minute," came the muffled, sleepy mumble.

God, how can anyone *sleep* so much? Benjamin wondered. He heard some soft stirrings, and then:

"Come on in. I'm decent."

When he pushed open the door, all he saw was a shape under the covers. "Come on out from under those blankets and talk to me," he started to say—but suddenly the door slammed into his back and he was knocked forward. He took a judo chop on his neck and went down heavily, sprawling half on the bed and half on the floor—but managing to keep his body rolling out of the way of whatever was coming next.

It turned out to be a cross with a sharpened point. With the zeal of a saint in his insane eyes, Mathew was driving the "holy" stake at Benjamin's chest.

Making use of his superior speed and his ability to slow down action (which he had used in his mortal combat with Elijah Alford in the parking garage), Benjamin seized both of Mathew's wrists. Not only was he not impaled, but he had reached out in plenty of time to stop the point of the crude weapon from grazing his shirt.

"Look at it! Look . . . at . . . it!" Mathew hissed through gritted teeth. "It's . . . supposed . . . to . . . make . . . you . . . weak . . ." His throat muscles bulged and his face and neck turned purple with the effort of doing Benjamin in. "Lord Jesus . . . and the Holy Spirit . . . help me . . ." he grunted in desperation. "Blessed Virgin Mary," he implored in one last gasp before he succumbed, dropping the thing he had fashioned from the suitcase rack to one side as Benjamin rolled him onto his back and punched him hard on his right temple. He went limp, all the fight gone out of him.

For a moment Benjamin feared that Mathew was already dead. But he was still breathing, a bit raggedly. And there was a pretty strong pulse in his wrist.

Benjamin froze, listening for any sign that the brief fight had alarmed the other tenants. As he recalled it, there hadn't been much noise, just an intense struggle. Anyway, one could usually count on people not to want to get involved. After a while, when he heard no footsteps in the hall and no one knocking on his door, he decided he was safe.

Using strips of hotel towel and the leather straps from the suitcase rack, he got Mathew tied up and gagged. Luckily, even in the heat of combat he had had the presence of mind to render Mathew unconscious by striking him in the temple—where he would logically shoot himself and where the damage done by a bullet would obliterate any evidence of a bruise or a concussion. Benjamin panicked all of a sudden, thinking he had chosen the wrong temple. But no. Mathew was right-handed. He would correctly place the muzzle of the gun against the right side of his head.

This is going to work out splendidly, Benjamin thought. To think I let this ungrateful rascal trouble my conscience, when all the while he was going to do unto *me*. Now all I've got to do is leave him here, trussed up on the bed like a Christmas turkey, while I case his apartment tonight. And then, if the coast is clear . . .

Instead of growing accustomed to the awful smells after being here six hours, Vargo was feeling sick to his stomach. The apartment stank of human perspiration and ejaculation on dirty sheets, moldy french fries and half-eaten hamburger on the coffee table, and a maggoty overflowing garbage can in the kitchen. Vargo had seen it all when he first got here, in the daytime. Now, not wanting to turn any lights on, he could imagine the maggots slowly crawling toward him.

Like most murderous punks with delusions of grandeur, Mathew Latham was a worm. A worm living in shit. He would go on smearing his shit on other people until he was put away for good.

Sitting in the dark with his .357 magnum on the chair arm, Vargo was resigned to waiting all night, hoping someone would come, hoping he'd hear footsteps on the concrete steps of this dank basement apartment, then a key turning in the lock. He had placed an old rusty floor lamp with a torn shade next to his chair, its gooseneck aimed at the doorframe so he could switch it on at the right moment, spotlighting whoever entered.

Judging by the maggots and the moldy leftovers, Mathew Latham hadn't lived in this wormhole for some time. But his clothes and his gun were here. His final paycheck, in a brown envelope from Zenko Janitorial Services, lay where it had fallen just inside the mail slot. His scrapbook was in a dresser drawer. And ten twenty-dollar bills were inside a cigar box taped under the kitchen sink. Worms like Mathew always hated to lose their "valuables." Sooner or later they usually came crawling back for them, after convincing themselves that it would be safe. Vargo intended to keep his vigil . . . today . . . tomorrow . . . maybe the next day . . . until Mordini and Demchak went ahead and released Mathew's description and photo to the media. Then his chance of catching anything in his trap would be gone.

Maybe it was a slim chance anyway. Yet Vargo had a hunch that something was going to happen. It was the same spooky feeling that had come over him on the stakeout at Angela Stone's place the night Weird Garth disappeared. That time he had been played for a sucker, as if someone had been looking over his shoulder laughing at him. It was almost enough to make him start believing in ghosts. His hunch that night back in Pittsburgh had been a good one, but somehow he had been cheated out of the payoff.

He wouldn't be cheated again.

If Mathew Latham crawled into his trap, he'd have the drop on him, but he wouldn't fire. He'd wait for him to come far enough into this foul-smelling room—then hit him with the spotlight. Before the worm could turn and crawl away he'd be stepped on, handcuffed, and having the shit beat out of him till everything he knew came blubbering out.

But if it wasn't Mathew . . . If by some stroke of luck it was the Vampire Killer . . .

Vargo knew beyond the shadow of a doubt what he would do. For his daughter Kathy. For all the pitiful, voiceless victims of madmen like Benjamin Latham . . . Mathew Latham . . . and John Hampton, the child-murderer who was still on the loose.

At three o'clock in the morning Benjamin let himself out of the Welcome Hotel by the side door. No one was around. The sidewalks were clear. By five A.M. the delivery trucks would start pulling up in front of the shops and restaurants, and the city would start to come alive. But now it was quiet . . . almost dead.

Walking quickly, making himself invisible to a loitering taxi driver and a couple of cops in a slowly cruising patrol car, he got to Front Street in about twenty minutes. He was satisfied that he could pull off the feat of carrying Mathew here in a rolled-up carpet.

When Benjamin looked at the mailbox number written on Mathew's keychain tag, he first thought that he must somehow be at the wrong place. It was an old, decrepit two-story brick building with all the windows boarded up, upstairs and downstairs. A realtor's signs were tacked onto the plywood: COMMERCIAL STORAGE SPACE FOR SALE OR RENT. Puzzled, Benjamin did a double take. Then he noticed the concrete steps leading down from the sidewalk. Glancing all around to make sure no one was watching, he walked down the steps, bits of broken glass crunching under his feet. He lit a match and saw a number scrawled in yellow chalk under a mail slot in a warped, weather-beaten door. It matched the number on the keychain tag. Perfect! A basement apartment with no tenants upstairs to notice Benjamin's comings and goings or to be disturbed by a gunshot.

He hadn't seen any signs of police. There didn't seem to be any good place from which they could maintain a surveillance without themselves being spotted. Benjamin figured that if they were lurking inside either of the two buildings next door—both big brick warehouses—they would have jumped out at him by now. And if they were on the first or second stories of *this* building, how could they see out through the plywood? Across the way was nothing but the girders of the Ben Franklin Bridge and the steps going down to Penn's Landing.

Still, something felt wrong. Benjamin's nerves were buzzing. But, telling himself that he certainly couldn't expect to see his plan through without incurring *some* risk, he twisted the key in the lock and opened the door. He was almost knocked back by the rotten odor that engulfed him. He turned his head away, trying to breathe fresh air. Certainly, he thought, no cops could be inside this place—how in the world could they ever stand it? Putting his hand into the darkness as gingerly as if he were reaching into a coffin, he groped for a light switch and found none. Damn! Probably there was a bare bulb in the center of the ceiling, with a pull-down cord. He took several cautious steps forward and suddenly he was blinded by light. "Don't move!" a voice barked. "Or I'll shoot!"

Benjamin slowly moved his hands away from his eyes. He was bathed in light while the other man was in pitch blackness. "Who are you?" he asked. "Do you live here?"

Vargo chuckled mirthlessly. The person in front of him wasn't Mathew Latham, although the resemblance was close. His heart was beating fast, his finger tightening on his trigger. But he had to be sure. He said, "I know who *you* are, Benjamin Latham, thanks to the snapshot we found in Andy Bonner's room. Did you think vampires couldn't be photographed? He must've taken it when you weren't looking." Getting up from the chair, Vargo said, "Just put your hands straight out in front of you, wrists together, and hold that pose till I get the cuffs on you."

The man must be bluffing. Andy Bonner didn't even *own* a camera. Or did he? Or might someone on one of the Manpower jobs have taken a candid shot and given it to Andy?

In any case, Benjamin couldn't afford to be taken into custody. Once the police had him, they would test his saliva, and electrophoresis would confirm that they had the right man.

It was too late to make himself invisible. Once he had already been seen, the power didn't work. He'd have to try to get away. Better yet, he'd have to kill this man who had a gun on him. This man who said he could recognize him, photograph or no photograph.

"You are right," he said. "I am Benjamin Latham. I will surrender peacefully."

But from the way Vargo chuckled, Benjamin knew he wasn't going to be arrested. He was going to be shot. He whirled and sprang for the open doorway just as the gun went off with a deafening roar. He could feel the surprising supermortal speed and agility of his escape. But he also felt a fat slug crashing into his back. The force of it slammed him to his knees on the concrete steps, his hands being lacerated and punctured by bits of broken bottles that still stank of cheap booze. Another deafening roar, and a second slug shattered his left shoulder as he clambered to get out of the pool of light.

Vargo ran, firing into the darkness, amazed that anything could run so fast once it was hit. The .357 magnum was designed to take a man down with one bullet. Vargo had to run for all he was worth to catch up with Benjamin, who was now across the street. He aimed but couldn't fire because his quarry zigzagged under a streetlamp and darted between some concrete pillars. Vargo chased him down the clanging steel steps that led to the wharf.

Penn's Landing was all lit up—open paved spaces—not

a very good place to hide. But Benjamin was outdistancing Vargo with his uncanny speed. Sweating and breathing hard even though he was in excellent physical shape, Vargo struggled to maintain his stamina and close in on his target. Fueling himself with the energy of rage, he pictured what John Hampton had done to Kathy and what Benjamin Latham had done to little Stephanie Kamin.

Benjamin started to stagger from loss of blood. It was a strange, eerie sensation—his leg muscles still being able to perform powerfully while the life of his internal organs was draining away. He couldn't go on much longer. An ordinary human would have succumbed as soon as those first two bullets had struck, but a superhuman aspect of himself that he did not understand would not let him go down.

His spirit kept him running. He thought of Lenora and wondered if he would ever see her again. Somehow he wanted to make it to where the *Gazela Primeiro* was anchored—the tall-masted sailing vessel was a refugee from the past, and so was he. He stumbled and fell, but pulled himself up by clutching the steel railing at the edge of the wharf. He kept going till the rigging of the big ship was within sight, black against the graying sky. Then he turned and faced his pursuer, no longer trying to escape but accepting the certainty that he must die.

Totally out of breath, Vargo stopped running just twenty feet away from Benjamin. They looked at each other the way a hunter and a deer sometimes look at each other just before the animal loses his life. Vargo realized that Benjamin was truly giving up, making himself helpless. Shaking from exhaustion, he raised his .357 magnum, assuming the standard firing crouch, pistol gripped in both hands. He squeezed off two rounds. The first slug struck Benjamin in the chest; the second blew away half of his skull. His arms flew up and his hips jerked in a weird death dance; then he folded over the rail. Vargo shot Benjamin in the back as his dead weight somersaulted him over the railing and down into the black, shiny Delaware River.

Vargo ran to a spot near the rail, and stared down at the body floating like a rag doll against the backdrop of the

Gazela Primeiro. Benjamin was face down in the harbor. He was undeniably dead. Vargo holstered his weapon. Lights were flashing aboard the big ship moored at the wharf. Vargo started shouting, hoping to arouse some crewmen who could lower a longboat and haul the Vampire Killer's body out of the water.

32

When Mathew Latham came to, he had a wet, furry gag in his mouth and his head felt as if it were being removed with a hammer and chisel. He was lying on his side with his hands tied behind him. His ankles were bound with leather straps and pulled up and tied to his wrists with strips of towel. His left shoulder ached from being twisted under him, and his knees felt as if they were being stretched apart at the joints.

The bedroom door was closed and there was no light on. But he could see daylight peeking through the one window where the heavy red curtains almost touched the sill. He listened hard, trying to focus his sense of hearing despite the fuzzy, throbbing pain in his skull. He couldn't discern any sounds of movement out in the anteroom. Was Benjamin in the shower? Mathew couldn't tell if the water was running. If Benjamin was on the couch reading, Mathew couldn't hear him breathing or clearing his throat or turning pages. He listened for a long time, and when he didn't pick up the slightest "human" sound he came to believe that Benjamin must be gone.

In a burst of groggy, incoherent panic he wondered if Benjamin had left him here to die. But no. Eventually the maid or somebody connected with the hotel would have to get in, even if there was a DO NOT DISTURB sign on the doorknob. He wouldn't die of thirst or hunger. If Benjamin was going to risk killing him right here in the suite, he'd already be dead. So Benjamin must be coming back. *That* was something to be afraid of. If he didn't manage to get loose before Benjamin got here, he was as good as dead. The stark realization made him sweat so much that he soaked the bed. His heart pounded wildly. His nose and sinuses burned as his hot breath wheezed in and out and he thought he'd suffocate because it was impossible to take in enough oxygen through his nasal passages. The ball of rag in his mouth, held there by a towel strip tied around his neck, tasted so slimy and sour that he started to gag, but he was afraid that if he threw up he would choke to death on his own vomit. He tried desperately to calm down.

The razor blade! The one he had used to cut the leather straps from the suitcase rack. It was hidden under a corner of the bedroom carpet—unless Benjamin had found it. Was he that psychic? Mathew wondered, fearful of Benjamin's special powers, real and imagined. But the razor blade seemed to be his best chance. He'd have to wiggle to the edge of the bed and drop off . . .

What if the razor blade really *wasn't* there?

Fighting his rising panic and his terrible aches and pains, he inched across the carpet to the corner next to the closet. Then he squirmed around and wedged himself against the wall and the closet door, and squeezed and twisted his hips until he managed to get his fingers in there and lift the carpet just enough. He felt the razor blade.

Cutting the strip of towel between his wrists and his ankles wasn't easy, but after hacking at it for a while he shredded it enough to pull it apart. It was a blessed relief. Now he could straighten his legs, get some circulation back, and ease the pain in his knees and his cramped hamstrings. When he felt able, he got himself into a sitting position on the edge of the bed, and at last he stood up.

He had to find a place to wedge the razor blade so he could rub his wrist straps against it and cut them away. Looking around the room, he thought he might make use of a dresser drawer, although it seemed doubtful. Bending his knees, he started moving toward it in little hops, hoping he wouldn't lose his balance and fall. Then he thought of the deadbolt on the door to the suite. If he could hop out there he could slide the bolt shut and the door would be locked from inside. If Benjamin came back he wouldn't be able to get in. And he wouldn't dare make a fuss in the hall or a hotel cop might come and investigate a little too closely.

Going slowly, taking time to get his breath every few feet and to control the urge to vomit, Mathew hopped to the bedroom door and got it open. He half expected to see Benjamin staring him in the face, having toyed with him. But it turned out that the suite really was empty. Nobody in the anteroom. Nobody in the bathroom.

Mathew made it to the main door and secured the deadbolt. After a number of bad tries, dropping the razor blade a few times and having to slide down the wall to pick it up, he succeeded in wedging it between the door and the jamb. He imagined that he would only have to cut through one strap and he could work the rest free, but it turned out they were knotted in several layers. It took a long time, and he was badly frightened the whole while, dreading the sound of a key in the lock. He cut his wrists several times, but at last the straps fell to the floor and he was able to tear off his gag and untie his ankles.

The first thing he did was rush to the bathroom and run cold water on his bleeding wrists. The cuts were numerous but not very deep. He plastered them with Band-Aids from the medicine cabinet, where Lenora had put them. That made him think of her, and she stayed in the forefront of his mind. Now that he was free, he was already itching for revenge. Exactly what form it would take he did not know. But he knew he wanted it badly.

He splashed water on his face, removed his bloody T-shirt and shorts, and put on clean ones. He combed and brushed his hair, frantically trying to look presentable, and dressed in a yellow long-sleeved shirt of Benjamin's, his own brown trousers, and Benjamin's tan corduroy jacket. He wanted to leave the suite in a hurry, but not without ransacking the dresser in the bedroom and the suitcase in the closet. He found about three hundred dollars in cash. Also a folder of traveler's checks cashable by Benjamin or Lenora Clayton—which was how he learned the last name they were traveling under. He stuffed the checks into his pants pocket. Then he undid the deadbolt and let himself out into the hall, still scared he might see Benjamin coming at him. But he made it onto the elevator and down to the lobby.

It was taking a risk, but he had to stop at the registration desk. He told the checkout clerk, a stringy-haired redhead barely out of her teens, that he wanted to have a look at the telephone charges for suite 403 because he wanted to be sure he wasn't being billed for a mistake the operator had made the other day when he was on long distance to New York. Responding to his good looks and his warm manner, the clerk handed the bills and records over with a smile. He memorized the digits that appeared several times after a 212 area code; it must be the number of the hotel where Lenora was staying. Then he handed the slips back, with a thank-you.

Outside in the street he felt a little safer from Benjamin, but not much. He flagged down the first taxi he spotted and asked the driver to take him to the Greyhound terminal. He almost considered going to his old apartment and cleaning out his stuff. But he decided not to take the chance. If the police had a make on him, they might already have the place covered.

"What time is it?" he asked the driver, a skinny little guy with a sickly complexion and a bald head.

"Let's see . . . I got nine-fifteen. Yep . . . nine-fifteen by my watch . . . if it ain't running slow." The driver glanced back over his shoulder. "My schedule's all fouled up today. No way I'm gonna make a decent buck. I lost too much time in that jam-up this morning because of the Vampire Killer being shot."

"What?" Mathew blurted.

"Ain't you heard about it? You must've been sleepin'. A cop from Pittsburgh by the name of Vargo. It was on the news—radio and TV. He claims to have shot the Vampire Killer, down on Penn's Landing. Right beside the *Gazela Primeiro.*"

"Is the Vampire Killer dead?" Mathew asked, his voice a mixture of hopefulness and awe.

"Yep. The cop plugged him four times with a .357 magnum, like what Clint Eastwood uses. Blowed half his head away and dropped him in the water. They got the dredging crews out, trying to pull up the corpse."

"Maybe he's still alive," Mathew said with a tremble.

"No way!" scoffed the taxi driver. "When a magnum slug hits you in the head it explodes your skull and brains to bloody bits, just as if a hand grenade went off inside. My buddy done it to a deer once when we was out huntin'—ruined an eight-point trophy. Same thing must've happened to the Vampire Killer. Then he was probably sucked under by the tide while Vargo was goin' for help. By the time he came back, he didn't see no body. But it don't mean a thing. Lots of folks drown in that harbor every year, and they dredge and dredge and don't come up with nothin'. There's such a powerful current down there . . . undertows and whirlpools, what have you. Whole ships and airplanes down there. Whatever don't wash ashore is lost forever."

The news story was on the television in a noisy, crowded bar near the Greyhound terminal. Sipping a couple of drafts, Mathew watched the special coverage. Trooper Ronald Vargo, from Pittsburgh, came on the screen. Mathew recognized the cop's name and face from his scrapbook of articles on the Vampire Killer case. It made Mathew angry to be looking at somebody who was bragging about doing in his ancestor, especially when there wasn't even any cadaver to prove it yet.

"There is absolutely no question that Benjamin Latham is dead," Vargo said. "I saw him with my own eyes floating face down in the water. The tremendous amount of blood he lost—about eight pints that we can verify—would be enough to cause death, regardless of the exact nature of his wounds. He left a trail of blood all the way across Penn's Landing. I shot him in the heart *and* in the head with a heavy-caliber weapon. We hope to recover his corpse for a morgue autopsy. But, even if we don't, the American public can rest assured that he won't be a menace any longer."

Shoving a microphone in Vargo's face, a reporter asked, "What about the people who believe that Latham is a *real* vampire? Is there any way, Detective Vargo, that we can prove to the superstitious ones among us that Benjamin Latham won't come back from his watery grave?"

Vargo shook his head disgustedly. "Even if they believe in the Dracula legend," he said, with a tone of sarcasm and ridicule, "then they'd be the first to claim that Dracula has to sleep in his coffin in the daytime. Well, the sun's been up pretty bright for four or five hours, and nobody's seen Latham come up out of that water. If he were Dracula, he'd be disintegrated to dust by now, on the bottom of the Delaware River."

"Are you a superstitious man?" asked the reporter.

"No," said Vargo succinctly.

"Are you religious?"

"That's *my* business and nobody else's."

The cop is a helluva smart mouth, Mathew thought. Then his heart jumped to his throat when suddenly his own face appeared on the TV. It was his ID photo from Magnum Security. He spun sideways on his bar stool, trying to put his face in the shadows. Lucky he wasn't in a brightly lit saloon. The television commentator said:

"Mathew Latham, believed to be somehow related to the so-called Vampire Killer, is wanted by the police in connection with one murder charge and one assault charge here in Philadelphia. Anyone having any information about Mathew Latham is urged to contact police headquarters immediately. He may be armed and is considered extremely dangerous. He is five feet eleven, one hundred and sixty-five pounds, with sandy hair . . ."

Mathew left a tip on the bar and walked out, trying not to call undue attention to himself. He was considering whether he should remain in Philadelphia and bump off this Trooper Vargo. Then, if Benjamin were *not* dead, he'd be honor-bound to forgive Mathew and grant him a reward. And Mathew knew just what he'd ask for.

He wanted to be like Benjamin. To have all the special powers: mind control, mental telepathy, astounding strength and speed, invisibility, immortality.

The next stop was a phone booth. He quickly dialed the number he'd memorized off the hotel bill.

"Good morning. Montclair Plaza."

"I'd like to speak with Lenora Clayton."

"Do you know her room number?" the hotel operator asked.

"No. I'm hoping she hasn't checked out yet."

"Just a minute, sir. No . . . she's still registered. I'll ring for you."

Mathew waited for six rings, and the Montclair operator got back on the line: "I'm sorry, sir, there's no answer. Would you like to leave a message."

"No, thank you. I'll call again later."

Oh, God, he had to talk to her, convince her that he was her only true ally. That she should make him into a vampire—that it was the only way to get revenge.

Then *he* would become the new Vampire Killer, resurrected in Benjamin's image. With his awesome occult powers, he would confront Vargo. Make him suffer and die. Drink his blood.

If Benjamin were truly dead, never to awaken again, never to arise and walk the earth, then Mathew would take Lenora as *his* mate. They would produce offspring . . . a new and mighty breed, intelligent and ruthless . . . ferociously prowling the wide land . . . hunting and pouncing upon lesser creatures . . . copulating at will with all the choicest, loveliest mortals . . . slaking superhuman appetites and passions in an insatiable orgy of blood and sex . . . down through the mystical eons of time.

33

Lenora Clayton didn't return to the Montclair Plaza Hotel until after five o'clock on Tuesday. All day long she hadn't bothered to look at a newspaper dated any later than 1942 and hadn't been near a radio or TV. From early morning on, she had been in the New York Public Library, insulated from the bustling turmoil of the contemporary world. As she stepped out of a taxi in front of the Montclair she was tired but she was also happy—because the search for Benjamin's relatives was over. The last of the line, James Latham, had died in World War II. It was disappointing that Mathew and Julia Latham were the sole survivors of the family, but now Benjamin and she could end the hunt.

Crossing through the lobby of the Montclair Plaza, Lenora hoped Benjamin wouldn't be too disappointed that their search had finally petered out. As soon as she got up to her room and unwound a little bit, she intended to phone him and relate all that she had discovered. Then, tomorrow morning, she'd fly to Philadelphia and convince him that they should ditch Mathew and live in New York.

She was passing by the hotel newsstand when she saw the big black headline on the *New York Times:* VAMPIRE KILLER SHOT, BELIEVED DROWNED.

She gave an involuntary gasp as her head swam. Pale and trembling, she forced herself to fumble in her purse for change and to buy a newspaper. The wording of the headline seemed to offer a faint hope that Benjamin might not be dead. Trying desperately to cling to that possibility, she staggered half blindly onto an elevator.

She threw the paper onto the bed and knelt over it, her heart racing, her eyes blurring with tears. After reading all of it, she was utterly devastated. How to begin facing up to a life without Benjamin? He must be dead. He had been shot four times, including twice in the chest and once in the head. Then he had fallen face down into the harbor.

Lenora flung herself onto her hotel bed and sobbed and sobbed, her face burning with hot, salty tears, her chest heaving and aching with each spasm of anguish.

Through her grief, she thought about Mathew. Somehow *he* must be to blame. He was still on the loose. Yet, according to the newspaper, Trooper Vargo had trapped Benjamin at Mathew's apartment. Why was Mathew still alive? Had the sniveling, cowardly rapist and murderer of women managed to sacrifice Benjamin in order to save himself?

Lenora vowed to return to Philadelphia to try to find out. She would deal with Mathew and make sure he got what he deserved. Intuitively she knew that it was within her power to do so, even though the news of what had happened to her lover had been a hard, terrible blow. It had weakened her. But it would not destroy her. She would rebound with the courage and strength of womanly rage.

She would do whatever was necessary to avenge Benjamin's death. His spirit would work through her so that for his enemies she would be the angel of death. She would see the red blood running from their veins, staining the earth.

Concentrating fervently on that imagery, she began to dry her tears.

34

On Wednesday Trooper Ronald Vargo drove home to Greensburg on the Pennsylvania Turnpike in his unmarked black sedan. His big case was over. Officially solved. Yet, because of its special mystique, it was never going to be forgotten. Especially since the body hadn't been recovered.

Benjamin Latham, the Vampire Killer, was going to be the new boogeyman. Realization of that fact had Vargo angry and frustrated. He wished he could bleed off part of his anger by hunting down Mathew Latham, but Mathew's crimes had nothing to do with his case, which had originated in Hanna's Town; Mordini and Demchak would continue to go after Mathew for the Ridenour murder and the Jensen assault, since those offenses fell under their jurisdiction. Vargo would go home and hope to eventually receive news that Benjamin Latham's body had washed ashore somewhere in the Philadelphia harbor. The only thing that would help close the case once and for all would be the recovery of a corpse.

Or would it?

Vargo thought about how Hitler's corpse had been found and positively identified in the Führerbunker in 1945 after he had committed suicide, but to this day the tabloids kept printing wild articles about how Hitler, Göring, and Bormann were all in Argentina building up a Fourth Reich to take over the world. Many people loved to believe in scary myths. Vampires. Werewolves. Devils. Voodoo curses. Abominable snowmen. Loch Ness monsters. The human race was still primitive, still ready to worship fire and lightning . . . or whatever it didn't totally understand.

As if to confirm Vargo's cynicism, one of the buttons he punched on his car radio located a talk show featuring as its guest Dr. Harrison Lubbock, the "vampire expert." Instead of punching another button, Vargo listened, dismayed and yet amused by what he heard.

"Contrary to popular belief," the doctor said, "vampires are not invulnerable to bullets or knives."

Damn right, Vargo thought. You have to admit that, because I proved it.

"They can be killed like ordinary human beings," the doctor went on. "But then the corpse must be destroyed, preferably by fire. Otherwise it will regenerate. Just as a starfish will grow a new limb to replace one that is amputated, vampires have the ability to regenerate missing parts and to heal wounds."

Yeah? Vargo thought. I'd like to see him grow a new head, and a new set of lungs since the ones he has are shot full of holes and filled up with water.

"But how would this be possible?" the talk-show host asked. "No human being can grow a new arm or leg."

"Not a whole arm or leg," said Dr. Lubbock. "However, it *is* scientifically proven that children can regrow portions of their fingertips if the amputation is left alone and is not treated, except to be bandaged. And, furthermore, electrical currents are now being used to successfully stimulate the growth of new bone tissue in men and women who previously would not have been able to heal certain kinds of bone damage to any great extent. Scientists working in these experimental areas postulate that the instruction to regenerate a missing limb could be locked in our DNA, and, once we discover how to do it, we *can* program our cells to produce a brand-new replacement for a part of the body that has been destroyed or amputated."

"Bullshit!" Vargo exclaimed out loud. "Nothing but farfetched bullshit!"

"Can you apply this theory to the Vampire Killer?" the talk-show host asked.

"Yes, I certainly can. I believe that creatures like Benjamin Latham, superior in some ways to ordinary humans, have the ability to regenerate once they are dead. They *die* . . . but they come back. The spirit, the 'glow of life' that can be witnessed as a radiant electrical entity, like a halo, by means of Kirlian photographic techniques, does not desert the vampire when he is killed. Instead, it remains a cohesive, invisible, plastic substance, a *soul* if you will, maintaining more of a life presence than humans are able to maintain after physical death, and acting as a blueprint whereby the wounds and deformities can be 'filled in,' replicating the original organism and thus enabling it to reanimate itself."

"Claptrap! Pseudoscientific jargon!" Vargo shouted at the radio as he sped along the turnpike.

"In other words, to live again," said the talk-show host. "If I follow you correctly."

"Precisely," said Dr. Harrison Lubbock. "That is what I am telling you. The vampire will reconstruct himself, as a starfish reconstructs its missing limb, and when he is ready he will live again."

"All right, let's take some calls from our audience," the talk-show host said.

The first caller wanted to know if Dr. Lubbock thought there was going to be a plague of vampires now, even though Benjamin Latham might be dead. "I mean, people he might have bitten but didn't necessarily kill," the caller explained. "I mean, I always heard those kind of people would *become* vampires. . . ."

"I don't think that biting a victim can be the correct method," said the good doctor. "Unless the saliva is not always poisonous. Otherwise, anyone who is bitten is going to be killed instead of being transformed. Actually, I have to admit that there is some question in my mind as to whether or not a vampire can be created in any other way except through heredity."

Angrily, Vargo turned his car radio off. He wished fervently that Latham's corpse would wash ashore and put an end to this nonsense.

35

Under the water, Benjamin's body turned over and over, his limbs buckling and unbuckling, fingers clenching and unclenching, agitated by the river currents, turning and turning, like an unborn baby in its cradle of amniotic fluid. He dreamed the dreams of the unborn who have once lived. Scenes of his two incarnations played through his semiunconsciousness, which existed independently of his wounded body. His aura—the electrochemical Kirlian glow or glue that holds body and spirit together—did not desert him as the soul leaves an ordinary man when he dies. Instead, the aura remained, like the "ghost" half of a leaf cut in two, and acted as a pattern for the healing of his wounds and the regeneration of his missing parts.

36

Mathew Latham waited in Christ Church Cemetery, where Benjamin Franklin was buried. The night was black and cold. He was anxious for Lenora Clayton to show up. He wanted, among other things, to gaze upon her beauty again. He felt that he was very close to mating with her in a supernatural union of fantastic orgasmic pleasure.

"It must be done in a cemetery," she had said over the phone. "Benjamin taught me how to do it properly."

"How?" Mathew had asked immediately.

"Be patient," she had replied mysteriously. "You will soon learn. I am ready to teach you. You are right when you say that Benjamin's death must be avenged. I'll help you see that the guilty one is punished. Your transformation must be inaugurated by a special occult ritual in a cemetery, three days before the full moon. That will be two days from today. I will meet you at three A.M. on Saturday night."

"Why not midnight?" Mathew had puzzled.

"Why does everyone think that everything esoteric has to happen at midnight?" Lenora had snapped back. "Forget all your preconceptions. This thing you desire must be accomplished at three A.M., approximately, and three days *before* the full moon. Will you meet me at Christ Church Cemetery, as I have told you to do, or would you rather remain a mortal?"

"Not one hunted by the police," Mathew had said. "I'll meet you at three A.M. at the entrance to Christ Church Cemetery. On Saturday night."

"And wear black clothing," Lenora had added, almost as an afterthought, before hanging up the telephone.

It was a lonely, quiet place, Mathew observed, even though it was in the heart of the Olde City. It would be perfect for some of the exploits he had planned for after he became a vampire. There were no tourists or churchgoers about at this hour. Across the street from the cemetery was the massively stolid United States Mint. And in the adjacent blocks were the First Quaker Meeting House and the Arch Street Friends Meeting House, the buildings and grounds silent and dark and no longer open to visitors. If the ritual of his transformation was going to be at all noisy, then this location was certainly private enough.

At last he saw Lenora coming toward him, dressed all in black just as he was, so that she seemed to simply materialize out of the blackness of the night. It was an eerie way to glimpse her again after not seeing her for a while. Even her face was wrapped in a black shawl.

"Good evening, Mathew," she said in a hushed voice, her breath white because of the cold.

He noted that she recognized him easily even though he had dyed his hair black and had grown a mustache. It would have shaken his confidence in his disguise had he not known that she had occult powers of perception.

"Good evening," he told her.

"Don't talk anymore now," she commanded. "If we are to succeed, you must follow me and obey without question, for I am your guru. I shall explain everything that is to be done as well as it is possible to explain these matters."

A thrill shot through him. He could sense so strongly that he was on the threshold of *becoming*. He nodded to show that he understood and was willing to comply.

She said, "Follow me," and led him to a place at the side of the old cemetery where an evergreen shrub grew right against the corner of the black iron fence. When she pulled the shrub aside, Mathew saw that a vertical rung of the fence had been removed, making it possible for a trim adult to squeeze through. Lenora went first, and then Mathew. "Come on," she said, her voice taking on a bit more urgency. "Don't talk, just follow."

She clicked on a black penlight that she had taken from her purse. Its weak beam was just bright enough to show them their way between clusters of sunken, eroded tombstones and monuments. Lenora was obviously looking for a special place deep inside the graveyard, and after a few minutes she found it. "Here," she told Mathew in a whisper. "This ancient carved cross shall be our altar. You must kneel and I must stand behind you to recite the prayers to Satan."

"Satan?" Mathew blurted huskily. "I didn't think he had anything to do with it."

"Shhh!" Lenora reprimanded. "You fool, you almost broke the spell. Now kneel, as I told you."

He got down on his knees in front of the ornate granite cross that formed part of a tall, tilted monument. Now he felt a rush of expectancy that told him he must *really* be getting close to what he wanted.

Taking something from her purse, Lenora said, "Now I am going to touch the back of your neck with a secret metallic charm that will help you to be transformed. You mustn't turn around and look at it, and you mustn't tremble when its coldness touches you."

Mathew waited stoically, but when the cold steel met his skin he shivered despite himself.

Lenora shot him twice in rapid succession at the base of his skull with the .25 automatic that had belonged to Janice Ridenour. The small-caliber weapon didn't make much noise—just a couple of loud pops similar to the sound of breaking blown-up paper bags. Mathew tipped forward and hit the top of his head against the side of the monument. Lenora jumped back so as not to get any blood on her. Mathew groaned and crumpled sideways, still breathing, but hoarsely and weakly. She didn't think he would breathe for long: he would soon be transformed from a living being to a dead one.

"Well done, love," Benjamin Latham said, stepping out from behind a shadowy array of large monuments.

Lenora smiled at him. She let the pistol drop.

He opened his switchblade knife and handed it to her.

Mathew looked up at Benjamin, seeing his ancestor's face out of the corners of his eyes just before they took on the glaze of death that he had enjoyed bringing to others.

Lenora tugged up the right sleeve of Mathew's black denim jacket and used the switchblade to slit his wrist. She knelt and drank his blood, her very first blood from a victim of her own.

Benjamin looked on approvingly, his heart filled with affection for her and all her bodily functions and appetites whose gratification kept her alive and beautiful and in love with him.

37

High above London, a commercial airliner circled and prepared to land. Sitting behind the wing, Benjamin Latham leaned forward, pressing his face close to the window, awed and excited by his first trip in an airplane. He still couldn't get over the fact that the clouds looked like a thick, billowy carpet substantial enough to walk on. The plane nosed through the clouds, and the capital of Great Britain was majestically revealed thousands of feet below.

Suddenly there was a great loud clunk that scared Benjamin into thinking they were going to nose-dive and crash. He looked over at Lenora. She reached out and held his hand.

"Just the landing gear going down, darling," she explained. "We'll soon be on the ground."

"Wonderful!" he exclaimed. "The city looks wonderful!"

"Don't expect too much out of it," she cautioned. "It's a lot like America now. They even have McDonald's."

The plane dropped its flaps, and with a mighty screeching roar it coasted smoothly onto the runway and began taxiing toward the terminal.

Benjamin and Lenora smiled at each other. They were both thrilled at the prospect of visiting the country where his forefathers had been born.